About a Girl

About a Girl

William Michael Stephens

Severline Press

ISBN: 979-8-9864612-2-9 (hardcover)

ISBN: 979-8-9864612-0-5 (paperback)

ISBN: 979-8-9864612-1-2 (eBook)

www.severlinepress.com

Front cover image by Romariolen. Licensed at shutterstock.com

Spine and interior painting by Mariia Aiiram. Licensed at shutterstock.com

Back cover illustration by Barandash Karandashich. Licensed at shutterstock.com

Background image by Yuriy Mazur. Licensed at shutterstock.com

Cover and interior elements licensed at canva.com

Cover design by William Michael Stephens

This book is dedicated to all of my students, both former and present, who have given me the drive and purpose to power through each day.
Special thanks to my AP English Language and Composition students who encouraged me to finish writing this book.
-Mr. Stephens

Contents

Chapter One
The Band

"**P**LAY IT RIGHT, GOD damn it!" Rob yelled as I stood there loosely holding my bass guitar in my hands. I stared at him for what seemed like a minute without saying a word. The silence in the garage was only interrupted by the sound of white noise ringing in my ears. Chris was twirling his drumsticks around with a curious, whimsical look on his face. I finally said, "this song is too fast, maybe I can play every other note..." Rob quickly cut me off.

"I don't care how you play it, just play it right!"

"What does that even mean?" I replied.

"Stop messing up. The only reason I let you in the band is because you're my friend. You just suck! Get better!"

"Thanks," I said as sarcastically as I could. "Nirvana doesn't even play it that fast."

"They do play it that fast when they play it live, and guess what? We're playing it live." Rob looked over at Chris and then back at me waiting for a response. I didn't say anything because I didn't know if that was true or not. "And stop being a bitch about it."

"I'm not being a bitch about it...shit, forget I said anything at all."

"That's right. Practice is over, my dad's gonna pick me up in a minute. Will, practice 'Breed,' and Chris, work on 'Teen Spirit.' You're still playing that too sloppy." Chris raised an eyebrow and moved his shoulders up and down but didn't respond. Rob always had the last word at practice. He was the band and we both knew it. He sang and played the guitar, taught me how to play bass, and taught Chris how to play drums. He wasn't physically imposing. In fact, he was a pudgier, spitting-image version of Kurt Cobain with dirty blond hair hanging in his eyes and a dull, grey grandpa sweater included. He had a good voice, but he was trying to emulate Cobain to the best of his ability. It was obvious without too much digging that he was the biggest Nirvana fan ever. Period. I often described our band to other people as a Nirvana cover band because we didn't play any songs from any other band. We also never wrote any original songs, which I thought was strange at the time, but I was happy to be in a band, even if Rob wasn't the most likable person. Chris got up from his drum set and set down his sticks on his snare drum. Rob's dad pulled up at the end of the cul-de-sac in front of Chris's house in his beige Dodge mini-van and Chris said, "all right, later Rob. See you tomorrow." I unstrapped my bass and set it down on my stand.

"Later." Chris and I watched the mini-van drive down the street and then looked at each other and kind of smiled.

"What a dick," I said.

"Yeah, total asshole," Chris replied. "Well, I have to go to football practice. See ya."

"All right, man, see ya." I got on my Redline Proline BMX bike and rode home.

I met Rob and Chris when I was in eighth grade and they were both in seventh grade. Rob was new to the school and I had seen Chris around, but didn't personally know him. I thought Rob was homeless the first time I saw him. He looked dirty. He looked like he hadn't taken a shower in years, if ever. His hair was so greasy it almost dripped from the tips at the bottom of his jaw. He had his signature grey, grandpa sweater paired with torn blue jeans and a dilapidated pair of Chuck Taylor all-star shoes, which he wore every day. He always kept to himself. I never saw him talk with anyone and he always ate his bagged lunch alone. It almost seemed like he was going out of his way to not fit in.

Chris was different from Rob. Chris was one of the cool kids. He was popular, played football, and everyone knew who he was and liked him. He was always hanging out with the jocks and cheerleaders. He was classically good-looking, had short brown hair, and a strong jaw-line. He dressed really well, which was described at the time as 'preppy.' He was part of the 'in' crowd.

I was not a part of Chris's group; in fact, I had more in common with Rob even though I thought I was better than him in every way. I tried to fit in. I tried to be popular. I had a very thin build, but I was athletic, even though I didn't play any organized sports at the time, like Chris. I looked at Rob as sloppy, or even fat. I had jaw length brown hair, but, unlike Rob, I kept mine clean. I wore Stussy shirts and blue Vans chukka boot shoes.

I had a best friend at the time named Donald. Donald had been my best friend since the beginning of the sixth grade. We hung out all the time. For two years we were almost inseparable. We always stayed the night at each other's houses and whenever there was something going on, we did it together. We had a falling out about a girl named Stephanie. We both liked her and, come to find out; she did not like either one of us. We blamed each other and stopped hanging out. I was about to be eating my bagged lunches alone. There was a trend in 1994 of sewing patches, placing stickers, and writing in Sharpie's and white-out our favorite bands or phrases directly on our backpacks. I was no different. The first patch that I had sewn onto my backpack was, thanks to my mom, Faith No More's symbol for their album, Fool for a Lifetime. It was a cool-looking picture with the silhouette of a cop and a barking dog. I was eating my lunch alone one day, like usual since I stopped hanging out with Donald, and Rob sat down next to me. "Hey," he said.

"Hey," I replied. *What kind of loser am I if this dude is talking to me?* I thought. It was nice that someone was talking to me though, even if it was Rob.

"That's a cool patch." Rob pointed to my backpack lying face-up beside me.

"Thanks," I said, but was still skeptical about him even being in my personal space. *What if someone saw me sitting with him? What would they think about me?* I was a little anxious.

"Where did you get it?"

"It came with the CD."

"Cool, did you know that Faith No More used to be fronted by Courtney Love?"

"Fronted? By who?"

"Courtney Love, Kurt Cobain's wife, used to be the lead singer of Faith No More."

"Yeah, I didn't know that." I knew who Kurt Cobain was and liked Nirvana, but I had no idea who his wife was at the time or that the Faith No More I was listening to wasn't the same Faith No More that had existed before. *How does he know all of this?*

"I'm Rob."

"Will."

"I got this documentary for Christmas on Nirvana and they talk about it. You wanna see it?"

"Sure," I said with some reservation in my voice, "when?"

"After school?"

"I have to call my mom."

"You can call her when we get to my house."

"Ok. Where do you live?" *It's something to do.*

"On Walnut, pretty close to the donut shop."

"Oh, all right, I know where that is." The bell rang. Lunch was over.

"Meet me at the front gate after school."

"Ok," I said, but I was already thinking about ways that I could get out of it. *I wonder if I could say someone died. Maybe my dog? Wait, I don't have a dog! Wait! That's perfect! Would he believe it? Ahh, who cares if he did!* Rob walked to his class and I walked to mine. It was 5th and 6th period core, a mixed English and History class. I walked into class and was confronted by Donald.

"I saw you hanging out with that little loser seventh grader," he said.

"I wasn't hanging out with him. He just sat down next to me," I replied.

Yeah, you were hanging out with a seventh grader."

"Whatever." *Why does he even care?*

"You're a loser!"

"You're a loser! You're the one hanging out with fat boy Barrett." Kyle Barrett was Donald's seemingly new best friend and also the fattest kid at school. Donald pushed me against the wall at the threshold of the classroom and before I had a chance to react our teacher, Ms. Peralta got between us and called the office. We both sat in the office for the rest of the day, but we didn't get in trouble. The bell rang and we went our separate ways but not before Donald got out one last insult.

"Later, loser," before running away down the hall. I met Rob at the front gate with my prepared story about my poor dead dog. *Damn, what's his name? Dude, you don't even know the name of your own dead dog? Idiot!* I had not thought this thing through. I had a change of heart, partially because I couldn't come up with a plausible lie fast enough and partially because I wanted to piss off Donald. Rob didn't have a bike so I walked mine along next to him. "Why don't you have a bike?"

"I don't need a bike; I don't live that far away." I didn't know Visalia that well, being that I had only lived there for a couple of years, but I knew that the Scotties Donuts was not close. *Maybe he likes to walk? Who likes to walk? Oh, Whatever.* We slowly made our way toward Rob's house when he pulled a pack of cigarettes out of his backpack. I was surprised and a lot disgusted. "You want a smoke?" Rob asked me this question as if it were rhetorical. The stern look on his face made it seem like there wasn't an option. *Shit. I'm allergic to smoke.* "Are you going to take one or what?"

"I don't really, um, want one."

"Don't be a pussy. Take one." I didn't want Rob to think that I wasn't cool so I took the cigarette. Rob also had a black Bic lighter, which he used to light his first and then mine. I coughed violently. *This is some bull-shit.* Rob started laughing at me. It was a really snarky laugh that made me feel like I was three feet tall.

"Shut up, man, this shit is gross."

"You'll get used to it." *Why would I want to do that?*

"When did you start smoking?"

"My mom has smoked all my life, so I guess; 13 years."

"You know what I mean…"

"This past summer." Rob looked down at his own feet as if he were embarrassed by the fact that he wasn't the professional smoker that he thought he was. He gradually looked back up at me and asked, "What did you do last summer?"

"I spent the summer in Camarillo with my best friend from fifth grade and his aunt. She's rich so we always spend summers with her. She didn't have any kids of her own so she spends her money on her nephews. I am like one of her nephews when I'm there."

"So, what'd you do over there?"

"Well, we did all kinds of stuff, but, yeah, I got laid."

"That's so much bullshit. You did not get laid."

"I did." *I knew he wouldn't believe me. I wouldn't believe me.*

"What's her name?"

"Rebecca."

"Rebecca who?"

"I don't know. I didn't ask for her life story."

"Bullshit."

"She was 15. That she told me."

"Dude, you don't have to lie. You're a virgin. It's ok, I'm a virgin too."

"Congratulations. I'm not a virgin, though. I don't have to prove anything to you anyways." I wasn't mad, but I knew I was wasting my time trying to convince him. "Why don't we change the subject?"

"Ok, but you're still full of shit. Have you ever gotten drunk?"

"Yeah, the first time I got drunk was last summer." *A lot happened last summer. Shit.* "Brad and I waited for his aunt to go to work and we took a bottle of whiskey out of the cupboard and took turns drinking."

"Shit, what happened?"

"I don't even know how much we drank, but after like an hour, the last thing I remember was falling out of the office chair and woke up three hours later."

"So, you blacked out."

"I must have. Brad too. He was still asleep on the couch when I got up. It was early afternoon when I woke Brad. We both felt like shit. Brad threw up. At least he made it to the bathroom. I remember saying, 'that was fucking stupid' and 'why the fuck do people like to drink?' We left the bottle on the kitchen counter. It was half empty. We were both like, 'oh shit, Peg is gonna be pissed.' We panicked and filled the bottle back up with water. It didn't look right, but we didn't know what else to do."

"Damn, man, you're hardcore. I've only drank a few beers. My mom lets me drink. They're always in the fridge."

"Your mom lets you drink? Holy shit! You have the coolest mom ever."

"Yeah, I think so too. Did Brad's aunt ever find out?"

"Not that I know of. I don't think she checked that cabinet the entire time we were there."

"How long were you there?"

"A month. The same as the year before. I had a pretty bad headache and when Peg got home that night, I wasn't even hungry, which she thought was weird. She told me to drink a bunch of water and I'd be fine."

"That's crazy. So, you guys got away with it?"

"I guess, but I felt like shit."

"Have you smoked weed?"

"No. I don't think it's a good idea. Have you?"

"Yeah, all the time. What do you mean? You think guzzling down a bottle of whiskey is a good idea?"

"You have a point there."

"We're going to have to get you high one of these days."

"Sure, I guess." We were still both smoking our cigarettes as we made our way towards Rob's house. I was doing more holding my cigarette than actually smoking, but I started thinking that it looked cool. "Do you like football?" I asked as we crossed onto Walnut Avenue. I don't know why I asked this question because it seemed obvious that he wasn't too concerned about sports.

"Yeah. I like the Chiefs."

"What?" I smiled and laughed. *How does this guy like football? This is California. How did that happen?* "I'm a Chargers fan. I was born in San Diego and my whole family is Chargers fans."

"I just like Joe Montana."

"Then the 49ers would make more sense. Again, we are in California."

"It doesn't matter where you're from. I can like any team I want."

"I guess. GO Chargers! The Chargers and Chiefs are playing soon, I think. You should come over to my house to watch the game."

"Sounds like a plan." We finally got to his house, and sure enough, it was right next to Scotties Donuts. It was a small, yellow house, probably really old, and had a small, curved driveway that ended with a single-car garage. "This is me," Rob said. "It doesn't look like anyone is home yet." Rob unlocked the front door and we went inside. There was a faint smell of ammonia that I couldn't figure out as the place seemed like it hadn't been cleaned in a long time. "So, what do you want to do? You wanna watch the Nirvana show?"

"Yeah, let's put it on. Rob led me to his bedroom and had me sit at the end of his bed. There were clothes everywhere, but what I noticed the most was all of the music equipment lining the walls; guitars, basses, and a few amps. "Where did you get all of this stuff?"

"Mostly from my grandpa. He doesn't use it anymore."

"So do you play guitar?"

"Yeah, I've been playing for a couple of years."

"Are you any good?"

"I can play."

"Play something then..." Rob had the video cassette of the Nirvana show in his hand ready to put it inside of the VCR. He put the tape down and strapped on one of the guitars propped up against the wall and plugged it into a large amp. He turned the volume up pretty loud and started playing a familiar song: 'Smells Like Teen Spirit.' He played through the entire 5-minute song, including the solo, and, something I really didn't expect; he sang too. "That was awesome!" I said. "Holy shit, man, you're actually really good. It sounded just like on the radio."

"That's what I told you. I've been practicing every day after school."

"Yeah, but it's not like I'm going to believe you until I see it. Have you ever wanted to start a band?"

"Yeah, but I don't know anyone who plays anything. Do you play anything?"

"No, I mean, my brother plays, and I've tried, but I never learned."

"I can teach you to play bass. We would still need to find a drummer and then we would have a band."

"Shit, how long do you think it would take for me to learn?"

"If you practice every day, probably not long. It's a lot easier to learn bass than guitar."

"All right, sounds good."

"First lesson starts right now."

"What? Are you serious?"

"Yeah, I've got a bass right over there that hasn't been played for years." Rob set his guitar down and walked over to the bass. It was black and definitely looked like it hadn't been played in forever. "It's probably out of tune." He plugged the bass into another amp on the opposite side of the room and began tuning it. He did it without using a tuner. I had seen my brother tune a guitar, but he always used a tuner. "Well, it doesn't sound great. It needs new strings, but it's good enough." Rob handed the bass to me and I wrapped the strap over my shoulders. "This is the E string, this is the A string, this is the D string and this is the G string." Rob pointed at each string as he told me to pull each one. "Each one of these inlays is called a fret and you hold your fingers over them to play each note. You don't have to know all the theory." *Theory?* "All you have to know is the tab or the numbers of the frets to learn to play songs. I'm going to teach you to play the easiest song ever first. It's called 'About a Girl.' It's off of Nirvana's first album." I spent two hours learning and practicing that song. Over and over and over again. Finally, what I was playing actually sounded like the song. The tips of my fingers were practically bleeding. They hurt so badly, and yet; I didn't care.

"Hey, man, I've got to go home, my mom's gonna be pissed. I'll see you at school tomorrow." I took the strap off of the bass and handed it to Rob.

"Do you wanna meet at my house tomorrow before school?"

"Ummm, I guess so..."

"You don't have to if you don't want to."

"No, I'll be here. What time?"

"Like 7:30. It'll give us enough time to walk."

"All right. I'll see you tomorrow."

"See ya." Rob walked me outside where I left my Bike. "Oh, hey man, wait up." Rob went back inside of his house and then came back out with the bass in his hands. "You can keep it. I don't play it and you need the practice."

"Damn, thanks, Rob," I said. "That's really nice of you."

"No worries, see you tomorrow."

"All right, see ya." I rode home with my bass strapped to my back and thought: *I'm pretty damn good at playing bass.*

The next day, I woke up early, took a shower, ate some Grape Nuts, and pedaled my ass over to Rob's house. Rob met me at his door in, seemingly, the same clothes he was wearing the day before. "Dude, are you wearing the same clothes as yesterday?"

"Yeah, so what?"

"Aren't you worried about stinking things up?"

"I changed my underwear," Rob responded quite matter-of-factly.

"Well, that changes everything." *That's so gross. I know he has different clothes. I saw them hanging in his closet!*

"I was thinking about what I said yesterday about starting a band. We need to find a drummer," Rob said.

"So we're really going to start a band then? Just like that?"

"Sure, why not? You got something better to do?"

"No, not really, but what I mean is, how are we just going to find a drummer?"

"I don't know yet, but it can't be that hard, right? I found a bass player yesterday."

"That's a good point."

"I have a drum set. I just have to find someone, I mean, we have to find someone that wants to play the drums, and loves Nirvana...And doesn't suck."

"What are we going to do, ask random people if they want to play drums?"

"Pretty much, yes. I have an idea though. I think if we go and scope out the band room at lunch, we'll find someone."

"The band geeks? You think we'll find someone that wants to play drums and likes Nirvana in that bunch of losers?" I inquired.

"Maybe. You have a better idea?"

"Nope." We started making our way to the school. I left my bike in Rob's back yard and we began walking down Walnut Avenue. We made it to Divisadero Street a lot faster than we thought. Divisadero was also the name of our school. *Why did they name the school after a street? Stupid.* It was 7:55. We still had 5 minutes to go check out the band room. We practically ran over to the room and found a bunch of kids standing around waiting for class to start. There were some kids warming up on their trumpets, clarinets, and trombones. The teacher, Mr. Bonner, pronounced by the students as Mr. Boner, was sitting behind his desk, staring at his computer screen, and not paying any attention to anyone. In the corner was a kid in a school football jersey playing a beat with his hands on a desk. "What's a jock doing in here?" Rob inquired.

"I don't know. Let's go see if he plays drums."

"I don't want a jock in my band!"

"I thought you were a Chiefs fan. What do you care if he plays football?"

"I am a Chiefs fan. What does that have to do with anything?"

"Ummm, duh..."

"I don't want a jock in the band because he won't have time to practice." I felt stupid pointing out Rob's hypocrisy because he actually made sense.

"Let's just go talk to him. You don't know if you don't ask. Would you rather put an ad in the paper? How would that read? MIDDLE SCHOOL KIDS LOOKING TO START A BAND NEED A DRUMMER. Yeah, that's going to go over well." Rob looked at me cross-eyed.

"Fine, let's go talk to him." We walked over to him and I said, "Hey, do you play the drums?"

"No, but I want to. Who're you guys?"

"I'm Will and this is Rob. We're looking for a drummer to start a band."

"That's Awesome! I've always wanted to be in a band. I don't know how to play, but that's so cool. I'm Chris, by the way."

"I can teach you," Rob said.

"What?" You know how to play the drums too? What the hell?" *How does he know how to play everything?*

"You'll teach me how to play the drums? Just like that...?" Chris asked.

"Yeah, I want to start a, we want to start a band and someone needs to play the drums. Wait. Do you like Nirvana?"

"Who?"

"Oh, shit, forget it." Rob turned around and started walking away.

"Psych!" Chris said. "Of course I like Nirvana. Everyone likes Nirvana."

"That wasn't funny. Don't joke about Nirvana," Rob insisted.

"No sense of humor," Chris responded with a handsome, self-assured smile. The bell rang and everyone started moving around to where they were supposed to be.

"Meet us on the field at lunch, Rob said. "We'll talk about setting up a practice."

"Ok. See ya later."

"Laters," I said as we all walked to our classes. The time between the morning classes and lunch was almost imperceptible. The lunch bell rang and I wasn't even thinking about the cafeteria. I was thinking about getting out to the field as quickly as I could without running and looking like a dumbass. I saw Chris waiting near one of the tetherball courts. "Hey, Chris, I had a question I was thinking about in class. Why were you in the band room? You play football, right?"

"There's this girl named, Angela, that I like and I was in there waiting for her. Turns out she's absent today. She's always in the band room though, most days."

"All right, I can see that. Wait. Angela Travers?"

"Yeah, that's her. She's so hot."

"She's in my math class. She's also an eighth grader."

"I know, but I still like her. I think I have a chance." *If any seventh grader did it was him.* "I don't think she has a boyfriend."

"Do you want me to ask her? We've been friends for a while."

"Yeah, find out for me."

"Ok, I'll ask her tomorrow."

"Cool, but don't tell her it's me asking."

"Dude, she's going to think I'm asking for myself."

"Yeah, you're right, I guess just say you're asking for a friend." *Yeah, that's going to work.*

"Ok, I'll do my best." Rob walked up to us.

"What are you guys talking about?" He said.

"Oh nothing, it's about a girl," I said.

"What girl?"

"Angela Travers."

"Don't know her," Rob said. "Anyway...Chris, can you come over to my house after school? Me and Will are going to start working on 'Come As You Are' and the drum part is really easy. The drums are all set up in my garage."

"No, I can't today. I have football practice."

"You can miss a day of practice, can't you?" I said.

"Coach is not going to be happy, but yeah, I can miss practice. I'll have to make up some excuse."

"So, you're coming then?" Rob asked with a hint of hesitation.

"Yeah, but I can't do this every day." I was glad that Chris decided to come to practice, but I worried that Rob was going to have a problem with him not being able to come every day. Rob didn't say anything though.

"Ok, let's go get some food. We'll meet after school. Chris, do you have a bike?" I asked.

"Yeah, I have a Mongoose."

"I meant; did you ride your bike to school today?"

"Yeah. I live too far away to walk."

"Ok, let's meet at the bike racks after school and walk to Rob's house."

"You guys don't have bikes?"

"Yeah, I do, but, it's at Rob's."

"I guess I can walk," Chris said with a sarcastic tone.

"Don't be a bitch," Rob asserted.

"Calm down, it was a joke. Again, no sense of humor," Chris added.

"Rob doesn't joke about music."

"Are you sure Rob jokes about anything?" Chris said. *I wasn't.* Rob didn't say anything else while we made our way to the cafeteria to get some lunch. After school, Rob and I took the lead with Chris trailing behind riding his bike. We were going so slow, I was sure that he would fall off, but he didn't. "Chris, where do you live?" I inquired.

"I live over on Laura Street at the end of the Cul-De-Sac."

"Where?"

"It's like on the opposite end of Mountain View. The elementary school."

"I went to that school. I think I know what you're talking about." We continued walking and Rob seemed completely disinterested in our conversation.

"Where do you live?"

"Close to Blain Park."

"You live in one of those rich-people houses? You're rich?"

"No, I'm not rich." *The opposite of that actually.* I didn't want either of them to know that I lived in an apartment. "Rob's the rich one. He's got all kinds of equipment."

"I'm not rich. My parents both have jobs, but we're still poor. All the equipment is my grandpa's." Rob had no shame. He didn't have a problem telling people he was poor. I did. If Rob considered himself poor, then I really didn't want anyone knowing about my situation.

"I think my family is middle-class. We're definitely not poor," Chris said. I just shook my head in agreement.

"Do you think your parents would buy you a drum set?" I asked Chris.

"Maybe. I'll ask," Chris said and then Rob interrupted.

"We'll see if you're good enough first. You don't want to waste your parent's money if you suck."

"I don't suck."

"How do you know? Have you ever played on an actual set?"

"No, but I can keep a beat."

"Yeah, on a desk." I looked back at Chris and he was just shaking his head with a frown on his face.

"Don't be such a dick," Chris quipped, "I'll prove it to you."

"You'll have to," Rob replied, "that's the point." After a while we got to Rob's house and Rob directed us into his garage. There was an older-looking, blue drum set in the back with some amps set up along the sides. Rob had already set everything up. "It looks old, but it's a good set." He directed Chris to sit behind the set and handed him a pair of drumsticks. Chris played a drum roll on the snare and it didn't sound too bad. Rob had a little boom box stereo set up and had Nirvana's Nevermind CD ready to play. "Listen to this song." Rob played 'Come As You Are' as he pointed out which drums to play while the song played in the background. Chris held the sticks over the drums and played air drums while taking Rob's instruction. After a second play through of the song, Rob told Chris, "Ok, now play along with it." To my amazement Chris had little trouble playing along. It sounded pretty good. "Not bad, really not bad at all. All right, Will, let me teach you how to play it." Chris kept practicing and I slowly learned to play 'Come As You Are.' After two hours of practice, we were able to play the song, as rough as it was, all the way through. Rob's parents eventually got home and practice ended for the day.

• • • ● ● • ● ● • • •

"I don't get it," Rob said. "We've been playing together for almost two years and you guys still suck." We had just finished playing 'Breed' for the fifth time and for the fifth time, we played it wrong, according to Rob. Chris and I, as was usually the case when Rob started on one of his rants, just looked at each other and rolled our eyes. "We are going to play this god damn song until you get it right!"

"You mean, until we get it right," I said while putting my bass on the stand.

"No! Shit! I always play it right. You guys play it wrong."

"Maybe we should just move on to a different song," Chris said.

"How about we play something that's not Nirvana? There are other bands," I said.

"Like who? No one is as good as Nirvana."

"Whatever, Rob, just forget it," I said.

"You need to get better! Rob pointed at me first and then pointed at Chris. "And you need to stop playing football and practice the god damn drums." He pointed back at me. "And I don't know what your problem is. You have the time to practice at home. Yet, you obviously don't."

"There is more to life than playing Nirvana songs in a cover band. That's what we are Rob, a cover band. We don't write our own songs. We don't do anything but learn Nirvana covers. What? Did you think we were going to get big and famous playing someone else's songs?" Chris looked at me with his jaw slacked open like he had seen a ghost. Rob set down his guitar.

"You can barely play Nirvana and you want to write your own songs?" I didn't really have a response. After a year and a half of playing, maybe I should have been better. I didn't know what to say. I looked out of Chris's garage down the street. A U-Haul truck was pulling up to a house a few doors down. "It looks like someone is moving into that house that burned down last year," Chris said.

"I wonder if they know it burned down?" I said. The house that burned down the year before was caused by an electrical fire, at least that's what we were told. The family wasn't home when it happened. We once walked through its charred remains. They rebuilt it, but I guess they decided to sell it.

"Who cares?" Rob said. "We need to get back to practice." We didn't pick our instruments back up though. We watched as the entire family got out of the moving truck. The first person to get out of the truck was a beautiful blond girl. She looked to be about our age, or a little bit older. All three of us were staring at her. I looked at Chris and then Rob and simply said, "whoa." I looked back toward the girl down the street and she smiled at me. She was wearing tight fitting blue jeans and a flower printed shirt. I had never seen a prettier girl. Her blond hair flowed lightly over her shoulders and glistened in the sun. She waved at me and turned toward a young boy, maybe 10 years old, probably her brother. An older man got out of the truck and looked at us; well, scowled at us, before turning back to a woman, probably his wife, and helped her out of the truck. They all went inside the house.

"Dibs," I said as I turned back to Rob and Chris. "You already have a girlfriend, Chris, and well, Rob, you have no chance." Chris had been with Angela since I hooked them up and Rob had never even talked to a girl. At least I had never seen him talk to a girl. Chris laughed and said,

"I don't think either one of you has a chance. Did you see her?" *Of course I did.*

"That's not going to stop me from trying," I insisted.

"Good luck, man, you're gonna need it," Chris said.

"Thanks, Chris. Thanks for the support," I said sarcastically.

"Any time, bro, any time," Chris said while smiling and shaking his head.

"You guys are stupid. I'm going home," Rob said and packed up his guitar. Rob still didn't have a bike and he didn't call his dad to pick him up. He started walking down the street with his guitar strapped to his back. "Practice tomorrow. Same time," Rob said without turning around.

"All right, Rob, see you tomorrow," I said.

"See ya, Rob," Chris said. Rob gave a slight wave and walked slowly down the street. We had been practicing at Chris's house more often since Chris's parents got him a drum set for Christmas. Chris's house was also bigger and had a bigger garage. It was a much better place to practice, especially being at the end of a Cul-De-Sac. Rob's house was on a main street so it was much noisier. I wasn't thinking about practice though, I was thinking about the beautiful blond girl that was moving in down the street. I wanted to go up to her and tell her how beautiful she was. I wanted to go knock on her door and talk to her. I wanted to go help her move into her house. I wanted to do whatever she wanted me to do. I didn't do anything though. I strapped my bass guitar to my back, got on my bike, and rode past the U-Haul truck.

Chapter Two

Hannah

T HE LAST DAY OF school that year was a relief. It was the last day of my freshman year and the last day that Chris and Rob would be at Divisadero. We would all be at Mt. Whitney and I could put the worst year of school behind me. I was basically alone the entire year while I was at school at least. I would ride my bike after school every day to meet Rob and Chris at Divisadero, the days that we all decided to go to school. For whatever reason, Mt. Whitney got out 15 minutes before Divisadero and gave me just enough time to ride over to the middle school. I failed all of my classes, except for P.E. I got a D in P.E. I didn't even know how that was possible. The days that we all ditched, which were a lot, we just hung out at Chris's house. I would ride my bike over to Chris's house in the morning and we would wait for his parents to go to work and then decide if we were going to go to school that day. Chris's parents were a lot like my mom. They were just too busy with work to have the time to keep track of us. The school did call when we were absent, but we were always home in time to intercept that call. Eventually we grew a brain and started calling in to the school for each other, pretending to be one another's dads. The school didn't seem to know that my parents were divorced and my dad did not live with us. Rob's parents found a way to keep better track of him. He ditched with us sometimes, but he would get caught more often than not, so he went to a lot more school than either Chris or me.

"Hey, man, do you want to go to school today?" I asked Chris like I did every morning that I got to his house.

"No, I've got a math test today."

"I just don't wanna go." We both laughed, but quietly. Chris's parents still hadn't left for work. They knew that Chris was failing, but they never made the connection with his lack of attendance. I guess they just thought he was stupid. I think my mom knew that I ditched all the time, but didn't know what to do about it. Chris's mom came into his room while we were getting ready. We had our backpacks open with our binders out organizing our school work.

"Hi, Will. Chris, don't forget to take out the trash on your way out," Chris's mom said.

"Yeah, mom," Chris responded. She walked over to Chris and kissed him on the cheek. They were a very affectionate family, unlike my own. They were also very religious. They called themselves Pentecostals and I even went to church with them a couple of times. I stopped going though because it was scary how people would talk to themselves and fall on the ground like they were having seizures. Chris never did any of that stuff, but it was expected that he be there. If I did spend the night at his house on Saturday, I ended up going to church in the morning. His step dad would cook us a big breakfast of eggs and bacon and then we would go to church and watch all of the crazy people. I started spending the night on Friday's, even though the breakfasts were really good. Chris's parents both left for work at the same time like they always did and right on cue Rob called.

"Hello," Chris said as he answered the phone. "It's Rob. Let me put it on speaker."

"Are you assholes going to school today?" Rob said.

"Why, no sir, we are not," I said. Chris and I both laughed. "Get your ass over here."

"No, I have to go to school today, there's a math test. My mom would kick my ass if I ditched again."

"Yeah, well, enjoy your test," Chris replied. "Mr. Theeble can kiss my ass."

"Fuck, what are you guys gonna do today? Rob asked.

"Shit, I don't know, Chris, what do you want to do with all this freedom?

"I think we should smoke a bowl and see where the day takes us."

"Sounds like a plan."

"I fucking hate you guys," Rob said.

"Then hoof your ass over here and stop being such a pussy," I said.

"I gotta go, I'm gonna be late. You guys better not be too fucked up to practice."

"Sure, Rob, no worries," Chris said.

"Later, Rob," I said. Chris hung up the phone and pulled out a dime-bag and makeshift pipe that he made out of a Pepsi can from his closet. We couldn't smoke in the house because the smell would never go away and then his parents would know exactly what we were up to. Chris had an oversized doghouse in his backyard that had the roof removed, but no dog. *I wonder what happened to his dog.* That was where we smoked. We smoked the bowl and then got on our bikes and rode in circles in the middle of the Cul-De-Sac. "Hey, man, I'm hungry."

"Me too, you got any money?" Chris replied.

"I've got 5 bucks. Let's go get some Burger King."

"Whopper Cheese heavy everything?"

"You know it." We rode our bikes down Whitendale to South Mooney and got to Burger King. It was about two miles. They weren't serving lunch until 11 and it was barely 10. We waited in the parking lot for an hour, sitting on our bikes, and laughing at all of the people ordering breakfast. I didn't know what was so funny. *Fat people, ugly people, shitty cars, shitty haircuts, random stray cats...* When there was nothing left to laugh at Chris said,

"Hey, man, thanks for hooking me up with Angela."

"Yeah, of course."

"I know it was a long time ago, but I never thanked you."

"You don't have to thank me; I was doing you a favor. So, have you hit that yet?"

"No, her mom doesn't let her hang out much. Haven't had the chance."

"Sorry to hear that. Things will get better next year when you're at Whitney."

"I hope so. We need to find someone for you. Interested in anyone?"

"No, but I'll take anyone at this point. As long as she's not fat."

"For sure, for sure." The time rolled around to 11 and we both ordered two Whoppers. *99 cents each; nice.* We sat outside and finished our whoppers and started on our ride back to Chris's house.

"What happened to your dog?" I asked. It randomly came to me that a giant dog house, without a roof, and no dog was suspicious.

"He died. Old age. He was like 15, which is like, what, a hundred years old?"

"Damn, that sucks. So, what's the deal with the dog house?"

"My step dad wanted to get another dog, but he hasn't done it yet. He tore off the old roof because it was leaking. He was going to build a new roof too."

"And now we use it to get high. It has a new life."

"Yes, it does."

"Maybe you could drop hints that maybe you don't want a new dog."

"Ha, yeah, I really don't. Who do you think was picking up all of the dog shit? That's right, it was me. Remind me to take out the trash when we get back too." We got back to his house in the early afternoon and watched MTV until Rob showed up for practice.

It had been a week since I had seen the beautiful girl with blond hair. We practiced every day after school and every day that week I would look out of Chris's garage, down the street waiting and wondering. Since school was out for summer, we would have a lot more time to practice. The problem was the timing. Chris's parents were fine with us practicing, but only if they weren't home. They always seemed to be home all the time on the weekend. We were all sitting in Chris's living room watching MTV just waiting for a chance to play some music when Chris's little brother, Mitchell said, do you guys want some cookies?" Chris's step dad worked for Keebler and they had copious amounts of cookies stacked in their pantry. We were regularly encouraged to eat as many cookies as we could.

"Yeah, Mitch, grab me some Fudge Stripes," I said.

"I don't need anymore cookies, Rob said. *Good choice. That's strange, he's never turned down cookies before.* I opened the package of Fudge Stripes and started eating the cookies. Chris's mom and step dad came into the room and told us that they were going to the store and would be gone for a while.

"Can we play?" Chris asked while twirling his drumsticks.

"Yes, but keep it down. I don't want the neighbors complaining again. And keep the garage door shut, his mom insisted. We'll be back in a couple of hours."

"Ok, see ya later," Chris said. His parents left and we immediately went into the garage and started playing 'Smells Like Teen Spirit,' which for me was a pretty easy song to play, but for Chris, the drum part through the chorus was rough. That day was no different. Chris struggled and Rob got irritated. Usually when Chris couldn't play something, Rob would sit down behind the set and play it and show us how easy it was. Chris was pretty competitive so this tactic worked to get him to practice harder. For 'Teen Spirit' though, Rob couldn't even play it that well. This was the one song where Rob didn't get totally pissed off when we couldn't play it perfectly.

"It's getting hot in here, let's open the garage," Rob pleaded.

"We can't, my parents said not to and the neighbors..."

"Who cares what your neighbors say!" Rob said as he wiped away beads of sweat that were dripping from his forehead.

"Yeah, it is kind of hot," I said.

"Fine, I'll open the garage, but we have to tone it down," Chris said adamantly. Chris pushed the button for the garage and I turned around to once again look down the street for the beautiful blond girl. As the garage got above my line of sight, I saw the girl, and who was obviously her little brother, walking toward the end of the Cul-De Sac.

"Will, 'Dive,'" Rob said. "Will...Will! Start the damn song." 'Dive' was one of the songs that started on bass so I had to be focused. But I couldn't focus with that beautiful girl walking toward me. *Don't look at her. Just don't look at her.* "All right, all right, relax," I said. I started playing the intro to 'Dive' just as the girl and her brother reached the end of the driveway. They seemed like they wanted to watch us play. *Don't mess up. Don't mess up!* I took my own advice and didn't look directly at her. I looked over her head, around her, at her brother, and even turned around to look at Rob. That focused me up pretty quick. It was an easy song, actually. It would be difficult to mess up. Rob started singing. For the first time in a while, I actually listened to Rob sing. I actually listened to the lyrics. I slowly turned around and looked at the beautiful blond girl right in her eyes. She gave me a little smile, which I returned to her. I guess I was lucky in that the way we were set up in the garage, I was playing at the very front. Chris had his drums set up in the back, while Rob was set up in the middle because of the orientation of the PA system. I had the perfect view. Out of the corner of my eye I saw some people walking towards us. They didn't look happy. There was an old man and a portly, middle-aged woman. They waited until the end of the song and then the portly woman started waving her finger in the air.

"Turn it down! You're too loud. Why don't you shut the door? Do I have to call the police? Where are your parents?" The woman said frantically. Chris got up from his set and put his drumsticks down.

"What's your problem, Karen? We're not even playing that loud."

"We'll see if the police agree! I'm going to have a talk with your parents too!" I took off my bass and looked back at the beautiful girl. She raised her eyebrows and shrugged her shoulders. *She is so cute!*

"Call the police! Like we care. What are they going to do? Nothing!" Rob said while strumming his guitar in defiance. The portly woman and man walked back down the street.

"She's gonna call the police! We need to stop for today," Chris said.

"So, we're just going to cut practice after two songs? Stupid waste of time," Rob said as he put down his guitar. "That pisses me off. I'll call my dad. Maybe we can practice at my house."

"Nah, I'm good for today. Let's just chill," I said. I had no intention of leaving that very spot.

"Fine. Whatever. I'm going home." Rob put his guitar away, strapped it to his back, walked past the girl and her brother without saying a word, and continued down the street. I walked toward the girl with an eagerness that I hoped wasn't apparent. She waved at me and said,

"Hi, I'm Hannah...this is my brother, Michael."

"I knew that was your brother. I saw you guys moving in last week. I'm Will, nice to meet you, Hannah." I pointed behind me.

"That's Chris, this is his house, and that was Rob." I pointed down the street. "He has an anger problem, but he'll get over it."

"Cool. How long have you guys had a band?"

"We've been playing together for like, what, two years, Chris?"

"Yeah, I think it's been almost two years," Chris replied quickly.

"You guys are really good," Hannah said. "What's your band name?"

"Ummm, we don't have a band name. We've never played an actual show." Chris and I looked at each other kind of perplexed. "How did we not think about having a band name?" I said.

"You should come up with a name. I could help if you wanted," Hannah said.

"Yeah, we should talk to Rob about it," I said.

"Yeah, for sure," Chris said, "and playing a show. We're good enough to play a show...Aren't we?"

"I think you guys sounded great," Hannah said.

"Yeah, you're really good," Michael reiterated.

"Cool, thanks!" I said. I was really enjoying my conversation with Hannah. *Hannah. Beautiful name for a beautiful girl.* I really enjoyed looking at her. She reminded me of someone...I thought about it for a split second and it came to me. *Gwen Stefani. That was it. Gwen Stefani with longer hair!* A police car slowly approached as I was coming to my revelation about Hannah. Both cops got out of the car and were looking around the neighborhood as if they were lost.

"We got a noise complaint," one of the cops said as he looked inside of Chris's garage. "You kids in a band?"

"Yeah, but were done playing for today," I said.

"Hannah. Michael. Get over here!"

"That's my mom, I gotta go. See ya later," Hannah said.

"All right, bye Hannah," I said.

"See ya," Chris said.

"Ok guys, just keep it down." The cops left without another word. I looked down the street and saw the portly woman shaking her head. She did not seem content with the outcome. I turned my gaze back to Hannah walking towards her house. Her hips swayed back and forth while her long, blond hair bounced from shoulder to shoulder. *Damn she's fine.* Chris and I looked at each other for a second and then went inside to watch some more MTV.

"Hey, man, do you want to spend the night?" Chris asked. I struggled with this question because on the one hand, I did not want to go to church the next morning, and on the other, maybe I would get to see Hannah afterwards. "You'll have to come to church..." *Thank you, Captain obvious.*

"Yeah, sure, why not?" I said not convincingly. "I haven't seen that many crazy-ass people in a small room since, well, the last time I went to your church."

"Shut up, man, they're not crazy." *They were.*

"Maybe not crazy, but what's that word...psycho, no, no, Ummm...right, schizophrenic. Schizophrenic, not their fault, just mentally ill." I let out a sarcastic laugh.

"Whatever, man, I don't have a choice, and so neither do you." *Awesome.* I was only 15, but something did not seem right to me to force someone to do something that they did not want to do. Chris was pretending to want to do it to appease his parents, but I had to pretend to want to go too just to be able to spend the night and hang out with my friend. Seemed shady. *I wonder if his parents even believed any of it.* I never saw them writhing around on the floor and chewing on their tongues. "We should call Rob and see if he wants to spend the night." Rob never spent the night at Chris's because he refused to go to church. Any church. He once told me that it was against his religion to go to church. I had no idea what to make of that, but I think he had the right idea.

"I don't think that he wants to. He never wants to hang out if it doesn't involve practice." *That's not totally true.*

"I guess you're right. He probably needs some time to calm down anyway. Dude has a serious anger problem."

"He does seem to lose his temper a lot."

"Yeah, he does. I can't figure out what's wrong with him. Anyway, I'm gonna call Angela and see what's up with her."

"Ok, I'll hang out and watch TV." Chris left to his bedroom to make the call. His parents still weren't home yet from shopping. I got up from the couch and walked over to the window. I pulled the curtains aside and stared down the street hoping that Hannah was outside. She wasn't though. No one was outside. She was all I could think about. I wanted to go knock on her door, but I didn't. I went and sat back down on the couch and continued to watch MTV. A little while later Chris came and sat down next to me with a smirk on his face.

"What's up, what are you so happy about?" I asked with genuine interest.

"Angela misses me, and oh yeah, she says hi. She wants me to sneak out and meet her tonight at Blain Park."

"Shit, are you gonna do it? Yeah, we're gonna do it."

"I'm not looking to be a third wheel, man. And what if your parents catch you? They'll bust your ass."

"They're not gonna catch me. I've got a plan. And you're not going to be a third wheel."

"Wait, what?" *I know what that means.*

"Angela has her friend, Vicki spending the night..."

"No, no way! Vicki Ramos? She's hella ugly and kind of fat. No, no, no, and one more no to be clear."

"Come on, bro, take one for the team. She's not that ugly." Chris let out a subtle laugh and literally coughed as he choked on his words. "Dude, it's gonna be dark anyway." It was strange. Although Chris did have a point, I couldn't get Hannah out of my head long enough to even consider it. *What the hell was wrong with me?* I had exchanged three words with Hannah. I had known Vicki since the sixth grade. Vicki was a sure thing. Not even close to what I wanted and Hannah made her look terrible, but she was a guaranteed hook up.

"So, let me get this straight...We sneak out without your parents knowing, pedal our asses over to Blain Park, you hook up with Angela, and I entertain the female version of Quasimodo...sound about right?" Chris laughed.

"Yeah, sounds like a plan."

"I am not letting that girl shove her used up tongue in my mouth. So gross, man. I'll talk to her, I guess. I admit, I thought about it for a minute, but I am so not going to hook up with Vicki."

"It's that new girl, Hannah, isn't it?"

"Maybe." *It was.*

"Dude, you don't even know her and like I said before, you don't have a snowball's chance in hell."

"We'll see about that. I think I do." *I hope I do.*

"Shit, are you going to help me out or not? Angela doesn't want to walk to the park alone. Vicki is part of the deal."

"Fine, but you're going to owe me." I heard the sound of car doors closing outside. "I think your parents are home."

"All right, I need to ask them if you can stay the night. Then we can make a plan for sneaking out."

"I'm not sure it's that complicated. Wait for them to go to sleep and then leave."

"We'll talk about it later...shhhh, they're coming in." Chris's parents, led by his step dad walked through the front door and into the living room where we were sitting. MTV, as always, was playing in the background.

"Chris! Your ass is grass and I'm the lawnmower!" Chris's step dad said while pointing his finger into Chris's chest.

"What'd I do?" Chris said while attempting to stand up. I just sat there on the couch in disbelief. *Ass is grass. Lawnmower?*

"We told you to keep it down. We told you to keep the garage door closed," Chris's mom chimed in. "The neighbors just told us that the police came."

"It wasn't a big dea…" Before Chris could even finish his sentence, his step dad turned around and walked towards the kitchen.

"You're grounded!" Chris's step dad said emphatically.

"Grounded? What the hell? I'm 14, you can't ground me anymore. I'm not a little kid," Chris pleaded.

"Will, I think it's time for you to go home," Chris's mom said.

"Wait, I was going to ask if he could spend the night."

"No, that's not going to happen," Chris's step dad interjected. I got up and walked toward the door. Chris looked at me and winked his left eye as if he were trying to convey to me that the plan was still on. The plan that still hadn't been planned was somehow still on.

"Later, Chris," I said.

"Wait. How long I'm I grounded for?" Chris asked his parents in an unusually high-pitched tone. Chris's mom looked at his step dad and they both nodded in agreement like this had been previously decided.

"Two weeks no practice, no phone, no friends over," Chris's mom said with precision. I think I may have been more disappointed than Chris when I heard the terms of his imprisonment. I needed Chris as an excuse to be close to Hannah. *Shit.* Rob was gonna be pissed too. As I was walking out the door, I heard Chris pleading for leniency and his mom was saying something about earning their trust back. I grabbed my bike off of Chris's lawn and started riding down the street. I slowed to a crawl in front of Hannah's driveway. An Isuzu Trooper and an old motorcycle were parked outside, but there were no signs of life. I picked up speed and continued home. As soon as I walked through the door, I picked up the phone to call Rob.

"Is Rob there?" I asked his mom.

"Yes, he is, just a minute."

"Hello?"

"Hey, it's Will. Chris got grounded. No practice for two weeks."

"What? How did that happen? What a dumbass!"

"It was the neighbors. They told his parents about the cops."

"Shit. Well, how are they going to stop us from practicing while they're at work?"

"Good question. I don't know. I don't think they really can. Tomorrow's off for sure though. I'll cruise by his house on Monday when his parents are gone."

"Ok, call me Monday if we can practice."

"All right, hey I gotta call Angela." *Shit.* "I think I should call Angela. I need to tell her what happened. Chris was gonna sneak out to meet her tonight."

"What a dumbass. Ok, talk to you later."

"Later, man." I hung up the phone and thought about whether I should call Angela or not. *Was it my business? Chris can't use the phone so I have to call her.* I couldn't decide what to do so I decided to relax to some 'Resident Evil.' I bought the game when it came out, but I hadn't had the chance to play it because of school and practice. I played for a couple of hours. Killed some Zombies. *Good times.* My mom was cooking some spaghetti for dinner, which I could smell aromatizing our entire apartment. My brother, Larry, wasn't home from work yet, and I wanted to maximize the time that I got to play in peace. We shared a room so any amount of alone time I got was a good thing. When he got home, I stopped playing the game.

"Hey bro, how's your little band going?" he asked me as he was changing clothes.

"Good. How's your dish washing job going?" Larry was always bouncing between jobs. As in, he was always getting fired. He graduated from high school but only managed a few classes at College of the Sequoias.

"It's a job, like any other. At least I have a job to help mom out. When are you gonna get a job?" Larry was 22. I didn't have much respect for him. He was a grown man living at home because of terrible life choices.

"I'll get a job when I can. I need a work permit from school."

"Yeah, you get on that." One of the things that bothered me the most about him was the fact that he treated me less like a brother and more like a son. He seemed to think that I needed a dad more than a brother. I went out to the kitchen to grab a plate of spaghetti.

"Welcome back stranger," my mom said as I approached. She would use that phrase a lot. I guess she said it because I wasn't home very often. My mom and dad got divorced when I was 4. I didn't remember him at all. The only thing I had to prove his existence was two family pictures. He supposedly lived in Louisiana, but no one talked to him or about him. I often wondered why they got divorced or whose fault it was, but I wasn't angry about it. It was strange though how my mom never talked about it.

"Thanks, mom, the food smells great."

"What were you up to today?"

"Nothing. Usual. Practice at Chris's."

"How's that going?"

"Fine." I grabbed my plate and sat down on the couch in front of the TV. Larry followed, and then my mom sat in her wooden rocking chair. I couldn't understand why she liked that thing. It was as hard as a rock. We all sat and ate while Star Trek: The Next Generation played on the TV. As I finished my spaghetti, I remembered that I needed to make a phone call to Angela. I rinsed off my plate and placed it in the sink while looking out in the living room at my mom and brother. I couldn't make that phone call. There was no privacy. I didn't want them to know what was going on. *It doesn't matter anyway. It's none of my business.*

I rode my bike over to Chris's house late Monday morning after I knew that his parents would be at work. When I turned the corner onto Laura Street, I saw Hannah shooting some hoops outside of her house. She was playing on one of those portable basketball hoops that people put in their driveways. As I approached, Hannah made a jump shot. *Not bad.* "Hey, Will, do you want to play?" Hannah said as she collected the ball. She was wearing black, loose-fitting sweat pants and a white sports bra. Her long blond hair was pulled back into a pony-tail. She kneeled down on the ground to tie one of her shoes while looking up at me. Her hair whipped around from behind her back. "Well, are you afraid to get beat by a girl?" She looked raw and athletic, but still hot. She wasn't wearing any makeup. She didn't seem to care about her less than pristine appearance. There was something very impressive about her. "Take a picture, dude, it lasts longer," she said with a smirk.

"Oh, sorry, I was just thinking...I need to go see about Chris. He got grounded on Saturday. I guess we were playing too loud. The cops. His parents were not happy."

"Oh yeah, my parents weren't happy about it either. They didn't want us hanging out down there." *That's not good.* "Play a game with me, to 21."

"Well, since you put it that way..." I smiled at her and put my bike down against the curb. I wasn't really dressed to play basketball. I was wearing a black White Zombie t-shirt and oversized blue jeans; they kind of drug on the ground when I walked and almost completely covered my Van's Chukka boots. "Do you have a thing for my hair?" I asked as I started pulling my hair back.

"Yeah, hold on." Hannah ran up the driveway and into her house. I was really beginning to like watching her from behind. She had the most perfect body I had ever seen. She came back outside almost immediately. "Here's a scrunchy, it's got some of my hair in it, sorry." *Not a problem.*

"Hannah, with the quickness," I said decisively.

"That's right, you wanna race?"

"Nah, maybe another time, thanks for the hair thing."

"It's a scrunchy."

"That's a weird word." Hannah smiled as she picked up the basketball.

"Ok, we're playing to 21. 2 points for lay-ups and 3 points for jump shots. And no dunking." The basket was low enough for me to dunk, but my pants would have prevented me from attempting it. "My dad hasn't put the sand in it yet."

"No problem."

"Your ball."

"Ladies first," I said assuredly with a smirk.

"Your funeral," Hannah replied. Her confidence was astonishing. I believed her. She took the ball and started dribbling toward me. I had my hands out to guard her going by me for an easy lay-up. She turned around and started backing into me to close in on the basket. *Really!?* I put my hand on her lower back right below her sports bra to prevent any more progress. She quickly turned and shot a lay-up into the backboard. It was good.

"Nice shot," I said.

"Thanks. Let's play losers. Your ball." I took the ball and did not attempt to dribble past where I already was. I could feel my pants wedging underneath my shoes and I had no intention of falling down and embarrassing myself in front of that girl. I took a jump shot and it was a terrible looking air ball. Hannah grabbed the ball and quickly shot another good lay-up.

"4-0," Hannah said with ruthlessness in her voice.

"I'm a little out of practice," I said while hoping to maintain some dignity. The next shot was indicative of how the rest of the game was going to go.

"Me too, I haven't played for months!" Hannah said with enthusiasm. *I'm screwed.* She took the ball and started dribbling it toward me and then picked up speed. She stopped dead in her tracks, pulled up, and took a distant jump shot. I fell backwards and lost my balance because my pants got caught again under my shoe. My hands hit the ground first in my search for balance. The shot was perfect. I heard the unmistakable 'Swoosh' sound. *Nothing but net.* I looked at my hands. They were torn up pretty bad but only bleeding a little. "Are you ok?" Hannah kneeled down next to me and took hold of my hands. I looked into her eyes. *Beautiful.*

"What color are your eyes?" I asked while admiring the outline of her face.

"Brown with green speckles," she answered quickly as if she had been asked this question before. "And your eyes are light blue almost hazel, but more blue than green. Much prettier than mine."

"That's not true, you have beautiful eyes."

"Thanks," Hannah said. It was apparent that this was not the first time she had heard this compliment. She did not blush. She continued to look into my eyes. "So, are you hurt? You want to keep playing?"

"I'm fine, of course I want to keep playing. I have to redeem myself."

"All right. Cool. 7-0. let me help you up." Hannah stood up, and reached out both of her hands. I grabbed on and pulled myself up. I leaned over and rolled up my pant legs to the point that they were no longer dragging on the ground. It didn't make a difference. "10-0, 12-0, 14-0, 17-0, 19-0, 22 and game." The score rang off of Hannah's tongue in quick succession. "Good game," Hannah said as she put her hand out.

"Good game for you. You're actually really good at basketball." I shook her hand and focused on how soft it was even though we had been playing for so long.

"Did you expect any less?"

"I guess not," I said with a subtle smile on my face. I was impressed. I didn't try to lose. She simply kicked my ass.

"Better luck next time."

"So, there's going to be a next time?" I looked into her eyes and then let go of her hand.

"Yeah. There has to be. You have to redeem yourself, remember?"

"Yup. So, I have to go talk to Chris." I walked over to the curb and grabbed my bike. "I'll see ya later."

"All right, cool," Hannah said as she took another shot at the basket. It too, was good. I rode down to the end of the street and placed my bike on Chris's lawn. There were no cars in the driveway so I knew the coast was clear. I knocked on his door and then rang the doorbell. Chris answered.

"Hey, man, what happened when I left?"

"They ruined my life, that's what happened. They took my drums."

"What!?"

"Yeah, man, it's such bullshit. Are you coming in or what?"

"Yeah." We walked inside and sat on the couch. MTV was playing in the background like always. "Rob is gonna be pissed."

"Rob is always pissed, but that's not the worst of it. They took the phone with them so I can't call Angela. Here, let me show you something." Chris led me to his bedroom. "Something missing?"

"Your door. Where's your door?"

"They took it. I don't know where it is..."

"So, that means..."

"Right! I couldn't sneak out to see her Saturday night. We were supposed to meet at Midnight. She's gonna think I stood her up. So, I have no privacy, no phone, and no drums. For two fucking weeks! Do me a favor, call Angela and tell her that I'm sorry."

"Sure thing. I need to call Rob too. I guess practice is off for two weeks."

"Yeah. This is fucking bullshit. You should probably go before my mom gets home for her lunch break."

"All right, man, give me a call as soon as you can."

"Definitely. See you later." I let myself out, picked my bike up off of the lawn and headed home. Hannah wasn't playing basketball anymore. *What am I going to do for the next two weeks?* I rode past her house and looked through her window to see if I could catch a glimpse of her. I couldn't see anyone through the curtains and continued riding home. My brother wasn't home when I got there. It was my chance. I called Rob. He was pissed and threatened to find a new drummer. I called Angela. She was pissed and threatened to break up with Chris. Things seemed to be falling apart around me, but I was calm. Life was good. As I lay down to sleep that night, I saw Hannah's beautiful brown eyes gazing through me and everything was right with the world.

Chapter Three

In the stars

I T HAD BEEN ALMOST two weeks since I had seen or heard from Chris or Rob. Chris was still grounded. I called Rob a couple of times, but his mom told me each time that he was out with his dad. I didn't really care what Rob was doing and who he was doing it with because I was much more interested in Chris calling me. I really wanted to see Hannah again. I picked up one of my brother's guitars. It was a sunburst Les Paul. My brother loved that guitar. He was at work though so as long as I didn't break anything he would never know. I strapped the guitar around my shoulder and began strumming the intro to 'About a Girl.'

• • • • • • • • • •

"Hey, Rob, I want to learn to play guitar," I said after practice.

"Really? Why?"

"I don't know. I've been playing the bass for like, what, a year now, and I'm just bored with it I guess."

"Hmmmm. Ok, I'll teach you how to play guitar, but you're still my bass player, and any practice you do is on your own time."

"Yes, sir, captain, sir!" I said sarcastically while letting out a little laugh.

"Shut up, I'm serious!" Rob said while taking off his guitar and handing it to me. "You're a bass player first."

"I got it. Now, what's the first thing I need to learn?" I strapped on his guitar ready to play.

"Ok, there's a lot of theory and stuff like that. You don't need to know any of that. Kurt Cobain didn't know all of that shit. What you need to know are basic chords. You already know the notes on the bass. The most basic chord is the power chord." Rob pointed at the fret board. "This is a B on the second string, second fret, and an E on the third string, second fret. You already know the open E, the first string. Play them all together and you've got an E chord." I started strumming and it sounded pretty bad. "You've got to press down harder on the frets." It started sounding a little better. "And then your G power chord is played at the third fret on the first string, and then the fifth on the second and third strings, like this." Rob pointed to what fingers belonged where. It was a stretch, but I was able to play it. "Now, practice moving between those two chords and play 'About a Girl.' You can move that power chord shape all over the fret board and play any song you want. Your index finger placement will dictate what chord you're playing."

"Wow, Rob, thanks, that's pretty simple, actually."

"It gets a lot more complicated than that, but those are the basics. Pretty much any song you know on bass can be played with power chords on the guitar."

"Cool." I stumbled through 'About a Girl' for a few minutes and then handed the guitar back to Rob. I was really excited to learn all of the songs I already knew all over again. The only problem was that I didn't have a guitar.

The next morning, I woke up to the phone ringing. *What time is it? Shit.*

"Will, it's Chris on the phone!" My mom yelled through the wall. I slowly got out of bed and headed to the phone.

"Hey, man, are you not grounded anymore?"

"Nope, I'm calling you, aren't I? Get your ass over here."

"All right, I need to take a shower. I'll be over in an hour."

"An hour? Seriously? What are you gonna do? You can jack off later."

"Nah, I got a lot of hair to wash. You wouldn't know anything about that with your preppy haircut."

"And I'm happy about that. Just hurry up." Chris hung up the phone and I jumped in the shower. *What's his problem?*

I passed by Hannah's house at about 11. She wasn't outside as I rode by. I was disappointed. I was looking forward to a rematch, but Chris was waiting anyway. Chris's garage was open when I rode up. He was sitting behind his drum set twirling his sticks. "I got my drums back," Chris said while putting down his sticks.

"What's wrong with you? Shouldn't you be happy?"

"Before I called you this morning, I called Angela. We got into a fight and she broke up with me."

"Shit. What'd she say?" I put my bike down in his garage and walked toward him.

"She said that it wasn't working out and that we should see other people...Shit! This is so messed up. I never even got any."

"Yeah, that sucks, man. Do you think it had to do with getting grounded?"

"She said it didn't, but I know it did. What else could it have been?"

"I don't know."

"Can you call her for me?"

"Yeah, I can call her later."

"Thanks, see if she'll change her mind."

"Are we going to practice today? We should call Rob."

"Yeah, let's call Rob."

"Cool. Let's play some music. It'll get your mind off of Angela."

"I doubt that." We went into Chris's living room and called Rob. He answered and said that he would be right over. As we were waiting for Rob to show up, we grabbed some cookies and headed back outside. Hannah and her brother were playing basketball down the street. She saw us standing under the tree in Chris's yard and started to walk over to us. I opened the package of cookies and looked at Chris.

"Damn she's hot," I said while eating a cookie.

"Yeah. I should ask her out." My cookie almost fell out of my mouth.

"Don't even try it! She's mine. I'm going to smooth things over with you and Angela. Don't worry about it."

"You should make a move then."

"I will, these things take time."

"Sure, sure, they do. Don't be a pussy."

"All right, all right, shut up, shut up, they're close." Hannah and her brother walked up to us.

"Hey, are you guys gonna play today?" Michael said.

"Yeah, we're gonna play as soon as our guitar player gets here."

"That's so cool. Can we watch you guys play?" Hannah said.

"Yeah, you're always welcome. Do you want a cookie?"

"Yeah, I'll have a cookie," Hannah said.

"Michael?" I asked.

"Yeah." Chris, Michael, Hannah, and I all stood in a sort of broken circle eating cookies. We were halfway through the package when I asked Hannah once more if she wanted another cookie.

"Are you trying to fatten me up?" Hannah said with a smirk on her face.

"Nah, I like you just the way you are." Hannah smiled. Chris audibly sighed.

"You like my sister?" Michael said with a mouthful of half-eaten cookies.

"Shut up, Michael!" Hannah responded.

"I just meant that I don't think you could ever get fat." I was feeling brave at that moment. "What, are you like 100 pounds soaking wet?" I asserted.

"Yeah, something like that," Hannah responded while taking another cookie and smiling. "But, you're just as skinny as me, dude."

"Oh, burn," Chris said.

"I didn't mean anything bad," Hannah said. Her demeanor changed. She seemed concerned that she had hurt my feelings.

"No worries," I said. "I weigh like 147 pounds..."

"Soaking wet?" Chris chimed in.

"Yeah, soaking wet," I agreed. "I can't gain weight no matter how much I eat."

"Same," Hannah said. The smile returned to her beautiful face. She placed her hand under my hand and took another cookie from the package. I could see Chris rolling his eyes.

"I'm gonna go tune my drums and wait for Rob," Chris said as he walked into his garage. At that moment Mitchell came outside from the front door. He walked up to us and I introduced him to Hannah and Michael.

"Michael, why don't you take Mitchell to play basketball?"

"Yeah, ok, Mitchell, do you want to play?" Michael asked. "It's set up at the end of our driveway."

"Ummm, Sure." Michael and Mitchell walked down the street.

"Best friends forever," Hannah said as they walked away.

"Yeah, that was easy. Kids...go play. Ok." We both laughed. I was able to really get a chance to look at her now that we were alone. She was wearing low cut blue jeans and a flower-patterned mid-drift t-shirt. It was so simple and yet so perfect. I could see every curve of her body. I could see the narrowness of her waist cascade into the tops of her hip bones. Her long blond hair was gently flowing in the afternoon breeze across her shoulders. Chris started banging on his drums which woke me from my dream-like state. I looked down the street and saw Michael and Mitchell playing basketball and then I saw Rob in the distance with his guitar strapped to his back. "There's Rob. It looks like it's time to practice," I said indifferently.

"Oh, cool, what are you guys practicing for? Are you going to play a show?" *Good question, Hannah.*

"Nah, we're just playing for fun right now." *Not that fun, actually.*

"That's cool. Hey, I have an idea. I'll go ask all of the neighbors if they want to come watch you guys play. Then you'll be playing a show!"

"Sounds good to me."

"Ok, cool beans." *Cool beans?* "I'll go get my brother and his new friend and then we'll go door to door." Hannah started walking back to her house, passing Rob in the process. Rob seemed to acknowledge her, but kept walking toward me.

"Hey, Rob, Hannah is gonna ask people from the neighborhood to watch us play."

"Ok, whatever...wait, maybe you won't play like shit if people are watching," Rob said with a smirk on his face.

"Oh, thanks, Rob, I appreciate the confidence."

"I don't have any confidence in you...or Chris, especially Chris, actually."

"Again, thanks, you're a great friend," I said while raising my left eyebrow."

"I am your friend, but this is business." *Is it?* "Speaking of business, I don't think Chris is gonna work out. He's not reliable. I found a new drummer. I met him last week and he seems coo..."

"Rob, we're not replacing Chris. It wasn't his fault he got grounded," I interjected. Chris was practicing the chorus drum fill to 'Teen Spirit' in the garage as I grew more irritated.

"It's not just that. He's not very good. Matt's much better."

"I'm not very good either. Are you gonna replace me when you find a better bass player?" *What an asshole.*

"Well, yeah, but luckily for you, not many people play bass. We can still be friends with Chris. Like I said, it's business."

"Rob, you're stupid if you think that's going to go well." *I'd rather be friends with Chris.*

"I don't care if it does anyway." The thing is...Matt won't be able to play until after summer, so we'll keep Chris until then."

"That's a dick move, I'm gonna tell him what you have planned right now." I turned to walk toward Chris and Rob grabbed my arm.

"You really want to fuck up his summer just to stick it to me?"

"No, I don't want to fuck up anyone's summer, but Chris should know. Actually, Chris should still be our drummer."

"He will be, for two more months, then I'll tell him. If he asks, I'll tell him that you didn't know anything about it."

"Fine, Rob, have it your way." A lot of things went through my head as we walked into the garage to set up for practice. *I could maybe start a new band with Chris...I could play guitar. We would need a singer.* I couldn't sing to save my life, or at least not well enough that anyone would tolerate listening to me. *We would need to find a bassist...If it were hard for Rob to find a bassist, how was I going to find one? Hannah...Hannah.* I didn't want to be anywhere else. *I have to figure out what I'm going to do by the end of summer... I have time.*

"Hey, Rob," Chris said, sorry about practice, my parents..."

"Don't worry about it," Rob interjected, "let's just play." Rob plugged in his guitar, I plugged in my bass and we both tuned up. "Let's play 'Teen Spirit' to start." I nodded in agreement. Chris didn't have much of a reaction, which usually meant he wouldn't have a problem playing it. Rob started the song off with the iconic guitar riff and then we joined. It sounded good. Chris was playing it right. I could see down the street, quite a few people walking toward us. Hannah was in the back of the group with Michael and Mitchell following. It looked like mostly neighborhood kids, but, to my surprise, there were a couple of adults. They were probably coming to tell us to keep it down. Everyone settled in, maybe 10 people total, around the driveway by the time Rob started playing the solo. Michael and Mitchell were running around the driveway seemingly playing tag. Hannah sat down in the grass and started talking with one of the girls in Chris's neighborhood named Casey Green. I had talked to her a few times before since she lived so close. She was a grade below Rob and Chris, so she was going to be an 8th grader. Hannah turned and talked to Casey in between making eye contact with me. *What were they talking about?* We finished playing 'Teen Spirit' and we got a small round of applause. *Wow, that's cool.* "Thank you," Rob said through the microphone and followed with 'About a Girl.' By that point, I had played 'About a Girl' a thousand times, and could play it blind-folded. We started playing the song. Because of the lack of attention I had to give the song, I was able to focus my attention on Hannah completely, with an occasional nod to Rob and Chris. Hannah was still intermittently talking with Casey. She would say something to Casey, Casey would say something to Hannah, they would laugh; they would smile. Hannah started pulling out blades of grass one at a time. *Why's she doing that? She's so hot.* We finished playing the song and again we got some light applause. "Thanks," Rob said. He looked at me and said 'Dive.' I started playing the song.

"Whoo-hoo!" Hannah blurted out while clapping, which brought a smile to my face. It was the intro to 'Dive,' not a guitar solo, but I appreciated her support. We then played 'Come as You Are,' 'Aneurysm,' and 'In Bloom.' Our audience had trickled down to just Hannah, Casey, Michael, and Mitchell.

"Breed," Rob said. I looked at Chris and he looked back at me. We both shrugged our shoulders as Rob started the song. 'Breed' was the fastest song that we played and I still wasn't that great at playing it despite practicing it all the time. I was determined to not mess up though because Hannah was watching. Rob started the song off with a healthy amount of feedback that had our audience wincing in distress. Rob started, then Chris, and then I came in.

I was feeling good. We sounded better than we ever had. I was playing it right, in time, with Chris. Rob allowed himself a small smile as we finished the song. It was only a 3-minute song, but seemed to go by even faster than that. Hannah and Casey were the only ones left watching at that point, but they both clapped enthusiastically for us. Michael and Mitchell had gone back to playing basketball down the street. "Not bad," Rob said through the microphone.

"Hey, Rob, let's take a break, I gotta take a piss," Chris said.

"All right, when you come back I wanna practice 'Heart-Shaped Box.' We haven't played it before, but it's not hard on drums and bass."

"Ok, I'll be right back," Chris said as he got up from behind his drums. I set my bass down and walked over to Hannah and Casey.

"You sounded great," Hannah said assuredly with a smile on her face.

"Yeah, you guys were great!" Casey followed. Hannah looked much older than Casey especially with them standing next to one-another. Casey was cute, but was flat-chested and seemingly still waiting on puberty. Hannah looked like she was 17. *How old is she? What grade is she in?* I wanted my questions answered, but I didn't want to seem obvious or desperate. Rob walked up to join our group.

"Dude, you sound just like Kurt Cobain!" Hannah said.

"Uhm, thanks," Rob said haphazardly. He then looked at Casey and said, "Hey."

"Hey, Rob, Casey said, you guys are awesome!"

"Thanks," Rob said as he turned around. "I need to detune my guitar." Rob walked back into the garage.

"What's his problem?" Hannah asked.

"I'll let you know when I figure it out," I whispered. All three of us laughed.

"He doesn't seem very social," Hannah said.

"More like anti-social," I said. "I don't think he talked to anyone until I came along. It's weird. We're friends, but I still don't get him." I heard Chris playing a fill on the drums so I knew he was back and practice was on.

"Hey, I'm gonna go over to Casey's house for a while," Hannah said. "I'll see ya later."

"Ok, see you later. Bye Casey, thanks for coming by."

"Anytime," Casey said as they started walking over to her house. Hannah looked back at me and caught a glimpse of me watching her walk away. She smiled and slowly turned back around.

"Hey! Practice is back on!" Rob said as he walked out of the garage. "You need to focus on the band and not on that girl!" Hannah and Casey overheard what Rob said and started laughing as they continued over to Casey's house.

"Thanks for your cock-blockery, Rob, I really appreciate it." I said while shaking my head.

"Give it up. You have literally zero chance."

"She seems to like me."

"She seems to like everyone!"

"What are you trying to say? Like, you think she's a slut?"

"They're all sluts, dude."

"Real nice, Rob, no wonder you've never had a girlfriend."

"Go ahead, make your move with her. You'll see. She'll turn you down quicker than the Chargers being out of the playoff race every year."

"We're you saving that one up?"

"Yup, and it was God damn perfect!" I didn't like what I was hearing. I didn't like the fact that Rob could be right. *Maybe Hannah was just being nice. Maybe she was just a friendly person. Maybe it was all in my head.*

"You're wrong," I said, which is all I could come up with. "Let's get back to practice. And, dude, the Chargers were just in the Super Bowl."

"And they got blown out so badly, I'm surprised you even mentioned it." We walked back into the garage. I didn't have any response to Rob at that point. "That's right. You've got nothing to say."

"Heart Shaped Box, right?"

It was the sixth week of school freshman year when I started noticing a girl in my English class named Kristi. Mr. Harden changed the seating chart, which put Kristi right in front of me. She was tall for a girl. She must have been like five-foot-nine. She was almost as tall as me. She had long brown hair that went past the middle of her back and it always ended up in a pool on my desk. I didn't mind though. She smelled really good. It was like walking through Macy's at the mall. Mr. Harden was having the class work on plot maps of 'Romeo and Juliet' and we were supposed to use colored pencils to make them look nice. Every time that Kristi would move her head, her hair would move across my paper. I tapped Kristi on her shoulder and she turned around. *She's really pretty.* "Ummm, Kristi, I think that I'm coloring your hair."

"Oh my goodness, I'm so sorry," she said in a very soft voice.

"It's ok, I just thought you should know," I said while moving my colored pencils.

"Oh, thank you. I'll move my hair." She carefully lifted her hair off of my desk and swung it over her right shoulder side-swiping me in the face. "Oh my god, sorry," she said while turning back around.

"Don't worry about it." I went back to work but couldn't help stare at her now bare neck. She had a really thin, long neck that I found appealing. I wanted to touch it, but I didn't. I didn't say anything else to her that day, but I thought about her every day at practice. I was a little jealous of Chris. He had a girlfriend and

I wanted one too. He had a girlfriend because of me and I knew that if I could do it for him, I could do it for myself. A few days had passed and I wanted to make my move with Kristi. I had an addiction to Starburst candy and decided that the best place for the wrappers was going to be in Kristi's hair instead of the pencil pouch of my backpack like usual. I would take out a square of the candy, unsheathe the wrapper, place it in my mouth, roll the wrapper into a little ball, and gently toss it into her hair. The first time I did it, the wrapper simply fell back down on my desk. Undeterred, I tried again and again until one stuck. I let out an obnoxious laugh.

"Will, are you ok?" Mr. Harden asked.

"Yeah, sorry, I was thinking of something funny."

"Would you like to share with the rest of the class?"

"No." The entire class was looking at me. *Awesome.* "It won't happen again." I pulled out another Starburst and continued working on disposing of the wrappers. At the end of class, Kristi got up, ran her fingers through her hair and all of the wrappers fell out. I laughed. I thought she would be mad, but she wasn't.

"You're a little devil," she said while smiling.

"You want a Starburst?" I asked.

"Sure, can I have a pink one?" *The pink ones are the best.*

"Yeah." I handed her the candy as we walked out of class. "What do you have next?"

"Math." She put the candy in her mouth but didn't bite down.

"Can I walk you to class?"

"Sure." Her math class was across campus. I had some time. We walked right next to each other. *It looks like we should be together.*

"So, Kristi, I was thinking. Do you want to go...?"

"I have a boyfriend," she quickly interjected.

"You do? But I haven't seen you with anyone."

"Yeah, he goes to Redwood." Redwood was Visalia's first high school and also, coincidentally, our arch rival. We had this Cowhide football game every year where the winner, in addition to bragging rights, literally got a Cowhide. Redwood seemed to win it every year. Mt. Whitney people and Redwood people had a healthy disdain for one another.

"I know some people that go to Redwood, what's his name?"

"You don't know him, he's a senior."

"You're dating a senior? Your parents are okay with that?"

"They don't know. Look, I've got to get to class, I'm gonna be late." *I'm gonna be late too, and for nothing.* Kristi walked faster and I slowed down.

"All right, see you later." She didn't respond and I turned around. I felt my shoulders round over and started walking to my P.E class. I gazed at my blue chukka boots as I counted each snail-paced step I took. One of the assistant principals yelled at me from across the hall.

"Hey, get to class! Hurry up!" The bell rang before I had the chance to respond. *Shit.*

After practice was over, I grabbed a box of cookies and went outside. I sat down on the curb outside of Chris's house. It was the perfect vantage point to see all the way down the street. I was sitting right in the middle. Rob walked out of the garage with his guitar strapped to his back.

"Later," Rob said as he walked right past me.

"You're not going to hang out?"

"No, I wanna go eat some food."

"All right, later." I watched Rob walk down the street and then disappear into the distance. Chris's step-dad pulled up to the driveway and we exchanged waves. "Chris is inside," I said.

"Did you guys keep it down today?"

"Yeah." *We didn't.*

"You can stay for dinner if you want. We're having tacos."

"Thanks, I'll call my mom to see if it's okay." The sun was beating down on my face. The heat was oppressive. The heat was always oppressive in Visalia during the summer, but it felt hotter than usual. I was uncomfortable, but I didn't move. I felt a weight that tied me to the concrete. Hannah sat down right next to me without warning. She didn't say anything before sitting down. It was almost like she knew that I was in a bad mood. "Where did you come from?" I said, while acting sort of startled. "I didn't see you walk up."

"I snuck up on you. Pretty good, huh?"

"Yeah, I guess I'm just not paying attention," I said while looking down.

"What's wrong?" Hannah whispered. She seemed concerned.

"Nothing. I don't know. Just depressed, I guess."

"Depressed about what?"

"I don't know, life, I guess."

"That sucks, dude, you should be happy." *Really?*

"Thanks, I should consider that." I cracked a smile and Hannah smiled back.

"See, it's that simple." *Is it?* "Happiness is a choice. My dad taught me that."

"Hannah, how old are you?"

"14."

"Wow, I seriously thought you were like 17. You seem so much older."

"My parents tell me the same thing. I suppose I am mature for my age. Age ain't nothing but a number...I think that's an Aaliyah song. It's true though. How old are you?"

"I'm 15. I'll be 16 in September. Then I'll be able to get my license and be able to stop pedaling my ass around all the time."

"September what?"

"September 28th."

"I knew it! You're a Libra!"

"I am a what now?"

"It's your astrological sign. I'm Aquarius. I have a book on astrology. I can show you. It all makes sense!"

"Does it?" I had no idea what Hannah was talking about but she seemed really excited. "Sure, Hannah, I'm always down for learning new things."

"Awesome. I'll bring the book by tomorrow. You guys are gonna practice, right?"

"Yeah, I think so. That's the plan. So, if you're 14 you're gonna be a freshman..."

"Yeah, Mt. Whitney." *Perfect.*

"I'm gonna be a sophomore at Whitney. We don't say the mount part. Insider tip."

"Thanks, good to know."

"I had a pretty shitty freshman year so I'm hoping that this year will be better."

"It will be. It's in the stars." *What is she talking about? I hope she's not crazy.*

"Yeah, well, I appreciate your optimism."

"It's true, you'll see." Hannah smiled and pressed her hand into my arm.

"Hannah, it's time for dinner!" Her dad yelled from their driveway down the street. He was a scary-looking man even from a distance. Hannah got up and rubbed the dirt off of her pants.

"I've got to go. See you tomorrow?"

"Yeah, see you tomorrow." Hannah began walking back to her house while her dad waited for her.

"Be happy!" Hannah said as she turned back towards me. I nodded my head in agreement and waved goodbye to her. I went back into the garage to put away my bass before going inside. I walked back to Chris's room and found him sitting on his bed with the cordless phone in his hand.

"So, did you ask her out? Chris said abruptly.

"No, I didn't get the chance. Her dad called her back home."

"Dude, I keep telling you, if you don't make a move, I'm going to."

"Shut up and hand me the phone." I dialed Angela's number. She picked up after the first ring.

"Hello," Angela said.

"Hey, Angela, this is Will, Chris is really sorry and he wants you back. He said that he'll make it up to you."

"I don't know, Will, I think I should be with someone older and more mature."

"Just give him another chance. You guys have been together forever." There was a long silence and then I could hear Angela talking to someone, but her voice was muffled like she was holding her hand over the receiver.

"Put him on the phone. I know he's there."

"All right." I handed the phone to Chris. "She wants to talk to you. I'm going to leave you to it." I left Chris's room and went to the living room and sat next to Mitchell. Chris's step dad was making dinner and the news was playing on the TV. Chris's mom had just gotten home from work and came inside the living room.

"Oh, Will, are you staying for dinner?"

"Yeah, Scott said it would be ok."

"Did you call your mom to see if it's ok with her?"

"Yeah, it's fine." Chris walked into the living room and placed the phone on the handset.

"Can I get a ride to the mall on Saturday? Angela wants me to meet her there."

"Sure, I have to go to Penny's anyway."

"Cool, thanks, mom." Chris's mom walked into the kitchen to help with dinner. Chris looked at me and sat down next to me. "She's gonna give me another chance. She wants to meet at the mall to talk."

"That's good." *Focus on your girlfriend.*

"Thanks for calling her."

"I don't think I had a choice..." Chris smiled and turned his attention to the TV and then back to me.

"Hey, did you want to meet us at the mall on Saturday?"

"I don't know. I don't know what I'm gonna have going on. Besides, you should be alone with her."

"I don't know if that's going to happen. Vicki's probably going to be there."

"Then definitely count me out."

"Angela didn't say Vicki was going to be there...so, yeah."

"We'll see. We have a few days before Saturday."

"Do you want to stay over tonight?"

"Nah, I don't have a change of clothes."

"Why does that matter?" *It matters.*

"Maybe...tomorrow night?" I said indecisively.

"Food's ready," Chris's dad said. He was a great cook. We ate our fill of tacos and I thanked Chris's parents for dinner. I handed my plate to Chris's mom and went back to Chris.

"I'm gonna take off. See you tomorrow for practice."

"Later, man," Chris said as I let myself out, picked up my bike off of the lawn, and rode home with the sun fading into the horizon.

Chapter Four
About a girl

S HE REALLY SEEMED TO like me. I definitely liked her. I was afraid though. I was afraid that she would turn me down. I was afraid that she would say yes. I spent a lot of time that night going back and forth. I was afraid of her. I was disappointed in myself that I was afraid. I stared at the ceiling like I always did. I was lying on my bed, motionless, when my brother came in and turned on the light.

"Hey, bro, what's wrong with you? Why are you just lying here in the dark?"

"It's nothing, I'm just thinking."

"About what?"

"It's about a girl."

"It's always about a girl, isn't it?"

"Yeah, it seems like it is. Anyway, I really like this girl and I'm afraid that if I ask her out, she's going to turn me down. I don't want that to happen again."

"Again? How many times have you been turned down?"

"I don't really want to talk about it..."

"Let me give you some advice; If you really like this girl, you need to act like she doesn't exist. Don't compliment her or do anything for her."

"Too late."

"It's never too late. Look, you have to make her believe that you have other options, even if you don't." Larry laughed but quickly caught himself.

"It's not funny. You should see this girl. She could get any guy she wants. It's not the other way around. Besides, how does it make any sense to act like a dick? She'll just move on to someone that treats her better."

"You've got a lot to learn little brother. It's complicated, but trust me, it'll work. Been there and done that."

"I'm going to sleep. Can you turn the light out?"

"Sure thing. Remember what I said, bro, you'll thank me later."

I had a crush on a girl when I was in the seventh grade named Courtney. Courtney was considered by everyone, including Donald, to be the prettiest girl in our class. She had shoulder-length blond hair and a thin, athletic body. She was cute, but not 'hot' as we would say, at least not like some of the eighth grade girls. I didn't really care about that though. I really liked her. "Courtney, you're the prettiest girl at school," I told her the day before we went on Thanksgiving break. We we're all standing around waiting for class to start and It seemed like a good time to tell her.

"Thanks, Will, that's cute." *What is that?* Her friend Michelle walked over to us. "Michelle, have you heard Ace of Base? I heard them on the radio...this song, I think it's called 'The Sign.' They're my favorite band now," Courtney said.

"No, I haven't, but I'll listen for it," Michelle replied.

"B95. I heard it on B95 twice last night. It's so good. I think they play it every hour."

"Yeah, Ace of Base is awesome!" I said even though I had no idea who they were. "I just bought their CD."

"You have a CD player?" Michelle asked.

"Yeah, I got it for Christmas last year."

"That's so cool. My dad has one but I don't have one of my own yet. Maybe I'll get one this year," Courtney said.

"If you ask for one, I'm sure you'll get one." Class was about to start, but I was already working on a plan to win Courtney's love. I could ride my bike down to Sam Goody's and buy Courtney the Ace of Base CD. I had a paper route and it was almost time to collect some money. That Saturday, after Thanksgiving, I rode around my neighborhood collecting the money. I got almost 100 bucks. I rode down to Sam Goody's in the Sequoia Mall and bought the Ace of Base CD for 12 dollars. *This is gonna be perfect.* I rode back home and waited for Monday to come. At school Monday morning, I confidently walked up to Courtney. She was talking with Michelle and eating an apple.

"Hi Courtney, hi Michelle. Ummm, Courtney, I got you something." I unstrapped my backpack, unzipped the front pouch and pulled out the CD. "Here, I bought you a copy."

"Oh my God, thank you so much," Courtney said. She gave me one of those one-armed, side hugs that girls seemed to do a lot.

"Yeah, wow, that's really nice of you," Michelle said.

"Well, she deserves it." I was really proud of myself at that moment. *She has to like me now.* The bell rang for class to start. "See you later, Courtney."

"Bye." Courtney and Michelle walked in the other direction. *That's not a good 'bye.'* The school week went by really fast. I was planning on asking Courtney out Monday after school, but I didn't see her. I didn't think much of it, but I didn't see her all day on Tuesday either. Then Wednesday, Thursday, and Friday. Nothing.

"Donald, have you seen Courtney lately?" I asked him at lunch.

"No, why?"

"I was going to ask her out, but..."

"Dude, I heard she was dating a ninth grader."

"What! She never told me anything."

"Was she supposed to?"

"Yes, I mean, I guess. I don't know."

"Are you going to Roller Towne tonight?"

"Yeah, I guess so." Roller Towne was a skating rink where a lot of people hung out on the weekend. We went there a lot even though I couldn't skate. It just happened to be where everyone was. "I'll meet you there at, like, 6."

"Meet me at my house. My mom can drive us. You don't really want to leave your bike in front of Roller Towne, do you?" We sat down outside of the cafeteria and ate our cafeteria 'food.' I looked left, right, up, and down the halls and I didn't see Courtney or Michelle anywhere. *What is going on?* There wasn't a single day that I didn't see Courtney...And Michelle. Courtney and Michelle were always together, like Donald and I. Divisadero had about one-thousand students, but the school wasn't that big. *Something's wrong.*

"No, not really. Ok, I'll meet you at your house." Roller Towne wasn't in the best neighborhood and people would get their bikes stolen all the time. After school, I rode home and ate two Hot Pockets. I watched some MTV while waiting for the time to pass. No one was home. My mom and my brother were at work. My mom coined the term for that type of day. She called it a 'fend for yourself night.' Most nights were 'fend for yourself' nights. At around 5, I rode over to Donald's house and knocked on his door. His mom answered. She was a jovial and portly woman.

"Hi, Will, Donald's in his room, come on in!" Donald and I had a lot in common. The biggest thing though was that our parents were both divorced. We had an understanding even though Donald seemed angry about it. He would always say that he hated his dad. I never knew mine so I didn't care.

"Hey, you ready?" I asked Donald while he was putting some Legos together.

"Yeah, I'm almost done with this..."

"I can't believe you still play with Legos. I mean, I used to play with Legos too...when I was 10!" I laughed sarcastically. "Grow up."

"I don't wanna grow up, I'm a Toys R Us kid..." Donald began singing out of tune as was usually the case. He did it, not necessarily because it was true, but because he knew that it pissed me off.

"All right, I get it, stop singing." I covered my ears and Donald laughed.

"Ok, let's go. Mom, we're ready!" When we got to Roller Towne, there were a lot of people standing outside waiting to get in.

"What time do you want me to pick you up?" Donald's mom asked.

"10 should be good. Yeah, I think it closes at 10."

"I'll pick you up at 9."

"Fine." Donald and I got out of the car and at the front of the line I saw Courtney with someone's hand around her waist. I circled around the line to get a better look.

"You were right! Look at that guy!" I said to Donald. *He has a mustache!*

"I told you so." *Shit.* My stomach sank deep into my bowels. I didn't want to be there, but Donald's mom had already left. We went to the back of the line and waited our turn to be let inside. Donald went over to the counter to check out skates and I sat down at a table overlooking the rink. Courtney and her 'boyfriend' eventually skated by. She made eye contact with me but quickly looked away. *Shit.*

I don't want to treat her like shit. She doesn't deserve that. Larry's full of shit. Maybe he has a point about making her think I have other options though. That kind of makes sense. I don't want to be a dick to her. This shit is complicated. I was riding my bike to Chris's house for practice that morning and I couldn't stop thinking about how to approach Hannah. I thought that I was having an anxiety attack even though I had no idea what that was. I didn't want to screw up my chances with her. She seemed to like me. *She seems to like me. Seems.* I focused on that word. Seemed. I really didn't know for sure. And my brother. *Shit! He says I need to treat her like she doesn't exist. He must be smoking on the crack pipe. How does that make the least bit of sense?* I went back and forth in my mind and finally snapped out of it as I turned onto Laura Street. I had no recollection of my ride over there. I just seemed to be there. Hannah, Michael, Casey, and Mitchell were all in front of Hannah's house playing basketball. "Will!" Hannah exclaimed. "Hold on! Let me grab my astrology book." Hannah practically ran inside of her house and then back out before I could blink my eyes. "Look!" She opened the book and pointed toward a section called 'The Libran Personality.' "Check this out. These are your positive characteristics and these are your negative characteristics." I looked closely at the negative side and saw the word 'indecisive.' *Yeah, no shit!*

"Wow, Hannah, this seems pretty spot on," I said.

"You can take it home and read it if you want," Hannah said. Out of the corner of my eye I saw Casey smiling. *What is she smiling about?* Michael and Mitchell weren't paying any attention to us.

"Sure, I'll read it tonight," I said as I put the little red book into my oversized pants pocket. "You going to watch our practice?"

"Yeah, of course!"

"All right, I'm going to head over there."

"See ya!" I continued riding down the street and watched Chris's garage door began slowly opening. Rob, much to my amazement was already there and tuning up his guitar. Chris sat down behind his set and started practicing 'Teen Spirit.' I rested my bike on the lawn and walked into the garage. I went to grab my bass and Chris stopped playing.

"Hey, man, you're late!" Chris said.

"Not even! I'm right on time."

"You're talking to that girl again." Chris pointed his drum stick outside of the garage, down the street towards Hannah.

"What if I was?" Chris smiled and continued warming up. Rob just shook his head in disapproval.

"I think both of you care more about pussy than this band," Rob said arrogantly.

"I still don't know why you don't care," I replied. Chris laughed. We looked at each other and knew exactly what the other was thinking.

"Whatever," Rob said. "Let's start with 'Come as You Are.' Rob started playing and then Chris and I came in. We played our usual set list of Nirvana songs and Hannah and Casey came to watch half-way through 'In Bloom.' They started singing the chorus along with Rob. I couldn't hear them though because we were playing really loud, but I could tell that they knew the lyrics. They seemed to be having a better time than me. We finished with 'Teen Spirit' like we always did. Hannah and Casey clapped enthusiastically like they had done before. Everything felt the same. Nothing had changed. We played the same songs over and over again. Rob decided which songs we would play, which order we would play them in, and which songs needed extra practice.

"Same time tomorrow," Rob said as he packed up his guitar. Chris and I walked out of the garage and said hi to Hannah and Casey. Rob simply said "hey," and proceeded to walk down the street.

"I'm so tired of this," I said. "Same thing every day. We should be writing our own music."

"We don't know how to write music," Chris said.

"You could learn. It can't be that hard, right?" Hannah said.

"Yeah," Casey added.

"That's right! We can do whatever we want to do. I know that Rob is the band, but at the same time, I think he's holding us back."

"You think so?" Chris said.

"You don't?" I replied.

"No, not really. I never thought about it," Chris said while shrugging his shoulders.

"Hey, I have an idea. I'll go get a notebook and you guys can start writing some stuff down." Without waiting for a response, Hannah started running down the street to her house. I smiled a little and turned to Chris.

"That's what I'm talking about," I said.

"Don't you think Rob's gonna be pissed that we're doing this behind his back?"

"I don't care and neither does he. He doesn't want to be involved. He's a stubborn asshole!" Casey's mouth dropped open like she was surprised about what I had said. Chris shook his head as if he disagreed with me. "Chris, I have to tell you something. Rob didn't want me to tell you this, but he found a new drummer."

"What the hell!?" Chris exclaimed.

"He was gonna kick you out of the band at the end of summer when school started."

"That's messed up. I'm going to kick his ass!"

"I have a better idea. Let's start our own band and kick Rob out."

"How are we going to do that? All of this stuff is his." Chris pointed in the garage at the amps and the PA system.

"We'll figure it out. He's a traitor, Chris, do you really want to be in a band with a traitor?"

"No, actually, it's kind of funny, kicking him out of his own band."

"It's perfect, really. He's going to get exactly what he deserves."

"I still think I should kick his ass. Where did all of this come from, anyway?"

"I've been thinking about it for a while," I said. Hannah came running back to us with a notebook in her hand.

"Oh my God, Hannah, you missed out," Casey said.

"What happened?" Hannah asked. Casey went ahead and told Hannah basically everything that we said while she was gone word for word. *Impressive.* "Wow. Here's the notebook. Where do you want to start?" Hannah said while handing me the notebook and a pen.

"I think you should start with a name," Hannah said and smiled at me as we sat down on Chris's lawn. Chris and Casey sat next to us forming a sort of semi-circle.

"What's a good band name?" I asked with the notebook in my lap and the pen in my hand. We all looked at each other and around the neighborhood searching for an answer.

"Bush fucking sucks! Gavin Rossdale is a pussy!" Rob said as he headed straight for my new Bush poster. He looked right in Gavin's eyes and spat in his face.

"Whoa! What the fuck are you doing, Rob? You can't walk into someone's house and spit on their walls!"

"Take it down and throw it in the trash where it belongs!"

"Dude, relax, it's just a poster," I said. It was the first time that Rob had been over to my house. It was a few months after we became friends. I had no idea that he hated Bush that much.

"Bush is a Nirvana rip-off band and doesn't deserve to exist."

"That's pretty harsh."

"It's true."

"That's your opinion."

"Not an opinion. It's a fact."

"I'm not sure that you know the difference."

"Sure, I do. Incesticide is a better album than Nevermind. That's an opinion. Bush is the worst fucking band ever. That's a fact." I shook my head and tore the poster off of my wall.

"There, happy?"

"Yes, I am, and you should be too." I decided that was going to be the end of that argument. Rob couldn't be reasoned with but I did respect his judgment on music. "Hey." Rob turned his attention to my closet. He went through my clothes. "You have some really cool shirts. This is an awesome White Zombie shirt and Megadeth? I've never seen you wear these shirts. Why don't you wear them?"

"I don't know. They're faded. Black shirts don't last very long."

"Who cares? You should wear them or give them to me." *Yeah, they're definitely not going to fit you.*

"Fine, I'll wear them."

"I want a Sex Pistols Anarchy in the U.K. shirt. I don't really like the Sex Pistols, but I like their shirts."

"'Anarchy in the U.K?' What's that?" I said. Rob started singing some lyrics.

"That's pretty cool. Why don't we play that song?"

"I don't really like it that much. I like anarchy, chaos, and destruction, but, nah."

"Ok, Rob, you don't make any sense."

"Sure, I do."

"Anarchy!" I said after a few minutes. "We should call the band Anarchy."

"That's a great idea!" Hannah said.

"It is?" Chris said suspiciously.

"Yeah, no Government," Hannah added. *What?*

"I thought it meant chaos, like how the world is crazy," I said.

"Nope. It means to not have a government. Government means to control the mind. Anarchy means no mind control," Hannah said. *Wow! What the fuck?*

"How do you know all that?" Chris said. Casey looked as if she was still confused.

"My dad told me. He watches a lot of political stuff and I was watching with him one day. He talks to the TV a lot." Hannah laughed.

"He sounds like a very smart man," I said.

"Yeah, he is. He didn't go to college or anything, but he's really smart." I was writing the word Anarchy on the notepad and stylizing it into a symbol. Chris looked over at the paper with a dumb look on his face.

"Dude, what are you doing? That looks like the Metallica logo."

"Yup, it does," Hannah said while Casey nodded her head in agreement. *Shit, it does.*

"Yeah, I can't draw for shit. I'm just messing around," I said as I put the pen down on the notepad. I was facing the street and saw Hannah's mom walking toward us. "Hannah, is that your mom?" Hannah turned around and checked.

"Yeah, what does she want?" This was the first time that I saw Hannah's mom up close. It didn't look like that could be Hannah's mom at all. There was no resemblance. She was wearing blue coveralls that did not hide the fact that she was a little overweight. She had very short, dirty-blond hair, cut above her ears and her face reminded me of an English bulldog. *Hannah must have been adopted.* "Hey, mom, what's up?" Hannah's mom did not respond to Hannah. She looked right at me.

"We don't want Hannah just hanging out down here. It's ok if you want to play basketball at our house, but no hanging out and doing nothing." *We are doing something.* "Hannah, it's time to come home. We're going to have an early dinner before your dad goes to work. Say bye to your friends." Hannah got up from the ground and I handed the notepad and pen back to her.

"Bye, guys, see ya later." Hannah and her mom started walking to her house.

"Bye!" Casey said. Hannah turned around while she was walking and made eye contact with me while mouthing the words, 'read the book.' I nodded to let her know that I understood and she turned back around and continued home.

"What was her problem?" Chris said.

"I don't know. I guess she's just overprotective. It makes sense if you think about it. It must suck for Hannah though."

"Yeah, sucks for her." I grabbed my bike off of Chris's lawn.

"All right, I'm gonna take off too." I looked at Casey and then Chris. "Rob can't know about any of this. Casey, can we trust you?"

"Sure, I won't say anything."

"Chris...?"

"Yeah, I won't say anything, but he still needs his ass beat."

"True, but we need time to work everything out like finding a new bass player and a singer. Rob went behind our backs and we should return the favor." Casey didn't say anything and Chris nodded his head in agreement. "See you guys later," I said as I started pedaling down the street. Chris yelled after me,

"Wait, what about practice tomorrow?" I turned around and saw Casey walking toward her house. I stopped in front of Chris.

"Same deal, we practice like everything's cool. Nothing's changed as far as Rob's concerned."

"I still don't see why we don't just tell him to fuck off."

"Because I still want to be able to play music while we come up with a plan, don't you?"

"Yeah, but I also want to punch him in his greasy forehead."

"It'll be better this way, trust me." Chris raised his eyebrows.

"I don't know, man."

"I'll see you tomorrow. Same time. Don't worry about it."

"Later," Chris said as I rode home. My mom was actually home when I got there and she was making my favorite dinner, tuna

melts. I ate four of them and went to my room. My brother wasn't
home either. He was probably still at work, but I didn't care either
way. I went to take my pants off, but remembered the little red
book that Hannah had let me borrow. I envisioned her beautiful
face as she reminded me to read the book. I took the book out
of my pocket and set it down on top of my dresser. I looked at it
for a minute. *Shit, I don't want to read.* I was tired and needed to
start planning my new band, but it was a small book. *This should
be a quick read.* I put on my Puma sweat shorts and sat down on
my bed with the book in hand. I looked at the table of contents.
I read about Zodiac types, predictions, astrological symbols, the
12 sun signs. *What do I care about all of this stuff? Aries? Let's see:
March 21st-April 19th. Do I know any Aries people? I don't know.*
I flipped through the book page by page, but without reading
anything completely. I finally came to the point that Hannah
pointed out to me. I read the section on Libra's completely and
it blew my mind how accurate it was. *This is some voodoo shit.* I
read about my positive characteristics: Charming, sincere, refined,
artistic, and very strong beliefs. And then I read about my negative
characteristics. Like before, the word indecisive stuck out. And
then, narcissistic: *What does that mean?* I continued: Fearful,
sulky, manipulative, and flirtatious. Sounds about right. I then
read about the typical Libra appearance: Is usually handsome,
but is never ugly. *Thanks, book.* I finished reading the section on
Libra and I was impressed. I was even more impressed than I was
when I started. *I wonder if this applies to everyone.* I thought of
everyone I knew and started comparing their birthdays to their
signs. My mom was a Capricorn. My brother was a Virgo. Rob
was a Taurus. Chris was a Sagittarius. I read a little bit about
each person and again, it seemed spot on. *This is very interesting,
very, very interesting. Hmmmm, Hannah told me that she was an
Aquarius, I think.* I turned to the section on Aquarius, and I almost
dropped the book when I saw a number at the bottom of the
title page with a little heart next to it. Both the number and the

heart were written sloppily, as if they were written in haste. *Did she just give me her number? That's a first. I didn't even have to ask.* I read some of her characteristics: Thoughtful and caring, loyal, inventive, perverse, eccentric...*Perverse huh?* I continued to the end of the section where they had the compatibility charts between the signs. Hannah had seemingly circled the section on Aquarius woman and Libra man. The first line read: Harmonious. An Aquarius woman and Libra man are an excellent compatibility match. I turned back a few pages and stared at her number until I had it memorized. I then grabbed a piece of paper out of my backpack and wrote it down, *in case I forget.* I stared at it some more. *I should call her right now. It's late, maybe I should wait, but if I wait...* My brother walked in and saw me holding the book.

"Hey, bro, what's that?"

"It's a book that the girl I was telling you about gave me."

"What's it about?"

"Astrology."

"That's some bullshit."

"It doesn't seem like bullshit and I've been reading it."

"Whatever, bro, you can believe in Santa Claus and the tooth fairy too if you want, but it's not going to make it true."

"All right, whatever, that's not the point. She wrote her number in here with a heart next to it." I showed Larry the number and he smiled.

"Isn't that cute, with a little heart and all."

"Yeah, well, I was thinking about calling her tonight, but I don't..." Larry quickly interjected.

"Don't call her now! You've got to wait a few days. Let her think about it. I already told you: You've got to make her think you have other options." Larry sat down on his bed across from me and started untying his shoes.

"But what if she loses interest?"

"Bro, she'll lose interest if you do call her too soon." *I'm so confused.* "Women are complicated." *I guess.*

"So, how long should I wait?"

"At least a few days, but a week is even better, in my experience."

"If you say so." I was growing tired of Larry's advice, but I knew he had to know more than me about women. Larry took off his shoes and headed to the bathroom for a shower. That was a good thing because the smell he brought into our bedroom was that of a dirty, swampy restaurant. I looked back in the little red book and stared at Hannah's number and the asymmetrical heart attached to it. *I hope he's right.* I put the book inside of my backpack and lay down on my bed and stared at the ceiling. *Shit, I didn't even plan for my new band. Maybe that's a bad idea. Maybe I should just stick it out with Rob. No. He's an asshole. He's gonna get rid of Chris so we need to get rid of him. But he's so much better than us, musically at least. Ahh, what are we gonna do? What am I gonna do? Where do I even start? What if Rob finds out I told Chris? What if Chris gets pissed at Rob? Shit, I need to stop thinking so much! Hannah, I should call Hannah. She's so pretty. Everything's crazy. Everything's changing.* My eyelids slowly started feeling heavy and I began falling asleep with all of the possibilities of what could be still on my mind.

Chapter Five

Summer vacation

"Hey, Will, isn't that your girlfriend over there?" Chris pointed toward Victoria's Secret. He had his arm around Angela and an evil smirk on his face.

"Real funny, Chris," I said. "Which mannequin were you referring to? The one in the green panties isn't too bad." Chris and Angela both laughed.

"No, Poindexter, I saw Hannah in there."

"Oh, shit! Are you serious?"

"Yeah, I think so. She was with some girl."

"Casey?"

"No, it definitely wasn't Casey."

"Will, I didn't know you had a girlfriend. I thought you were saving yourself for Vicki," Angela said and smiled.

"It's too bad she couldn't make it today," Chris followed.

"Hannah's not my girlfriend, yet...and you know I'm not into Vicki."

"She's into you." *Yes, I know.* "What do you mean yet?" Angela said. "Are you going to ask her out? Vicki will be pissed."

"Yeah, I just haven't found the right time. We practice every day and her parents keep her on a pretty short leash. Her parents are probably here...somewhere." I looked up and down the mall corridor. Chris and Angela did the same. I didn't see Hannah's parents, but it was hard to see through the crowd. On the weekends in Visalia, everyone that was anyone was at the Visalia Mall. There wasn't really anything else to do but hang out at the mall. It was also extremely hot in the summer and a lot of people came to the mall for the free air conditioning. Sometimes we would hang out at the Sequoia Mall down the street if there was a movie playing that we wanted to see. There wasn't a movie theater at the Visalia Mall, but it was newer and much nicer. Some people would spend their entire day at the mall eating, shopping, and sometimes, sleeping...They had beds set up at J.C. Penney and Sears. I don't think the stores thought that people would sleep in them, but they did.

"You have the time right now, not that I want you to because Vicki would be crushed," Angela said.

"Yeah, get your ass in there!" Chris laughed.

"Yeah, no, I'll wait for her to come out." Everyone knew that it looked creepy for single guys to be walking around Victoria's Secret, especially in the summer.

"We could go in there and find her for you," Angela said.

"Nah, it's ok, don't worry about it. Let's go get some food. I'm getting hungry."

"Are you sure you don't..." Angela began to say, but was interrupted by Chris.

"Let's just go in there and get her." Chris's hand slid from Angela's shoulder and moved to her hand and they started walking towards the entrance.

"You can do whatever you want. I'm hungry. I'll be at the Chinese Gourmet," I said as I walked away and toward the food court. I waited in line and then ordered a chicken bowl. I found a seat in the middle of the food court away from other people and started eating. Before I had a chance to finish my food, I felt a tap on the back of my arm.

"Hey, Will, your friends told me that you were looking for me," Hannah said.

"Well, Chris said he saw you and I thought I would say hi," I said. "Hi."

"Hi! Oh, this is my friend, Jessica." I looked up at Jessica. She was wearing a purple, long-sleeved shirt and tight-fitting black jeans. She had long brown hair which was one of the only contrasts to Hannah. She was a pretty girl; not as pretty as Hannah, but attractive. She reminded me of someone... Like with Hannah and Gwen Stefani. I studied Jessica's face and body and tried to make a connection. *That's it! Fiona Apple.*

"Nice to meet you, Jessica," I said.

"You too," Jessica said. She was fidgeting with her shirt and looking around the food court.

"Wow, Hannah, you make friends fast."

"Actually, we've been friends for a long time. Our dads are best friends."

"That's cool. You guys wanna sit down?"

"Yeah," Hannah and Jessica said simultaneously and then sat down across from me. I continued working on my Chicken bowl.

"Jessica goes to Redwood."

"Does she now? How do you like it at Redwood, Jessica?"

"It's fine, I guess," Jessica replied in a hurried tone. I took my last bite of chicken and placed the plastic bowl on the table.

"I was going to call you yesterday, but I..."

"It's ok, call me whenever you want," Hannah quickly interjected.

"Is there a time that's good for you? I asked. I mean, I don't want to call you if you're busy."

"My mom works days and my dad works nights. So maybe call me when my dad's not home." Hannah looked over at Jessica and they smiled at each other. *What's that supposed to mean?* "He usually leaves for work around 4:30," Hannah said while folding her hands on the table. "What'd ya think of the book?"

"I thought it was very interesting."

"Did you read the whole thing?"

"Most of it. I read the Aquarius section really closely," I said and smiled. "That's the part that matters..."

"Oh my God, Hannah, you're getting him into that stuff?" Jessica said.

"Yeah, he asked for it." *I did?*

"Seems pretty accurate from what I've read."

"I don't believe any of it," Jessica said. Hannah leaned in to me and whispered in my ear.

"She doesn't want to believe it." *She smells so good.*

"Hey, I heard that!" Jessica said.

"I said it loud!" Hannah replied with a smile. "She's a Cancer." *That doesn't sound good. What does that mean? I should have read that part.*

"Ahh, I see," I said. Hannah and I both laughed a little.

"Whatever," Jessica said and pouted.

"Did you need the book back?"

"No, you can keep it; I have a better one at home."

"Thanks. I'll be sure to finish it..."

"Anyway," Jessica interjected, "we should go find my parents."

"Yeah, it's been a while since we saw them, and they're our ride so..." Hannah said. They both stood up and then I followed.

"I should go find Chris; his mom is my ride." I said while looking around. "I can't wait to get my license so I can come and go as I please."

"September 28th!" Hannah said excitedly.

"That's right, I'm getting that thing as soon as I can."

"Jessica turns 16 next month, but she doesn't want to drive," Hannah said.

"Really! Why not?" I inquired.

"I don't want to all right!" Jessica pleaded. Hannah once again moved in close to me and whispered,

"She's scared."

"Shut up, Hannah! We need to go right now," Jessica said. Jessica grabbed Hannah's hand and led her away. Hannah looked back at me. I waved at her and smiled. She waved back at me.

"Call me," Hannah said as she was whisked away. I nodded while holding my wave until Hannah turned back around. I could hear Jessica scolding her, but couldn't make out exactly what was being said. *She's in trouble.* I threw my plastic bowl away and began walking back down towards Victoria's Secret. *Where could they be?* I walked to J.C. Penney because that seemed like it was the best place for people to hang out. I went upstairs and found Chris and Angela making out on a queen-sized bed in the back of the store.

"Excuse me, sir, please get a room," I said as loud as I could without yelling and started laughing. They stopped making out and got off of the bed.

"Thanks for the cock block, man," Chris said.

"Thanks for finding Hannah and telling her where to find me," I replied.

"You're welcome. Wait. That's a good thing. I did you a favor."

"Maybe, but I told you not to."

"Yeah, yeah, yeah..." Angela turned to Chris and said,

"I should get going anyway. My mom was expecting my call an hour ago. Let me borrow a quarter," Angela said and Chris handed her a quarter. We all headed down to the first floor to use the payphone. Angela called first and then Chris. We sat down on a bench and waited for our rides. Chris and Angela held hands and we watched the hundreds of people quickly rush by in front of us.

The next morning, I woke up to my mom nagging me. "Will, wake up. Your friend Brad is on the phone. Get the phone!" I slowly got out of bed. *Brad, oh shit!* I grabbed the phone with one hand while cleaning the sleep out of my eyes with the other.

"Hey, what's up man?"

"Hey, what's up with you?"

"Not much, just catching up on some sleep. Band drama."

"Oh, right, you've got that band. How's that going?"

"A lot of drama…"

"So, you wanna hang out this summer?"

"Uhm, yeah, what's going on?"

"Peg's here and she's driving us back to Camarillo tomorrow. She says you're welcome to come. She has season passes to Magic Mountain."

"That's awesome! I'm down."

"Peg wants to know if your mom is ok with it."

"She has been every other summer…Mom, is it all right if I go to Camarillo with Brad?" My mom looked at me perplexed.

"You always spend summers there. It's ok with me."

"Yeah, it's ok."

"Ok, Peg says we'll be there around 3."

"All right, cool, I'll be ready."

"Ok, see you tomorrow."

"All right, later." I hung up the phone and started packing my clothes. *Oh shit, Hannah…Should I call her…To tell her what, that I won't be here, shit. What am I gonna do about Rob? Chris will be cool, though.* I finished packing my clothes and toiletries and then I grabbed the little red book. I opened it to the page with Hannah's number. *Should I really leave this summer? Of course you should. Wait, maybe it's a bad idea. On the one hand…shit, I've got to stop with this shit.* The last thing that I packed into my bag was the little red book. *I'll call her when I get back.* I called Chris after I took a shower.

"Hey, Chris, what's up?"

"Hey, what's going on?"

"I'm going to Camarillo tomorrow with Brad."

"Oh, right, it is about that time. Your boyfriend's back…" Chris laughed.

"Very funny. Anyway, we'll have to put off practice while I'm gone."

"That's fine. It's not like I want to play with Rob without you here. I might try to kill him. Yeah, I'll kill him. Are you going to tell your girlfriend?"

"So now I have a girlfriend? Which is it?"

"You play for both teams."

"Yeah, no, I only play for one team."

"I don't know why, but Hannah really likes you. Yesterday at the mall, she was stupid excited when I told her that you were there. I was going to tell her to calm down, but she was already out."

"I don't know what I would tell her. I don't think it's a good plan to tell her that I'm leaving on vacation and I don't know when I'm coming back."

"Shit, you don't know when you're coming back? Rob is gonna shit."

"It's usually like a month, right, I mean, what was it last year?"

"I don't even remember, but I do remember Rob talking shit."

"That sounds about right. So, I guess I'll be back in early July..."

"What are you going to do down there for a month?"

"I guess we got season passes to Magic Mountain..."

"Oh, fuck you! Can I go too?"

"I could ask, but I don't know if..." Chris cut me off before I could finish.

"No, don't worry about it. My parents would never let me go. You lucky son of a bitch."

"Yeah. All right, I'm gonna call Rob and tell him. I'll see you when I see you."

"Ok. Later." I hung up the phone with Chris and began to dial Rob's number. *This is not going to go well.*

"Hey, Rob, I called to let you know that I'm leaving for Camarillo tomorrow." I heard silence followed by a click. *He hung up on me!* I immediately called him back.

"Hello," Rob said.

"Listen, Rob, don't hang up on me!"

"Every god damn summer!"

"Brad was my first best friend and we like hanging out. What's your problem?"

"Yeah, it has nothing to do with his rich aunt, if that's what you're thinking. This is why you've never gotten better at bass. Fuck off." Rob hung up on me again and I decided not to call him back. *He'll get over it.*

The next day, Brad and his aunt showed up at 2:30 in her brand-new Acura. It was really nice. I felt rich just being in that car.

"So, Will, how's school? How are your grades?" Peg said as she made eye contact with me through the rearview mirror.

"It's all right, I guess, and my grades are awful."

"Why are you getting bad grades?"

"I don't know. I don't really care about school."

"You should. Don't you want to be able to go to college and get a good job?" *Wow, Peg is more of a mom than my own mom.*

"Yeah, I mean, I think so." *I'm 15. I don't need to think about this stuff right now.*

"It may seem too early to think about, but it's never too early to think about your future." *What? Is she reading my mind? That's creepy.*

"I'll do better next year, Peg, I just had a hard year."

"It's never too late to turn your life around." It sounded like Peg was speaking from experience, but I couldn't help but think that she never struggled a day in her life. *She's rich. What does she know?*

"Thanks, Peg." Brad didn't say anything. He was playing Tetris on his Gameboy, and seemingly, couldn't be bothered. "Hey, Brad. How are your grades?" I asked. He didn't say anything for a couple of seconds and then simply said,

"Straight A's."

"That's good," I said. *Why do my grades suck so bad?* Brad continued playing his game as we drove down the freeway.

"Music?" Peg asked.

"Sure," I said. "You got any Nirvana?"

"No, but I've got Whitney Houston." *Great.* Peg pushed a button on the dash and I heard Whitney Houston's unmistakable voice. I heard the lyrics to 'I Will Always Love You' and I got a strange feeling inside my gut. *Hannah. What am I doing?* Peg handed the cassette jacket back to me. It read: The Bodyguard Soundtrack. I really liked that song even though I wasn't a big fan of pop music. I liked Mariah Carey, because she was hot, but I was into rock so that wasn't really my thing. *I miss Hannah. What? Wait. She's not your girlfriend. She could be...She will be. What if she finds someone else? What am I doing here? Holy Shit! Stupid.* I looked outside of the window and watched the parched earth go by at a pace that was truly frightening. We got to Camarillo at 6.

"What do you guys want for dinner?" Peg asked as we pulled into her driveway. She had a really big house. *For one person?* Every time that I saw her house, I asked myself the same question.

"Pizza," Brad said without hesitation.

"Round Table?" Peg asked.

"Yeah, it's the best," Brad said. I was really hungry and would have been happy with Little Caesars at that point, so Round Table was perfect.

"I'll order an Italian Garlic Supreme and a vegetarian," Peg said as she parked the car in the driveway. *I love me some Italian Garlic Supreme.* We moved our bags from the car into the house and Peg made the call to Round Table. She set us up in the guest bedroom like she had done in past years and we waited for the pizza to show up. I opened my bag and pulled out the little red book. *Hannah...*

Brad and I met on the first day of school at Mt. Shasta Elementary in Ms. Hackley's class. Ms. Hackley was a terribly bitter old woman and an even worse teacher, but I did have her to thank for introducing me to Brad. The first thing we did in class was an activity where Ms. Hackley paired everyone up into groups to introduce ourselves and put paper bag book covers on our books. She gave us a script to follow in case we didn't know what to say.

"Hi, my name is William Smith, I was born in San Diego, California, and I like to ride my bike and play Nintendo," I said to Brad.

"Hi, my name is Bradley Woods, I was born here and I also like to ride my bike and play Nintendo," Brad replied. "How did you end up in Mt. Shasta?" Brad asked off script.

"My parents got divorced and then my mom moved us up here. My aunt, uncle and cousins live here too. I guess that's why."

"My parents are divorced too. I live with my dad. My mom works at Round Table. She gives me free cheese bread when I go down there."

"I love Round Table. Best pizza ever! And the arcade is cool too."

"I have to go after school, you wanna come?"

"Yeah, but I should call my mom to ask first. I'll call her from the office at lunch."

"Ok, do you have your bike?"

"Yeah, at the bike racks."

"Me too, it should only take a few minutes to get over there then?" Ms. Hackley interrupted our conversation when she had us change partners.

"Ok, class, thank your first partner and find another partner on your own. I said bye to Brad and then walked to the other side of the room. I saw a really pretty blond girl by the window overlooking the playground. Before I could say anything, she followed the script.

"Hi, I'm Sasha Sanders, I was born in Yreka California, and I like to go camping with my family." *She's really pretty.*

"Hi Sasha, I'm Will..." I went through the script with Sasha much like I had done with Brad, but after the script there was an awkward silence.

"Are you going to put the book cover on?" Sasha asked.

"No, I don't know how."

"I can help you. Here, hand me your book." Sasha cut the brown paper bag and then put the book inside. It only took her a minute to do. She made it look easy.

"Thanks, I owe you," I said. Ms. Hackley once again asked us to move on to another person. "Bye, Sasha, see you later." Sasha handed me my book and smiled.

"Bye, Will." After that, a kid named Bryan walked up to me and we went through the script. The morning went by so slowly that I could have been convinced that the minute hand on the clock was going backwards. Ms. Hackley had a math lesson and then spelling and then what she called 'SSR' which was short for silent sustained reading. When it was lunchtime, I went to the office to call my mom with Brad following closely behind.

"What'd she say, can you go?" Brad asked.

"Yeah, she just told me to be home by 5."

"That's good. My mom gets off at 4. She's gonna take me home to my dad's. Maybe she can drop you off on the way."

"Cool, food and a ride," I said as we walked to the cafeteria to get lunch. After school, Brad and I rode our bikes over to Round Table Pizza and I met his mom. She looked too young to be a mom. She looked much younger than my mom.

"Hi, mom, this is my friend, Will," Brad said.

"Hi, Will, you guys want some cheese bread?" She asked.

"Yeah," I said.

"Yeah," Brad followed. Brad's mom went behind the bar. "She can't give away free pizza, but we can have as much cheese bread as we want."

"That's cool." After a few minutes Brad's mom brought out the cheese bread and soda. It smelled really good and tasted even better. It was garlic infused mozzarella cheese on toasted bread sticks. I hadn't had them before, but I quickly became a fan. "Hey, did you see that blond girl in class, Sasha?"

"Yeah, what about her?"

"I think I like her. I'm gonna ask her out," I said after taking a drink of soda.

"Ask her out where?"

"Uhm, I...don't know." *That doesn't make sense.* "That's just what people say. You know, ask her to be my girlfriend."

"Good luck. I think she's too good for you."

"Maybe...I'm too good for her." Brad laughed as he took another bite of cheese bread. "Seriously, she talked to me first today."

"She had to because the teacher made her." *Hmmmm.*

"Well, I'm gonna ask her tomorrow." Brad shook his head and finished his food.

"You wanna play Ninja Turtles? My mom gave me quarters."

"Sure, I love that game." We went to the arcade and played until his mom got off of work at 4.

"Will, do you want a ride home?" Brad's mom asked.

"Yeah, thank you."

"Where do you live?"

"On Sheldon Street."

"Ok, no problem." Brad and I put our bikes in the back of his mom's truck and she drove me home.

"Thanks for the ride, see you at school, Brad," I said.

"See you tomorrow," Brad replied as I pulled my bike out of the truck and headed down our gravel driveway.

"Hey, Will, what's with the little red book?" Brad asked while unpacking his bag.

"It's this book that a girl named Hannah gave me."

"You've got a girlfriend?" Brad inquired.

"No, I mean, yes and no. I'm going to ask her out. I just haven't done it yet. She's just so freaking hot that I'm afraid she's going to say no. She seems to really like me. She wrote her number in this book. I just don't know."

"You remember Sasha from fifth grade?"

"Yeah, of course."

"You asked her to be your girlfriend the second day of school and now you're having a problem?"

"It's different now. I can't explain it. We were just kids then. I didn't care if Sasha said yes or no. It didn't matter."

"She said yes though. I was actually pretty surprised. I did not expect that at all. I thought she was going to run away from you screaming, but that's not what happened. And then Rebecca...I still don't know how you pulled that off."

"That was all her. I didn't know what I was doing."

"You're a lucky bastard."

"Yeah, I wonder if she's still around." Brad laughed.

"I bet she's been around, that's for sure."

"You're probably right about that. She was pretty slutty."

"That's the understatement of the year."

"We should go to her house and see what's going on."

"If you want to, I guess, but we're going to Magic Mountain tomorrow, so definitely not tomorrow." The next morning, I was startled awake by loud music. It was 'Conga.' *Oh Shit, Gloria Estefan?* I jumped out of bed and looked at Brad.

"Peeeeggggggg!" Brad yelled. I saw a speaker in the doorway that was definitely not there when we went to sleep.

"What's going on?" I said. Brad and I went outside of the room to find Peg laughing her ass off.

"Good morning, guys!" Peg said.

"Not cool, Peg, not cool," Brad said. *Wow, unbelievable.*

"It's 8. Time to wake up! I have to get you guys over to Magic Mountain early. I have a meeting." *Wow, Peg, nice.* "Take your showers, we're leaving at 9," Peg said while walking toward the kitchen.

"Shit, all right, you shower first," I said to Brad as I was still trying to collect myself.

"All right, fuck. Fucking Peg, right?"

"It definitely worked though. No doubt there."

"Yep, shit." Brad went into the bathroom and took a shower. I went into the kitchen where Peg was still laughing and making waffles.

"Will, how long were you planning on staying?" Peg asked. I helped myself to some waffles that Peg had already made. I poured a healthy amount of syrup on my waffles and then grabbed a glass from the counter.

"How long do you want me to stay?" I asked while pouring myself a glass of milk.

"As long as you want."

"No, for real," I said. *She can't be serious.*

"Yeah, I'm kidding. I'm going to fly Brad back on July 1st. His dad wants him home for the 4th. I can fly you back or you can take the bus if you want. I'm not sure if there's a direct flight to Visalia. You may have to go to Fresno and then have someone pick you up. Brad's dad is going to have to pick him up in Redding."

"I'll take the bus. I think that'll be easier."

"All right, if you change your mind, let me know."

"For sure. Thanks again for letting me stay this summer."

"Anytime. You know I like having you guys here." I finished my breakfast just in time for Brad to get out of the shower.

"It's all yours," Brad said as he pulled up a seat at the table.

"Cool, I'll be quick."

"You better be, or we're leaving you here," Peg said with a slight smile on her face. *Well, that would suck.* I put my dishes in the sink and went to take a shower.

The drive from Camarillo to Valencia took about an hour so we got to Magic Mountain right when it opened at 10. "Ok, guys, here's some money." Peg handed each of us 40 bucks. "Do you guys have your season passes?"

"Yes, Peg," Brad and I both replied.

"Ok, I'm going to be in Burbank for the rest of the day. Call me when you want me to pick you up."

"All right, Peg, thanks!" I said.

"Bye, Peg," Brad followed.

"Have a great day," Peg said as we shut the car doors. Peg drove away and we looked behind us at all of the roller coasters.

"This is awesome!" I said. We walked toward the front gates and there was a special, and much shorter, line for season pass holders.

"I think we have to get our pictures taken. Peg was saying something about that," Brad said as we continued forward. Peg was right. They took our tickets and told us that we would need to get our ID's and pointed us toward the building where they took the pictures and issued the cards. The ID cards only took about 10 minutes and we were free to explore the park.

"What do you want to ride first?" Brad asked.

"'Viper,' of course," I said. Brad and I both smiled and we made our way over to the massive orange coaster. That day went by as quickly as any day I had remembered. We rode 5 coasters, which was really good considering how busy it was. We also got sun burned pretty badly. The one thing that we forgot was sunscreen. We called Peg at about 7 to pick us up.

"Did you guys have fun?" Peg said as we got in the car.

"Yeah, it was awesome," I said.

"It was fun, but I got burnt pretty bad," Brad said.

"Yeah, it looks like you got your sun for the day," Peg responded.

"More like the week," Brad said as he looked over his bright-red arms. He looked like a lobster. He definitely got the worst of it. I was burnt, but I wasn't changing species.

"I have some aloe at home. You'll be fine. Don't forget the sunscreen next time," Peg said with a slight smile on her face. On the way home Brad fell asleep in the front seat and I watched the scenery go by in the back seat. Peg's Acura smoothly glided down the 126 as I contemplated what the next day held. *I wonder what everyone's doing at home... I wonder what Hannah's doing. I wonder what she's wearing. I hope nothing at all... Wait, how does that do me any good here? Maybe I should call her...*

The next day, Brad and I woke up to the sounds of birds chirping. I looked over at Brad and somehow, he was even redder than he was before. *Shit.* I walked out into the kitchen and peg had left a note and 40 bucks. "Brad and Will, I have an emergency meeting that I have to go to this morning. Cake on some aloe, order some pizza, and take it easy today. Love, Aunt Peg," Peg wrote. *Good call.* I wasn't burnt as bad as Brad but I didn't feel like standing in the sun all day either. I took a shower and then ate a bagel for breakfast. Brad still hadn't gotten out of bed so I decided to take a walk down the street to see about Rebecca. She only lived a few doors down so I didn't tell Brad I was leaving. I got to her house and an older man answered the door. *This guy doesn't look familiar.* "Hi, is Rebecca home?" I asked.

"Rebecca? No, I don't know any Rebecca. You sure you have the right house, young man?"

"Yeah, I think." *Yes, I remember this house.*

"My wife and I bought this house last year." *Oh, shit.*

"Sorry, I didn't know she moved," I said. "Do you know where they moved?"

"No, I didn't know them. The house was empty when we bought it."

"Sorry I can't help. Good day."

"Yeah, thanks." The older man shut his door and I walked back to Peg's house to check on Brad. *Well, shit.* I went back inside of the house to find Brad still in bed but awake. "I went to see about Rebecca and she doesn't live there anymore."

"That sucks," Brad said as he slowly sat up on the bed. *Dude, put your balls away. Unbelievable.*

"You wanna put some pants on?"

"I'm gonna take a cold shower. This sunburn is killing me."

"What are we gonna do today?"

"I don't want to do anything. I just want to stay inside and out of the sun."

"Peg left us money for pizza. I guess we'll just hang out today."

"All right," Brad said as he walked to the bathroom to take a shower. *Shit, I could do this at home.*

The next three weeks went by fast. Brad and I spent most days at Magic Mountain and every few days we just hung out at Peg's. On July 1st, Peg drove me to the bus station and bought my ticket home.

"Thanks, again, Peg, for everything."

"No thanks necessary, have a safe trip," Peg said.

"See ya," Brad said. Peg gave me a hug and I shook Brad's hand. I got on the bus and took my seat. I could see Brad and Peg waving. I waved back and then pulled the little red book out of my bag. I started reading the rest of the book, but I started by re-reading the entire section on Aquarius. The trip back to Visalia took about 4 hours and I called my brother from the station to pick me up.

"Hey, bro, how was it?"

"I had a good time, but I don't know. This sounds crazy with season passes to Magic Mountain and all, but it got boring after a few days."

"Too much of a good thing can be a bad thing."

"I guess that's true. I'm happy to be home." We got inside of my brother's 1973 Ford truck and headed home. It was always fun to ride in my brother's truck. It had a three-speed manual, that my brother called a 'three on the tree.' It was a terrible transmission. Every time he shifted to second gear; he could never find it. By that time, the truck had slowed down so much he had to shift back to first. It was always a hilarious ride.

"Son of a BITCH!" My brother growled. "Get your ass in gear." Every time we would come up to a stop sign or stop light, it would happen again. I knew that it wasn't funny to him, but I couldn't help but laugh every time we would slow down to a crawl out of first gear. And every time, my brother would curse his truck's existence. We eventually did make it home. *Hannah...I have to call Chris.*

"Hey, Chris, what's up homey?"

"Hey, what's up?"

"I'm back, bitch!"

"Didn't even know you were gone...nah, just kidding, man."

"Right, so what's going on?"

"Not much. I haven't heard from Rob. I tried calling him but his mom said he wasn't home. Hannah asked about you."

"Did she?" *Nice.*

"Yeah, man, she literally knocked on my door to ask about you..."

"What'd you tell her?"

"I told her that you were on vacation and then she asked when you were coming back and then I told her that I didn't know."

"That was it?"

"Yeah, she walked back home and I went back to watching MTV."

"Ok, I should call her."

"That's probably why she's bothering me."

"Yeah, yeah. So, I'm gonna call Rob, practice on Monday?"

"Sure, if you can get a hold of him."

"I will. I'll see you Monday morning."

"Call your girlfriend."

"I will, see you later."

"Later." I hung up the phone and dialed Rob's number. No one answered. *Shit.* I hung up again. I started dialing Hannah's number and then stopped. *What if she's mad at me? I didn't tell her I was leaving. 3 weeks and nothing. Yeah, I fucked up. What time is it?*

Chapter Six

Independence Day

I TURNED THE CORNER onto Laura Street and saw Hannah, Casey, Michael, and Mitchell playing basketball. I rolled up on their game, stopped my bike, and rested my foot on the curb of the sidewalk. It was already 90 degrees outside and it was only 10 in the morning. I waved to them but didn't say anything. It looked like it was Hannah and Casey versus Michael and Mitchell. *That's not fair at all.* It also looked like Hannah was taking, and making, every one of her shots. *That seems about right.* She was wearing sweatpants and a tight-fitting sports bra. She was sweating like she was running a marathon. I watched the sweat bead off of her perfectly flat stomach and envisioned my hands around her diminutive waist. Casey passed Hannah the ball and then took a 10-foot jump shot. "That's game," Hannah said and tossed the ball to her brother. "Practice up, Michael." Michael and Mitchell started playing against each other. Hannah and Casey walked over to me. "Hey, stranger, where have you been?" Hannah said while undoing her pony tail, letting her beautiful blond hair fall to her shoulders.

"I thought Chris told you. I was on vacation in Camarillo."

"I didn't know you were in Camarillo. Where's that?"

"It's pretty close to Ventura."

"Oh, ok, yeah...So, what did you do there?"

"We spent most of our time at Magic Mountain."

"That's cool. Who are 'we?'"

"My old best friend, Brad."

"Your old best friend, huh, so who's your new best friend?" *Hmmm. Shit.*

"Good question. I guess it has to be Rob or Chris. Yeah, I'll go with Chris. I have a question for you, Hannah..."

"Do you? Casey looked over at Hannah and kind of smiled. "Shoot," Hannah said.

"Isn't it too hot to be playing basketball?" I said. Casey's smile faded and Hannah's expression changed. *She doesn't look happy.* "Did I say something wrong?" I said as I pointed at my own chest.

"No...I'm going to go take a shower," Hannah said as she walked back across her lawn and into her house. Casey looked at me like I had killed someone and the police had been called to take me away.

"Why haven't you called her yet?" Casey said with disappointment in her voice.

"I don't know, Casey, I've been busy."

"You know she really likes you, right?"

"Yeah, I mean, I thought so, but I wasn't sure."

"Would you consider going out with her?"

"I don't know. I guess so...She is a lot younger than me." *That's stupid.*

"Not really, and besides, girls mature faster than boys so it makes sense." *Yeah, it does. What am I doing?* "If you ask her out, she'll say yes. She talks about you all the time." *Really?*

"Ok, Casey, I'll ask her out."

"When?"

"I don't know. Today, tomorrow..."

"Ok, just do it!" Casey said as she walked away toward her house. I rode past Michael and Mitchell who were still playing basketball even though it was too hot to be outside, let alone play sports. I got to Chris's house and set my bike down on his lawn. I knocked on the door and Chris answered.

"Hey, man, I tried to call Rob again, but no one answered."

"Yeah, I don't think he's coming. I tried calling him this morning too...I have some shitty news. I'm moving."

"What!?"

"Yeah, my parents told me last night. We're moving to a house over on Ben Maddox. I'm going to have to go to Golden West." *Shit.*

"Why!?"

"I don't know. It's something about my step dad's job."

"When are you moving?"

"In two weeks."

"Shit, that sucks, man."

"I haven't told Angela yet. This is not good."

"Yeah, shit, dude."

"You wanna smoke out?"

"Yeah, let's hit that." Chris and I went through his living room and into his back yard. We went and sat in the doghouse and Chris pulled a real pipe and a dime bag of weed out of his pocket. We smoked the bowl and then got out of the doghouse. "You feel better?" I said as we walked back to Chris's living room.

"Yeah. We'll still be friends, right?"

"Of course, man, you're not moving that far."

"But I'm going to a different school."

"It's fine. I'll still come over."

"You're a good friend, Will. I wonder if Rob..."

"I doubt it," I interjected.

"Yeah, fuck Rob!"

"Fuck Rob, indeed," I said as we sat down and turned on MTV. No Doubt's 'Just a Girl' was playing. *Hannah. Shit. I should talk to her.* "What are you doing tomorrow? It's the 4th."

"My parents are having a barbeque and they bought some of those shitty fireworks. Are you coming over?"

"Yeah, I'll be here. I don't have anything else going on."

"Cool." I heard some playful screaming in the distance. Chris looked at me with a disconcerting look on his face. "What the hell was that?"

"I don't know, let's go check it out." Chris and I went outside and saw Hannah, Casey, Michael, and Mitchell running around in the sprinklers. Hannah was wearing an orange, two-piece bikini. *Holy shit!*

"Holy shit!" Chris said. "God damn, Hannah is stupid hot."

"Yes, yes, she is." I felt extra stupid after seeing Hannah's body in a bikini. *Good lord! This can't be legal.* "What is happening right now? I think I smoked too much."

"Yeah, for real. Go talk to her. I'm gonna go call Angela." Chris pushed my arm and went back inside his house. *Shit.* I walked toward Hannah's house feeling very overdressed. I got close and Hannah ran toward the front of her house. *What is she doing?* She grabbed a hose and turned the water on. She walked toward me with the hose in her hands. She stopped and aimed the hose at me before I got to her lawn.

"Don't do it!" I said as I watched Hannah approach with a smile on her face. *This is not good.* I was wearing my black, baggy jeans and knew that it would be a problem if I got wet. "Don't even think about it."

"Don't even think about what?" Hannah said as she unleashed the full fury of the hose on me. She soaked me from head to toe. She took extra special attention to soak my Chukka boots. She laid into them as she stared directly into my eyes. I didn't move. I didn't try to run away. I stood there in the middle of the street and didn't say a word until Hannah seemed satisfied that I was sufficiently drenched and pointed the hose down at the grass.

"It's so hot today. Luckily, I have this hose to cool you off," Hannah said as she returned to turn the water off. *She is something else...*

"Thank you, I was getting hot, I needed that," I said with a smile on my face. Hannah smiled too. I stared at her body as I shook my arms violently as water flew everywhere.

"My eyes are up here," Hannah said as she pointed towards her face."

"Yeah, but give me a break, your body, you're beautiful," I said without thinking. Casey, Mitchell, and Michael all looked at each other and stopped moving around.

"Thanks," Hannah said as she put the hose down. She walked up to me with a smile on her face. Casey, Mitchell, and Michael ran away toward Chris's house at the end of the Cul-de-sac.

"Hey," I said as she got closer. I looked into her beautiful brown eyes and knew what was about to happen. Hannah raised her arms and I saw the door open out of the corner of my eye. It was Hannah's dad.

"Hannah, get inside. NOW!" He yelled. I froze. I stood there soaking wet. Hannah's dad was as scary as ever. He was as mad as I had ever seen another person. His lip was trembling. His full lumberjack beard was shaking. "NOW!" Hannah stopped in her approach.

"Sorry, I've got to..." Hannah started to say but was quickly interrupted.

"NOW!" Hannah's dad insisted. Hannah stopped and started walking toward her house. She walked by her dad and he slammed the door behind them. *Wow, fuck.* I looked up at the sun. It unleashed its oppressive fury on my face and I decided to walk back to Chris's house. I was still soaking wet and moved very slowly. I felt my jeans scrape against my legs. *This sucks.*

"What happened?" Michael said as I made my way onto Chris's lawn.

"Your dad is pissed," I said while shaking the water off of my arms.

"I better go home." Michael ran past me and back home. Mitchell's eyes were bugging out of his head. He turned around and went inside. Casey stood there and looked through me.

"Did you ask her out," Casey asked.

"No, I didn't get the chance," I said. "Her dad..."

"Ok, call her tonight," Casey said as she started walking home. She turned around quickly. "I'm serious, call her!"

"Ok, ok, I'll call her." *Shit.*

"Good." Casey continued walking to her house and then closed the door behind her. *Shit.* I went to knock on Chris's door and he opened it before I got the chance.

"Hey, man, I've got to go. Hannah soaked me up pretty good."

"All right, I'll see you tomorrow then?"

"Yeah, I'll be back over tomorrow," I said. "Later, man."

"Later." Chris shut the door and I went and picked up my bike from his lawn. Still soaking wet, I rode my bike by Hannah's house and rode home. *I need to call her.*

After dinner that night, I took the phone into my room and held it in my hand and sat on the edge of my bed. *You have to wait until her dad goes to work. What if he doesn't go to work? It's after 6. He must be at work by now. He was pissed though. Oh well. Shit. I guess I'm doing this.* I dialed Hannah's number and it sounded like Michael who answered.

"Hello?"

"Is this Michael?"

"Yes, who is this?"

"It's Will, Is your sister there?"

"Oh hey, yeah, hold on, I'll get her." I heard some muffled voices and then Hannah got on the phone.

"Hello?"

"Hey, Hannah, it's Will."

"Yeah, my brother told me. I've been waiting for you to call." I heard her mom ask her who was on the phone. "It's Jessica, mom." *She said that like she believes it.*

"Lying to your mom, Hannah?"

"Yeah, trust me..." Hannah trailed off. "Mom, I'm gonna take this in my room...Hey, sorry about that."

"Nothing to be sorry about. Your dad was pissed today. Are you ok?"

"Yeah, silly, my dad has a bad temper but he doesn't beat me." Hannah laughed. *I'm glad she can laugh about it.*

"That's good, I was a little worried about you."

"He was mad that I was outside in my bikini. Duh, it's the middle of the summer, dad. What does he expect? They bought it for me."

"Maybe it has to do with the fact that a skinny, grungy, punk rock kid with long hair is hanging around his daughter." Hannah laughed again.

"Maybe...I don't care what he thinks though."

"That's good, because well, *Shit, why is this so hard?* I really like you, and..."

"I really like you too!" *Thank God.*

"So, I was wondering if you would want to go out with me..."

"...Ummm, well, I'm not sure if...*Shit.* Yes! Ha-ha, I had you going there, didn't I? *Wow, she's got jokes. Almost gave me a heart attack.*

"Yeah, ya did...funny girl."

"You deserve it, dude. I've been waiting for a month for you to ask me out."

"You could have asked me out..." *Why did you just say that? Idiot!*

"That's not the way it works, dude." *I know.* "What are you doing tomorrow? It's the 4th."

"Chris's parents are having a thing so I'll be down there. Barbeque and fireworks."

"Cool, my parents are having Jessica and her family over and we're going to do the same thing."

"Jessica, huh? Oh, good times...We should call in the fun police to keep her in check." Hannah laughed.

"She's not that bad...She's just shy. Besides, she's good cover so I can see you tomorrow, Billy."

"Billy? Seriously?"

"Yep, seriously. What? You don't like it?"

"Ummm, it's ok, I guess. I just haven't heard that since I was little when that's what my mom called me."

"Ha-ha, nice, I like it. So, are you guys going to play tomorrow?"

"I don't think so, not unless Rob shows up."

"Ok, well, I should probably go before my mom gets suspicious. I'll see you tomorrow, Billy." I laughed a little.

"Ok, Hannah, see you tomorrow, bye."

"Bye." Hannah hung up the phone. *Holy shit, I did it. I actually did it.* A smile slowly encroached on my face and I kicked up my feet on my bed. *What was I even worried about? I could have done that weeks ago. So much wasted time.* I grabbed my Pearl Jam CD and put it in my stereo. I played the track 'Alive' and found new meaning in the lyrics. The phone rang interrupting Eddie Vedder's soulful vocals. I hit pause on my CD player and answered the phone.

"Hello?"

"Hey, it's Rob."

"Hey, what's up, Rob?"

"I just got off the phone with Chris and he said you were back."

"The fuck, man, why didn't you call me?" *I did, didn't I?*

"I did. No one answered, besides, I thought you were still butt hurt."

"I wasn't butt hurt."

"Yeah, you were butt hurt."

"Whatever. Chris said his parents are going to be home late tomorrow so we can practice."

"Ok, that's cool, I'm down to play, but we need to talk about the band."

"You mean Chris? He told me he was moving. That's a good thing. Now we don't have to kick him out. He'll quit."

"Why do you even want to practice then?"

"We might as well as long as we can."

"He's not even moving that far...Whatevers, we'll talk about it tomorrow. I gotta go."

"All right, later," Rob said and I hung up the phone. *Asshole. I don't care what Rob thinks. I'm going to tell him exactly what's up tomorrow.* I hit the play button on my CD player and continued listening to Pearl Jam. *I'd like to play some Pearl Jam songs and Soundgarden! And maybe...some Bush!* I smiled and started going through all of my CD's. I came across Metallica's Black album. *Shit, I haven't played this in a while.* I advanced the tracks to my favorite song on the album, 'Nothing Else Matters.' *Hannah. Nothing else matters.* I lay back down on my bed and stared restlessly at the ceiling.

I got to Chris's house early the next morning. I wanted to beat Rob there to talk to Chris about what we we're going to say to Rob. The garage was already open and Chris was tuning his drums. I set my bike down and walked inside. "Hey, Chris, we need to talk before Rob gets here." Chris put his drum sticks down and stood up.

"Uh oh, it sounds like I'm in trouble."

"Nah, but I talked to Rob last night and he thinks you're going to quit the band because you're moving...so he doesn't have to kick you out."

"I hadn't thought about it, but it's not a bad idea. Think about it. If I quit then you can quit too. It serves the same purpose of kicking him out." *That's pretty smart.* "Then we can start our own band."

"That's not a bad idea. Rob won't get pissed because he'll think it was his idea. I'll still have to come up with a good reason to quit."

"Or not, maybe you're just tired of his shit."

"That is a good reason."

"Rob's coming." I turned around and saw Rob walking down the street with his guitar strapped to his back."

"So, you still want to play after you tell him that you're going to quit."

"I'll tell him after we play. He's got to move all his shit anyway."

"Yeah, that's true." *This is sad. Our last practice.* "We don't have a name and we don't write our own songs, but we had fun."

"And we'll have even more fun without Rob." *Yeah, but will we be any good?*

"For sure, we don't need Rob yelling at us." Chris walked back behind his drum set and continued tuning. I took my bass out of my gig bag and plugged it in. Rob finally got to the garage. He took his guitar off of his back and set it down. "Take your time, Rob."

"I will, thanks," Rob replied with a smirk. "Let's see how rusty you fuckers are."

"I don't know, Chris, what do you think? Are you rusty?" I said.

"Yup, probably real rusty. What about you?"

"Yeah, it's gonna be bad." Chris and I both smiled and then laughed.

"I hate you guys so much," Rob said under his breath while shaking his head. "All right let's play through the set. 'Teen Spirit.'" Chris and I looked at each other and rolled our eyes. We started playing the song and didn't sound too bad. I was surprised because we hadn't played in so long. I looked at Rob, who was looking into the void, doing his best impression of Kurt Cobain. I looked back at Chris and shrugged my shoulders. We worked through 'Come as You Are,' 'Breed,' and 'Lithium,' before Hannah, Casey, Mitchell and Michael gathered outside the garage. Rob called out the next song, "About a Girl.'" *Does he do that on purpose?* We started playing the song and I locked eyes with Hannah throughout the song, occasionally looking down at my bass so I wouldn't mess up. We played through five more songs and then Rob set down his guitar. "Let's take a break and then practice 'Heart Shaped box.'" *That makes no sense.*

"Nah, I think we're done, Rob," I said as I put down my bass.

"Yeah, Rob, we're done," Chris said. "I have to quit the band." I could hear a collective gasp from our audience. Hannah and Casey walked closer to us. Michael and Mitchell started pushing and chasing each other. *Kids.* Hannah walked up to me and gave me a hug.

"Hey, Billy," Hannah said. She pulled me close to her and I could feel her breasts smash against my chest. I moved my hands down to her waist and looked across the garage at a very confused-looking Rob.

"Hey, Hannah, you smell great," I said as we separated.

"It's Sun, Moon, Stars." *Of course it is.* I smiled.

"That's a perfume, right?"

"Yeah, what else could it be?" Hannah reasoned.

"I just thought you naturally smelled like flowers."

"Ahh, that's so sweet, Billy!" Hannah went in for a second hug and her hair brushed across my face. Rob, Chris, and Casey watched us and Rob abruptly said,

"Billy? What is happening right now?"

"So, you finally asked her out?" Chris said. "It's about damn time."

"You can say that again," Hannah said as she rubbed her hand against my arm. Casey nodded in agreement.

"Maybe we can double date sometime," Chris said.

"Great. Everyone has a girlfriend but me," Rob said.

"Wait, you like girls?" Chris quipped.

"What! Yeah." Rob turned a shade of red I hadn't before seen on him. He looked down at his feet and then back at Chris and said, "So you're quitting the band, huh?"

"Yeah, I have to move in two weeks. We have to get all of this stuff moved out of here."

"Ok, that's fine. I'll call my dad to pick up the equipment." Hannah put her hands over my right ear and whispered,

"Did you know about this?" I looked at her and nodded my head. Rob packed up his guitar and turned back to Chris.

"Can I use your phone?" Rob asked and made his way toward Chris."

"Yeah, you know where it is," Chris responded. Rob walked in to Chris's kitchen and Chris followed. I put my arm around Hannah and then rested my hand on her hip. Casey looked at us and smiled.

"I'm happy for you guys," Casey said. "You look so cute together."

"Thanks, Casey," Hannah said.

"Yeah, thanks, Casey," I said.

"Like Chris said, it's about time," Casey reiterated. I looked into Hannah's beautiful brown eyes.

"Thanks, Casey...I wonder if I'll ever hear the end of it," I said sarcastically.

"Nope. I'll be here to remind you," Hannah said. *Great.* She pulled me closer to her and put her hand in my back pocket. *Nice.* Casey laughed.

"Are you still gonna have a band with Rob?" Casey asked.

"Well, actually, Chris and I plan to start our own band, but Rob doesn't know that yet, so keep quiet."

"Oh, ok, wow," Casey said.

"Rob's still my friend, but musically, I think we're going in two different directions. I've been thinking about this for a while." Rob and Chris came back into the garage and Rob started unplugging all of his amps.

"Are you going to help or are you just going to stand there?" Rob said.

"Yeah, I'll help," I said.

"I don't use any of that stuff, but yeah, I'll help," Chris said.

"Hannah, do you wanna come over to my house for a while?" Casey said while walking out of the garage.

"Yeah, Ok, Billy, I'll see you later." Hannah hugged me and our hands touched as she turned away.

"See you later," I said. I watched her walk away until I couldn't see her anymore and then started rolling up speaker wire. We packed all of the equipment up and then waited for Rob's dad to come pick it up. After about 15 minutes of us standing around, Rob's dad showed up in his pale beige Dodge van. We loaded the van with the equipment and after we were done Rob turned back and faced us while his dad started the van.

"I'm going to help my dad unload the equipment and then I'll be back later."

"All right, later, Rob," I said.

"Later," Chris added. We watched the van drive down Laura Street for the last time. "You wanna watch some MTV?"

"Yeah, let's grab some cookies while we're at it." We walked inside of the house and Chris shut his garage door. We grabbed the cookies off of the counter, sat on the couch and turned on MTV.

After about an hour of staring at the TV watching music videos, there was a knock on the door.

"I'll get it," Chris said as he quickly got up from the couch and put the cookies down. He answered the door and yelled back to me, "It's Hannah and Casey." He turned back to them and said, "Hey, you wanna come in and hang out?" *Why does he have to be so loud? Oh well...*

"Yeah," I could hear Hannah say. Hannah and Casey came into the living room. Hannah sat right next to me on the couch. Casey and Chris sat across from each other in chairs on either side of the room. Hannah put her hand on my thigh and slowly moved it up and down. *What is happening right now?*

"What are you guys doing?" Hannah said.

"Just watching MTV, eating some cookies," I replied.

"That's cool. We just found out that they're going to shut down the entire street for fireworks tonight. It's gonna be like a block party," Hannah said.

"Nice. I'll be there. Well, I'm already here and I'm not going anywhere...hmmm, here or there?" I said.

"You're so cute, Billy," Hannah said while squeezing my leg.

"Why do you call him, Billy?" Chris said.

"Because I want to, got a problem, dude!?" Hannah said with authority. Chris put his hands in the air as if he were being arrested.

"No, no problem, just wondering," Chris said. Casey smiled at Chris and he quickly looked away from her and toward me. "Hey, I'm gonna call Angela again. No one answered the last time I tried. I need to tell her I'm moving."

"Yeah, good luck with that," I said.

"When I tell her I'm going to Golden West, she's so gonna break up with me...again. I should just break up with her first."

"You don't know that," I said. "I mean, it's probably going to happen, but you've been together so long. It's just sad."

"Yeah, I'm gonna go get this over with," Chris said as he grabbed the phone and walked down the hallway to his bedroom.

"Hey, Will," Casey said as soon as Chris left the room. "Do you think Chris and I...If he breaks up with his girlfriend? Hannah looked at me with a special curiosity. *Shit, what am I supposed to say?*

"I don't know, Casey, maybe." *Not going to happen.*

"Could you, maybe, talk to him for me?"

"Casey, you heard that he's going to Golden West, right? That's on the other side of town."

"That's ok. Do you think you can talk to him?" Hannah was still staring at me, waiting patiently for my answer.

"Come on, Billy, don't you owe her a favor?" *Shit, I think I do, but I don't want to get her hopes up. Well, shit.* I turned back to Casey and I could almost feel her nervous energy infecting the room.

"Sure, Casey, I'll talk to him, but only if they break up. I'm friends with Angela too and I wouldn't do that to her," I reasoned.

"I understand, thanks," Casey said. Hannah's demeanor changed as she moved her hand from my leg to behind my head on the couch."

"How long have you been friends with Angela?"

"A long time. A lot longer than she's been with Chris."

"Really. Just friends?"

"Yes, just friends. You'll meet her soon enough, at school."

"I think I already met her that time at the mall, but she didn't say anything to me. What's her sign?"

"I have no idea, Hannah; I don't know what her birthday is." *Is she jealous? Already?* I put my arm around her and looked into her eyes, "You have nothing to worry about, trust me." A slight smile returned to Hannah's face.

"I do trust you; I just don't trust her." *This is a weird conversation. You don't know her.*

"Like I said, no worries. I don't even hang out with her." Chris came back into the room and put the phone down on the table.

"Yeah, we broke up," Chris said.

"That sucks," I said. "Did she..." Chris quickly interjected.

"I broke up with her. I told her that I'm going to a different school and that we should break up. She wasn't even mad..." Casey perked up from her seat and immediately made eye contact with me. *Shit.*

"Oh my God!" Hannah said. "I love this song." No doubt's 'Just a Girl' came on MTV. Hannah started singing along. She even mimicked Gwen Stefani's facial expressions. *I was right!*

"Holy crap! You can sing!?" I said.

"Yeah, I got it from my dad. He's a triple threat." *That's not good.*

"What's a triple threat?" I asked.

"It means someone can sing, dance, and act." *That's a relief.*

"That's cool. You've got a really good voice; better than Gwen."

"Thanks, Billy, but it's Gwen. I'm not better than Gwen." *Yes, you are.*

"What do you guys think? Better than Gwen?" I looked at Casey and then Chris. Chris nodded his head in agreement and Casey said,

"I agree with Will, Hannah, you are better than Gwen."

"Thanks for the backup, Casey!" I squeezed Hannah's arm. "See, Hannah, we have a consensus." *I think that's right.*

"Thanks, guys, I appreciate it, but I don't think I'm that great." *Wow, really?* Chris's parents came through the door before I could get another word out.

"Chris, come help unload the groceries! Oh, wow, we've got a full house," Chris's mom said. "Will, you can help too; you're staying over, right?"

"Yes, ma'am," I said as I got up from the couch. Hannah laughed and looked over at Casey.

"Hey, Billy, we're gonna go get ready," Hannah said. *Ready? What is she talking about?*

"Ok, ready for what?"

"The block party, silly." *Hmmm, I am ready.* Hannah gave me a hug and Casey stood at the door and waited for her to let me go. "See you later."

"Remember..." Casey said and they walked out the front door and toward Casey's house. I met Chris out at his mom's car and we grabbed a few bags of groceries each.

"Hey, man, are you ok? With Angela and everything..."

"Yeah, I guess I have to be."

"Well, if it makes you feel better, Casey likes you."

"What!? She doesn't even have tits yet." *Yeah, I knew he would say that.* We both laughed as we walked to his kitchen.

"She's cute, and she's nice. Something to think about..."

"Nah, I'm good." *I tried.* Chris's dad came into the kitchen and started putting beer in the refrigerator. "Hey, Scott, can I have a beer?"

"No, you can't have a beer. I'm not contributing to the delinquency of a minor and besides, your mom would kick my ass. Go set up the grill in the front yard."

"All right," Chris said and pointed at me. "Come help me." We went in the back yard and grabbed the grill, some tools, and charcoal and set it up in the front yard. Chris's dad came outside loaded up with hot dogs and hamburgers to grill. Chris whispered in my ear, "let's go get those beers." *Shit.* I followed Chris back into the kitchen and he pulled a Corona out of the refrigerator. "Hurry up, grab a beer."

"Won't your dad notice?"

"Scott doesn't care; we just have to keep my mom from finding out. Hurry up!" I grabbed the beer and we went to Chris's room. He shut the door and said, "let me get the bottle opener...let me see." Chris opened one of his desk drawers. "Here it is." We opened our beers and started drinking. "Drink it up fast," Chris said and started gulping it down. I followed his lead and then he hid the bottles in his closet. Have you drunk beer before?"

"Yeah, my brother lets me drink with him. He only buys Budweiser though and that tastes like ass. Your dad's Corona's are much better."

"Yup, let's see if the coast is clear to grab another one."

"No, man, I'm good. I don't want Hannah to think I'm an alcoholic."

"Ha-ha...whatever, man, suit yourself." Chris got up from his bed, opened the door, and then returned with another beer in his hand. He drank that beer faster than the first. I was feeling pretty good and without warning Chris said, "Fuck, Angela!"

"Ok, shit, are you sure you're ok?"

"No, I don't want to move! Fuck!"

"Yeah, it sucks, but it'll be fine. At least you're staying in Visalia. It could have been worse."

"Like what, Fresno?"

"No, like Bakersfield." We both laughed and Chris put the empty beer bottle in his closet. "Let's go check on the food, man, I'm getting hungry."

"All right. Hey, thanks."

"We'll always be friends, man, and we have to focus on our new band. What do you think about Hannah...?"

"She's stupid hot and too good for your skinny-ass."

"Ha-ha. First, stay away from my girlfriend." *I really like hearing those words come out of my mouth.* "Second, I was going to say what do you think about Hannah singing for us?"

"Yeah, sure, do you think she wants to sing for us?"

"I'm actually not sure, but I'm gonna ask her anyway. It might be a problem because of her parents, but it's worth a shot...And, we still need a bass player."

"You are a bass player."

"Thanks, Captain obvious. I'm gonna play guitar. I thought I told you that."

"I don't know, maybe you did. Were we smoking when you told me?" *That's a good question.*

"I don't know, doesn't matter. I'm gonna play guitar."

"You don't have a guitar, or an amp."

"I'll figure it out. Worst case, I can borrow one from my brother." *He may just give me one.*

"Now for the real question: Do you think you're good enough to play guitar? I've never even seen you play." *That's a fair question.*

"Maybe, but I want to play so that's going to have to be enough for now. I'm gonna have to practice a lot more that's for sure."

"Why not just find a guitar player?"

"Simple; I don't want to find another Rob telling us how to run OUR band."

"Yeah, fuck Rob."

"Let's go get some food, seriously this time."

"Yeah, I'm getting hungry too." Chris and I went out into the living room and didn't see anyone. "I guess everyone's outside." We opened the front door and saw all of the neighbors out in their yards. Everyone had the same idea to Barbeque on their front lawns. The sun was getting very low in the sky, but it was still sweltering hot outside. Chris's dad was manning the grill and stacking meat on a large plate next to him.

"It'll be a few minutes," Chris's dad said. I looked down the street and didn't see Hannah. *What is she up to?*

"Didn't Rob say he was going to be back?" Chris said.

"Yeah, but it's Rob, so who knows. Wait, who cares?"

"He's coming; that's his dad's van," Chris said as he pointed down the street. The van pulled around the Cul-De-Sac and Rob slid open the door and got out.

"Hey, Rob, you're just in time. The food's almost ready," Chris said.

"Good, I'm starving." *I highly doubt that.* Rob responded with a slight smile on his face.

"Food's ready, boys. Chris, go get the buns from inside," Chris's dad said. Chris went into his house and got the buns while Rob and I stared at each other. *I should just tell him right now and get this over with. Nah, he'll probably make a scene.* Chris brought back the buns and we all took turns loading up our paper plates with food. We stood at the end of the driveway and ate while we people-watched all of the neighbors. After I finished my first hotdog, I saw Hannah and Jessica walking toward us.

"Your girlfriend's coming." *Thanks, Chris, I can see that.* Hannah hugged me and I set my plate down on the ground. She grabbed my hand as soon as I stood back up.

"Hey, babe," *Babe?* "did you miss me?" Hannah said.

"Of course I missed you," I said. Hannah squeezed my hand tighter and looked over at Jessica.

"This is Jessica."

"Yeah, I remember, from the mall," Chris said. Rob didn't say anything and continued eating.

"Hi," Jessica said. I looked at Hannah and smiled.

"Do you guys want some food?"

"I'm good, Jessica?" Hannah said.

"No, I ate earlier," Jessica replied. It was getting darker outside and people started setting off fireworks in the middle of the street. I could see Michael and Mitchell in front of Hannah's house and looked to my left to see Casey running up to us.

"Hey, guys, this is so cool," she said. "Hi, Chris."

"Ummm, hi, Casey," Chris said as he walked away from our group to get more food. Rob also grabbed another plate of food. The sun continued its final descent into the horizon and the fireworks picked up intensity. We all stood in a half-circle looking down Laura Street with Hannah and I holding hands in the middle of the group. Hannah's mom and dad came outside and saw us standing at the end of the Cul-De-Sac. Her dad stared right at me and walked into the middle of the street to set up a firework. Her mom walked down the street toward us.

"Shit, Hannah, your mom's coming," I said as I pulled my hand away. Hannah reached for my hand and held on tight with both of her hands.

"I don't care if she knows about us." *You probably should.* "What's she going to do?" *Lock you up.* Hannah's mom got closer and closer to us and then stopped short. She moved her finger in a 'come here' motion without saying a word. "Come on, mom, leave me alone," Hannah pleaded.

"Would you rather that your dad come over here?" *Shit.* Hannah let go of my hand and gave me a hug.

"Fine, whatever." Hannah walked past her mom and Jessica followed behind. Her mom maintained eye contact with me, but didn't say anything. *What the hell? What is that look on her face? Disappointment? Disgust? Hatred?* She turned around and walked back to her yard. Hannah and Jessica sat down on the curb in front of her house. *Shit! I never gave her my number.*

"Hey, Casey, I need you to do me a favor. I need you to give Hannah my number."

"Ok, but I don't have your number," Casey said.

"Chris, do you have some paper and a pen?"

"Yeah, hold on." Chris went inside his house and came back with a piece of binder paper and a pen. I wrote my number on it, folded it up, and gave it to Casey.

"Give it to her on the down low, Casey," I said. She ran over to Hannah and sat down next to her. She slowly slipped the note into

Hannah's hand. Hannah smiled and we stared at each other over the distance of the street. I looked at Chris and then at Rob and then back toward Hannah. I sighed as darkness filled the sky and the fireworks gradually diminished to a whimper.

Chapter Seven

Adoration

I WOKE UP THE next morning with a massive headache. Chris's living room floor didn't do me any favors even with a sleeping bag underneath me. I looked over to my right and saw Rob still asleep. His ratty blond hair clung to his greasy, pimpled face as he turned over on top of his sleeping bag. I sat up and saw Chris still sleeping on the couch. I could hear Chris's parents getting ready for work. I got up, rubbed the sleep out of my eyes, and went to the bathroom. I walked back out to the living room and tapped Chris on the shoulder. "Hey, man, I'm gonna go home and take a shower, I'll be back later." Chris barely opened his eyes.

"Ok, later." I went out the front door to find my bike exactly where I left it near the tree. I grabbed the handlebars and headed down Laura Street. I looked to my left and right cruising along as slowly as possible. Empty fireworks littered the street with occasional scorch marks scattered throughout. I passed by Hannah's house and saw her mom getting into her Isuzu Trooper to go to work. She stopped short of getting inside of her truck as I rode by. She scowled at me but didn't say anything. I scowled back at her and continued riding home. My mom and my brother weren't there when I walked through the door. I immediately went to take a shower. *I wonder if Hannah's going to call...I wonder if she can call.* Half-way through my shower, I heard the phone ringing. *Oh shit!* I hadn't even rinsed off completely but decided to shut the water off. I quickly wrapped a towel around my waist, bulldozed the bathroom door and answered the phone.

"Hello...Hello?" I said frantically.

"Oh, yes, is Patricia Smith there?" *Shit, not Hannah.*

"No, she's at work," I said.

"Do you know when she'll be back in?" I was already growing impatient as I stood in my living room dripping soapy water from my hair.

"Look, I don't know, call back later," I said and hung up the phone. *Fuck! What a mess.* I looked at the floor and saw that the carpet was flooded beneath me. *That wasn't worth it.* I went back into the bathroom and finished taking my shower and then cleaned up the sopping mess I had left by the phone. *This day is going great.* I looked over at the clock on the wall and it read 9:15. *I've got some time before I go back to Chris's. Maybe Hannah will call.* I brushed my hair out and got dressed before putting Soundgarden's Bad Motor Finger into my CD player. I advanced the tracks to 'Jesus Christ Pose.' It was my favorite song on the album. Chris Cornell belted out the lyrics and I pictured Hannah's mom staring at me like I needed to be saved. *Like I'm not good enough.* I played the song and then played it again and again. I felt myself getting angrier and angrier as the song played on. *They don't have a right to judge me! Who the fuck do they think they are?* The phone rang and I snapped out of it. *Shit.* I went into the living room to answer the phone and was reminded of my previous mistake as the floor was still damp against my feet.

"Hello?"

"Is Will there?"

"Hannah?"

"Yeah, it's me, Billy. I saw you ride by my house this morning."

"Your mom mad dogged me something fierce."

"She doesn't want me anywhere near you."

"I figured that much after last night."

"You don't even want to know what my dad said." *I really don't.* "I don't care what they say though. I wish that they would just chill. They can't control the guys I go out with." *Guys?*

"Especially when school starts, what are they even thinking?"

"I really like you and I don't care how long it takes for my parents to understand that. Why can't they just be happy for me?"

"I guess they're just worried about you."

"I can take care of myself." *I don't doubt that.* "Hey, I need to tell you something..." *That's never good.* "Chris asked me out when you were gone on vacation."

"What!?"

"I just thought you should know. I don't want to cause any problems."

"I don't believe it! That traitor!"

"I turned him down and told him that I liked you."

"Did he try anything?"

"No, I would have kicked his ass." Hannah laughed. *This is not funny.* "He just made fun of you and basically said I was stupid."

"What'd he say?"

"It doesn't matter."

"It does matter. I want to know. We've been friends for years and to find out he went behind my back. He knew that I liked you."

"He said you were skinny and weak and that I could do better, like him. I told him that he was stupid and that was it."

"He was still with Angela then too. What the hell!?"

"That's the way guys are..."

"That's not the way I am. I would never cheat on anyone."

"That's why I like you, you're different."

"I feel the same way about you."

"No matter what, I'd always pick you over Chris; I just hope that he doesn't come between us."

"That's not going to happen. I guess it's a good thing that he's moving." *Shit, what about the band? I do not need this right now.*

"Are you going to stop being friends with him?"

"I don't know." *This sucks.*

"Maybe it's best if you guys aren't friends."

"I don't know. I don't know what to think right now." *I need to call him and see what he has to say for himself. Mother Fucker.* "I need to see you."

"My dad's asleep right now, but if he woke up and I wasn't here he'd probably lock me up for good."

"Yeah, we're going to have to figure this out..."

"If you want, I can try to sneak out tonight after my dad goes to work and my mom goes to bed."

"Do you think you'll get away with it? That sounds risky as hell."

"It's not as risky as my dad being here. He wakes up a lot. My mom sleeps like a baby."

"Well, in that case, I'm down. What time?"

"Meet me outside of my house at midnight." *Shit. Is she serious?*

"You know there's a 10 O'clock curfew, right?"

"No, I didn't know that. If you don't want to..."

"No, I do, I really want to see you." *I need to see you.*

"Ok, it's settled then. Midnight. What are you going to do about Chris?"

"I guess I should call him. We we're going to practice today, but I don't really feel like doing that anymore."

"Are you going to tell him that I told you?"

"I would like to hear him admit to it..."

"What if he lies about it?" *That's a good question.*

"I don't know...I guess I won't even bring it up. He's moving in two weeks. Why should I care, right?" *I totally care though; I care a lot.*

"Exactly. I like that, Billy, be the bigger person. But, hey, I should get off the phone before my dad wakes up and takes it from me."

"All right, babe, I'll see you tonight."

"Babe? I like it. Ok, sweetie, don't be late. Bye!"

"Bye," I said and hung up the phone. *What am I going to do about Chris? Shit. I should call him. I don't want to call him. Shit.*

I'll just wait for him to call me. I poured myself a bowl of Life cereal and sat down in front of the TV. I did some channel surfing until I settled on MTV. They were showing a marathon of Beavis and Butthead. It was a stupid show, but I still watched it because it was funny sometimes, and I didn't have anything better to do. I watched two episodes and the phone rang in the middle of the third. I looked over at the clock. It was after 11. *Shit.*

"Hello?"

"Hey, man, get your ass over here, I wanna go to the bike jumps," Chris said. *Don't bring it up...*

"I don't really feel like it today, I've got a headache." *Don't bring it up...*

"Headache? What are you talking about? As if you've never done anything with a headache before..." *Don't...*

"I'm just not feeling it." *Don't...*

"This doesn't sound like you at all...What's wrong? Don't you want to see your girlfriend?" *Shit.*

"Did you ask Hannah out when I was in Camarillo?"

"...Ummm, so she told you?"

"So, it is true! How could you do that to me? I thought you were my friend."

"You weren't making a move and I thought that..."

"That what? You're a piece of shit. And on top of that you were still with Angela."

"That was going to end anyway. None of this matters; she said no to me and you still got her so who cares?"

"I do. I can't trust you."

"You can't trust me? You're starting to sound like a girl..."

"You went behind my back. You knew that I liked her and that didn't stop you."

"You're getting your panties all in a bunch because of a girl?"

"Fuck you, Chris." I hung up the phone and unplugged it from the wall. I didn't want to even hear the phone ring let alone talk to Chris again. *Melancholy and the Infinite Sadness.* I decided that I was more angry than sad and grabbed my brother's Motley Crue cassette, put it in my stereo and blasted 'Kickstart My Heart' as loud as I could. I wasn't really a fan of hair bands, but I really liked that song. I let the tape play after the song was over, but I turned it down before one of the neighbors complained. I could hear my mom's voice in my head. *The walls are as thin as paper! Turn it down!* I went into the kitchen and made myself a turkey sandwich and walked back and forth between my living room and bedroom while eating. After the music stopped, I flipped the tape over and played the other side. I heard a loud knock on the door and turned the music off. *Shit, the neighbors.* I heard a second knock, but louder. *Shit.* I walked over to the front door and hesitantly opened it.

"Rob, what are you doing here?"

"Chris told me what happened. It's fucked up."

"Yeah, it is, but who cares, right? He's moving. Thank God for that."

"You're not going to be friends anymore?"

"How could I?"

"I don't know. It is pretty fucked up."

"You wanna come in and hang out?"

"Yeah." Rob came in and sat on my couch.

"You want some water or something?"

"Yeah, thanks, water's good. I walked all the way over here."

"I told you that you needed a bike, man." I got Rob a glass of water and handed it to him. "You're a good friend, Rob, I know you'd never pull this shit on me."

"Yeah, I really wouldn't." *He really couldn't.*

"I'm just saying that I trust you."

"That's why I came over. I wanted to make sure that we're good."

"We're good, Rob."

"Do you wanna meet our new drummer? He can play this weekend; Saturday afternoon."

"Yeah, let's do it." *Why not?*

"Cool, just be at my house at noon Saturday. Matt is so much better than Chris." *I don't even care, fuck Chris.*

"All right, I'll be there." I turned on the TV and the Beavis and Butthead marathon was still going strong. I sat down in my mom's chair. Rob and I watched until about 4, somehow mesmerized by the stupidity that was in front of us.

"Hey, man, I have to go; I have to get home for dinner. My mom is making lasagna."

"Oh, all right, let me give you a ride."

"What do you mean?"

"On the back of my bike. It'll be faster than walking."

"True. All right, let's go." I grabbed my bike and drug it downstairs. Rob put his hands on my shoulders and stood on the foot pegs. We rode up Court Street and down Walnut until we got to his house. "Damn, dude, that was fast."

"I told you. Get a bike, man." We walked inside of Rob's house and his mom was making dinner. It smelled great. *Very Italian.* Rob's mom looked over at me.

"Hey, Will, are you staying for dinner?"

"I think so, something smells great."

"You're more than welcome; we have plenty of food," Rob's mom continued.

"Ok, thanks," I said. Rob and I sat down at the dining room table and his mom brought out the lasagna from the oven. She cut it into pieces and plopped them onto our plates. I took a bite and looked at Rob. "This is fantastic," I said.

"My mom's a great cook," Rob responded.

"Yeah, she is," I agreed. We finished our food and Rob said,

"Hey, you want to stay over?"

"Nah, I can't, I'm meeting Hannah tonight."

"Oh yeah? Shit, ok."

"Yeah, we already made plans. I'll call you tomorrow though."

"Ok, yeah, call me tomorrow. What are you going to do with her?"

"I don't know." *Shit.* "I'll figure it out. She wants me to meet her tonight and I'm going to be there."

"Shit, man, you're just gonna do it then?"

"You're God damn skippy! Have you seen her? You know..."

"Yeah. I get it. Just don't get caught or end up in jail." *What is he talking about?*

"It'll be fine." I finished my food and handed my plate to Rob's mom. "Thanks for dinner, see ya later, Rob," I said as I walked out of his house.

"See ya. Call me tomorrow," Rob said as I pulled my bike off of the ground. "Don't do anything I wouldn't do." *Huh?*

"For sure, see ya." I rode away from Rob's house, and down Court Street. When I got home, my mom was already there.

"What do you want for dinner?" She asked.

"I'm good, I already ate at Rob's," I said as my mom's face relaxed.

"Leftovers for me then," she said. I went to my room and turned on the radio. *I don't have any condoms. I wonder if Larry does.* I went through his stuff and didn't find anything that I could use. *Shit. I should probably go to the store.* There was a liquor store right down the street from my apartments. *Nah, I don't want to do that.* I put my hands inside of my pockets and felt around. *I don't have any money anyway. Shit.* I heard my brother come in. I went and sat down on the couch. My brother grabbed some leftovers from the refrigerator and sat down next to me. *Shit. How am I going to get out of here without anyone noticing?*

"What's up, bro?" My brother said before he started eating.

"Nothing, just chilling," I said as he grabbed the remote, turned on the TV, and changed the channel to the Nightly News. A long time passed as we watched the news and then some terrible sitcoms, but my mom and my brother eventually got tired.

"Hey, bro, are you going to bed?" My brother said.

"Nah, I think I'll stay up for a while and watch some MTV."

"All right, good night," he said. My mom and brother each went to their rooms to go to sleep. *I just have to wait for my chance.* I waited until 11:30. I didn't hear anything coming from the bedrooms. I turned off the TV, slowly got off of the couch, and headed for the front door. I turned around and looked back toward the bedrooms and waited a minute. I didn't hear anything so I slowly opened the door and then closed and locked it, being as quiet as I could. I grabbed my bike and headed downstairs. I started riding down Court Street to meet Hannah. *It's the middle of the night. What are you doing?* It wasn't as dark as I had hoped for as I made my way to Laura Street. Cars were constantly buzzing by me. *I hope it's not the cops.* I got up to Whitendale and a car pulled up beside me.

"Hey, what are you doing?" A voice said from inside of the car. *Shit.*

"I'm just going home," I said as I coasted to a stop.

Someone rolled down the back window and threw a bottle at me. The bottle hit the ground and shattered. I heard laughing as the car sped off into the distance. *Shit. Not the cops. Just some assholes, but shit.* I got to Beech Street and ditched my bike in someone's bushes and walked the rest of the way to Laura Street. I stood outside of Hannah's house and waited. It was almost midnight. I didn't usually wear a watch, but I did that night. I stood behind the Isuzu Trooper in Hannah's driveway checking the time every few seconds. Around 12:05, I saw Hannah walking toward me from the edge of her driveway. *Wow, I didn't even hear the door.* There was a full moon that night which reflected brilliantly off of Hannah's beautiful, flowing blond hair. She walked up to me and gave me a hug and slid her hand down my arm to hold my hand. "Hey, babe, we should probably go somewhere," Hannah whispered in my ear.

"I didn't know you were a ninja," I said and smiled.

"It's not the first time I've snuck out." *Really?* "Let's walk down to that school." Hannah pointed down the street.

"Mountain View. Yeah, I went to that school in sixth grade. There's a park over there too." Hannah and I held hands and walked down the middle of the street toward the school. We waited for all of the cars to pass on Court Street and then ran across the intersection still holding hands. We approached the school and realized that the gates were locked.

"What are we going to do?" Hannah asked.

"We're gonna have to jump the fence. I'll go first and then help you over."

"I think I can jump a fence without help."

"It'll make me feel better," I said as I jumped onto and over the fence. As I jumped down to the ground, I heard Hannah grab onto the fence. She was standing right next to me before I had the chance to say anything.

"See, I'm not just a girl..."

"But you do look like Gwen Stefani."

"Yeah, sort of, a little bit." We walked toward the concrete benches on the playground.

"Nope, more like a lotta bit. It's a good thing."

"Ok, I can do that too. Hannah stopped walking and dropped my hand. She looked me up and down and then walked around me in a circle."

"What are you doing?" I looked straight forward.

"Trent Reznor, the Nine Inch Nails guy. You look exactly like Trent Reznor."

"Oh yeah...I guess that's not too bad."

"I was messing with you. I thought you looked like Trent Reznor the first time I saw you playing Bass in Chris's garage." *Chris...*

"We should probably talk about Chris."

"Talk about what? I told you what happened. It's not a big deal." I put my hand on Hannah's lower back and we continued walking to one of the concrete benches. We sat down next to each other on top of the bench and stared out at the darkened playground.

"I called him and asked him about it. He didn't deny it. It wasn't good. I said some things..."

"I thought you were going to let it go..."

"Why did you turn him down? I guess what I'm saying is why me and not him?"

"...Honestly..." Hannah looked into my eyes and moved her hair from her right to left shoulder. "He reminds me of my ex-boyfriend, Joe." *Oh shit.* "He was a jock too; good looking, athletic, you know, like an Abercrombie and Fitch model." *A what? I wouldn't exactly call Chris a model.* "He also treated me like shit. When he broke up with me, I told myself that I would never date another jock."

"So, I'm the anti-jock." *Awesome...*

"You're different, in a good way. That's what I like about you." Hannah grabbed my hand and held it tightly. "And, you're a Libra, which makes us perfect for each other." *Yeah, I read.*

"It's just that everyone keeps telling me that you're too good for me."

"That's not true, I think that you're too good for me." *Come again...Is this girl for real?* "I can't believe you're my boyfriend. You're so sweet and such a nice person, it's hard to believe that you would go out with me. I'm only saying this because I've never really felt the same way with a guy like I feel with you. So many guys treat me like shit, it kind of was a shock that you didn't. I think it's because you're almost 16 and more mature."

"I knew that you liked me, but I didn't know why."

"Now you do. I was afraid you didn't like me. I didn't think you were ever going to ask me out."

"Well, I was a little intimidated by you. You're super-beautiful, smart, nice..."

"That's so funny," Hannah interjected, "I was intimidated by you, but you make me feel so comfortable." She jumped off of the bench still holding my hand. "Let's go on the swings."

"All right." We walked over to the swings, sat down, and started swinging. Hannah reached over and put her hand over mine.

"I feel so safe with you."

"That's a good thing, because you never know what could be out here at night." I laughed. "It's ok, though, I'll protect you."

"Maybe I'll protect you." Hannah stopped swinging, got up and sat in my lap sideways. I laughed.

"That doesn't look comfortable." Hannah put her arm around my neck and I started swinging. She rested her head against my chest.

"It's perfect." The moonlight filtered through the trees and onto my shoes as I slowly swung back and forth. After a few minutes, I slowed down to a crawl and put my feet on the ground. I wrapped my arms around Hannah and rested my head on top of hers. *I think she's asleep.* I felt her breathe in and out against my chest and smelled her perfume as I started feeling my eyelids getting heavy.

I heard a car horn which woke me from my blissful slumber. I looked around and didn't see anything. I checked the time on my watch and it read 2:18. *Shit.* I grabbed a hold of Hannah tightly underneath her legs and stood up. I looked around for somewhere to set her down, but my whole body was numb from the swing so I set her down right where we were in the dirt underneath the swing. I sat down next her and she woke up.

"Hey, babe, what time is it?" Hannah asked.

"It's almost 2:30."

"We should go back. My dad gets off at 4."

"All right, give me a minute. My legs are asleep."

"Ahh, poor baby," Hannah said and started rubbing my legs. *Ummm, Ouch much.* I felt the pins and needles as the blood came back. "Better?"

"Yeah, much better." *Nope.* "You ready to go back?"

"Yeah, let's go." Hannah jumped up from the ground and brushed herself off. She put her hand out and I grabbed on. She pulled me up and I stumbled forward until I was able to balance myself onto the frame of the swing. "You ok?" Hannah laughed as she continued dusting herself off.

"Of course," I said while walking over to her. "What are you talking about? Hey, you missed a spot," I said and brushed the dirt off of her jeans.

"Was there really dirt on my butt or did you just want an excuse to touch it?"

"Yes," I said and smiled.

"Smooth." *Is she being sarcastic? I can't tell.* We headed back to the front of the school and jumped the fence. I put my arm around her waist and she put her hand in my back pocket. "I have to check for dirt," she said and smiled back at me.

"Really, what'd you find?"

"Nothing, actually..." *Wait, what? This girl...*

"Ha-ha," I said. Hannah smiled and I once again admired her beautiful blond hair reflecting the moonlight.

"Let's go," she said and we made our way back down Laura Street. "Do you think you're going to work things out with Chris?" *Huh?*

"I don't know. I don't think so. Why?"

"I know that your band matters to you and you've been friends for a long time so I figured that you would want to fix things." I laughed.

"Well, I did tell him to fuck off so that might be a problem."

"I know you're not the type of person to hold grudges."

"I'll think about it, Hannah, but I don't think it matters. I think I'm gonna start hanging out with Rob more."

"Rob, really? I thought you didn't like him."

"He is really hard to get along with sometimes, but at least I can trust him."

"What's his birthday?"

"You mean for the astrology thing? I think it's like May 10th or something like that."

"Yeah, that would make him a Taurus; stubborn and bull-headed, but also loyal, so that sounds exactly right." *Interesting...*

"The thing is that I want to play guitar so I'm going to have to talk to him. I also want us to write our own songs and come up with a band name. You know, to be legit."

"'2 Legit 2 quit,' Hammer time!" *I remember that. She's quick.*

"You're so cute," I said while squeezing her waist. *So hot.* We got to Court Street and did not have to wait to cross because there wasn't any traffic. *Shit. We're almost there.*

"No, you're so cute," she responded as she grabbed my butt and smiled. *Let's go!* "So, you're going to give him an ultimatum then?" *This girl is smarter than me...*

"Ultimatum?"

"Yeah, like, if he listens to you then you'll stay in the band with him and if he doesn't then you'll start your own."

"That's exactly right. It also reminds me...Would you want to sing for my band? I mean, you have a great voice."

"I would love to sing for your band, even though I don't think I'm very good, but my parents hardly ever let me out of the house now."

"Yeah...that sucks."

"I'm so happy that school starts in a couple of weeks, Billy, we'll be able to see each other every day. No parents breathing down my neck." *Just me...*

"Yeah, just the teachers." *Get to class!*

"They don't care."

"Yeah, probably not, at least most of them." We got to Hannah's house and stopped behind her parent's truck. I hugged her close to me and then let her go. "You want to see a movie this weekend?" I whispered.

"Yeah, what do you wanna see?" *You.*

"Doesn't matter, we can decide when we get there."

"I'll have to bring Jessica."

"I'll bring Rob. Call me tomorrow, we'll figure it out."

"Ok, I'll call Jessica in the morning." Hannah looked into my eyes and I felt a sense of anxiety that I hadn't felt in a long time. I looked back into her eyes and I knew that I had to kiss her. *Don't fuck this up.* My heart pounded. *Shit. What if she doesn't want to? Don't be a pussy. Shit.* Time seemed to stop. *How long have you been standing here?* I moved my hands up to her face and slowly pushed her hair back behind her head. I let my hands settle on the back of her neck and pulled her closer. I watched her close her eyes and I moved in. *It's a go.* I pressed my lips into hers and tasted her cherry lip gloss. I pulled back away from her and smiled. She pulled me back and I felt her tongue slide past my lips. She pinned me against her body and held onto my back with claw-like precision. *I'm not going anywhere.* Silence and moonlight engulfed us. There was nothing else. I felt Hannah release her grip from my back and then slowly pull away from me. "I should probably go inside, Billy; you don't want me to get caught, do you?" She grabbed my hand and led me over to the fence. She carefully opened the gate and then turned back towards me. Her lips met mine once again for a moment. She looked into my eyes and then rested her hand on the gate. "I'll call you tomorrow."

"What time?" I whispered.

"Noon. Bye, Billy."

"Bye, Hannah." She shut her gate and I turned around, walked past the Isuzu Trooper, and back down the street. I found the random bush where I stashed my bike and fished it out. I headed home down Court Street and went over every detail of the night in my head. *I think I love this girl. Wait, what?* I was unlocking my front door before I knew it. It was still quiet. I took off my shoes and sat down on the couch. *Did that just happen? Yeah, yeah it did.* I smiled and put my feet up. I pulled my mom's fluffy blanket over me and fell asleep.

Chapter Eight

Follow the leader

"Hey, man, do you want to go see a movie this weekend with me, Hannah, and her friend, Jessica?" I asked Rob on the phone.

"Jessica, that girl from the other night?"

"Yeah, she's single."

"That doesn't mean anything. It doesn't mean she likes me."

"True, but it doesn't mean you shouldn't try. She's cute, she's single, why not?"

"All right, what movie?"

"I don't know, I was thinking Batman or something like that."

"I've been wanting to see the new Batman. I'm down."

"Ok, we're going to meet them at the mall at 2 on Saturday. Do you think your mom will give us a ride?"

"I think so. I'll have to ask."

"All right, what are you doing today?"

"Nothing."

"Ok, I'm coming over."

"All right, later."

"Later," I said and grabbed my bike. I quickly rode to Rob's house. I had a lot to talk to him about and I didn't want to waste any time. Rob answered his door almost immediately after I knocked.

"Hey, man, my mom said she'll take us on Saturday."

"Oh, all right, cool."

"Are you coming in or what?"

"Yeah," I said and Rob led the way to his bedroom. I sat down on Rob's chair and he sat down on the edge of his bed. He picked up his guitar and strummed a song I hadn't heard before. "What's that song?"

"It's called 'Verse Chorus Verse.' It's Nirvana. It wasn't even released on an album."

"Well then how did you get it?"

"I have my ways." *That's some shady shit...*

"Anyway, I want to talk to you about our band...I'm ok with this new drummer, but I don't want to play bass anymore. I want to play guitar."

"Matt is out. His parents won't let him play anymore; something about focusing on school. What a loser. I was thinking we keep Chris around..."

"That's not going to happen. It's either me or him."

"I know you're pissed at him, but get over it." *What the hell!?*

"Ok, so let me get this straight: You wanted to kick Chris out of the band because supposedly, he wasn't reliable and now when I want him out because he's a back-stabbing piece of shit, everything's good. Did I miss something?"

"Nope, I just don't care about all that girl bullshit. He knows the songs and we need a drummer, period."

"Then we'll find a new drummer, period."

"Because that's the easiest thing to do...And if you want to play guitar, you're going to have to find a bass player to replace you, also super easy...NOT."

"I'm telling you that's what's going to happen. School starts in two weeks and we'll find a bass player and a drummer. I'm not playing with Chris anymore; besides, he's going to Golden West. And you thought he was unreliable before..."

"...Fine, have it your way, but it's on you to find these people."

"It's on us, Rob, we're a band. Also, we need a name and we need to write our own damn songs. I'm tired of being a Nirvana cover band." I could see Rob's face turning its classic shade of red. His greasy blond hair hung uneasily in front of his eyes and I knew that he was angry.

"You need to slow down with all this shit."

"What shit, Rob? I'm not backing down."

"You're not good enough to be telling me how to run my band."

"Again, this is our band, not your band! If you can't see that then I think I should leave."

"Calm down." *Rob's telling me to calm down?*

"Seriously, things are gonna change, or you're gonna be playing by yourself."

"I was playing by myself before I met you and I'll be playing by myself long after we're friends." *What is he talking about?*

"So, you don't think we're going to be friends one day?"

"Maybe, I don't know. I can't tell the future. Look at what happened with Chris."

"That's different..."

"Is it?"

"Yeah, Chris can't be trusted..."

"And you trust me? Why?" *Because, dude, you're gross and kind of fat. I have nothing to worry about.*

"You haven't given me any reason to not trust you." *Well, you did spit on my wall. So gross. Not a trust issue though.*

"Whatever, man, no one knows what's going to happen in the..."

"Yeah, you already said that," I interjected. "But right now, we need to make some changes. I have to go; I don't want to miss Hannah's call. Think about what I said. I'll call you later." Rob didn't say anything else and I let myself out of his house, grabbed my bike, and rode back home.

Hannah called me at exactly noon, just like she said she would. "Hey, babe, what's up?"

"Not much, I guess you didn't get caught last night..."

"They've never caught me sneaking out. I don't think the thought has ever crossed their minds." *Is this a regular thing?*

"That's good, I don't think my mom cares."

"If I got caught, that would be the end of my life."

"That would be a damn shame. There is a lack of beautiful girls in the world."

"Smooth, Billy. I called Jessica earlier and she said she would go to the movies on Saturday. Did you call Rob?"

"Actually, I went over to his house and told him how it was."

"How'd it go?"

"I thought it went pretty good. He said he wanted to see a movie and that his mom would drive us, but that was before..."

"Before you told him off..."

"Yeah, well, I'll call him later to check."

"Guess what, Billy?"

"What?"

"No, I said guess."

"Ummm, ok...the Chargers are going to win the Super Bowl this year."

"No, silly, I miss you..."

"I miss you too."

"And it's obvious to anyone paying attention that the Packers are going to win the Super Bowl..." *The Packers? That's random. This girl...*

"Nope, not gonna happen."

"You should talk to my brother about it." *Sure...* "So, what are you wearing?" *Huh? Clothes...*

"Is that a trick question? I'm wearing clothes."

"What type of clothes?"

"A t-shirt and jeans, why?"

"That sounds sexy..." *No it doesn't. Wait...* "I'm just lying here in my bra and panties thinking about you." *Oh shit! Hannah on her bed, half naked.* I pictured the time that I saw her in her orange bikini. *Shit.*

"What color are they?" *Really? That was stupid.*

"It's a white bra and white panties with purple flowers. I got them at Victoria's Secret." *I wonder if she got them...ah, who cares when.*

"Now that sounds sexy," I said. *That does not sound right coming out of my mouth.*

"So, what do you want to do to me?" *Is this a dream? What am I supposed to say?* "Shit, my dad's awake, I gotta go. I'll try to call you later. Bye, Billy." Hannah abruptly hung up the phone. *Wait, what!?* I hung up the phone and looked around the living room to make sure that no one heard our conversation. No one was home, but I had to make sure. I went into the kitchen and poured myself a glass of water. *What am I supposed to do? Shit.* I couldn't get the image of Hannah in her bikini out of my head. *Does she really want to...?*

Later that day I called Rob and his mom answered. "Hi, is Rob there, this is Will."

"Yeah, honey, just a minute," his mom said. *Honey? Gross.*

"What do you want?" Rob said.

"I wanted to check if you still wanted to see the movie on Saturday."

"I guess so, but that was a dick move this morning."

"I learn from the best. And if there's any confusion, I mean you."

"Yeah, I got it, thanks...I thought about what you said, and, you're right." *I am? I mean, I am. Wait, about what?*

"What am I right about?"

"Chris, the band, you know, finding new people."

"And..."

"And if you want to name the band and play different stuff, that's fine." *Well, shit. How about that?*

"And that's it; just like that...What made you change your mind?"

"I talked to my grandpa and he told me that I need to be more flexible." *God Damn Skippy!* "He likes you too for some stupid reason and told me not to fuck it up, in those exact words."

"Nice, I always liked your grandpa." *I think I've talked to him like once.*

"I respect what he says. Without him, I wouldn't know anything about music."

"Well, shit, I didn't think that you respected anyone, but that makes sense."

"So, you want me to come by tomorrow? We could start writing stuff down and make a plan, or something."

"Yeah, all right, come by tomorrow."

"All right, later," I said.

"Later," Rob said and hung up the phone. *Cool, everything's cool. I wonder if Hannah's going to call. What am I going to say to her? Shit.* My brother walked through the front door wearing slacks and a nice shirt. *What the hell?*

"What's with the clothes?" I said while putting the phone down on the counter.

"I got a promotion to waiter," my brother said. "I don't have to wash the dishes anymore thank God."

"Congratulations, Larry; thinking about getting your own place?" *I really want my own room.*

"We'll see, I'm not sure how much money I'm going to make yet." *That makes no sense. You took a job and don't know how much you're getting paid? What a dumbass.* "I know you snuck out last night," my brother said as he went to the refrigerator and grabbed a beer. *Shit.* "I woke up and you weren't here."

"Are you going to tell mom?"

"Well that depends..."

"Depends on what?" *Damn it. What does he want?*

"Why were you sneaking out in the first place?" *Shit. Just tell him.*

"I snuck out to see my girlfriend."

"Girlfriend, huh? Is this the same girl you were talking about..."

"Yeah, we had to sneak out. Her parents have her on lockdown. I don't think they like me very much; actually, I think they hate me."

"Nice, bro, nice, that means you're doing something right." *I am?* "The more her parents hate you, the more she's going to like you." *What is he talking about? More shit not making sense.*

"Hey, Larry, can I ask you a question?"

"Sure, bro, what's up?"

"How long?" *Shit.* "How long should I wait before I ask her to have sex?" My brother spit out his beer all over the floor and let out a boisterous laugh.

"That shit's hilarious. Ask her? It should just happen. What happened last night?" *We mostly just slept. Don't say that.*

"We just made out. It was the first time we were alone." *What does he expect?*

"Don't wait too long. She'll find someone else, trust me."

"I didn't have protection."

"What? You need condoms?" My brother walked to our room and then came out with a handful of condoms. "Here." *Shit.*

"Thanks, Larry," I said as I stuffed the condoms in my pocket.

"You know how to use those?" *Fuck.*

"Yeah, they had this thing at school." My brother laughed and took another drink of his beer.

"School...ok, I'm sure you're good to go then." *I hope so...*

"Well, I'm going to watch some MTV now," I said as I grabbed the remote and sat down on the couch. *That was freaking embarrassing.*

"All right, bro, and don't worry about mom, I won't say anything."

"Thanks," I said and changed the channel to MTV. *Damn it. Do they even play music videos anymore?*

The next day, I headed out the door, jumped on my bike, and rode down Court Street. I rounded the corner around Mountain

View Elementary and slowed down. *Hannah. I should just go over there right now. I need to see if she's all right. Shit. Her dad. Nope.* I continued on to Rob's house and knocked on his door.

"Hey, man, what's up?" Rob said. *Hannah.*

"I've got a band name for us."

"Well, get your ass in here." We walked back to Rob's room and he shut the door.

"Anarchy. What do you think?"

"Anarchy? Just anarchy?"

"Yeah."

"Actually...I like it."

"Good, you can thank Hannah."

"Your girlfriend came up with our band name?" *Not really. Kind of...*

"Yeah, she did. You know, she's a really good singer."

"I'm happy for her." *Hmmm.* "Ok, so we're Anarchy. We just need a plan to find a bass player and a drummer."

"We already know what we have to do."

"Yeah, what's that?"

"The same thing we did before. We need to scope out the band room at Whitney when school starts for some talent."

"I guess so. What are we gonna do for the next two weeks?" *He can't even wait two weeks...*

"We're going to start writing some songs. You write the music and I'll write the lyrics."

"You want to write the lyrics?"

"Yeah, I can write."

"This is going to be a disaster."

"If by disaster you mean awesome, then I agree," I said. Rob just shook his head. "Have some faith, man; it's going to be great. Are you ready for Saturday?"

"What do you mean ready?"

"You've got a date with a pretty girl."

"Jessica...She thinks it's a date?"

"I don't know, maybe, the point is to seize the opportunity."

"I've never even been on a date." *Yeah, I know.*

"Now's your chance, trust me, it'll be good."

"I guess. So I should trust you like you say you trust me."

"Let me use your phone. I'm gonna call Hannah and see what's up."

"All right, you do that." Rob left his room and came back with his phone. He handed it to me and I dialed her number. *Please let it be her, please let it be her...*

"Hello?" *Thank God, it's Michael.*

"Hey, Michael, is your sister there?"

"Yeah, hold on." Hannah answered the phone.

"Hey, babe," I said. "I hope this isn't a bad time."

"No, we're good; my dad's still asleep, but my brother is bugging so I can't talk long, what's up?"

"Well, I just wanted to call to say I miss you." I could hear Rob mumble in the background. *Eat a dick, Rob.*

"Ahh, you're so sweet...Michael, leave me alone, sorry..."

"It's ok. I also called because Rob is down for Saturday."

"That's good, I'll tell Jessica."

"Rob wants to know if she thinks it's a date." Hannah laughed.

"Dude!" Rob whispered.

"Oh, is he there? That's funny. I didn't exactly put it that way to her..." *Shit* "...But, she's a Cancer and he's a Taurus. It's a good match." *I really should have read that book more closely.*

"Perfect, I'll tell him not to worry about it."

"Ok, I should call Jessica," Hannah said. "You know, to make this call legit." I laughed.

"Of course..." I said. "Talk to you later, babe."

"Bye, Billy," Hannah said and hung up the phone. I handed the phone back to Rob.

"No worries, man, she didn't tell her it was a date, but she said you shouldn't worry because she's a Cancer and you're a Taurus and that's a perfect match. Again, you have to trust me."

"What are you even talking about?"

"Astrology," I said, "you just have to trust me." Rob and I spent the rest of the day drawing logos of our band name and started writing our first song. I went home that night picturing myself playing guitar and rocking out on stage. *I am a Bad-ass guitar player with a stupid-beautiful girlfriend. Well, that last part is true...*

I woke up Saturday morning to what was already oppressive heat. It must have been 100 degrees outside. I looked over at my alarm clock and it read 10:08. *Shit, I have to get ready.* Hannah had called me the night before and told me that we were going to meet for lunch before the movie at 1. I rushed into the bathroom and took a shower. I used extra Pantene conditioner and took my time blow drying on low. My mom always complained that I took longer in the bathroom than her, but I don't think she cared how she looked. I decided to skip breakfast because it was almost time for lunch anyway. I jumped on my bike and headed to Rob's house. When I got there, Rob was sitting on the two steps outside that led into his house. "Oh, shit, Rob, is that you?" I said. "You washed your hair!"

"Yeah, I figured it was about time." *It was time two months ago.*

"You must really like Jessica; you never washed your hair for me." I laughed as I set my bike down.

"I don't even know her."

"But you want to know her..."

"She didn't say much that night. I do like that about her; she's quiet, as opposed to your girlfriend..."

"You don't know Hannah like I do." Rob got a funny look on his face like he was trying to solve a complex math problem."

"You're not saying what I think you're saying are you?"

"Not yet, but she has dropped hints that she wants to."

"Like what?"

"I don't think your virgin ears can handle it." I laughed again as I leaned against the garage.

"Dude, you're a virgin too."

"No, no I'm not. I already told you."

"Whatever...I don't believe you."

"That's ok. I said it before and I'll say it again: I don't care if you believe me." *I kind of do though.* A confident smile appeared on my face. "You will, though, in time," I said and stood up straight from the garage. "Dude, check on your mom, we gotta go."

"All right, hold on." Rob got up from the steps and went inside of his house. A few minutes later, he came out with his mom.

"Hi, Will, are you guys ready?" Rob's mom said. *For a while now.*

"Yeah, thanks for giving us a ride."

"What are you guys going to see?"

"Batman, probably," I said.

"Yeah, Batman," Rob added. We all got inside of the car and headed to the Sequoia Mall.

"What time does the movie start?" Rob's mom said.

"We don't know, we're going to get some lunch and then catch the one that's playing the earliest," I said.

"Oh, ok, call me when it's over." We pulled up to the front of the mall, got out of the car, and walked through the automated doors. I looked at my watch.

"We're early, man, let's go sit down on that bench over there." I pointed to the seating area in the middle of the mall and we went and sat down.

"This is exciting..." Rob said sarcastically.

"At least we're not outside in that scorching heat."

"Always looking on the bright side..."

"Yeah, so, it's better than being depressed all the time."

"Is it?" *Such a pain in the ass.* "There they are." Rob pointed to the entrance.

"All right let's go." Rob and I got up and we walked toward them. Hannah and Jessica were both very similarly dressed. They were both wearing low-cut blue jeans and mid-drift shirts. I loved those short-cut shirts on Hannah. Every time that she would raise her arms to stretch it would reveal her perfectly sculpted waistline. Jessica couldn't pull it off as well as Hannah, but she tried. Hannah looked like a super-model on a catwalk coming toward me. She smiled as her hair bounced back and forth. Jessica followed her lead even though she seemed to be a step behind. Hannah wrapped her arms around me, hugging me tight. She pulled away and then kissed me.

"Hey, Billy, I missed you so much."

"I missed you too." Rob and Jessica looked at each other and Jessica rolled her eyes. *What's her problem?*

"I like your hair, Rob," Jessica said. *Nice, maybe he'll wash it every day now.*

"Thanks," Rob replied.

"Oh, shit, Jessica speaks!" I said. Hannah laughed.

"Yes, but only when she wants to," Jessica said. *Huh? That's weird.*

"So, Hannah, Rob wants to thank you for naming our band," I said.

"Yeah, it's a cool name; Anarchy."

"Cool, you guys are going to use it? That's awesome!"

"We'll be sure to give you credit when we release our album," I said and then smiled and held Hannah's hand. Rob rolled his eyes.

"It's not that easy to just release an album." *Relax, Rob.*

"I'm sure you're right," I said. "I'm hungry; you guys wanna get some food?"

"Yeah," Hannah said. "What do you wanna get?"

"Subway sounds good to me," I said. "I'm thinking about a meatball sub."

"Ok, let's go," Hannah said.

"Sure," Rob added. Jessica didn't say anything but followed us as we made our way to Subway. I ordered a meat ball sub, a bag of Lays potato chips, and a soda. Rob ordered a roast beef combo and Hannah and Jessica didn't order anything.

"I'll share with my Billy," Hannah said.

"Jessica, did you want me to get you something," Rob said.

"No, I already ate," Jessica replied.

"No, she didn't," Hannah whispered in my ear.

"Hannah! I heard that," Jessica said. Hannah laughed.

"Just get something," Hannah said.

"Yeah, I've got it," Rob said. Jessica looked down and then back up at Rob.

"No, it's ok, I'm not hungry." We left it at that and got our food. We found some seats close to the restaurant and sat down. I dove into my meatball sub and Hannah opened my bag of chips and ate one at a time. Rob started eating his sandwich as well and Jessica sat with her arms folded across the table.

"What movie are we gonna watch?" Jessica asked.

"Batman," Rob quickly answered.

"I don't want to see Batman. Why don't we see something funny?"

"The only thing I want to see is Batman," Rob insisted. Hannah and I looked at each other and smiled.

"What do you guys want to see?" Jessica said as she looked left and right at Hannah and then me. I looked at Hannah and smiled. I looked back at Jessica,

"It doesn't matter to us," I said. "Anything is fine."

"Hannah!" Jessica said.

"It's up to you two."

"How about Nine Months? That looks good," Jessica said to Rob.

"Nah, isn't that a stupid chick flick?" Rob said. "Will, back me up here."

"I really don't care, man, we're down for whatever," I said.

"Rob, let's make a deal." *A deal? Rob doesn't really negotiate.* "We'll watch Nine Months today and next time you can choose," Jessica reasoned. *Oh shit! There's going to be a next time...*

"Fine, have it your way," Rob said. "We'll watch the chick flick." *Nice work, Jessica.* Hannah and I smiled. We finished our food and headed toward the theater to check the show times. Nine Months was playing at 2 so we bought our tickets and were able to walk right into the theater and wait for the movie to start. Rob and I sat on the outside of the girls in the very back row.

"I'm gonna go get some popcorn," Rob said.

"I'll come with you," Jessica added. "You guys want something?" Hannah handed her 5 dollars.

"Yeah, get me some Milk Duds."

"I'm good, thanks," I said. Rob and Jessica got up and walked back to the snack bar. "What do ya think?"

"About Rob and Jessica?"

"Yeah, do you think she likes him?"

"Maybe. Jessica's kinda weird. Sometimes I have no idea what she's thinking. But, she is the perfect alibi to see you, Billy." Hannah put her hand on my leg and leaned in over the seating console and kissed me. "My parents trust Jessica more than they trust me." *Is that a good thing or a bad thing?* "I've got a surprise for you, Billy."

"Really? I love surprises." *No, I don't.*

"Casey's family went to Disneyland this weekend..." *Okay.* "Guess who is house sitting for them?" *House sitting?*

"You?"

"That's right, Billy, you know what that means right? *Nope.*

"Not really, I don't even know what house sitting is."

"It's no big deal. I just have to feed their dogs and water their plants," Hannah said. She got closer to me and whispered in my ear, "The good part is I have the key to their house..." Hannah pulled back away from me, looked into my eyes, and raised her eyebrows. It took me a minute of her staring at me but I finally figured it out.

"Oh, ok, I get it, you want me to sneak out again."

"Yup, tonight." *Is she crazy?*

"But won't your dad be home?"

"Yeah, but Jessica's spending the night. He never bothers me when Jessica's over. It's perfect."

"Ok, I guess I could get Rob to spend the night too."

"Someone's got to keep Jessica busy while, well, you know..." *Shit, this is happening.* The movie previews started playing and the trailer for Clueless came on. "Oh my God, Billy, I want to see that so bad."

"Ok, I'm down." Rob and Jessica sat down with the popcorn and candy. Jessica handed the Milk Duds to Hannah.

"Jessica, we have to see this movie." Hannah pointed towards the screen.

"Oh, yeah, Clueless, that looks good," Jessica replied. Rob and I looked at each other and we shook our heads. *Another Chick Flick as Rob likes to say.* I put my arm around Hannah and rested my hand on her leg. The theater went dark as Nine Months started. *This guy is in a lot of these movies. I wonder if Rob's gonna make a move with Jessica? Nah. 10 bucks Hannah falls asleep...Am I making a bet with myself? Dumbass. Hmmm, I would have rather watched Batman.*

"Hey, babe, you want some candy?" Hannah said.

"Sure," I said. *Not really.* Hannah took one of the Milk Duds out of the package and put it in my mouth. I chewed down on it and Hannah grabbed another one and put it in my mouth. I could already feel the cavities forming. Hannah grabbed another one out of the box. "Ok, babe, I'm good," I said as I swallowed the salty, sweet concoction. Hannah put the box of candy in the cup holder and leaned in to kiss me. After about 10 minutes of making out with Hannah, Jessica intervened.

"Hey, Hannah, you guys are loud, stop it! People are trying to watch the movie," Jessica whispered with authority. We both turned and looked at her. I hoped that she could see the disdain in my eyes. I whispered in Hannah's ear, "I can see why your parents like her." Hannah started laughing.

"Shut up!" Jessica reiterated. *Damn, all right, grandma.* Hannah put her hands in my lap and then rested her head against my chest. *Yeah, she's going to sleep.* I looked over at Rob and then at Jessica. *I really don't like her.* I turned back to watch the movie. *I really don't like this movie either.*

We finished watching the movie and the credits rolled. "Hey, babe, the movie's over." I softly shook Hannah awake.

"Oh, ok, what happened?"

"You fell asleep."

"No, with the movie..." Rob and Jessica had already made their way to the theater lobby.

"They got married." *Who would have thought?*

"I knew it!" *Yeah, duh.* "Where are Rob and Jessica?"

"Probably waiting on us," I said as I held Hannah's hand and walked with her into the lobby. Jessica was standing in line at the payphone and Rob was standing alone by the arcade. I walked over to Rob and Hannah went to stand in line with Jessica.

"What's up, man?" I said.

"That movie was stupid," Rob said.

"Yeah, same old shit."

"Seriously, I knew exactly what was going to happen 10 minutes into it."

"Yup," I said, "we should have watched Batman."

"Dude, I told you, but you've got those pussy-blinders on."

"Relax, man, we can watch Batman next week. There's still time before school starts. Hey, you wanna spend the night tonight?"

"Sure, I guess."

"Hannah wants us to sneak out and meet them."

"Where?"

"Casey's house. They're at Disneyland."

"She wants us to break into their house? Your girlfriend is insane."

"Nah, she has the key."

"Well, this keeps getting better...How did she get their key?"

"Are you down or what? Jessica likes you. It'll be the chance to make your move."

"...How do you know she likes me? You don't."

"You're right, I don't know, but do you really want to regret not making a move? You may not get another chance." I looked back over at Hannah and Jessica. The line had moved and Jessica was on the phone.

"You've got to man up. Don't be a bitch."

"Fine, I'll do it. Shit." Hannah and Jessica walked over to us.

"All right, shut the hell up, they're coming over," I said. "Hey babe, what's up?"

"Jessica called her mom to pick us up. We need to wait outside for her," Hannah said.

"And you guys need to stay in here until we leave. I don't want my mom to see us with you," Jessica said. *Wow, thanks.*

"Ok, we have to go, Billy," Hannah said, and then whispered in my ear, "see you tonight, same time." She quickly hugged and kissed me. "Bye, Rob," she said as Jessica pulled her away by her arm.

"Bye," Rob said. "I guess I'll call my mom."

"Yeah." *Fucking Jessica...*

Chapter Nine

Secrets

ROB'S MOM DROPPED US off at my house after Rob asked to spend the night. Before driving away, she rolled down the window and said, "what are you guys going to do for dinner?"

"We'll just order a pizza," I said.

"Ok, have a good time."

"Bye, Mom," Rob said. He looked at me sideways. "This is a bad idea."

"No way, man, this is a great idea. Come on," I said. We went upstairs and found that my mom and my brother were both home.

"Hey, mom, is it cool if Rob spends the night?"

"Yeah, it's ok with me. Are you guys going to sleep out here?"

"That was the plan. Can we order a pizza?"

"Yeah, bro, we already ordered a pizza. Have a seat. What were you guys up to today?"

"We saw a movie," I said.

"What'd you see?" My brother said.

"Nine Months," I replied.

"What the hell is that about? Sounds like one of those chick movies," my brother said.

"Thank you!" Rob said. "His girlfriend's friend talked us into it."

"You have a girlfriend?" My mom interjected. "When do I get to meet her?"

"I don't know..." I said.

"You should have her over for dinner sometime," my mom said. *Yeah, that's not going to happen.*

"Sure, mom, we'll see," I said.

"Yeah, bring her over. I want to see if she's as hot as you say she is," my brother added.

"She is," Rob quickly said. "He's not lying." *Thanks, Rob, shit...*

"Be careful, bro, that kind of girl is trouble," my brother said. *Yeah, I know.*

"I know what I'm doing," I said. Rob and my brother both laughed. *Great...*

"Whatever you say, bro," my brother said. Before I had the chance to respond there was a knock on the door. "It's probably the pizza." My brother got up from the couch and got the door and the pizza. We all ate pizza while watching the evening news. My mom and brother always seemed to be watching the news. They especially enjoyed watching the weather report. *What a waste of time. Stupid hot today, stupid hot tomorrow, and stupid hot next week.* Rob and I went to my room after we finished our pizza and I put Nirvana's Bleach CD into my stereo.

"All right, man, they're going to want to go to bed right after Touched by an Angel. They watch it every week and then go to bed at 10 like clockwork. Then, we'll go set up our sleeping bags in the living room and make it look like we're going to sleep. We need to leave at 11. I want to get there early."

"This is crazy. Your brother is right, that girl is going to get you in trouble."

"He's probably right, but she's worth it."

"I don't think any of them are worth it."

"Then why are you here right now? That's right, because you think you have a chance with Jessica. You don't have to pretend that you don't care."

"I don't care, I'm just helping my friend out." Rob looked around the room with a smug, coy look on his face. *As if, Rob. Your shit stinks too.*

"So if Jessica dropped her panties in front of you, you wouldn't do anything."

"I didn't say that."

"That's what I thought. Why do you have to be so damn stubborn? Just admit that you like her."

"I don't know her well enough to like her." *You're impossible.*

"I hope she changes your mind tonight."

"Doubt it..." *Wow, what is his deal?*

"Anyway, thanks for coming. I think Hannah wants to have sex tonight and I need you to keep Jessica busy."

"Dude, you've known her for like 10 minutes and you think she wants to have sex..."

"Yeah, I do. I mean, she hasn't said the words outright, but you should hear the way she talks."

"I think it's all talk. Do you even know if she's a virgin?"

"No, it hasn't come up."

"And you don't think it's weird that a 14-year-old girl wants to have sex with someone she just met, assuming you believe that, and not be a ho?" *Shit.*

"I'll ask her tonight."

"Yeah, man, because she would totally tell you the truth..."

"Why would she lie?"

"Why wouldn't she lie? I don't think she's stupid. I'm really sure she would want everyone to know she's whoring herself around town."

"Ok, that's a good point, but she's not like that. Remember, she turned Chris down."

"Really, did she? Is that what she told you?" *What the fuck.*

"That's what they both told me. You think they're both lying to me?"

"I don't know, but I think it's kind of strange that you don't trust Chris anymore, but Hannah you trust without question." *Shit.*

"Well, shit, I'm going to figure this shit out tonight."

"What are you going to do?"

"I'm not going to be an asshole. I'm just gonna ask her some questions."

"And hope that she tells you the truth..."

"I'll be able to tell if she's bullshitting me."

"Sure, man, whatever you say." *This is messing with my head.*

"Let's change the subject; this shit is pissing me off. Why don't we write some music?"

"All right, you got some paper?" I handed Rob some paper from my binder and I started working on song lyrics for our first, yet to be named, song. "Hey, can I play that guitar?"

"Yeah, it's my brother's, he doesn't care." Rob played some chord progressions and wrote them down on the paper. We continued working on our music until 10 and then set up our sleeping bags in the living room. I said good night to my mom and brother. Rob and I sat on the couch and turned on MTV. *Nice, they're actually playing music videos.* At 11, I got up from the couch and turned off the TV.

"Time to go," I said and Rob got up. We walked out my front door and I gently closed and locked it. We walked up Court Street and watched all of the cars go by.

"We better not get caught," Rob said.

"You worry too much, man."

"Apparently, I don't worry enough."

"What are you talking about? You worry enough for both of us." As we got to the end of Laura Street, I pulled the condoms out of my pocket and handed one to Rob. "Here, just in case."

"Where did you get those?"

"My brother gave them to me. Just take one."

"Ok, but I'm not going to need it. Neither are you." Rob took the condom and put it in his pocket. We continued walking down Laura Street and I turned to Rob.

"You know, your negativity is getting really old."

"Reality Bites." *The movie or your life?*

"Ok, we're gonna go wait in front of Casey's house...And be quiet, we don't want to attract any attention."

"Ya think?" We sat down on Casey's porch as I checked my watch.

"We still have 15 minutes. Just chill, they'll be here." Rob looked at me slack-jawed and seemingly confused.

"What other choice do I..." Suddenly, the front door opened. Rob and I jumped up and looked at each other before focusing our attention on the door; Hannah and Jessica were standing there smiling. *Fuck.*

"...Scared the crap out of me," I said.

"Yeah, you got me too," Rob added.

"I didn't know you were already going to be here..."

"Surprise!" Hannah said. "Get in here before someone sees you." We walked into Casey's house and Hannah closed the door behind us. She hugged me tightly and then let me go.

"Do you guys want a beer?" Hannah said.

"Well, yeah, but do you think it's a good idea to drink their beer?" I said.

"They're fully stocked. They even have another refrigerator in the garage filled up. They'll never know." *This girl*...We walked into the kitchen and Hannah took two beers out of the refrigerator and handed them to us. "The bottle opener is on the table." She pointed to the dining room table where Jessica was now sitting. Jessica was already working on a beer. Hannah grabbed another beer and started drinking it. She walked over to the stereo and turned on some music.

"What're you playing?" I asked and took another drink of my beer.

"Veruca Salt, they're my favorite." *Veruca Salt, huh?* I looked over at Rob and I could tell that he was not pleased with the music selection for the evening, but he didn't say anything. I smiled. I was very pleased with Rob's discomfort. I looked over at Jessica and she was nursing her beer but seemed to be having a good time. Hannah started singing along with one of the songs called 'Seether.' She sang through the entire song while we all watched her performance. I slowly drank my beer as I watched Hannah's hips shake in a pair of cutoff jean shorts. Lines of fabric were hanging from her shorts and dancing along with her body. The song ended and Hannah grabbed my arm. "Come on, Billy." She walked us back to what looked like Casey's parents' bedroom. *Spiderman? What did I just hear? Weird ass band. I'll bet Rob is pissed. Nice.* Hannah shut the door behind us. "They'll be fine." *Not if that music's playing.*

"This is nice, Hannah, but aren't you worried that your parents are gonna find out?"

"Nope, and I don't care. I just want to be here with my Billy." Hannah fell back on the bed. "It's a water bed, lay down next to me." I sat down on the bed and felt the waves gently roll beneath me.

"Hannah, babe, this bed is awful."

"I like it...Take off your shoes and put your feet up. It's like you're floating." I did what Hannah asked and then she quickly mounted me. She leaned in to kiss me and I grabbed her by the waist and moved my hands up to her bra. She slowly moved off of me and lay down next to me. I looked into her eyes. *Just ask her.*

"Have you ever done this before?"

"What do you mean?"

"I guess...what I'm asking you is, are you a virgin?"

"Yeah, I'm a virgin," Hannah answered abruptly. *Hmmm.*

"So, you've never had sex before?"

"No; I've done other stuff, but not sex." *What does that mean?* I almost did it with Joe last year but it didn't happen."

"Why? What happened?"

"I was at my friends Halloween party and we were playing 7 minutes in heaven. Joe and I were in the closet making out and he started taking my clothes off, I didn't really want to do it, but..."

"But what?"

"I would have. Joe's friend opened the door and we were both in our underwear. Joe was pissed. Everyone was laughing at us. I was so embarrassed that I grabbed my clothes and ran outside and then all the way home. I've never told anyone that, Billy." Hannah ran her hand through my hair. "I feel so close to you."

"I'm glad you told me. Maybe we should slow things down."

"No, it's ok, that was a long time ago." *Not really.* "I don't want to lose you." *She's worried about losing me?*

"You're not going to lose me, no matter what. You're the best thing that's ever happened to me."

"You're everything I've ever wanted." Hannah moved in and kissed me and then pulled back. "You asked me, so I'm going to ask you..."

The girl I lost my virginity to wasn't the prettiest girl in the world but she did catch my attention almost immediately. She was wearing an American flag bikini the first time that I saw her. She had a really nice body that was accentuated by her long brown hair. Brad and I were walking Peg's dog, Gloria, an old Afghan hound, around the block the second day I was there that summer. We had to do chores as our keep to stay there and one of them, maybe the most important to Peg, was walking that dog twice per day. We approached a house that afternoon, a few doors down from Peg's, and there were two girls sunbathing in the front yard.

"Hey, what are you guys doing?" One of the girls said. Brad and I stopped in our tracks but Peg's dog pulled hard on the leash and yanked Brad's arm. "What are you guys doing with Gloria?"

"Walking her, obviously," I said.

"Yeah, I can see that, but where's Peg?"

"She's making us do it," I said.

"Who are you guys?"

"This is Brad, Peg's nephew and I'm Will. What's your name?"

"Rebecca. This is my sister, Stacy." Rebecca took off her sunglasses and stood up revealing all of her stars and stripes. Stacy didn't move from her towel. "You mind if I tag along?"

"Sure, it's a free country," I said. I smiled about the reference to her bikini.

"Yes, it is," Rebecca said as she stepped into her flip-flops.

"Let's get this over with," Brad said as he let the dog pull him forward. I walked next to Rebecca behind Brad.

"What are you up to this summer?" Rebecca said.

"We're mostly just hanging out. We were gonna go to Magic Mountain sometime. I've never been there before."

"It's so much fun. Let me know when you go and I'll come with you." I was intrigued by how aggressive that girl was. She literally invited herself to Magic Mountain with us and we had just met her. I didn't know that people actually did that.

"Brad, what do you think about that?" I said.

"I don't care," Brad said.

"Cool, I guess you're invited," I said.

"When were you thinking you wanted to go?" Brad looked back at Rebecca.

"Maybe next week," Brad said.

"How long are you guys going to be here?" Rebecca said.

"I think until after the 4th of July. I think we're leaving that Monday," I said.

"Cool, so we'll have some time to hang out," Rebecca said.

"Yeah, we'll be here," I said. We eventually made our way around the block and back in front of Peg's house. "I guess we'll see you later."

"Yeah...wait, what are you doing later?" I looked at Brad and then down at Gloria.

"After dinner, we're probably just gonna chill in the hot tub. That's what we did last night," I said.

"Cool, I'll come by. I'll probably have to bring my sister," Rebecca said.

"I don't think Peg's gonna be ok with..." Brad started to say.

"She let us use her hot tub before. She's friends with our family. It's all good," Rebecca interjected while walking away.

"She's pretty hot," I said as I watched her walk away.

"She's ugly and a pain in the ass," Brad whispered.

"She's not too bad. She has a nice body," I reasoned.

"She bugs, man, but whatever," Brad said. Brad and I went inside and waited for Peg to get home. Peg walked through the door about an hour later.

"Brad, Will, I've got Round Table coming for dinner."

"Peg, who's that Rebecca girl?" Brad asked as Peg walked into the living room.

"Oh, that's Frank's daughter, why?" Peg asked.

"She invited herself over here later and to Magic Mountain with us..." Peg laughed and sat down on the couch.

"She doesn't have anyone her age in the neighborhood to hang out with, except for her sister. You guys need to be nice."

"Of course, Peg, always," I said. Brad shook his head but didn't say anything. The pizza arrived shortly.

"Get it while it's hot," Peg instructed. We ate our pizza and then Peg put The Bodyguard on. In the middle of the movie, we heard a knock on the door. Peg got up and answered it. "Oh, hi girls, come on in, do you want some pizza? I can nuke it for you?"

"No, thanks, Peg, we just wanted to know if we could use your hot tub," Rebecca said.

"Yeah, of course you can. I heard you guys met Brad and Will." Peg led Rebecca and Stacy into the living room where we were still watching the movie.

"Yeah, we met when they were walking Gloria," Rebecca said.

"I'm going to finish the movie," Brad said.

"I'll watch it some other time," I said. I went to the bathroom to change into my board shorts and then met Rebecca and Stacy who were already in the hot tub. I got inside of the water and sat down.

"Nice abs," Rebecca said.

"Thanks," I said, "I try." The water was perfect. The sun slowly went down over the horizon and Rebecca got prettier the darker it got.

"You wanna skinny dip?" Rebecca asked.

"You mean like get naked in here?"

"Oh, gross, Becca, what's wrong with you?" Stacy said.

"Fine, forget it, what a baby," Rebecca said. "Sorry, she's still in junior high." I wanted to tell her that I was still in junior high too, but I didn't.

"You're such a bitch, Becca," Stacy said.

"You love me and you know it," Rebecca said.

"Should I leave you guys alone, or?"

"No, we're good, right sis?"

"Yeah, we're fine," Stacy said.

"It's a sibling thing, I get it. I fight with my brother all the time."

"Is he younger or older?" Rebecca asked.

"Older, he's 20; always telling me what to do."

"It must be nice being that old...I can't wait to get my license. I'll be 16 in August then I can do whatever I want to."

"That's cool...So have you guys been to the beach this summer?"

"Yeah, we went to Silver Strand Beach when summer started," Rebecca said. "You wanna go?"

"Yeah, I haven't been to the beach in a long time. Where's Silver strand?"

"It's in Oxnard, like 20 minutes away," Rebecca said.

"Oh, all right, cool." Brad joined us after a while and we all hung out until Peg came and told us we had to come inside.

The next three weeks revolved around the four of us hanging out. We spent a lot of time in that hot tub, but we also went to Magic Mountain, the beach in Oxnard, and one day, we went to the mall in Thousand Oaks, all thanks to Peg. Another day we walked around Camarillo without a plan or a place to be. Nothing happened between Rebecca and I during that time and nothing happened with Brad and Stacy. We were just all friends hanging out and having a good time. On the 4th of July, Rebecca's parents planned a barbeque at their house with a truckload of fireworks. Peg, Brad, and I walked over to their house at around 6.

"The food's in the back," Rebecca's dad said as he pointed to their front door. Everyone had a beer in their hand and it was obvious that they had been drinking for a while. Brad and I walked into their house and Peg stayed in the front yard. Their sliding glass door was open to the back yard and Rebecca and Stacy were getting food.

"Hey, Rebecca," I said. "Let me get some of that food."

"Here you go," Rebecca said and handed me a plate with a hamburger and fries. She gave the same plate to Brad. Rebecca was wearing her American flag bikini just like the first day that we met. We all went back to the front yard where everyone was. There were a lot of people there that I hadn't seen before. Some of them were lighting off sparklers and other small fireworks to pass the time before it was time for the bigger ones. After we finished eating, Rebecca grabbed my arm.

"Come on, I wanna show you something."

"Ok," I said and looked at Brad and then Stacy. "Let's go," Rebecca said and led us to her bedroom and pulled a bottle of Vodka out of her closet.

"Shit, Becca, where did you get that?"

"Uncle Carl brought a bunch of it and I snatched a bottle."

"You want some?" Rebecca asked me as she took a drink. She started coughing violently and then handed the bottle to me.

"I don't know," I said and looked at Brad. He looked back at me. "We didn't tell you, but we got really messed up last week. It was not a good time." I held the bottle up to my nose. "Well, it doesn't smell as bad as that whiskey."

"How much did you drink?" Rebecca asked.

"Shit, I don't know, Brad, half the bottle?"

"Yeah, I don't remember," Brad said.

"You guys are stupid," Stacy said and left Rebecca's room.

"Don't be a rat!" Rebecca yelled in her direction.

"I'm gonna go back outside," Brad said. "I don't want any of that." Brad left Rebecca's room and then Rebecca shut and locked her door.

"So, are you going to drink?"

"Yeah, I guess so." I turned the bottle upside down and drank. I felt a burn in my throat that was even worse than the whiskey, but I powered through. I handed the bottle back to Rebecca and she took another drink. She passed it back to me and I took one more drink. "Ok, I'm good; I'm not going to screw up like last week." Rebecca took one more really long drink and then put the bottle back in her closet.

"Come here, sit down," Rebecca said and sat down on the edge of her bed. I sat down next to her and she moved as close to me as she could. Her thigh pressed against my leg and she went in to kiss me. I stopped her before she got too close.

"What are you doing?"

"I like you. I think you're cute...and you're leaving tomorrow, right? I just thought..."

"What about your parents? Your sister?"

"They're all outside watching the fireworks. No one's going to bother us, they don't even know we're not there." Rebecca reached around her back and undid her bikini top. I froze and she went back in for the kiss. She shoved her tongue in my mouth. I was paralyzed. She pulled back away from me.

"Have you ever? It seems like..."

"Yeah, I'm a virgin."

"Oh, it's ok, you don't have to do anything, just lay down," Rebecca said as she pushed my chest. She got on the floor and unzipped my pants. I felt very uncomfortable and was deathly afraid that we were going to get caught, but I think my brain stopped working after that. She stood up, dropped her bikini bottoms, and got on top of me. It was over before I even knew it. Rebecca laughed slightly as she got up off of the bed.

"Don't worry, you'll get better...So, you know, you can last longer."

"Ummm, sorry," I said awkwardly as I zipped up my pants.

"Don't worry about it, I'm gonna get dressed and we can go watch the fireworks." Rebecca put her bikini back on and then put on some cut off shorts. "I'm going to go to the bathroom, give me a minute." I sat on Rebecca's bed and looked around. I couldn't believe what just happened. Rebecca came back into the room and grabbed my hand. "Let's go." We walked out to the front yard and sat on the grass next to Brad and Stacy. Brad looked at me and then leaned in.

"What are you smiling about?" Brad whispered.

"I didn't even realize that I was smiling...I'll tell you later."

"That was two years ago."

"Wow, Billy, that's crazy."

"It's more embarrassing than anything else. I actually can't believe I just told you all of that." *Yeah, that did not make me look good.*

"No, I'm glad that you told me. We have to be honest with each other, right?"

"Yeah, I agree." *We're sure doing a lot of talking.*

"So you were just in Camarillo, right?"

"Yeah, that's where I spend my summers."

"Did you see Rebecca?" *And, here we go...*

"Nope, she doesn't live there anymore."

"How do you know that she doesn't live there anymore?" *Because I went to her house.*

"Peg, Brad's aunt, told us when we got there. They were family friends and since we had hung out before, I guess she thought we would want to know. I didn't ask. I was thinking about coming back to you."

"But you would have seen her if she did..."

"No, babe, like I said, I was thinking about you the whole time I was there. This was the first summer that I actually wanted to come home early."

"So you haven't talked to this Rebecca girl for two years..."

"I didn't say that...I saw her last year, but she had a boyfriend so we didn't hang out."

"Do you have her number?" *Why is she so worried about her?*

"No, I don't have her number." *I do.*

"Really? You have sex with a girl and you don't get her number?" *Well, I actually had her number way before that happened.*

"There wasn't any need. We were practically neighbors." I no longer heard the faint sound of Veruca Salt in the background. *Uh oh, I guess Rob got tired of it.* "Babe, you have nothing to worry about. Rebecca is in the distant past."

"Okay, yeah, sorry, I'm trippin...I need to trust you, it's just hard. Joe lied to me all the time. I'm just paranoid."

"I'm not Joe; I'm not anything like that."

"I know...that's why I'm with you." The smile returned to Hannah's face. I heard Nirvana's 'Come As You Are' playing from the living room. *Huh, Casey's parents have Nirvana?* Hannah rolled over the top of me and then took her shirt off as she sat up. *This is more like it.* She was wearing a pink Victoria's Secret bra. *Is that one of those push up bras? She doesn't need that.* Hannah laid back down and we started kissing again. I moved my hands up and down her body feeling every soft curve along the way. She moved her hands onto my chest. I raised my arms and she took off my shirt with one smooth motion. She wrapped her hands around the back of my neck and moved in to kiss me. She slowly slid down the bed and kissed the middle of my chest and then further down, my belly button. The bedroom door opened and Jessica walked in. Hannah sat up quickly.

"What the hell, Jessica?"

"Sorry, I just can't...be out there with him. He tried to kiss me. I didn't know what to do...Sorry, I didn't mean to..." Hannah looked at Jessica and then back at me. *It figures.*

"Jessica, just go back out there. What's the problem?" Hannah said.

"He's so gross, Hannah. He smells like cigarettes." *That's true. Can't blame her, but shit.* "Sorry, Will."

"I guess I should go talk to him," I said. I got up off of the bed, grabbed my shirt, and put it back on. "I'll be right back." I walked into the living room and no one was there. "Rob?" I walked into the kitchen and called his name again. "Rob, where are you?" There was no response. I walked over to the stereo, turned it off, and went back to the bedroom. "He's gone."

"Oh my god, I'm so sorry guys," Jessica said.

"He left because Jessica wouldn't kiss him?" Hannah said to me while putting on her shirt. *Shit.*

"I guess so, it's not like I can call him to find out. Jessica, what happened?"

"We were just talking. You know, about school and stuff. Everything was fine. He changed the CD because he didn't like it and then he sat down right next to me on the couch," Jessica said.

"What's wrong with Veruca Salt!?" Hannah said.

"Hannah!" Jessica said. I smiled. *That's kind of funny.*

"Sorry, keep going," Hannah said.

"Ok, so, we kept talking and he said how much better the music was. He shut his eyes and came closer to me. I saw his yellow teeth and smelled the smoke and almost threw up in my mouth. I jumped up and ran down the hall. I didn't know what else to do. What was I supposed to do?" *Take one for the team? Nah, that is gross.*

"Wait, shit, maybe he's outside," I said and walked to the front door. I opened the door fully expecting Rob to be sitting on the porch smoking a cigarette. He wasn't there though. I walked out onto the yard a little bit so I could see down the street, but all I saw was darkness. I walked back into the house. "Yeah, he's long gone. Don't worry about it, Jessica, he'll be fine."

"I feel bad though," Jessica said.

"He'll get over it," I said. *I think he will.*

"I didn't mean to hurt his feelings," Jessica said. I laughed.

"Before tonight, I didn't think that Rob had feelings," I said.

"Well, he obviously does or he wouldn't have left without saying anything," Hannah said. *True story.* I sat down on the couch and Hannah sat next to me. She put her hand on my leg and Jessica sat down in the chair across from us.

"I'm sorry, guys, I messed up your night," Jessica said. *Yep. Wait, didn't I know this was going to happen?*

"It's fine, there'll be other nights," Hannah said.

"Exactly, don't worry about it," I said. *Damn, Rob's never going to want to see Jessica's face again.*

Chapter Ten

Shelter from the storm

"HEY, BABE, WHAT'S UP? Did you get a hold of Rob?"

"Nope, I called him yesterday, but his mom said that he doesn't want to talk to anyone...I hope he doesn't kill himself," I said.

"What!? Oh my God. You don't think he would actually do that do you?"

"...I don't know, Hannah, I mean, the more I think about it, the more possible I think it is." *Nah, he wouldn't...*

"Over one girl? There's someone out there for him..." *I don't even know if I believe that, but, yeah...*

"I'm thinking about it like this: Kurt Cobain killed himself and Rob is his biggest fan. Even though it might not make sense to anyone else, it might make sense to him."

"It didn't even seem like he actually liked her."

"You're totally right. I was the one that put the idea in his head, but I was never able to get a good read on him."

"Jessica shouldn't have led him on." *She led him on?*

"It's not her fault. Rob's just weird."

"You should go over to his house and see if he's ok."

"Nah, it's Rob, I think I'll just leave him alone for a while."

"You think that's a good idea?"

"Babe, he's not going to kill himself...at least not with his family around."

"Wow, that's comforting." *Why does she care so much?*

"Trust me, I'll make sure he's ok. I think he just needs some time."

"Ok...I don't want to be responsible for someone's death."

"It wouldn't be on you. It would be on me."

"I would still be at least partially responsible...right?"

"Nope, it would not be your fault at all." *Nothing's even happened...* "So, I don't think the whole double date thing is gonna work out for us anymore." I laughed.

"Yeah, for real, we need to be alone."

"What about tonight? I was thinking we could find a spot at Whitendale Park. We could bring a blanket and lay out underneath the stars...just us and the insects biting our asses."

"That sounds fun, Billy, do you want me to bring the blanket?"

"Why don't we both bring a blanket?"

"Perfect! I should probably get off the phone. Promise me that you'll call Rob sometime today. *I'm getting tired of hearing his name.*

"Yeah, I'll call him later, I promise."

"Thanks, babe, remember, you might be the only person he has." *Yeah, no, he has his mom. Wait, does that count?*

"No worries, I'll see you tonight."

"I'm looking forward to it, bye Billy."

"Bye." I hung up the phone and went to sit on my bed. I looked around my room. *Why does she care so much? She is really nice. She's much nicer than me. I guess that's it, she's just a caring person. I don't understand how someone cares about someone else that really doesn't matter to them, though. I don't. Shit. I promised her.* I got up from my bed and went back to the phone. I stood over it for a while before picking up the receiver and dialing Rob's number. *Shit. I don't want to deal with this.* "Oh, hi, is Rob there?"

"Yes, honey, but I don't think he wants to talk. I don't know what's going on with him. He locked himself in his room...Will, do you know what's going on?" Rob's mom said.

"I think I do. It's about a girl."

"Oh, well, that makes sense. Let me check on him, hold on...Rob, it's your friend, Will on the phone." I heard the sound of a door opening.

"I'll take it. Hello?"

"Hey, man, are you all right? You dipped out the other night."

"I'm fine."

"But you just left without telling anyone."

"Fucking girls! They have no idea how hard it is to make a move...She just jumped up like there was a snake under her ass. Dude, I slept in the park. I couldn't go home in the middle of the night."

"You didn't have to do that. She just wasn't ready. She's sorry. She said it a million times. She was worried about you."

"Yeah, right, worried...These bitches don't care about anyone but themselves."

"Dude, that's not true, Hannah's the most caring..."

"Your girl's a fucking slut," Rob quickly interjected.

"Hannah isn't a slut; the fuck is wrong with you?"

"They're all sluts."

"Look, I know that you're pissed about Jessica, but Hannah doesn't deserve that."

"I don't care what you think about it, it's true."

"It doesn't even make sense...Your 'all girls are sluts' thing. Jessica turned you down, which would make her the opposite of a slut."

"Fuck you, dude." Rob hung up the phone. *What's wrong with him? All girls are sluts because they don't want to hook up with him? Whatever. I don't know why Hannah cares what happens to his ass. Shit. What am I going to tell her?*

I waited for Hannah at midnight behind her parent's Isuzu Trooper. She stealthily came around the truck after closing her gate. She was wearing her cut off jean shorts that left nothing to the imagination, and a halter top. *She kind of looks like Madonna in one of those 80's videos.*

"Hey babe, are you wearing a bra?" I whispered.

"Why ever do you ask?" Hannah whispered back.

"Because I can see your nipples." I brushed my hand over her right breast and she smiled.

"I have a surprise. I'm not wearing panties either." *What the...fuck. If there was ever a doubt, that's gone.*

"Ok...I don't really know what to say," I said and smiled.

"Let's go." *This is so much against the law. What is the punishment for sex in a public place? I don't know. Shit...It's probably worse at a school. I don't know where the school ends and the park begins. Shit.* Hannah and I held hands and slowly walked across Court Street to the school.

"I think, maybe, we should walk around the school to the park, you know, so we don't have to jump the fence."

"I can jump the fence."

"I know you can, I've seen you do it before, remember, but, I'm thinking, if you tear your shorts or even your shirt, we're going to have a problem."

"How is that a problem, Billy?" *God, I love this girl.*

"I guess it isn't, but it would make me feel better if you didn't have to run around naked out here."

"We were born naked and we'll die naked." *I'm not sure that last part is true.* Hannah smiled and started walking to the fence. I grabbed a hold of her arm.

"Please, babe, do it for me, it's not that much further."

"Do you think it's a better idea to walk along the street and maybe get caught or go right through the school? And besides, we have these blankets, just in case," Hannah reasoned. *Yeah, that makes sense.*

"You're right. And when you're right, you're right, but be careful."

"Ok, dad," Hannah laughed.

"Ouch, that's not funny."

"Sure it is, let's go." Hannah threw her blanket over the fence and jumped up onto it and pulled herself over. I did the same thing and followed her to a grassy spot underneath a big tree. We laid down both of the blankets and then sat on top of them.

"This is so cool," I said. "Beautiful girl, beautiful night." I put my hand behind Hannah's neck and moved closer to her. I looked into her eyes. "You're the most beautiful girl I've ever seen." Hannah smiled.

"That's not true." I looked away for a moment. *Yes, yes it is.*

"Babe, just say thank you...and, it is true. Like, if you look up the definition of beauty, you get a picture of you next to it." Hannah smiled again. *Nice.*

"Thanks, Billy." She moved in closely and our lips met in perfect harmony. We fell over side by side on the blankets and frantically made out. I slid my hand into her shorts and felt how wet she was. *I should have brought a towel to go with this blanket.* I started laughing and pulled back a little from Hannah's face. Hannah smiled.

"What's so funny?" She inquired.

"Nothing, it's nothing, I was just thinking of something," I said.

"Shouldn't you be thinking about me?"

"I was, I mean, I am, I'll tell you later..." I smiled. "Trust me, it's not a bad thing."

"Ok, do you have a condom?"

"Yeah, hold on." I pulled the handful of condoms out of my pocket and then Hannah laughed.

"How many do you have? Sheesh, I guess it's going to be a long night."

"I thought that was what you were all about?" I pulled one of the condoms out of its package and then undid my belt. I went to put the condom on but it was backwards and wouldn't roll down. Hannah laughed.

"Ummm, did you want some help?"

"I fucking hate condoms." I slowly lost my erection as I tried to figure out the latex demon. "What is the problem with this thing?" Hannah looked at me with a quizzical curiosity on her face.

"You know, there's this thing called VCF that my mom told me about. We could get some of that."

"What's VCF?" *Unbelievable.*

"Vaginal Contraceptive Film." *A what now? Shit this is embarrassing.*

"Hey, what are you guys doing?" A voice called out from the darkness. *Oh, fuck!* Hannah and I jumped up. I dropped the condom and then fixed my pants.

"Who's there?" I asked. I bent down and picked up the blankets and stood in front of Hannah. "Get behind me." Hannah stood behind me and held on to my arm with both of her hands.

"Hey, man, no worries, no worries." An older man approached us. He was wearing dirty, tattered clothes and had his hand out. *Homeless?* "Do you have any change you can spare? I'm really hungry."

"No, we don't have any money," I said. The man had a very sad look on his face and turned around and walked away. "That scared the crap out of me."

"I feel bad for him. He just needs help."

"I'm glad he wasn't some kind of serial killer or something."

"In Visalia? Really?"

"You never know, shit, what if that guy had a knife?"

"Yeah...Let's walk closer to the park," Hannah said. I held both of the blankets and Hannah walked in front of me. We went past the parking lot to the far side of the park and laid the blankets down again.

"Now, where were we," I said. We lied back down and continued making out. After a few minutes we stopped. "Did you hear that?"

"Yeah, it sounded like a car." We turned over and looked toward the parking lot. There was a car parked with its engine running and

lights on.. A flood light from the side of the car lit up the grass. A
dog started barking frantically.

"Shit, it's the cops. I don't think they've seen us yet. We have to
make a run for it," I whispered.

"Ok, but where are we going to go?"

"We're going to run through the baseball diamonds and get back
to the street on the other side. Follow me." We got up slowly and
I grabbed the blankets. "Ok, let's go!" We jogged at a good pace at
first but picked up to a full sprint when the sound of the dog got
louder. I turned around to look at the car and saw the spotlight still
moving around the grass. The sound of the dog barking got louder
and louder. We ran past the first backstop and then hid behind the
second backstop on the far side of the field. "Shit, let's just stay
down right here."

"They're going to find us if we stay here!" Hannah pleaded.

"No! They're going to find us if we're moving around. We'll be
safe. They're not coming over here."

"I don't know..."

"Trust me, it's going to be ok." Hannah held on to my arm
with vise-like precision. *Please go away. Leave us alone. Nothing
to see here.* I sat up just enough to see out of the bottom of the
backstop and watched as the spot light turned off. *Is that a good
thing?* The sound of the barking dog became faint as the car drove
away. "Thank God, they left."

"Now that scared me," Hannah said. "I would never see the
outside of my room if I had to call my parents from the police
station."

"For real, I don't think anyone would even bail me out...We
should go back."

"Yeah, it isn't a good idea to hang around." Hannah and I stood
up and walked back towards the school and the fence that we scaled
to get in. I threw the blankets on the other side of the fence and we
both jumped over. We took turns dusting each other off and then
began walking back to Hannah's house.

"Let's walk really slow and keep our eyes open for those cops. If we see any car, and I mean any car, we need to find a place to hide."

"Damn, Billy, we're like Bonnie and Clyde out here." *Bonnie and Clyde?*

"I don't know who that is."

"The outlaws, Bonnie and Clyde...They were rebels. It's a movie."

"Never heard of it, but we're definitely rebels, I like that." *Hannah and Will breakin the law...Oh Yeah, Beavis and Butthead, but not exactly...still funny though.*

"I like it too, Billy. It was scary, but it was fun." Hannah wrapped herself in her blanket and we made our way around the school and back onto Laura Street. Before we got to Court Street, a car crept up behind us and we didn't have time to react. The red and blue lights flashed. I looked around for a bush to jump in, but there was no escape in sight. *Shit.* "What are we gonna do?"

"It's too late to run, just follow my lead." I put my arm around Hannah and held the blanket tightly against her body. The cop got out of his car and started walking toward us. I didn't hear a dog barking. *This must be a different cop. That's good.*

"What are you guys doing out here this late?"

"We were at a party and it got out of hand. Our ride left without us...so we had to walk home," I said. *That makes sense.*

"How old are you?" The cop pointed his flashlight at me.

"17." The cop then pointed his flashlight at Hannah.

"And you?"

"16." He pointed his flashlight at the ground.

"And why didn't you just call your parents?"

"We didn't want to bother them. They work early." *Yeah, that's good.*

"You know there's a curfew, right?"

"Yes, sir, we know, but we had to leave that party." *Sir, yep, keep it respectful.*

"Where was this party?"

"Over off of Goshen." *Shit, I don't know.*

"And you've walked all this way?"

"Yes, sir."

"Where do you live?"

"My girlfriend lives right down the street and I live off of Caldwell."

"Is that right? Well, it doesn't seem like you've been drinking..."

"No, sir, we haven't. That's why we left the party." *Come on dude, really?* The cop shined his flashlight into my face and then Hannah's.

"Ok, I'm gonna let you go. Go straight home. I don't want to find you back out here in the middle of the night again. If I do, I'm going to take you in and make you call your parents. Am I clear?"

"Yes, sir, thank you." The cop turned off his flashlight and walked back to his car. He turned around and drove the other way and we continued walking to Hannah's house.

"Nice work, Billy. I thought we were busted. You were super-smooth."

"Super-smooth, huh? I can't believe he bought it."

"Now we can add lying to the cops to our resume," Hannah said and I laughed.

"That's not the first time I've lied to the cops, babe."

"I guess that's why you're so good at it."

"I didn't think I was that convincing...He didn't even ask about the blankets. I mean, seriously, I didn't have an answer for that."

"It's a good thing he didn't ask then."

"I honestly don't think he even cared. Arresting a couple of 'kids' would require paperwork that would take away from his donut eating time, and Scotty's is right around the corner," I said and smiled. Hannah laughed.

"You're funny, Billy."

"Seriously, though, we shouldn't come out here again. We shouldn't push our luck."

"Yeah, but what are we going to do?"

"We'll have to figure something else out. For a small city, we sure do have a lot of cops." We got to Hannah's house and stopped behind the Trooper.

"Are you going to call me tomorrow?" Hannah whispered.

"Yeah, I'll call you in the morning," I whispered back. I pulled on Hannah's blanket and kissed her. I hugged her and whispered in her ear, "We'll figure it out, don't worry."

"I'm not worried." Hannah smiled and walked back to her house.

Hannah and I spent the following two weeks talking about finding a way to see each other. Two weeks apart and all we had was the phone. We had ideas, but everything we came up with was so risky that we decided it wasn't worth it. It was the last weekend before school started and we had yet to figure out what we were going to do. Hannah called me every day at 10 and every day I patiently waited by the phone for her call.

"Hey, Billy, I miss you," Hannah said.

"I miss you too," I said.

"It's Friday! Be happy, babe!" *Friday...*

"It's Friday, and I still don't have a job." Hannah laughed.

"I didn't know you were looking for a job..."

"No, the movie, you know, Friday, Ice Cube..."

"Yes, babe, I know." Hannah laughed again. "I can be funny too."

"So, are you ready for school?"

"Yeah, my mom gave me money for clothes and I went shopping yesterday at Miller's Outpost with my brother."

"Ahh, how cute, clothes shopping with your brother."

"Yeah, well, I needed a ride, so..." *Two more months...*

"Chris and Mitchell came by this morning."

"Did they?" *Not like I care.*

"Yeah, Mitchell wanted to say bye to Michael. They're gone, Billy, they moved."

"Yeah, we knew they were moving."

"Michael's still sad though. Mitchell was like his best friend. Chris told me to tell you that you should call him." *Nah, I'm good.*

"Really? I don't see that happening."

"Well, I hope you guys work things out." *Why?* "Anyway, I have an idea, Billy."

"What's that?"

"We've been talking about finding a place and I think I found one."

"What are you talking about?"

"Chris's back yard." *The fuck?*

"Are you serious?"

"Yeah, it's perfect. No one lives there anymore and there's that patio area in the backyard..."

"I'm listening..."

"I could bring a sleeping bag..." *That's right! Fuck Chris, and his back yard. I wonder if they took the dog house.*

"All right, I'm down. I just have to be careful not to get caught on the way over there. I'm sure that cop will be cruising around."

"Ok, I'll see you tonight, Billy."

"I can't wait to see you tonight, bye, babe."

"Bye," Hannah said and hung up the phone. *Oh shit! I've got to have sex with her tonight. Once school starts...it's going to be hard. What was she saying about that vaginal something or another? Shit.* I hopped on my bike and rode up Court Street to the Walgreens. *It has to be in the condom section...doesn't it? There it is.* I picked up the box of VCF: Vaginal Contraceptive Film. *Gross, but I hate condoms. How much is this shit? 10 bucks? God damn! Oh well.* I bought the VCF and headed back home. I took the box into the bathroom and pulled out the instructions. *Fold in half, and then fold in half again. Insert into Vagina. Wait 15 minutes before sexual intercourse? 15 minutes! Why does this shit have to be so complicated?* I went into my room and removed two VCF packets from the box and then carefully hid it in my Chukka Boot shoe box under some pictures of when I was little. I put the packets in my pants pocket and then went into the living room to watch some MTV. *This is going to be a long day.*

It seemed like a lifetime of waiting even though it was only a matter of hours. I went over every detail of the possibilities that the night had in store for Hannah and I while I sat on my couch. *Don't fuck this up.* It was 11:30 when I opened the door and as soon as I walked outside, I heard a loud rumble in the distance. *Thunder? It's going to rain? It's July. What the hell?* It felt like a storm was coming. The air was thick and it was hard to breathe. My Ramones T-shirt clung to me as I rode down Court Street. A hot, sticky breeze blew across my face as I picked up speed. *This is too weird.* I saw a pair of headlights coming toward me. I turned down Paseo Street and rode through the rich-people neighborhood. *I can't get caught. Stick to the side roads.* A flash of light lit up the sky. *One one-thousand, two one-thousand, three one-thousand, four one-thousand, five one-thousand...*I counted it off like I had learned in science class. A roar of thunder surrounded me. *Five miles...*I took La Vida Street back onto Court and then quickly made a right onto Evergreen. I rode around to Garden Street and approached Laura Street. *I think I'm ok.* I rode past the Isuzu Trooper and down to the end of the cul-de-sac. I put my bike down under the tree in the middle of the yard. *This is crazy.* I looked up at the sky and saw an eerie darkness. There weren't any stars and there was no moon. Another flash of light illuminated the sky. *4 miles.* I felt a tug on my arm and turned around to find Hannah in a long-sleeved shirt and Jeans. She hugged me and then stepped back. *That's a lot of clothes.* "Hey babe, what's with this weather?"

"I don't know; I've never seen anything like it this time of year," I said.

"Ever?"

"Ever, ever."

"Yeah, we never got anything like this in Santa Maria."

"That's where you're from? That's funny..."

"What's funny?"

"I didn't even know where you were from."

"That's true...where are you from?"

"I was born and raised in San Diego."

"That's awesome! How did you end up in Visalia?"

"Ask my mom."

"Maybe I will. Come on, I have the sleeping bag set up on the patio. The gate was open."

"Cool. Hopping fences was getting old." We walked through the gate and then I closed it behind us. I looked straight ahead and could see the outline of the dog house. "They didn't take their doghouse..."

"They had a dog?"

"No, not for a while. Actually, we hung out in there."

"How did that work?"

"Very carefully."

"It sounds like you miss your friend. Just call him."

"We had some good times, but times change." Another round of lightning lit up the sky. *2 miles...Hey, what happened to 3?* I took off my shoes and got inside of the sleeping bag. The concrete was ridiculously hard and I got back out. "Babe, I think we should move this to the grass."

"Ok, but what if it rains?"

"It's never rained in Visalia during the summer..."

"I don't know, Billy, it really seems like it's going to rain."

"If it does, we'll just move back. No big deal." I moved the sleeping bag to the grassiest piece of the yard which was about 10 feet away from the patio. "This is better." I got inside of the sleeping bag once again. "Come on, Hannah; get your cute butt in here." Hannah took off her long-sleeved shirt and then her pants. She put her hand on her hip and posed for me like a model on the runway. *Nice.* Another lightning strike filled the sky and illuminated Hannah's beautiful blond hair and white bra and panties. *God damn...* The thunder roared almost immediately. *1 mile?* "Babe, get over here." I reached down and took my pants off and placed them next to the sleeping bag. Hannah got inside of the sleeping bag and I looked into her eyes. "Hannah, I've got something very important to ask you."

"What's that?"

"Hannah...what's your favorite color?" I laughed and she smiled as she pulled my hair back behind my head.

"My favorite color? It's orange, but why...what's yours? I was not expecting that."

"Blue. The whole Santa Maria thing has me thinking. I don't really know much about you, which is kind of crazy, don't you think?"

"I don't know...maybe." Hannah smiled again and then kissed me. We became lost in each other's embrace as the lightning danced and the thunder roared all around us. I reached for my pants pocket and a packet of VCF. "What are you doing?"

"I got those things you told me about."

"Oh, ok, do you want me to..."

"No, I got it." I reached down and pulled Hannah's panties off with one hand and then tore open the package of VCF. *This shit is kind of sticky.* I folded it in half and then in half again like I had read in the instructions. I put the square of VCF on the end of my fingers and then slowly slid it inside of her. *Oh shit, it's stuck to my fingers. What the hell?* I worked it around until it came loose and stayed where it belonged.

"Problems?"

"Nope, not anymore, but that's a sticky bastard." I laughed and then went down on her. She grabbed a hold of my head and started moaning. I moved my hand up over her face and put my finger over her lips. "Babe, the neighbors..."

"What neighbors?" Hannah said and put my finger in her mouth." *Oh shit!* I moved up to her face.

"Babe, my tongue is numb!" Hannah laughed.

"The price you have to pay..."

"Let me give you some of this payment," I said and kissed her. The rain started falling as she opened herself up to me. *Thank God.* I was slow and meticulous. The rain steadily built to a torrent soaking my hair and bouncing off of Hannah's face. The rhythm was perfect until the song ended. My pace slowed and I looked into her eyes. "We should move to the patio."

"Yeah, or we could just stay here." *This girl...Have you lost your mind?*

"Yeah, no, I'm gonna go get some shelter." I unzipped the sleeping bag enough for me to get out and then grabbed my pants off of the ground. *Shit! They're soaked through.* I walked over to the patio and struggled to put my pants on. Hannah got up and wrapped the sleeping bag around her. When she got to the patio, she bent over and grabbed her clothes off of the ground.

"Nice, my clothes are still dry." Hannah put her clothes on and then we sat down against the sliding glass door and wrapped the sleeping bag around us."

"That was awesome, Hannah."

"Yeah, it was."

"I was starting to think that this was never going to happen. It seemed like the entire world was conspiring against us. We even had to beat this freak show of a storm..." I wrapped my arm around her shoulder. "At least it's not cold. That would have sucked. I love you, Hannah." I pulled her close and kissed her forehead with my numb lips. I reached down and held her hand while she rested her head against my shoulder. We watched the rain slowly subside to a trickle over the roofless doghouse.

"I love you, Billy."

Chapter Eleven

Freedom

"HAPPY BIRTHDAY, BRO," MY brother said as I woke up. "I have something for you." I rubbed my eyes and yawned.

"You didn't have to get me anything. I think I'm too old for birthday presents."

"You're going to want this one, trust me." My brother pulled a piece of paper out of his pocket and handed it to me. "It's the title to the Malibu."

"Are you serious right now!?" *No Freaking way!* I looked at the title carefully.

"I already signed it. It's yours bro." I gave him a big hug which I don't think had ever happened before.

"Thanks. This is huge. Now I actually have a reason to get my license." *I have to pass Kirkendall's class.*

"It's not all good news though." *Shit, I knew there was a catch.* "It needs a lot of work. You're gonna have to do a lot of work to keep it running." *Yeah, I already knew that.*

"It's cool, I have auto shop and our teacher lets us bring our own cars in." *And now I can too! I have to tell Hannah!*

"Sounds good."

"Thanks, again Larry, I really appreciate this."

"Don't mention it. You're actually doing me a favor. I don't have time to fix it up and it deserves some love."

"Yes, it does. All right, man, I have to get ready for school."

"Sure thing, I'll let you get to it." My brother walked out into the living room and I sat on my bed for a minute and stared at the title to my car before heading to the bathroom. *Holy shit! I have a car. My car! I can take Hannah on dates. I can take her anywhere I want. Oh shit; I won't have to pedal my ass to school anymore...*

I got to Rob's house at 7:30 like I had done every morning and stashed my bike in his back yard. He came outside and said bye to his mom before shutting the door. "Where's your girlfriend?"

"She got grounded again. Her dad found out she was walking with me in the mornings so now her mom's gonna drive her to school before she goes to work. They're tripping hard."

"That sucks."

"Guess who's getting a car?"

"Your mom." Rob laughed.

"No, smart ass, I am. My brother's giving me the Malibu for my birthday."

"It's your birthday?"

"Have I mentioned how much of a good friend you are lately?"

"No."

"Good." *What an asshole.*

"Well, that is a cool car, but it's kind of a piece of shit too."

"Yeah, I know. I'm gonna have to fix it up."

"When are you going to get your license?" Rob asked as we started walking to school.

"Shit, I have to get my permit first and then log some driving time. I think after that I just have to pass the written and driving test and then I'll be good to go. I got 100 out of 100 on the written test in Kirkendall's class, so I'm sure I'll be fine."

"What about gas and insurance? What about fixing it? That's a lot of money and you don't have a job." *Shit, what a buzzkill. Fucking Rob.*

"I guess I'll have to get a job."

"What about the band? How are you going to find time for both?" *Jesus Christ, Rob, you're killing me.*

"I'll figure it out, besides we've only been playing on Saturdays anyway since finding Aaron and Nate Dog."

"...And since you're going to have a car, we could go over to Nate's house every day after school. This might just work out." *You forgot about the job part.*

I met Aaron the second week of school when our English teacher, Ms. Jackson had the class do a 'get to know me' activity. We all went through the motions of sharing our interests and hobbies. When it was my turn, I went in front of the class and kept it simple.

"I'm Will Smith, I play guitar and I'm looking to start a new band. Thanks." I took my seat while the class completed their obligatory clapping. Aaron was next up to present. He had blond hair that was neatly parted down the middle of his head and covered the tops of his ears. He had an average build and was dressed in a collared shirt and khaki shorts. *That is next-level preppy. What a dork.*

"Hi, I'm Aaron Rossi, I like to work on my VW bug on the weekends. I want to have it running by the time I get my license, but I won't be 16 until May. Oh, I also play the bass. *No Shit! That was easy.* Aaron sat down behind me and I turned around in my desk.

"Hey, man, are you looking to join a band?"

"Maybe..."

"All right, let's talk after class." After class ended, Aaron and I stopped outside the classroom. "How long have you been playing bass?" I said.

"About a year. My dad plays drums and one day when he was playing I picked up the bass and started to learn," Aaron said.

"I haven't seen you around. Are you new to the school?"

"I'm from Morgan Hill...It's close to San Jose. That's where my dad lives. My mom lives here though...so now I live with her."

"Ok, that's cool, so what are you doing at lunch?"

"Nothing."

"All right, I want you to meet Rob; he's the other guitar player and our singer. Meet us at the stage at lunch."

"Ok, cool."

"All right, later."

"See ya." Aaron and I went in separate directions down the hall. *Shit, I have to walk Hannah to class!* I ran down the hall and found Hannah in the middle of the crowd.

"Hey, babe, sorry, I was talking to my new bass player...Well, maybe my new bass player." I held her hand and started walking her to her math class.

"Who is it?"

"His name's Aaron, from San Jose."

"Really? I bet Rob will be happy..."

"Babe, is Rob ever happy?" We both laughed as we made our way down the hall. We passed a lot of people that I knew, some people that I knew of, and some people that I didn't know. Everyone that we passed seemed to be staring at us, more specifically; everyone that we passed seemed to be staring at Hannah.

"Billy, why is everyone staring at us?" *I love this girl. She has no idea...*

"Because, babe, you're the prettiest girl at school and I'm the luckiest guy at school. Mystery solved." I smiled as I dropped my hand and wrapped it around her waist.

"That can't be true...except for the last part; you are the luckiest guy at school." *How can I be the luckiest guy at school if you're not the prettiest girl? You make a no sense...*

"It's true, babe, I keep telling you." We got to Hannah's math class and I kissed her goodbye. "See you at lunch." I looked back across the courtyard into the thinning crowd. *Shit, I'm gonna be late.* I started running to the auto shop, but kept stepping on my pants which slowed me down. I pulled up on my belt to try to increase my speed but the bell rang before I made it to the wing of shop classes. *Shit.* I walked into class and my teacher was already taking attendance. "Sorry I'm late Mr. Graff."

"Smith! You were late yesterday too. Why can't you get to class on time?"

"Honestly...I was walking my girlfriend to class and it's on the other side of the school." The entire class was silent during the exchange.

"I'm sure your girlfriend can find her own way to class. One more tardy and it's detention." I heard some murmurs around me. "Take your seat, Smith." I walked through the middle of the class and sat down on the second stool in the third row. *Why does he have to be such an asshole about it? What am I supposed to do, not walk her to class? He must be crazy.*

After class, I walked out to the stage in the middle of the school's courtyard where Hannah and Rob were waiting for me. The stage was where all of the band geeks and drama nerds hung out. Also in attendance were the goth kids that we referred to as the Trench Coat Mafia. They wore black trench coats and stuck to themselves. We thought they were strange but usually didn't give them a second glance. I walked up to Hannah and gave her a hug.

"Hey, babe," I said. "Hey, Rob, guess what?"

"What?"

"I found our bass player."

"That was fast. How'd you manage that?"

"I met him in my English class. His name is Aaron. I told him to meet us over here right now." I saw Aaron fighting his way through the crowd and pointed his way. "There he is; the blond dude."

"Seriously? He looks preppy as fuck," Rob said.

"He's cute," Hannah said. Rob and I both looked at her with disdain. "What? He's not as cute as you, Billy."

"Yeah, right, nice save, Hannah." I shook my head in disappointment. I looked back at Rob. "Anyway, you said yourself how hard it was to find a bass player so let's at least give him a chance."

"You're right, I did say that. Fine." Aaron found his way over to us and I shook his hand.

"Hey man, this is Rob and this is my girlfriend, Hannah."

"Hey," Rob said.

"Hi," Hannah added. I put my hand around Hannah's waist.

"So, Aaron, how long have you been playing bass?" Rob asked.

"About a year or so," Aaron said.

"What kind of music do you play?" Rob said.

"All kinds, mostly rock though," Aaron said.

"Do you like Nirvana?" Rob said. *And there it is.*

"Yeah, who doesn't? I haven't played any of their songs, but I can learn."

"Cool," Rob said. "We should meet up this weekend."

"Ok, yeah, I'm not doing anything," Aaron said. I pulled some paper out of my backpack and we exchanged numbers. We walked towards the front of the school to find a place to hang out away from all of the freaks.

"Hey, check that out," I said. In front of the band room was a kid thrashing away on a snare drum like I had never seen or heard before. "He's awesome, let's go talk to him." *I'm feeling lucky.*

"Ok, but the marching band is not the same thing as a real band," Rob said. We all walked up to the kid banging on the snare. He was on the short side and had dirty, oily brown hair. *I thought Rob looked dirty.*

"Hey, man, you're really good, how long have you been playing?" I inquired.

"Like 2 or 3 years."

"What's your name?"

"Nate. My friends call me Nate Dog. Don't ask me why."

"I'm Will, this is Rob, Aaron, and my girlfriend, Hannah."
Everyone responded with a chorus of 'hey.'

"Do you have a set?" Rob asked.

"Yeah, I have a 7-piece Pearl set with a Tama double bass pedal and Zildjian cymbals. *That's very specific.*

"I'm impressed," Rob said. "Have you ever been in a band?"

"No, I mostly just play for my church."

"Do you want to be in a band?" I asked.

"Yeah, that sounds awesome," Nate replied.

"All right, let me get your number and I'll call you later. We're going to get together this weekend," I said.

"Cool, you wanna come over to my house? It's a pain in the ass to move my drums." I looked around at everyone and didn't see any objections.

"Yeah, we can do that," I said. "Write your address down too." I took out another piece of paper and a pen from my backpack. Nate wrote down his information and then picked up his drum sticks.

"I have to get back to practicing for the pep rally on Friday."

"Cool, we'll talk to you later," I said.

"Later," Nate said. Rob, Aaron, Hannah, and I walked over to the grass area in front of the school and then sat down.

"I told you, man, simple," I said.

"I have to give you credit, you were right for once," Rob said.

"For once? Try all the time, son!" I pulled a hacky sack out of my backpack and got up. "Anyone down for some hacky sack?" Aaron stood up.

"I'll play." Hannah followed.

"Me too."

"Rob?" I said.

"Nah, I'm gonna eat my sandwich." Aaron, Hannah, and I kicked the hacky sack around for a minute when I saw two girls approaching us from the corner of my eye.

"Hey, Will, I thought that was you." I turned to my right and saw Angela and Vicki. *That cannot be Vicki...She looks kind of hot...What happened? Her hair's longer, she's skinny now; no acne...*

"Hey Angela, hey Vicki, what's going on? Oh, this is Aaron, and you guys know Rob, and this is my girlfriend, Hannah." Rob waved his sandwich at us and took another bite.

"Girlfriend? Since when?" Vicki said. *Oh shit...*

"I don't know, Hannah, what has it been, like a month?"

"Almost," Hannah said and smiled. She reached out her hand to Vicki. "Nice to meet you..." Vicki just stared at her in return. Hannah put her hand back down and then reached for my arm. She hugged me closely and then held my hand. Vicki and Angela looked Hannah up and down as if they couldn't believe what they were seeing. Vicki looked back at me and smiled and then Angela turned her attention to me. Aaron stood like a statue still holding the hacky sack. There was an awkward silence and then Angela said,

"I just wanted to let you know that Chris and I are back together. He still wants to be friends with you."

"I know, Angela, I just don't think..." I could feel Vicki mad dogging Hannah as I tried not to make eye contact with her.

"What happened between you guys? You were like best friends...Chris won't tell me. Well, he hasn't told me yet," Angela said.

"Just drop it, Angela."

"Ok, I did my part, see you later." Angela turned to Vicki and said, "Let's go."

"Bye Will, see you around," Vicki said and smiled. Angela and Vicki walked away from our group and I watched Vicki's newly tight ass walk away in her low cut jeans. *I did not expect that.*

"What was that about?" Aaron said. Rob seemed completely oblivious as he continued enjoying his sandwich.

"Yeah, for real, what was that about?" Hannah reiterated.

"I've been friends with Angela forever and Vicki, well..."

"Well, what? Did you see how she looked at me? I'm pretty sure she wants to kill me."

"Yeah, she's had a crush on me since the dawn of time. She's probably just jealous."

"And you never hooked up with her?" Hannah said and slowly pulled away from me.

"No, never, she was gross. I was never attracted to her."

"She doesn't look too bad to me," Aaron said. *Thanks, Aaron.*

"Yeah, it's weird, she used to look a lot different," Rob said. *Damn it, Rob.* "In a bad way." *This is great.* I turned to Hannah.

"Babe, you don't have to worry about Vicki. I never liked her and that's not going to change."

"She obviously likes you though," Hannah said.

"So...She'll get over it and I'll just avoid her."

"I'm not so sure. How long has she liked you?"

"Ummm, yeah, the dawn of...Nah, since like the 6th grade..."

"I think I've made my point," Hannah insisted.

"Babe, you worry too much."

"I actually don't think I worry enough." The bell rang and everyone moved around in a frantic rush. I held Hannah's hand and whispered in her ear,

"You're the most beautiful girl in the world." I kissed her on the cheek and then turned back to Rob and Aaron. "Meet after school?"

"Yeah, I'll be here," Aaron said.

"Yep," Rob muttered. I held Hannah's hand as we walked to her health class. We stopped at the classroom door and Hannah let go of my hand and turned away from me. I gently grabbed her arm.

"Are you mad at me?"

"No...I'm not mad," Hannah said. "I love you."

"I love you too..."

"You should go to class, you're gonna be late."

"That doesn't matter; I want to make sure that we're good."

"We're good, Billy, I'm just worried..."

"Worried about what?"

"Everything…It's fine, I'll be fine." Hannah kissed me. "I should go inside."

"Ok, I'll see you after class."

"Babe, I've got great news!" I said as I walked up to Hannah. She was sitting alone in the hall at the front of the school. It looked like she had been crying. *Oh shit, what's wrong?* "Are you ok?"

"I had a fight with my mom this morning. She doesn't really have the time to take me to school and I definitely don't want her to, but my dad, well, you know. So, she's blaming me for everything. And last night, someone called my house and left a message for me. A girl said, 'Hannah, you're a fucking bitch and I'm going to kick your ass when I see it.'" *What the hell?*

"Who would do that? Seriously, it doesn't make sense. How would they even have your number?"

"I think it was Vicki or Angela; probably both. The only way they would have my number that I can think of is Chris. Michael, Mitchell, Chris, Angela, Vicki…"

"Yeah, but why would Chris just give your number to Angela, unless…"

"Chris wasn't happy that I turned him down."

"Do you think that he told Angela about it?" *Shit.* "Wait, why would he do that?" *I'm so confused.* "What would he have to gain by telling her that he asked another girl out while they were together and that he got turned down?" *He's not the brightest bulb on the tree but he's not stupid either.*

"I don't know but I'm so tired of all this drama," Hannah said as I sat down next her. I put my arm around her and said,

"Look, babe, everything is going to be fine." Hannah looked over at me and smiled.

"Oh my God, I feel so stupid, happy birthday, Billy."

"Thanks. That's what I wanted to talk to you about."

"I just got so caught up in all of this shit...You said you had good news."

"No worries, babe, and yes, I have awesome news. My brother gave me a car!"

"That is so cool, I'm so happy for you." Hannah smiled and then kissed me.

"I'm happy for us! We'll be able to go anywhere we want..."

"As soon as I'm not grounded that is...And I'm always grounded." *Yeah.*

"I still need to get my license, so it's not going to be tomorrow or anything." I leaned in to Hannah and whispered in her ear, "I miss you."

"Babe, I'm right here," Hannah said.

"No, I mean, we haven't been 'together' since that night..."

"Ahh, in that case, I miss you too." Hannah smiled. "Since my dad started working days, it's been hard. I really could use some sexual healing, but I don't know how..."

"You don't think you could sneak out Friday night?"

"I don't think I can...If I get caught..."

"You've never got caught before...right?"

"Yeah, but with my dad home at night, it's different...I wasn't going to say anything because I didn't want you to worry, but..." *This does not sound good.* "My parents are talking about moving me to Redwood if things don't change."

"Wait, they can do that?"

"I don't know. They seem to think so. They think that having Jessica around will be good for me." *Jessica, huh?*

"Yeah, we can't let that happen..."

• • • ● ● ● • ● • • •

"So that's the plan then? We're gonna meet at Nate Dog's house tomorrow morning?" Rob said.

"Yup, he said his parents are cool," I said. "We talked about working on some simple songs to get started and then go from there."

"What songs?"

"'About a Girl,' and 'Come As You Are.' Even Aaron can play those." *I think.*

"Cool."

"There's Hannah." Rob and I walked across the school to the front gate where Hannah was waiting.

"Happy Friday! We made it through the first week," Hannah said and hugged me tight. I wrapped my hands around her waist and then slid my hands down and cupped her ass. I pulled back and then kissed her.

"Did you guys want to get a room? I'm going home..." Rob said. I stopped kissing Hannah and turned to Rob.

"All right, Rob, relax, don't get your panties in a ruffle." Hannah and I both laughed. "We're coming." We all crossed Tulare Street and headed home. On Johnson Street, right before Walnut, I started playfully slapping Hannah's ass while we were walking.

"Stop it," Hannah said. She smiled as she slapped my hand away.

"What are you going to do about it?"

"You guys are stupid," Rob said.

"Stop it," Hannah said. "I'm going to kick your ass!" I laughed. We stopped at the edge of someone's garage. Hannah punched me in the arm and I laughed even harder.

"Is that it," I said. I grabbed her by the top of her jeans and pulled her towards me. I kissed her aggressively and Rob made an audible groan.

"I'm going home, later," Rob said and ran across Walnut Street. Hannah and I continued making out in the driveway. I was able to negotiate my hand into Hannah's pants from behind and ran my fingers over her panties. Hannah, in turn, slid her hand down the front of my pants. *Oh shit!*

"Breakin the law," Hannah whispered to me. *I love this girl so much.* We heard a noise that startled us apart. The garage door opened and someone popped out from underneath it before it had fully opened. The middle-aged woman looked at us and then we looked at each other.

"Oh...Ummm, sorry, I didn't mean to interrupt," the woman said. Hannah and I looked back at each other and then busted up laughing. We walked away from the driveway and then waited for traffic to subside before crossing Walnut.

"I think we scared her more than she scared us," I said.

"Oh, for sure, that look on her face was priceless," Hannah said.

"I know, right? kind of like the look of walking in on someone in the bathroom." Hannah and I both continued laughing as we made our way to Rob's house. I walked over to his fence and grabbed my bike out of his back yard. I got on my bike and then rode alongside Hannah while holding her hand. Before we turned down Encina Street, an old pickup truck pulled up next to us. *Who is that? Oh shit, I recognize that truck...*

"Hannah, get in the truck! Now!" Hannah's dad peered through the passenger window of his truck at Hannah and then at me. I had never been that close to him. He looked huge behind the wheel of that truck. *Shit.* "Right now!" He yelled.

"Dad, I'm almost home, why do I?"

"Now, Hannah, get in the truck," Hannah's dad interjected. I didn't say anything. I was frozen. Hannah looked back and lipped 'sorry' to me. "Do I have to drag you in here?" Hannah let go of my hand and then stepped up into the truck. Hannah's dad sped away and down Laura Street. *Shit, that's not good.*

Chapter Twelve

Fighting

I SAT IN MY Auto shop class that day as unfocused as ever. *Hannah can't move to Redwood; that would ruin everything. I need to be alone with her...Maybe I should just go talk to her dad...reason with him...Yeah, that's gonna work...Shit.* I heard different parts from Mr. Graff's lecture about brakes and brake fluid, but I couldn't concentrate. I looked out into the shop where all of the cars were. *I can't wait to get the Malibu in here!* I started feeling a little better and paid more attention to what Mr. Graff was saying. *I'm going to need to know this shit...*

After class I made my way across campus and saw a rush of people gathering in the middle of the school. *Another fight...What's new?* I went and waited for everyone at the stage. No one was there. *I hope they're not over there watching that fight. So stupid...*I looked over at the crowd that had developed and saw some administrators run into the fray. I leaned against the edge of the stage and I could see Aaron running toward me. *Aaron? What is going on?* "Dude, it's Hannah!" Aaron said while catching his breath.

"What are you talking about?"

"She was the one in the fight..."

"What? With who?" Shit, is she ok?" I started running over to the crowd. Aaron caught up with me and said,

"It's that girl, Angela, I think that was her name..." *Oh shit...what is going on?* By the time I got over to the crowd of people, it was over. Hannah and Angela were being escorted to the office. I found Rob and Nate standing and talking on the outside of the disorganized circle.

"What happened!?"

"I'm not really sure how it started," Rob said, but Hannah definitely finished it." Aaron and Nate both shook their heads in agreement.

"Yeah, your girlfriend beat the shit out of her," Aaron said.

"So, she's ok then?" I said. *Thank God.*

"She's fine...Angela not so much," Rob added.

"What the hell happened? Did anyone see how it started?"

"I got here late, I don't know," Aaron said.

"Same," Rob said.

"I got here before them, but I'm still not sure...I thought I heard something about Chris or something like that, and then your girlfriend punched the other girl square in the face. *Chris? They're fighting about Chris? What the fuck...*

"Angela..." I said.

"That punch knocked her to the ground, I saw that happen," Nate said.

"And then everyone started running over here and I saw Hannah on top of her," Rob said. Angela was pulling her hair but it didn't seem like it made a difference.

"Yeah, your girlfriend got in some good shots," Aaron said.

"Then the APs broke it up, and now here we are," Nate said.

"Shit, I need to talk to her," I said. Why would she do this? Her parents are going to freaking send her to Redwood!"

"Good luck getting in the office, dude," Nate said.

"Shit, you're right, what am I supposed to do?"

"Ummm, nothing, there's nothing you can do," Rob said. The crowd had thinned out and gone about their normal business when I saw Vicki walking toward me. *Shit, she does not look happy.*

"Your girlfriend's a fucking bitch, Will!" Vicki said. *What the fuck*...I put my hands up and shrugged my shoulders. Rob, Aaron, and Nate looked on but didn't say anything.

"Look, Vicki, I don't even know what happened or even why it happened. Hannah's one of the nicest people I've..."

"Nicest people!?" Vicki interjected. "You really don't know do you?"

"Don't know what?"

"Hannah and Chris hooked up this summer, which is why Chris broke up with Angela, duh," Vicki said.

"Oh, I fucking knew it!" Rob said.

"No, that's not what happened. She turned him down. They both told me that," I said. "Why would Chris tell me that he got turned down?"

"That's not what he told Angela. Why do you think they got in a fight? You daffy bastard..."

"I thought I told you, I don't know!" I said.

"Angela called your girl out for being a whore and I guess she didn't like it." *She's not a whore. What is going on!?*

"All right, Vicki, get out of my face. Something's not right here." Vicki backed up.

"Fine, but the something not right is your girl. Just break up with her already. Don't be stupid," Vicki said, turned around, and walked away.

"Shit," Rob said. "What are you going to do?"

"Yeah, that was intense," Nate said.

"You really think your girlfriend's cheating on you?" Aaron said.

"I think she is..." Rob said.

"Yeah, thanks, Rob, I know your opinion. Shit, we weren't even together when all of this happened, or supposedly happened, but no, I don't think she's cheating on me now or lying to me about what happened then. This is stupid. None of it makes any sense. I need to call Chris."

"Shit, dude," Nate said.

"Hey, I'll catch up with you guys later. I'm not feeling very well. I'm gonna go home," I said.

"She's just a girl, man," Rob said. *She's not just a girl...*

"See you guys later," I said and walked towards the front gate of the school.

"Later, Will," Nate said.

"Yeah, later," Aaron said.

I had a terrible feeling in the pit of my stomach when I got home and went immediately to lie down on my bed. *Can I fucking trust anyone!? I need to figure this shit out tonight.* I skipped dinner that night. The feeling in my stomach got worse. *Fuck it.* I dialed Chris's number and he picked up after the 2nd ring.

"Hello," Chris said.

"Chris, is that you," I said.

"Will? Oh shit, man what's up?"

"I think you know what's up..."

"Nope. Hey, I got back together with Angela." *What the fuck? Maybe he doesn't know...*

"Yeah, I know, she told me...Have you talked to her today?"

"No, I was going to call her later tonight."

"You might as well hear it from me...Hannah and Angela got in a fight today at lunch."

"What!? Why?"

"That's what I'm trying to figure out...What did you tell Angela about this summer?"

"I told her the truth."

"Which is what?"

"I don't know what you're getting at. I already told you, and I told her the same thing. I really liked Hannah and I asked her out, but she turned me down." *Yeah, that is what you told me...*

"That's really interesting because Angela told Vicki that you told her that you and Hannah hooked up."

"Bullshit; I never told her that. It didn't happen." *I want to believe you...*

"Somebody's lying. None of this makes sense. If you're telling me the truth then Angela is running around lying. She called Hannah a whore and then Hannah beat the shit out of her."

"Oh, fuck, is she all right?"

"I don't know. I didn't see the fight, but she seemed ok after the AP's broke it up."

"All right, I need to go, I have to call her. Look, man, I'm not lying to you, but I don't know why Angela would lie about it either."

"Ok, Chris, do what you have to do, I'll talk to you later."

"Later, man." Chris hung up the phone and the knot in my stomach relented. *Why would Angela lie? It doesn't make sense. I should call Hannah to make sure she's ok...Shit; her parents will never let her talk to me.*

The next morning, I woke up and decided that I wasn't going to school. I needed to see Hannah and I knew she wasn't going to be there. I had no idea what happened to her after the fight, but I assumed that she got suspended. Most people that got in fights were suspended for 3-5 days. I got on my bike at 7:30 and rode down Court Street. *Should I just go to school? Hannah...I need to see her.* I made a right onto Laura and headed to Hannah's house. *Please don't let her parents be home.* I slowed down and saw that her driveway was empty. *Shit, I have to risk it.* I put my bike down on Hannah's lawn and then walked up to the door. *Shit, please...* I knocked on the door very softly and there was no response. I knocked again a little harder. The door opened and Hannah stood there with a smile on her face. She was wearing an oversized orange t-shirt and it seemed like that was it. Her beautiful blond hair was as messy as I had ever seen it. She wasn't wearing any makeup. It was like she had just woken up. *She looks as beautiful as ever.* "Billy, I'm so happy you came over, get in here!" Hannah shut the door behind us and then hugged me ferociously. She started crying and rubbed her eyes into my shoulder.

"Babe, your parents are at work, right?"

"Ummm, yeah, I think so. I hope so." *Yeah, me too.*

"I'm sorry, Billy, I shouldn't have hit her. I should have just let it go." Hannah pulled back away from me. Tears rolled down each of her cheeks. "She started talking shit. She called me a whore and said something about me being with Chris. I'm with you, Billy; I couldn't listen to her bullshit anymore." She started crying again and I hugged her close.

"I know, I'm not mad at you, I'm just glad you're ok. You are ok, right?"

"Yeah, well, my parents are pissed, but there's nothing new about that...And I got suspended for 5 days."

"It looks like I'm taking the next 5 days off..."

"I love you, Billy, you're so sweet." She leaned in and kissed me while I wrapped my hands around her waist.

"So, I heard you kicked her ass." I smiled as I pulled back away from her.

"Yeah, it wasn't my first fight." *I did not expect to hear that...What else don't I know about this girl?*

"Really, well, I'll keep that in mind for future reference. Don't piss Hannah off."

"You know it." Hannah smiled and softly punched me in the arm. "So, what do you want to do?" I stepped back a little bit and looked around Hannah's living room. I saw a deck of playing cards on the coffee table.

"I don't know, how about a game of cards." I smiled and then laughed.

"Are you serious?"

"Nope...babe, seriously?" I turned back to her and then kissed her. Hannah smiled and then walked down her hallway. I watched her walk away from me as her orange t-shirt flowed gently over the curves of her body. She moved her hands to the bottom of her shirt and then pulled it off and dropped it on the floor. *Oh shit. Damn she's hot.* She stopped in the middle of the hallway, bent over, and pulled her panties off. She turned around and smiled.

"Are you coming, or what?" *I was enjoying the view, but...* I smiled and walked toward her. She turned around and continued walking into her room. I followed her in and she shut the door behind us. *You should get suspended more often.*

"Babe, I don't have those VCF things with me..."

"It's ok, just pull out, I'm not worried about it." *I'll try. Shit.*

"Are you sure?"

"Yep." Hannah grabbed a hold of me and kissed me while I slowly took off my clothes. The world seemed to disappear around me as Hannah and I fell onto her bed and into each other. There was no school. There was no Chris and Angela. There was no band. There was only Hannah.

Chapter Thirteen
Harsh times

"WILL, I NEED YOU to clean the grease trap." *The what trap?* "Finish up those buns and then meet me in the back," my boss said. She was a middle-aged woman named Maggie. I applied for the job at McDonald's after I got my license and Maggie called me back the next day to offer me the job. It was my second week of work and I was getting good at making the buns.

"All right, I'll be done in a minute," I said while putting in my last batch of bread. After I pulled the buns out of the industrial toaster, I walked back to the dish washing area where my boss was standing. She had a pair of really long rubber gloves in one of her hands and a small trash bin lined with a thick plastic bag in the other. She handed the gloves and trash bin to me and kneeled down to the floor in front of the sink.

"Ok, so you may want to get some tissue to put in your nose. This smells pretty bad," my boss said. *Wonderful.* She unscrewed a cover on the floor and I looked over her shoulder to see what was inside. A nauseating stench flowed up to my nose and I immediately felt sick. My boss looked back at me. I was trying to hold my breath and it was apparently obvious to her. "I told you...You should really get some tissues for your nose." *Shit, I do not want to do this at all. I'd rather work the fryer.*

"Are you sure you want me to do this? This doesn't seem like a good idea if I'm going to be back on buns," I reasoned.

"Yeah, that's true, which is why I'm sending you home after this." *Well fuck me.* I went to the restroom and packed my nose full of enough toilet paper to prevent me from breathing. I looked in the mirror and saw the toilet paper dangling from my nose covering my upper lip. *This shit is so embarrassing.* I walked back to the kitchen and found my boss still standing over the hole. "Ok, what you need to do is pull all of the chunks out of the trap so that it flows freely. Put all the chunks in the waste bin, tie off the bag, put the cover back on, and then take the bag out to the dumpster." *Son of a bitch, fuck my life.*

"Ok, no problem," I said. *Ummm, no, this is a big fucking problem.*

"Great, let me know when you're done." My boss walked back to the front and I put the gloves on and put the trash bin next to the hole. I looked into the abyss and saw what looked like the most ridiculously chunky vomit that I could ever imagine. *Fuck me. Just get it over with…*I kneeled down on the floor and the smell overwhelmed my senses. *It's like a homeless man shit himself and then rolled around in it for a week.* I had never smelled anything so horrendous in my life and I knew that I should not be anywhere near that abomination if I had any concern for my health. I plunged my hand into a handful of chunks and started coughing. My eyes watered as I plopped the first load into the trash bin. *This toilet paper isn't working for shit!* I pulled out all of the chunks until I could see the sewage flowing. I put the cover back on, tied off the bag and threw it in the dumpster just like I was told. I carefully removed the gloves and set them down on the ground outside. I removed the toilet paper out of my nose and then looked down at my teal work shirt, which had a curious new design. *It's all fucked up and it stinks like the God damn grease trap!* I shook my head and stood outside for a minute before going back inside. I found my boss in the front office counting money.

"I'm done," I said. "It was the worst thing I've ever done in my life, but I got it done." My boss laughed.

"Yeah, I know. That's what I said the first time I did it."

"You've cleaned the grease trap!?"

"Yeah, I haven't always been the manager." *Well, shit.* "We've all had to do it."

"I need a shower."

"Yeah, you're free to go home, thanks."

"Yep, see you tomorrow," I said and walked out of the store and into the parking lot. I stared at the Malibu for a minute. *Is all of this worth it? Life was so much easier pedaling my ass around.* I got in my car and pumped the gas a few times before turning the key. It roared to life, but didn't sound right at low idle. *I'll ask Mr. Graff about it on Monday.* I drove home and immediately got in the shower. *What am I going to do with that shirt? Burn it?* When I got out of the shower, I put my work shirt in a plastic grocery bag and tossed it in the corner of my room. *I'll deal with it later.* After I got dressed, I called Nate Dog to see what was going on with practice. We were still practicing every Saturday, and despite the lack of practice days, we sounded pretty good.

"Hello," Nate said.

"Hey, man, I just got off work. Are we practicing today or what?"

"Yeah, Rob's already here. You just have to go pick Aaron up and we're a go."

"All right, I'll see you around 3."

"Ok, later." I got in my car and headed to Aaron's house. He lived all the way on the other side of town in a new development off of Akers. Nate Dog lived in the middle of all of us so it made sense that we practiced at his house. I pulled up to Aaron's house and his garage door was open. I could see that he was working on his car. He had a 1969 VW bug that he got from his dad. Even though he wasn't old enough to get his license, he still drove around his neighborhood. I parked next to the curb and then walked up his driveway.

"Hey, man, what's up?"

"I'm doing some wiring work. I want to put a pair of subs in the back and I need more power," Aaron said. *Nice.* "So, are we practicing today?"

"Yeah, are you ready?"

"Yeah, give me a minute."

"Man, you are not going to believe what I had to do today..." Aaron put some tools away and washed his hands.

"What's that?"

"I had to clean the grease trap at work. It smelled like a blended-up mess of shit and dead animals. It was the worst thing ever."

"Sounds gross, I'm glad I don't work there. I do need to get a job though."

"McDonalds is always hiring..."

"No, thanks, I'd rather work anywhere else."

"Yeah, me too, but a check's a check." We got inside the Malibu and I drove us over to Nate's house.

"When are you gonna put a system in this thing?"

"When I get paid...Shit, look at this radio." I pointed to the center of the dash. "I'm going to have to cut that entire thing out just so something new will fit."

"It looks like it'll be a pain in the ass."

"Yeah, so you can see why it's not at the top of my to-do list."

"It's just so quiet..."

"Quiet? You don't hear that monster V8 under the hood?"

"Yeah, I can feel that...but you know what I mean."

"Yeah, I do...I started working on a new song. I'm calling it Tread safe, after the stupid shoes that they make us wear at McDonalds." Aaron laughed.

"Those are pretty bad."

"Anyway, Rob's kind of still being a bitch about us writing our own songs so I need you to have my back."

"Even if your song sucks?" I smiled and looked over.

"Especially, because my song does suck," I said and we both laughed.

"Yeah, man, I've got your back."

"Cool, Nate will play anything and make it sound awesome, so Rob's shit out of luck on this one."

"Did you write lyrics?"

"Yeah, I started to..."

"What if Rob won't sing them?"

"He can re-write some of the lyrics if he wants...a little bit. That's what bands do; they figure things out." I pulled up to Nate Dog's house and Rob and Nate were waiting outside. Nate jumped up on the hood of my car and put up the devil horns.

"Check this out," Nate said. Aaron and I got out of the car.

"Nate Dog, what are you doing?"

"Nate's crazy," Aaron said.

"What's up, guys?" Rob said. We all looked up at Nate as he posed on top of my hood.

"This would make an awesome album cover," Nate said.

"I guess, but get off my damn car, man." Nate jumped down.

"Dude, your car is bullet-proof." *Yeah, I don't think it is.* "American Muscle..."

"All right, all right, let's go play some music," I said. "Rob, you're really gonna like my new song." *And if you don't, I don't care.*

"I'm not, I can pretty much guarantee that," Rob said.

"I don't know, man, you may like this one, it sounds like Nirvana," I said. We all laughed except for Rob. We went into Nate's house and walked into his bedroom.

"You can play it for us at the end of practice," Rob said. *Thanks, Master. I CAN play it...What a dick.* Nate Dog climbed over one of his floor toms to get behind his set, Aaron and I plugged in, and Rob set up the PA speakers. Rob turned on the microphone. "Ok, check, mic check, check 1...ok, we need to have 5 songs down perfectly for Tuesday." Tuesday was Halloween and ASB wanted us to play a show on the stage at lunch. Everyone at school knew we had a band, but we hadn't played a show yet. "I was thinking that we would start with 'Teen Spirit,' since Nate can actually play it," *Unlike Chris...* "and then 'About a Girl,' 'Breed,' and Come as You Are.' And then we need a 5th, any suggestions?" *Well, Hell has officially frozen over.*

"Let me get this straight, you're asking for our opinion?" I said.

"Yeah, I am, what's the big deal?" *Normally you're a straight up dictator, special emphasis on the dic.*

"All right, I want to do 'Negative Creep.' I think that's an awesome song to close out the show."

"That's actually a really good choice," Rob said. "I thought you would say something about the song you wrote."

"Well, now that you mention it..."

"Nah, 'Negative Creep' is perfect," Rob said. "All right, we've got our set list. Let's go through it. If anyone messes up, we're doing it again." *And he's back...*

After practice, we went outside to wait for Rob's dad to pick up the guitars, amps, and PA system. He said that he would be able to drop everything off at school. Nate Dog didn't have to move anything because he was able to get permission to use the school's set in the band room. "That wasn't bad, guys, I think we're ready for the show," I said.

"It was all right; we still need to be tighter. We should be practicing every day," Rob said. "And Will, your song does suck." *Thanks!*

"Then make it better, rock star..."

"Nah."

"My parents won't let us practice during the week," Nate said. Nate and I leaned against the hood of my car.

"We could play at my house, but, yeah, the drums..." Aaron said.

"We're fine. We don't need to practice every day," I said. *We're not going to be professional musicians.*

"Yeah, man," Nate said. "We've got school to worry about. I know that If I don't pass my classes, my parents won't let me play at all." Aaron and I shook our heads in agreement.

"There's my dad, let's load up the van," Rob said. We all went back inside Nate's house and moved all of the equipment into the van one piece at a time.

"Later," Rob said as his dad drove them away.

"I'm getting kind of bored playing Nirvana all the time," Nate said.

"Yeah, I like Nirvana, but we should mix it up," Aaron reiterated.

"I'm with you guys, but Rob's a stubborn asshole. I think we're starting to wear him down, but it's going to take time."

"How much time? We've been playing together for over two months," Nate said. *This feels like Déjà vu for some reason...*

"I don't know...What other stuff do you want to play?"

"I want to play some Korn or 311, stuff like that."

"Then just start playing it and I think Rob will have to come around...You're an awesome drummer. What choice does he have?"

"That's a good point. You guys wanna learn 'Blind' and 'Down?' I really want to play those songs."

"Yeah, I'll try to learn them tomorrow after work," I said.

"...I'm down," Aaron said.

"You did that on purpose, didn't you," I said.

"Did what on purpose?" Aaron said.

"You're down to play 'Down,'" Nate said.

"Yeah, it's a pun, like 'no pun intended,' but you totally intended," I said.

"I guess I did," Aaron said. We all smiled. "So should we be ready to play these songs on Tuesday?"

"No way, man, Rob would shit. Besides, I think it would be a good idea for us all to practice together before playing anything live. We're going to have 2000 people watching us."

"Yeah, you're right," Aaron said. *Oh shit, Hannah!*

"So...I gotta get home, Hannah's probably trying to call me," I said.

"Ok, I'm getting hungry anyways, I'll see you guys later," Nate said. Nate waved as he walked back toward his house. Aaron and I got in my car.

"Hey, man, do you want me to take you home?"

"Yeah, I should go home and eat too." I fired up the Malibu and let it run for a minute to smooth out the idle and then drove Aaron home.

When I got home, I went into my bedroom and grabbed my brother's guitar and then went back into the living room to turn on MTV. I had the VCR set up to record on a blank tape when' Blind' or 'Down' came on. I found it much easier to learn songs by seeing the bands play live versus listening on the radio. *Jesus Christ, there's more 'Real World' than real music videos.* I sat in front of the TV with my brother's guitar in my hands for two hours until my mom got home.

"How was work?" My mom said.

"Terrible," I said. "I had to clean the friggin grease trap. It was the worst thing I have ever smelled in my life." My mom laughed.

"Yeah, you're going to have days like that." *Shit, Hannah still hasn't called.* "How's your little girlfriend?" *That was spooky...*

"She's fine, I guess. Her parents are doing their best to keep us apart."

"When am I going to get to meet her?" *Did she not hear what the problem is?*

"When her dad let's her outside, I guess."

"Have you ever tried talking to him?" *That's just crazy talk.*

"No, I value my life." My mom laughed again.

"Maybe he's just being overprotective because he doesn't know you." *Maybe...*"That's my advice, just go talk to him, what's the worst that can happen? " *My death... But, maybe...I am getting tired of this shit.*

I woke up the next day and drove to work for another 10-2 shift. I spent the entire four hours toasting the buns, which I was more than happy to do. It was very robotic work. I could literally do it blind-folded. After work, I went home to shower and then stared at the phone. *Hannah probably tried to call me all day while I was at work. I got this job because of her...and, well, shit...*I fired up the Malibu and drove to Hannah's house. I parked on the curb right outside of her door and started walking through her lawn. I looked to my left and the Isuzu Trooper and her dad's old truck were both parked in the driveway. *Shit, you've lost your mind.* I took a deep breath and then knocked on the door. Hannah's mom opened the door and she scowled at me with her sunken bulldog eyes. "Patrick!" Hannah's mom yelled. Hannah's dad walked over to the threshold of the door.

"I thought we made it clear, we don't want you anywhere near Hannah," Hannah's dad said. Hannah walked up to the door and stood behind and between her mom and dad. She looked more afraid than I had ever seen.

"Billy..." Hannah said.

"You shut up, Hannah," her dad said.

"It's ok, I'm not here to talk to Hannah, I'm here to talk to you." I looked her dad square in the eyes. Hannah opened her mouth slightly and tilted her head to the right. It was a peculiar look. I couldn't tell if she was pissed at me or happy that I was there to stand up to her dad. Hannah's dad laughed and her mom smiled.

"There's nothing to talk about," her dad said.

"Yes, there is. Why do you hate me so much?"

"We don't hate you..." Hannah's mom said. *Could have fooled me...*

"What is it, my hair?" I said. Hannah's dad looked behind me at my car.

"It's not your hair. I had long hair when I was your age," her dad said.

"Then what's the problem?"

"Is that your car?"

"Yeah, why?"

"That's the problem...Hannah's 14...and I know she looks like she's 17, but she's not. She's too young to date anyone. It's not about you, it's about her."

"What are you going to do, keep her locked up until she's 17?"

"Yes," her dad said decisively. Hannah looked distressed and tears began to fall down her cheeks.

"You can't just lock her up!"

"This conversation's over," her dad said and then shut the door in my face. *Well fuck. This means war.* I walked back to the Malibu and fired it up. I revved up the engine a few times so that Hannah's parents could feel my frustration. I drove around the end of the Cul-De Sac and then back towards Hannah's house. I stopped in the middle of the street and stared at her door. I put my transmission into neutral and revved my engine up a few more times. *I have to free her from that prison...*I slammed my gear selector into drive and then sped away toward Court Street.

The next day at school, I found Hannah alone in front of the band room waiting for me. When she saw me, she ran over and hugged me. "Hey, babe, you're in a good mood. I thought after yesterday you would be mad at me."

"What!? No, that was impressive. I never thought you would actually confront my dad...and neither did he." Hannah laughed.

"What happened after I left?"

"They got mad like they always do, but this time it was different. They talked about how they didn't know what they were going to do. I didn't know before, but they called the school to see if they could transfer me to Redwood, and I guess they can't." Hannah hugged me again.

"That's great news."

"I know, right, I was so afraid that they were going to get their way. So, you guys are going to play tomorrow...First show, are you nervous?" Hannah smiled and I smiled right back at her.

"Not even a little bit. After telling your dad how it is, I think I can do anything. That's a scary man."

"Yup, you don't have to remind me, Billy, I have to live with him."

The next day was Halloween and I was in auto shop right before lunch. I walked around the shop going over every song that we were performing in my head. *I should really be checking my carburetor. I have to stop over thinking this.* The bell rang and I walked out to the stage. *Man, I didn't get shit done today. I hope everything's set up.* I fought my way through the crowd and got to the stage. Rob's dad was setting up the PA system and Nate was tuning up his drums. *Here we go.* I went up the short set of stairs and pulled my guitar out of my gig bag. I plugged in my guitar and saw the crowd start forming around the stage. *Shit, that's a lot of people. Isn't anyone hungry?* Rob and Aaron worked their way through and climbed up on top of the stage. Rob went over to his dad to check that everything was working. Aaron plugged in his bass and started tuning up. I turned the volume of my guitar all the way down and walked over to Rob. "Hey, man, you're going to start 'Teen Spirit' clean and then I'll come in," Rob said.

"Sure, Rob, I got it," I said. Nate looked out over his drums at me and then at Rob and Aaron.

"We ready?"

"I think ASB wants to say something," I said. Christian, the ASB president walked on stage.

"All right, everyone, are you ready for our very own Anarchy!" A few people in the crowd whistled and yelled 'yeah.' "Ok guys, a reminder, ASB is pre-selling tickets to the Winter Ball. They're 25 bucks per person or 40 per couple." *40 bucks? What the hell?* "Get your tickets in ASB before they're gone! Ladies and gentlemen, Anarchy!" Rob looked over at me and nodded his head. I slowly turned the volume of my guitar up and played the intro to 'Teen Spirit.' Everyone let out a loud 'Yeah,' and clapped obnoxiously. *Oh shit.* I was startled by their reaction but I still played the intro perfectly. Everyone else came in and we were rocking. *Damn, we sound good. We might as well be Nirvana. This is awesome.* I looked out into the crowd and saw Hannah staring at me with a smile on her face. I also saw Angela and Vicki on the other side of the quad. *Shit.* When we finished playing 'Teen Spirit' everyone went crazy with applause. *Damn.* We played 'About a Girl,' 'Breed,' and 'Come as you are' to the same fanfare. Rob stepped up to the Mic and said,

"Ok, everyone thanks for being here. This is our last song, 'Negative Creep.'" Everyone cheered and Rob started playing the song. We all came in and Rob started singing. When we got to the chorus, I really felt the lyrics. Rob sang it perfectly. He sounded just like Kurt Cobain on Bleach. At the end of the second verse, I made my way over to the center of the stage where Rob was. At the beginning of the second chorus, I started singing with Rob into his Mic. I looked out at Hannah and saw her rocking out. I smiled and continued singing with Rob through the end of the song. "Thanks," Rob said to the crowd and then turned to me and gave me a fist bump. "That was fucking awesome, man, where did that even come from?"

"I don't know; best show ever though." Nate got up from his drum set and Aaron put his bass down. They both quickly joined us at the front of the stage.

"We fucking rock," Nate said.

"Yeah, man, that was better than I thought it would be," Aaron said.

"Everyone was on point," Rob said and walked over to his dad. I jumped down off the stage and hugged Hannah.

"You were awesome, babe," Hannah said.

"Thanks, we were ok...yeah, no, we were awesome!" I smiled. Random people walked up to me and patted me on the back and shook my hand. I didn't know most of their names, but they knew mine. They kept saying how great we were, one after another.

Angela and Vicki walked up to us through the dispersing crowd. *Oh shit.*

"Will, you were amazing up there," Vicki said.

"Yeah, you guys were great," Angela said. Hannah didn't say anything while staring directly at her. Angela and Vicki didn't make eye contact with Hannah. *This is really awkward.* "Well, we gotta go."

"Bye, Will, see you around," Vicki said. Angela and Vicki walked in the other direction and I could feel Hannah's eyes burning right through me.

"Why did you talk to those fucking bitches?" Hannah said.

"Babe, they talked to me. What was I supposed to do?"

"They're so lucky I can't get suspended again."

"That wasn't so bad...I remember a very specific benefit to you being suspended." I smiled.

"Yeah, but I can't get in trouble anymore."

"Come on, babe, smile. Don't worry about them. We can't change what happened in the past."

"I want you to stay away from them. I don't trust them." I wrapped my hand around Hannah's waist.

"Neither do I. So, to change the subject on you, do you want to go to the Winter Ball? I was thinking since I have a car now, and a license, and a job that we could go on actual dates..." Hannah smiled but then quickly looked down.

"I don't think my parents will let me." *Jessica...*

"Yeah, I figured that much, but what about Jessica?"

"What do you mean?"

"Just tell your parents that you're going stag with Jessica. The dances are open to all the high schools."

"I could try...It sounds like it would be fun."

"Yeah, I mean, if you can't, you can't, but if you can I'll buy the tickets." Nate Dog walked over to Hannah and I.

"Hey, man, are you gonna help move stuff to the van? The bell's going to ring in five minutes," Nate pleaded.

"Yeah, it's all good though, we have late passes. I'll be right there, man," I said.

"Ok, hey, there's gonna be a party tonight that I guess everyone's going to, did you guys want to go?" Nate said.

"I can't," Hannah said.

"If Hannah can't go then I can't go."

"Come on, you guys," Nate said. "This stupid school won't let us dress up for Halloween so I thought it would be cool to..."

"If you want to go, you can go," Hannah interjected.

"I'm not going without you."

"That's sweet but you should go have fun."

"I'm not going to have any fun if you're not there," I insisted.

"If you change your mind, let me know," Nate said.

"Look, Nate, you guys can still go..." I said.

"Nah, the party's in Dinuba and you're the only one with a car...well, a car and a license. It's cool, man, later." Nate walked back to the stage and continued helping move equipment. *Shit.*

"I think you should go," Hannah said.

"Babe, I'm not going without you and that's the end of it." Hannah smiled and hugged me.

"How did I get so lucky?"

"Babe, I'm the lucky one." Hannah pulled me close to her by my belt and kissed me.

"Hey, get a room!" Rob yelled from the back of the stage. "Get your ass over here and help!" The bell rang and I hugged Hannah.

"I should go help; I'll see you after school."

"Ok, Billy, see you later." I kissed Hannah and then walked to the back of the stage and grabbed my guitar off of the stand. I looked out across the quad in front of the stage for a minute before putting my guitar away. *That was wild.*

After dinner that night, the phone rang and my mom answered it. "Will, it's Hannah," my mom said. *Shit.* I got up from the couch and took the phone into my room.

"Hey, babe, what's up?"

"I can't talk long, but I asked my parents about the dance and they said no." *What's new?*

"Did you mention Jessica?"

"Yeah, they didn't buy it. They know I want to go with you." *Well shit.*

"We have to figure something out. I miss you. We can't really do anything at school."

"I miss you too, but what are we gonna do?"

"I'll think of something..."

"Shit! My dad's coming, I gotta go." Hannah hung up the phone and I sat down on my bed and stared at one of the only blank spots on my wall that wasn't covered by posters. *What are we going to do? Wait! If I could convince her to ditch, I could bring her back here and call the school and pretend to be her dad...Just like Chris and I used to do. It's risky, but it just might work.*

I woke up early the next morning. I wanted to get to school before Hannah got dropped off so I could talk to her about my plan. I took a shower, ate some Grape Nuts, and was in the Malibu just after 7. When I got to school, I parked on the street to provide for a quick escape, and then waited in front of the band room for Hannah. At 7:45, I saw Hannah walking toward me and I immediately got up and walked toward her.

"Babe, I have an idea. Let's go to my house."

"You mean right now? Like, ditch school?"

"Yep, I want to be with you...if you know what I mean..." Hannah smiled.

"Yeah, I know what you mean, Billy, but that's the kind of trouble that will get me sent to one of those religious convent things."

"You're not gonna get sent to a convent. It's simple, I'll call the school when we get to my house and pretend to be your dad. No one will know the difference."

"I don't know. Do you really think that will work?"

"I don't just think it will work; I know it will work. I've done it before. Well, Chris and I used to do it all the time. We always called and pretended to be each other's dad."

"But you said that your dad doesn't live with you."

"That's my point exactly; they never questioned it. They never found out. They're stupid and we can take advantage of their ignorance."

"I don't know…"

"I promise you; no one will ever know."

"Is anyone home at your house?"

"Nah, everyone's at work. Trust me. Let's get out of here…"

"Ok, I trust you, let's go." I held Hannah's hand and we walked out across the front of the school to Conyer Street where I had parked my car. We got inside of the Malibu and I looked over at Hannah.

"It's going to be fine." I moved her hair off of her shoulder. "Buckle up for safety," I said and laughed. Hannah grabbed the seatbelt and then started looking around as if confused.

"Where's the shoulder belt?" I laughed again.

"All you get is a lap belt, this is an old car."

"Is that safe?"

"Babe, this car is a solid chunk of steel. If we were to get in an accident, the other car would be paying the price. All these new cars are made out of plastic…" Hannah snapped her lap belt shut and I pumped the gas a few times and fired it up. We drove down Conyer Street to Walnut and then Walnut to Court. I put my left hand on the bottom of the steering wheel and my right hand on Hannah's thigh. She put her hand over the top of mine and said,

"You look so cool driving, Billy." I smiled. "I would be so nervous…I am not looking forward to getting my license." *That's weird.*

"Yeah, but as soon as you get your license, your parents won't be able to control you like they do now."

"That's true, but I'm just scared, I guess. I'll probably run someone over." I laughed. "What? That's not funny."

"Sure it is; you're not going to run anyone over..." I turned the corner onto Caldwell Avenue and into my apartment complex.

"You live here, babe?"

"Yep," I said as I parked in the center parking lot area.

"It looks kind of shady."

"That's because it is." I laughed. "Don't worry about it though, let's go." I opened the door and then Hannah followed. "Hold up, I have to lock your door from the outside." I put the key into the door and turned the lock. "Yeah, I need to fix that." Hannah and I walked upstairs and into my apartment. Hannah walked around my living room and looked at all of the pictures on the wall. She pointed to a picture of my brother and I when we were both kids.

"Is this you?"

"Yeah, I think I was like 4 years old in that picture."

"You were so cute! And you had blond hair!? What happened?"

"I don't really know. It started darkening up when I was like 12 or something like that."

"That's crazy. So, what do you wanna do?"

"Is that even a question?" I smiled. "Come on." I grabbed Hannah's hand and led her back to my room. "What do you wanna listen to?"

"I don't know, maybe something romantic..." I smiled. "Well, let me go through my CD's here..." I shuffled through my CD's. "I don't have anything 'romantic.'" I continued looking around and found a Guns N Roses CD. *This has that 'Don't Cry' song, right. That's about as close as I'm going to get to romantic.* "Guns N Roses it is." I smiled and put the CD into my stereo.

"I was thinking something like Jewel, but sure...wait, aren't you going to call the school?"

"Right, yeah, let me get the phone." I walked out into the living room and grabbed the phone and the phone book. "Let me see here. Mt. Whitney high school...attendance...ok, it's right here."

Hannah came out into the living room and stood next to me. "All right, babe, watch me work." Hannah smiled and I dialed the number.

"Good morning, Mt. Whitney high school, how may I direct your call?" A receptionist said. *Wait, I thought I dialed attendance...*

"Attendance, please." I waited a minute.

"Mt. Whitney attendance," another receptionist said.

"Hi, this is Mr. O'Connor, Hannah's father." I made sure to adjust my voice down an octave to make myself more believable.

"Yes, sir how can I help you?"

"Yes, Hannah's not feeling well today, and I'm going to keep her home. Please excuse her absence."

"Yes, no problem, thank you for calling."

"Thank you, have a great day, bye," I said.

"You too, bye," the receptionist said and hung up the phone.

"And it's that easy, babe." I looked at Hannah and smiled.

"Damn, Billy, that was awesome, I almost believed you myself."

"Thank you, thank you, I try."

"You're sure they're not going to call my house, right?"

"I'm sure, we're good...One thing though. We can't do this all the time. They give us like 10 days per year to be absent before they start digging around."

"How do you know all this?"

"If you're going to break the rules, you have to know what the rules are..."

"You are literally the smartest person I know and you're mine." Hannah hugged me. "So, we have 9 more 'ditch days' then?"

"Well, yeah, I mean, we could falsify medical notes and shit like that...They don't check that stuff either, but to be on the safe side, yeah." Hannah pulled at my arm and we went back into my bedroom and shut the door. Hannah jumped on my bed and lay down. I pressed play on my stereo and skipped to 'Don't Cry.' Hannah took off her shirt and motioned for me to come to her.

The music started playing and I pulled off my shoes and took off my shirt. I got on top of Hannah and kissed her. She started pulling at and undoing my belt; I helped her slip off my pants. I undid the button on her pants and then with one swift motion, pulled her pants and underwear off.

"Damn, Billy, careful," Hannah said and then laughed. I smiled and we both got underneath the covers. I reached down underneath my bed where I had stashed the VCF and tore open a packet.

"I love you, Hannah."

"I Love you too, Billy." We fell into each other once more as the music became background noise. 'November Rain,' started playing as we lay in my bed soaked in sweat. Hannah rested her head on my chest and then looked at me and said,

"Do you think we'll be together forever?" *I hope so.*

"Yes, I do, I would never want to be with anyone else."

"I feel the same way, but my parents..."

"I'm not worried about them. Like you said, we're perfect for each other."

"Yeah, it almost feels like we were meant to be."

"Not almost...we are meant to be, which is why I'm going to do whatever I have to do to be with you." Hannah snuggled closer to me.

"Hey, babe, I'm kind of hungry. I didn't eat breakfast."

"What would you like, my lady?" Hannah laughed.

"I could really go for some pancakes, smothered in butter and maple syrup!"

"You know what, I can totally do that."

"You can cook!?"

"Well. I've never made pancakes before but I've seen my mom do it so I think I can. How hard could it be?" Hannah reached down into my boxers.

"Not hard at all," Hannah said and smiled.

"I see what you did there. I see you still have jokes." *I'm so in love with this girl.* "Well, put some clothes on...I'm gonna make you some pancakes." I got out of my bed and got dressed and headed to the kitchen where I took the box of Bisquick out of the cupboard. *Simple, just follow the instructions.* I made a stack of pancakes as Hannah looked on. "I think this is how my mom makes them." I planned on making the entire batch but Hannah grabbed a fork and started eating them before I was done. "Babe, I'm not even done yet."

"These are so good, Billy," Hannah said as she poured more syrup. I turned off the stove and took a bite.

"Yeah, not too bad," I said. Hannah stopped eating and stared into my eyes.

"Wow, Billy, a girl could get used to this kind of thing..."

"I'm glad you like it." We finished eating the pancakes and I rinsed off the dishes. Hannah walked up behind me and grabbed my ass.

"Are you ready for round two?" Hannah said as she leaned in and kissed the side of my neck. I put the plate down and turned away from the sink.

"I was just going to ask you the same thing..."

Chapter Fourteen

Anniversary

I T WAS THE SUMMER of 1996 and Hannah and I were looking forward to our one-year anniversary. It was a hard year but as time went on Hannah's parents lightened their grip and allowed Hannah some semblance of freedom. They allowed her to talk on the phone even if they knew it was me. Hannah told me that her mom was starting to warm up to the idea of her going out with me, but her dad still didn't like me. It was June 28th and I called Hannah that morning before I went to work. "Hey babe, I just thought I'd call to say I love you before I go to work."

"Ahh, that's so sweet, what time do you get off?"

"At 4, unless they keep me longer."

"What are you doing tonight?"

"I was gonna hang out with Aaron. He got his license and wants to cruise around in his car."

"That's cool. Jessica got her license too." *I remember when she was scared to get her license...I wonder what changed...* "We're gonna go to the mall if you wanna meet up. Maybe Aaron and Jessica could..."

"Babe," I interjected, "You know how that worked out last time."

"I think it'll be different this time." *What does that mean?* "Aaron's a Taurus, right?"

"Yeah, but so is Rob..."

"I think that Aaron is more Jessica's type though."

"Why, because he takes showers?" We both laughed.

"Yeah, that's a pretty good reason."

"No argument from me…So, what's up with your parents?"

"They think that I'm going out with you just to experiment sexually," Hannah said. *Sounds good to me.* "My mom said, 'you're curious, that's why you keep going back for more.' I thought that was totally unfair of them."

"I don't know, I think they're just looking out for your best interest," I said.

"But they're wrong. I love you and I've never been in love before. It's more than just sex."

"The sex is really good though."

"It is, but they don't understand. They would totally kill me if they knew I wanted to spend the rest of my life with you…That I wanted to marry you." *Marry?*

"They'll come around. Look at how much better it's gotten in the past few months…"

"Yeah, you're right. It's just that every time I bring you up, they try to put you down in some fucked up way. My mom asked me to explain in detail why I love you so much. I told her that words cannot and never will explain my love for you."

"Not bad, babe, what'd she say?"

"She said she had to give me credit for such a clever answer. She's acting like things are all right, but my dad on the other hand, is still going retarded."

"Hmmm, well, progress is progress. I'll take what I can get." I laughed. "Hey, I gotta go to work, what time are you guys going to the mall?"

"Around 6, I think."

"Oh, yeah, which mall?"

"The Visalia Mall."

"Ok, cool, I'll see you later then."

"Ok, I love you."

"I love you too." I hung up the phone and then put on my teal McDonald's shirt. I walked into the bathroom and stared at myself in the mirror. My hair was starting to grow out at the roots revealing what looked like a brown stripe going down the middle of my head. *I look like a skunk.* I hadn't died it in a very long time. I took one more look before heading out. *I need to get a better job.*

After work, I drove back home to wash the McDonald's smell off of me and then headed over to Aaron's. Aaron, as usual, was in his garage working on his car. "Hey, man, what's up?" I said as I walked up the driveway.

"Nothing, I'm just wiring up this new amp. My car is gonna be bumpin," Aaron said.

"That's cool, man. So, Hannah and her friend, Jessica, want to meet up at the mall. You wanna go hang out?"

"Yeah, you wanna take my car?"

"Yeah, I thought you wanted to cruise around."

"I do; I was thinking around the airport and Plaza Park."

"All right, cool, then we can cruise by the mall."

"What's this Jessica girl look like?"

"She looks like Fiona Apple...and that's pretty damn spot on."

"That's cool. Wait, she's not fat, is she?" I laughed.

"Dude, do you think my girlfriend would be hanging out with a fat chick?"

"I don't know, maybe, but I guess not."

"Birds of a feather, you know?"

"Yeah, I've heard that before. All right, get in, man, let's roll." I got inside Aaron's VW bug and he closed the hood before getting in after me. His car was much smaller than mine, which made for a tight fit. It was cool though. He had it primered in white and it had red vinyl seats. He started the car and turned to look at me. "Once I put in my new engine, we're gonna race." He headed out of his driveway and down the street toward the airport.

"You got a new engine? What's wrong with this engine?"

"It's weak. My car's too slow."

"I didn't think you had room for a bigger engine."

"It's not really that much bigger. It's a Porsche engine though..." *Shit.*

"How'd you get the money for that?"

"My mom bought it for my birthday."

"You lucky bastard, I want a new engine...shit, I need a new transmission first. That damn thing is slipping pretty bad."

"You wouldn't have that problem if it were manual."

"That's true, I'm pretty sure I could do a swap, and I'd have to learn how to drive a manual transmission."

"I could teach you, it's not that hard."

"All right, I'm gonna take you up on that." Aaron turned down a back road near the airport and then handed me a stopwatch.

"I want to get the 0-60 time to compare it to my new engine. I'll tell you when I hit 60." Aaron put it in gear and slammed on the gas. *Yeah, this car is slow.* "And, that's 60. What's the time?"

"18.3 seconds." Aaron and I looked at each other and laughed.

"That's ridiculously fucking slow. It's ok though, I'm gonna fix it." Aaron stopped on the side of the road and got out. "Ok, your turn."

"Are you serious?"

"Yeah, why not?" *Ok, but don't blame me when I burn out your clutch.* I got in the driver's seat and looked down at the clutch pedal. Aaron got in on the passenger's side. "Ok, I'm going to teach you just like my dad taught me. Don't even touch the gas. You want to get the car moving with just the clutch. *Ok.* So push the clutch in and it's left and up for first gear. Now slowly release the clutch until..."

"I stall it out..."

"It's all right, push in the clutch and turn it back on. This time, release it even slower and hold it when the car starts rolling." *If it starts rolling...* I practiced a few times until I had the car moving with just my left foot. "Now add the gas while completely getting off the clutch...and push the clutch in and shift down and to your left for second...and release the clutch."

"Oh shit, not too bad..."

"And that's all there is to it. It's just a matter of practicing now..."

"Just like music..."

"That's right. What time were we supposed to meet your girlfriend?"

"Like around 6."

"All right, pull over and trade places, I'll drive us over there."

"And I was just getting good..."

"Yeah, you're fine with no traffic around, but get one of those big-ass SUVs behind you and it could be a different story..."

"It sounds like you have some personal experience with that."

"Yup, I sure do," Aaron said as he drove us back out to Walnut Avenue toward The Visalia Mall. We pulled into the mall parking lot and Aaron found a space to park at the top of the garage. "Where do you think they are?"

"I'm not actually sure; they might be in Macy's." We walked across the parking garage bridge into Macy's. The women's section was on the top floor so Aaron and I walked around there for a while and then gave up. "They're not up here, let's go downstairs."

"All right, maybe they're getting some food. I'm getting hungry myself."

"Let's find them first." We went down the escalator and walked by Claire's. I stopped and looked inside because I knew that Hannah loved that store. "Hey, there they are."

"So that's Jessica? Not bad."

"Yeah, I told you, just play it cool." We walked over to Hannah and Jessica who seemed distracted with some costume jewelry in the back of the store. I snuck up behind Hannah and wrapped my arms around her. She turned around and smiled.

"Hey, Billy, I've got something for you."

"Babe, I don't have any more fingers for anymore rings." I laughed and held up my fingers revealing eight plastic rings that Hannah had acquired for me.

"Yes you do, your thumbs are still free...but that's not it." Hannah reached into her front pocket and pulled out a bunch of scraps of paper. She placed them in my hand and smiled. I opened them one at a time and saw phone numbers with dudes' names on them. *What the hell?* Hannah looked over at Aaron and then back at Jessica. "Jessica, this is Aaron." Aaron waved at Jessica.

"Hi, nice to meet you Jessica," Aaron said.

"Nice to meet you," Jessica replied.

"Hannah, what do you want me to do with all of these numbers?"

"I don't know, I thought you'd want them. I'm not going to call any of those guys."

"Then why'd you take their numbers?"

"Oh shit," Aaron said.

"...I didn't want to be mean..." Hannah said. *Unbelievable.* I walked over to the closest trash can and threw the numbers in and walked back to Hannah.

"Sometimes you should be mean."

"She told them she had a boyfriend, Will," Jessica said.

"There were like 20 numbers. I guess they didn't believe her," I said and looked over at Hannah hoping that my disappointment translated through to my face.

"It's not a big deal. You're here now so they won't bother us anymore," Hannah said. *20 dudes want to fuck my girlfriend and there's nothing to worry about...*

"Jessica, did you get any numbers?" I said.

"Yeah, but I already threw them away," Jessica said. *Yeah, right...*Hannah leaned in to me and whispered in my ear,

"You have no reason to be jealous, I love you." *Then why did you accept their numbers in the first place? What's so hard about...* Hannah grabbed ahold of my hand. "Hey, guys, let's go get some food."

"Yeah, I could eat," Aaron said. We walked over to the food court and decided to get pizza. After ordering we sat down and waited for it to cook. Aaron and Jessica made conversation and Hannah chimed in every now and then. I wasn't able to focus on anything they were saying.

"Babe, why aren't you saying anything?" Hannah put her hand on top of mine. I looked around the food court at all of the guys that probably hit on Hannah. *I don't have anything to say to you right now.* "You're not still thinking about the numbers, are you?" *No, I'm thinking about the super-awesome mall pizza I'm about to eat...*

"Look, I get it, you're the hottest girl here, no offense Jessica, and other dudes are gonna hit on you, but you don't have to encourage them," I said and Hannah let go of my hand.

"What do you mean encourage them?"

"Uh oh," Jessica muttered.

"I could be wearing a winter coat and sweat pants and they would still hit on me," Hannah continued. *Yeah, you're kind of making my point.*

"That's not what I mean. You shouldn't take their numbers. You should just say, 'thanks, I have a boyfriend,' and move on." *Simple.*

"Jessica told you; I did, but they insisted," Hannah said. *Don't be so weak.*

"Yeah, Will, sometimes it's just easier to take the numbers. Some of those guys are super scary," Jessica said. *That's just awesome.*

"Fine, whatever, let's just change the subject," I said.

"Babe, I don't want you to be mad."

"Then maybe you should have just thrown the numbers away and not told me at all."

"Are you saying that you don't want me to be honest with you? I don't want to hide anything from you," Hannah said. *Well fuck me.*

"No, I want you to be honest with me...Look, I'm sorry, I overreacted, and I'm making it awkward for everyone."

"Yeah, you are..." Aaron said. *Thanks, man.*

"All right, I'll shut up now, the pizza's coming anyway," I said. The pizza guy put the pizza down on the table and then walked away. Aaron was the first to grab a slice followed by Jessica and then Hannah. I stared at the pizza and then looked out across the food court. *Shit, Camarillo...I don't think...*

"Are you going to get some pizza?" Hannah asked me.

"I'm not really hungry," I said.

"More for us," Aaron said.

"Babe, what's wrong? You're not still thinking about..."

"No, well yeah, but that's not it," I said.

"Ok, what is it then, Billy? I'm not going to be able to eat anything if you don't tell me. I'm worried about you."

"...It's Brad; he's coming next week. I don't know if I should go this summer."

"You're leaving us, man?" Aaron said.

"It's a long story, I'll tell you later," I said to Aaron. I looked back at Hannah and then held her hand. "I don't want to be apart from you again like last summer." I mean, we weren't even together and I missed you a lot."

"It's ok, Billy, you should go."

"I don't think it's a good idea..."

"I'll be fine, Billy, I've got Jessica to keep me busy," Hannah said as Jessica momentarily looked up while choking down a bite of pizza.

"Ummm, yeah, we could go to Wild Water Adventures or something," Jessica said. *Oh hell no. Hannah's perfect ass walking around half naked at a water park...*

"That sounds fun!" Hannah said enthusiastically. *I'll bet it does.*

"I don't even think I can get the time off from work."

"Then quit," Hannah said. "What's more important, your friend or Micky D's?"

"Brad, but I still have my car insurance to pay and gas and food."

"Then get a new job when you get back. Babe, I know you don't like working at McDonalds."

"I don't know…" I said. *Why is she so anxious for me to go with Brad? Something's not right.*

"Well, let me know what you're going to do, babe," Hannah said.

"Yeah…I'll have to think about it." Hannah continued eating and I grabbed a slice of pizza while looking out past Aaron and Jessica. I looked back at Hannah and she smiled at me. I couldn't find it in me to smile back. *What is she up to?* After we finished eating, we all stood up and Jessica turned to Hannah.

"You wanna go find a new bikini?"

"Yeah, you guys wanna come with us, or…" Hannah said.

"No, I need to get home," I said. "I've got to work early."

"Why don't we hang out for a while?" Aaron said.

"You can come back if you want, I just need a ride to my car."

"All right, then, let's roll," Aaron said. Hannah walked up to me and hugged me goodbye.

"Bye, Billy, call me this weekend."

"All right, see you later, see ya Jessica."

"Bye! Aaron, are you coming back?"

"Yeah, I'll come back, where're you gonna be?"

"I don't know, Hannah, Victoria's Secret?" Jessica said. *Wonderful.*

"All right, I'll see you later." Hannah and I locked eyes and she waved goodbye to me as unenthusiastically as ever. I did the same.

"Let's go," I said to Aaron. We walked outside of the mall and over to the elevator.

"So, what's the deal with Brad?" I told Aaron about my summers in Camarillo and my friendship with Brad on our way up the elevator and out to the top of the parking garage. We got inside of Aaron's car and I looked over at him.

"Hey, man, do you think it's weird that Hannah had 20 numbers from random dudes and just gave them to me?"

"Yeah, that is weird. It seemed like she was trying to make you jealous."

"I hope that's it."

"What? You think she's cheating on you?"

"No, I mean, I don't have any proof that she is."

"But you're still worried about it?"

"Yeah, look at her. Wouldn't you be worried about it?"

"Yeah, I guess I would." Aaron started his car and we headed back to his house. He smiled and looked over at me. "I'm thinking about asking Jessica out."

"You should. It seems like she's into you."

"Any advice?"

"Yeah, don't tell Rob."

"Why not?"

"It was this whole thing. Long story short, Jessica turned him down and he was pissed about it for a long time."

"Shit, all right, thanks, I'll keep that in mind." We got to Aaron's house and I got out of the car and leaned back into the window.

"Are you gonna go back to the mall right now?"

"Yeah, I think I am, I wanna get Jessica's number and..."

"Well, shit, man I could give you Jessica's number, but yeah, you should ask for it yourself. Do me a favor, man, keep an eye on Hannah for me..."

"Yeah, no problem. I'll call you tomorrow."

"All right, man, later."

"Later," Aaron said and drove away. I got in the Malibu, fired it up, and drove home.

The next day at work, I asked for time off from my boss. "Maggie, I need to take a couple of weeks off. I have this friend..."

"That's not possible; not now," Maggie interjected.

"But I go to Camarillo every year," I said.

"This is our busiest time of the year and you want time off?"

"That's what I'm asking," I said.

"...When do you need to leave?"

"Next week...Tuesday."

"I can't do that. I need you here."

"Then I'm sorry, but tomorrow will be my last day." *Not sorry.*

"...All right..." Maggie sighed. "Two weeks, but I'm not holding your job after that...If you weren't the fastest..."

"Thanks, Maggie, you got it," I said and walked back to the kitchen to continue making buns. *Damn this job sucks.*

When I got home after work, the first person on my list of phone calls to make was Hannah. I picked up the receiver and dialed her number.

"Hello?" Michael said.

"Hey, Michael, it's Will, is your sister there?"

"Yeah, hold on...Hannah!" Michael yelled. *Awesome Michael, announce it to the whole world.*

"Hello?" Hannah said.

"Hey, babe," I said.

"Hey, Billy, so did you decide what you were going to do this summer?"

"Yeah, I'm going. I got the time off of work."

"...I was kind of hoping that you would decide to stay." *What the hell!?*

"Hannah, you told me I should go."

"Yeah, but I changed my mind. I would miss you too much." *I'm so confused right now.* "Jessica and Aaron are together now," *oh shit*, "and, I don't know, I don't want to be their third wheel."

"It's too late, I already put in for my time off and I'm going to take it."

"So you can hook up with other babes in Camarillo?" *It's so funny that she's worried about me.*

"I'm not going to hook up with anyone else. I'm gonna hang out with my friend and that's it. I don't get you. Have I ever given you a reason to not trust me?" *The answer is no.*

"No, but, I'm just worried that you'll find someone better." *That's not even possible.*

"There is no one better." *What is her deal?*

"I don't want you to go."

"I'm going." Hannah didn't immediately respond and I could hear her starting to cry very softly.

"I didn't mean what I said about you hooking up with other girls..." Hannah's voice cracked. "I guess I just have to deal with the fact that you're going to do whatever you want, whenever you want to, and I can't stop you."

"I told you that it was a bad idea for me to go and yet you insisted..." *I fucking knew that it was going to be a problem.*

"I know, I'm sorry, I was wrong." *I think I'm going to go insane.*

"It's too late for all that."

"I guess I just need to be happier about life...Life goes on, right?" *What is she talking about?*

"Look, babe, it'll be fine. I'll call you every day and I'll be back before you know it."

"I know it's only two weeks, but it's going to feel like two years."

"It's going to go by so fast that..."

"Just promise me that your butt will think about me the whole time, well not your butt exactly, your dick." *All right...* "And get me something wherever you go..."

"You mean like a t-shirt or something?"

"Surprise me."

"Ok, yeah, I can get you something."

"...Do you think we could get together before you leave so I could say goodbye?"

"Ummm, yeah, you mean like sneak out?"

"Yeah, you could come pick me up, at like, midnight."

"Do you think that's a good idea? Isn't your dad gonna be home?"

"I don't care. I have to see you."

"Ok, I'll be there Tuesday night. Brad will be with me though, so..."

"It's ok, I just want to say bye." I agreed and then told her that I had to go. I could hear the sadness in her voice as we got off the phone, but for the first time, I wasn't too concerned.

On Tuesday afternoon, I was watching MTV when I heard a knock on the door. I got up from the couch and opened the door. "Oh, hey, what's up man? I thought you were going to be here later," I said to Brad as I invited him inside.

"I left early this morning to avoid the hottest part of the day. It's stupid hot outside and I don't have AC in my car."

"Yeah, you and me both. What are you driving?"

"My dad's old Honda CRX."

"That's got a manual transmission, right?"

"Yep, you wanna check it out?"

"Yeah, later though. What time do you want to leave for Peg's?"

"Probably before 6, man, like I said, no AC."

"All right, you mean 6 in the morning, right? I have to go meet up with my girlfriend tonight...She wants to say bye. You wanna meet her?"

"Yeah, I wanna see this girl that you think is so hot."

"I don't just think so, everyone else thinks so too. You'll see."

"What time are you meeting her?"

"Midnight. She's sneaking out. You want something to drink...I've got water and...water; yeah, just water."

"Sure, I'll take some water." I got Brad a glass of water and we sat on the couch to watch MTV. The time went by quickly as Brad and I caught up on the last year of school and traded stories about working on our cars. My mom got home from work at about 5 and we ordered a pizza from Round Table for dinner. We watched TV until it was time to go meet Hannah.

"Hey, man, let's go," I said to Brad at 11:45. My mom had gone to bed at around 9 and my brother still wasn't home.

"All right, are we taking your car?"

"Yeah, we can take the Malibu." We went downstairs and got in my car. I drove down Court Street and then took Beech to Garden. I put my car into neutral and then shut off the engine as I approached Laura Street.

"What are you doing?"

"As you can hear, my car is loud; I don't want to wake up Hannah's parents. That would be all bad."

"Stealth huh? You do this a lot?"

"Not really anymore. We used to sneak out a lot more when I pedaled my ass down here. We ditch school a lot to fuck though." I rolled the Malibu to a silent stop on Garden Street well before Laura and got out. "Come on, let's go."

"All right...we're gonna walk?"

"It's right around the corner." We walked up Garden and before we got to Laura Street, I could see Hannah walking toward us. She was wearing cut off shorts and one of her patented mid-drift shirts. She was holding what looked like a bottle in her hand which she raised up as we approached. *What is that? Is she drinking?* Brad looked over at me with the widest eyes I had ever seen on his face.

"Dude, that's your girlfriend? You weren't lying..." Brad whispered. Hannah walked up to me and gave me a hug. I could hear the sound of the liquid in the bottle sloshing around. I pulled back away from her and looked at Brad.

"Hannah, Brad; Brad, Hannah..."

"Hi," Hannah said and smiled.

"Hey," Brad said nervously. I looked down at the bottle of vodka in Hannah's hand and then back up at her face.

"Whose vodka is that?"

"My dad's...Hey, can we go somewhere?"

"We can't stay long, we have to leave early."

"Please, Billy, can we maybe go back to your place?" I looked over at Brad and he shrugged his shoulders.

"I guess so, I mean, my brother's not home, but my mom is...we'll have to be really quiet."

"Ok, I can be quiet," Hannah whispered. *No, you can't...but I have pillows.*

"All right, let's go, but lose the vodka first...Why are you even drinking?"

"I don't know," Hannah said and then turned around. She set the vodka down in her neighbor's bushes and then came back to me and held my hand. We walked back to the Malibu with Brad following.

"Babe, you should sit in the back," I said. I moved my seat forward and held Hannah's hand as I helped her into the back of the Malibu. Brad got in and shut the door. I fired it up and it sounded like the end of the world on a desolate street without another sound. *Shit, so loud...*

"Damn, Billy, I hope that my parents don't wake up," Hannah said and laughed. *That's not funny at all. She must be drunk.*

"Babe, how much did you drink?"

"I don't know...a lot..." she said and laughed again. *Shit.* "I'm fine though...let's go." *Right...*I shook my head, turned the Malibu around and drove back to my house. When we got inside, Brad sat down on the couch and said,

"Is this where I'm sleeping?"

"Yeah, there's pillows and blankets on the chair over there."

"I don't think I'll need blankets, but thanks," Brad said. Hannah walked back to my room and I followed her. I shut the door behind us and then sat down on my bed next to Hannah.

"Babe, what's wrong? You're drinking and you don't seem to care if your parents catch you..." Hannah looked at me but didn't say anything. She pulled her shirt off and then undid her bra. *So, you're not going to answer my question...ok then.* I got up and turned off the light and sat back down next to her. After we had sex, Hannah put her head on my bare chest and I moved her hair away from her face.

"I hope I didn't wake your mom up," she whispered.

"No, you were really good, with the help of the pillow that is...Are you going to tell me what's going on with you?"

"I'm not mad. I just keep thinking about how much I'll miss you. I just feel that you'll have so much fun without me or that you're trying to get away from me. I know you're really looking forward to going away and I'm trying to be cool about it...but, it's hard." I hugged her tightly against me.

"Babe, it's two weeks...and I'll be thinking about you the whole time."

"I know, Billy, I love you, I'm just going to miss you so much. I wish I could be the one going on vacation with you. I think I'm jealous of your friend..."

"We'll go away together soon, I promise."

"You mean when I'm 18?"

"Yeah...it seems like a long time from now...I should probably take you home. I need to get some sleep before we leave tomorrow." Hannah and I got dressed and then went into the living room where Brad was already fast asleep. I drove Hannah home and then watched her stumble into the bushes where she had stashed the bottle of Vodka. She grabbed the bottle and then waved in my direction. I slowly drove away back towards my house. *Bye, Hannah.*

Brad and I left at the break of dawn as the sun was just coming up over the horizon. "Shit, man, it's already getting hot," Brad said as we merged onto the 198 west.

"Yeah, it's the valley, what'd you expect," I said. "You've been here before."

"I know, but it sucks."

"I just got used to it, I guess." Brad looked over at me and had a curious look on his face.

"Your girlfriend is ridiculously hot."

"I know. You seem surprised."

"I am. I don't know how in the hell you landed that girl or how you've kept her." I looked down at the floor of Brad's CRX and shook my head." *Neither do I...*

"Honestly, I don't know why you're coming with me right now. If it were me, I wouldn't let that girl out of my sight."

"She wanted me to go."

"Shit, that can't be good." *I know...fuck.*

"It'll be fine. Two weeks. What could possibly happen in two weeks?"

"You really want me to answer that question?" *Shit...*

"No, not really...Hey, man, turn on the radio, I don't even want to think about this anymore, let alone talk about it."

"Yeah, for sure, I get it." Brad turned on the radio and Alice in Chain's 'Would' played through the Honda's sub-par stereo. *This stereo sucks...God damn it! How am I going to get my head straight?*

We got to Camarillo just after 10 and the first thing that I did after Brad parked the car on the street was head for the door. I didn't grab my bag. I just made a beeline for the door. I rang the doorbell and Peg answered. "Hi, Will, where's Brad?" Peg said.

"He's still in the car. Can I use the phone?" I said almost in a panic.

"Yeah, you know where it is."

"Thanks, Peg, I need to call my girlfriend." Peg laughed and walked outside to meet up with Brad. I went into the kitchen, picked up the phone, and dialed Hannah's number. "Hannah?"

"Hey, Billy, are you in Camarillo?"

"Yeah, we just got here, and calling you was the first thing on my mind."

"That's so sweet, Billy, but you should really focus on having fun with your friend." *What the hell? I thought you wanted me to call you...* "Don't you think you're being rude to your friend?" *What the literal fuck?*

"I guess so, but you're more important..."

"Don't worry about me, I'll be fine..." *I'm so confused.*

"I don't understand…last night you…"

"I know, but I was thinking; I'm just being selfish."

"What's wrong with that? I love you. We shouldn't be apart."

"I love you too, but it's not fair of me to ask you to put your life on hold for me especially when you've been friends with Brad forever." *What is that supposed to mean? Who said life was fair?*

"Ok…I guess you're right…"

"I am…now go have some fun with your friend."

"Ok, babe, I'll try. I'm going to be thinking about you the whole time."

"Me too, but it'll be good. Absence makes the heart grow fonder, right?"

"Huh?"

"Nothing. It's just something my mom used to say."

"Ok, I guess I'll call you later…"

"Yeah, call me later…you don't have to call me every day, though. Try to have some fun."

"Ok, bye, babe, talk to you soon."

"Bye, Billy, have fun!" Hannah hung up the phone. *Yeah, have fun…*Brad came into the kitchen and set down his bag.

"Hey, man, you forgot to get your bag out of the car."

"Yeah, I'll get it right now. I just got off the phone with my girlfriend. Something doesn't seem right."

"What do you mean? You think she's cheating on you?" *This is becoming redundant.*

"I don't think so…not yet, at least, and I want to trust her, but I don't know if I can. She could be with anyone if she wanted."

"Yeah, she could…" *Thanks, Brad; real helpful.* "What are you going to do about it though? You're here and she's there. Don't worry about it."

"It's easy for you to say."

"Maybe…look, let's go to Six Flags and you'll forget about her." *No, I won't.*

"All right, let's go, I guess it's better than feeling sorry for myself here." Brad and I spent the day at Magic Mountain and we did have a good time, but I was constantly thinking about the possibility of Hannah with another guy. It made me mad, but I hid it well. We spent the next two weeks splitting time between Magic Mountain and the beach. Time seemed to drag on. I called Hannah every couple of days, but didn't get to talk to her. Her brother always answered the phone and told me that she was with Jessica. At the end of the two weeks, Brad dropped me off at my house and decided not to stay. "Are you sure you don't want to stay?" I asked Brad as I grabbed my bag and got out of his car. "It's a long drive, man."

"No, it's cool, I need to get home," Brad said.

"All right, man, I'll give you a call next week sometime," I said.

"Good luck with your girlfriend."

"Thanks, see ya." Brad drove away and my mind raced as I pictured Hannah handing me more phone numbers. *I need to see her tonight.* I went upstairs and practically knocked my door down to get to the phone. I dialed her number and no one answered. *Ahh, what the fuck...*I hung up the phone and then dialed Aaron's number.

"Hello," Aaron said.

"Hey, man, I'm back."

"That's cool, you want to come by?"

"Yeah, I'll come by later. I need to get a hold of Hannah first. I tried calling her right now but no one answered."

"...shit, man, I have to tell you something." *I don't like the sound of this...* "Shit, Jessica made me promise not to say anything, but I saw Hannah hook up with some guy named Keith."

"What the fuck!"

"I guess he goes to Redwood. Jessica knows him."

"Where...when...where did you see her with him?"

"It was at the mall the other day. I met Jessica there and Hannah was with that dude. She was sitting on his lap at JC Penny."

"Did you say anything?"

"I said something to Jessica, but not to Hannah. I didn't think it was my place. Seriously, dude, I barely know her."

"Shit! I should have never left. That's all it was...she sat on his lap?"

"No, they were kissing before we left."

"And you just watched it happen?"

"Well, yeah, like I said, what was I supposed to do?"

"Shit...Well, thanks for telling me...Wait, did Hannah tell you not to tell me?"

"No, she didn't seem to care." *God Damn it.*

"Well, fuck me. All right, man, I'm gonna try to call her again, but I'll be over later."

"All right, man, I'll see you later."

"Later." I hung up the phone and then sat on the edge of my bed. My heart felt like it was sinking into my stomach. Tears started filling my eyes and rolling down my cheeks. *I fucking knew it.*

Later that night after getting home from Aaron's house, I worked up the nerve to call Hannah again. "Hello?"

"Is Hannah there?" I asked. It sounded like her mom.

"Yes, she is, hold on, is this Will?"

"Yeah, I just need to talk to her for a minute."

"Ok, hold on," her mom said. "Hannah, it's Will, make it fast."

"Hey, Billy, are you back from your vacation?"

"Yeah, I am...Is there something you wanna tell me?" *I felt as angry as I had ever felt in my life, but I didn't show it.*

"So, Aaron told you..."

"Told me what?" *I want to hear you say it.*

"That I hooked up with another guy while you were gone." *Nope I was wrong, I did not want to hear that shit!*

"Keith?"

"Yeah."

"Who the hell is Keith?" I could feel my voice raise a little bit as I was having a very difficult time containing my anger.

"He's a senior at Redwood. I met him at the mall and Jessica knew him from school."

"Wow, Hannah, you don't even sound like you're sorry. You cheated on me and you don't even care."

"I do care. I made a mistake. We just kissed. That's not cheating." *A mistake...not cheating...what planet?*

"So, you're not breaking up with me?"

"No, I love you; I just made a stupid mistake. I don't even like Keith."

"Then why would you..."

"I just really missed you. I don't know why I did it, but I did, and now it's over." *What the literal fuck, again. I think I'm going crazy.*

"Babe, I don't want to lose you...you're the best thing to ever happen to me. I told you that I shouldn't have gone away."

"You're not going to lose me...I thought I was doing the right thing by encouraging you to go away, but I was wrong. I was just lying to myself."

"I knew it. Why didn't you just trust me? I knew you didn't want me to go."

"Yeah, I know, I'm sorry."

"And we need to talk about this kissing thing...that is so cheating."

"Ok, so we never talked about that before...It won't happen again...so are we good, or are you just gonna be mad at me forever?"

"No, we're good; I couldn't stay mad at you. *You really shouldn't trust her...*

"I'll be honest with you from now on...I don't want you to leave me again."

"Thank you, was that so hard?"

"Actually, yes, yes it was," Hannah said and we both laughed.

"I'll be honest with you too...It pisses me off even thinking about you with another guy. And Keith...I guess if you didn't have sex with him or anything I'll get over it."

"I didn't have sex with Keith."

"All right, I won't mention him again."

"Thank you, Billy, I love you, you're so understanding." *More like Pussy-whipped.*

"I love you too, Hannah."

Chapter Fifteen

Showtime

M Y JUNIOR YEAR WENT really well. Hannah and I didn't
have a single argument and her parents seemed to be
warming up to the idea of us being together. They still didn't
allow her to go out at night, but they did let her hang out on
the weekends at the mall and local shows. Our band played some
of those local shows that were mostly at churches, which some
people thought was ironic being that our band name was Anarchy.
I didn't really care though. I was just happy to be playing shows.
Rob, Aaron, Nate, and I all became closer friends and a pretty
tight band. Rob opened things up musically and we started playing
some nu-metal and even some classics like 'Sweet Home Alabama.'
We also played every couple of weeks at school, which was more
like an extra practice for real shows. We got good enough that
we even got paid a couple of times when we played shows Friday
and Saturday nights. It wasn't a lot of money; maybe enough for
gas, but it was better than playing for free. I didn't like the fact
that Hannah was never at those shows, except for one time when
Jessica brought her. I guess her parents hadn't figured out that
when she spent the night at Jessica's house she would go out. I
never understood exactly why Hannah's parents trusted Jessica so
much, but I guess it was good that they did. Aaron and Jessica were
still together and seemed to have a pretty good relationship. Nate,
through my introduction, started dating Casey. Rob still couldn't

get a girlfriend. As far as I knew, he never even tried. It was as if the entire Jessica situation ruined all hope of him ever attempting to try again. Hannah and I ditched school every couple of weeks for some alone time, and despite that, my grades were really good. I was starting to think about college which I had never done before. At the end of the year, I decided to quit McDonalds and focus spending my summer with Hannah and on playing music with my band. I had saved up enough money for a few months. I figured that I would just get another job in the Fall. I called Brad the day after school ended to tell him that I couldn't go to Camarillo with him that summer. I made up an excuse about the band getting big and playing a summer tour. He didn't believe me and he was right not to because it wasn't true. I couldn't leave because I was worried about Hannah cheating on me again and I think he knew that. After I got off the phone with Brad, I fired up the Malibu and drove to the mall where everyone was meeting. I walked into the mall and saw Hannah, Jessica, and Aaron hanging out in the middle of the food court. I walked up and waved at Aaron and Jessica and hugged Hannah. "Hey, babe," I said.

"Hey, Billy," Hannah said and kissed me.

"I called Brad. He did not take the news well, but I think he understands."

"I'm sorry...It's my fault, isn't it?"

"No, I would rather be here with you than with Brad. It's as simple as that," I said. *And I kind of have to...*

"Brad's your old friend," Aaron said, "We're your new friends."

"Nah, at this point, you're old too." Everyone laughed. "Where's everyone else?"

"Rob's dad is supposed to drop him off," Aaron said.

"I still can't believe he doesn't want to get his license," I said.

"Yeah, that is weird," Aaron said. I looked a Jessica and she looked down and seemed quite uncomfortable at even the mention of Rob. We all had been hanging out all the time, but I could tell that Jessica still had a problem with Rob even though she didn't show it when he was around.

"What about Nate and Casey?"

"I talked to Casey before we left and her mom is dropping them off," Hannah said.

"Ok, cool, let's get some food," I said. "I want some pizza."

"Shouldn't we wait for everyone else to get here?" Hannah said.

"Yeah, I suppose..." I said and smiled." We all sat down at a table in the middle of the food court and waited. After about 20 minutes Nate and Casey joined us and Rob followed 10 minutes after that.

"Hey, what's up?" Rob said. "We have a show in Fresno tomorrow. A real show."

"Oh shit, how'd you pull that off?" I said.

"My dad knows a guy. Anyway, it pays 500 bucks. That's 125 a piece!"

"Dude, no fucking way," Nate said.

"Yeah, that's like a week working at McDonalds."

"It's legit. We just have to get there, play a couple of hours, and bank the cash."

"Wait, what's this place called?" I inquired.

"It's at Shakey's pizza."

"Ummm, I didn't know that a pizza place...Does our Shakey's pizza have bands play?" I said.

"Not sure, but my dad knows the owner of the one in Fresno," Rob said. *Whatever you say...* "So we just need a way to get there...and move our equipment. My dad can take the amps, but Nate's drums aren't going to fit..."

"Well, shit," Nate said. We all stood there dumbfounded as if someone had asked us to solve a complex equation.

"...I can borrow my grandpa's van," Aaron said. "I think he'll let me borrow it; he doesn't use it."

"Why didn't you say something earlier?" Rob said.

"I just thought of it," Aaron said.

"What kind of van is it?" Rob asked.

"It's one of those big white bank-robbing vans," Aaron said.

"It sounds perfect," I said.

"Yeah, it does...we need to get a practice in today. Let's get to Nate's house," Rob said.

"Ok, but can we eat first?" I said.

"Yeah, let's get some food, but we need to make it fast, I wanna put our set list together," Rob said.

"All right," I said. Hannah, Rob, and I went over to get pizza, Aaron and Jessica went to get Chinese, and Nate and Casey went for hot dogs. We all got our food and then met back up in the middle of the food court. "This is gonna be a great summer, guys," I said and took a bite of my pizza.

"Fucking right!" Nate said.

"Less talking, more eating," Rob said. *Yeah, still an asshole.* I put my hand on Hannah's leg.

"Babe, do you think you can come to the show tomorrow?"

"I don't know...If I stayed at Jessica's..." Hannah said while looking at Jessica. Everyone stopped eating at that moment and stared at Jessica. "Do you think your parents will let you go?"

"I can ask them, but probably...yeah, they'll let me go. We just have to hope that my parents don't tell your parents," Jessica said.

"Yeah, my parents would never let me go if they knew...I wish my parents were cool like everyone else's parents. I always have to lie to them."

"And I can't tell them not to tell your parents...that would make them suspicious."

"That's true, and I want to go see them play, so, yeah," Hannah said and softly placed her hand on top of mine and we intertwined fingers.

"It's all right, babe, your parents have been really cool lately. Why would they even ask?"

"Yeah, Will's right," Jessica said.

"So, we're going to Fresno tomorrow?" Hannah asked.

"Yeah, I just have to ask my parents..."

"Aaron, ask your grandpa if we can use his van after we finish lunch," Rob interjected over Jessica. *Real smooth, Rob.*

"Oh, for sure, but he's cool. He won't care if I want to take the van," Aaron said while Rob nodded in agreement. We all finished our food and then walked out to the parking garage. Because I had the bigger car, Rob, Casey, and Nate rode with Hannah and I. Jessica left her car at the garage and rode with Aaron. We headed out of the mall parking lot and towards Nate's house. Aaron turned in the other direction towards his grandpa's house.

The next day, I drove over to Aaron's house around 9. He had indeed procured his grandpa's van and it was parked outside of his house when I pulled up. It was a big, white van. It looked exactly like one of those bank-robbing vans from the movies, just like Aaron said. Aaron met me outside and opened up the back doors. "Oh shit, man, there's no seats!" I said in astonishment.

"Yeah, the good thing is we can easily fit all of our equipment in there. The bad thing is two of you are going to be sitting on the floor," Aaron said. *Fuck that, not me.*

"Jessica's coming right?"

"Yeah, she's taking her mom's car."

"Well, shit, I guess Rob and Nate could ride with her and Hannah."

"Yeah, that works. You ride with me and the rest will go with Jessica."

"You think she'll be cool with that?"

"Yeah, I guess. It's not like she's gonna say no..."

"All right, call her to make sure though. We have to be at Nate's house to load up at 10." Aaron went back inside of his house to call Jessica. I waited outside and looked the van over. *The Band Van...*Aaron came back outside and tossed the keys to the van in the air and then caught them.

"We're good," Aaron said. "They're gonna meet us at Nate's, let's roll." We got to Nate's well before 10. Rob was already there and we loaded the van up right away. We started with the drums and then loaded in the amps and guitars. Finally, we put the PA system in the back.

"Do we even need the PA system?" I said. "Doesn't Shakey's have their own system for us to play through?"

"It's better to have something and not need it than not have something and then need it," Rob reasoned.

"Very philosophical of you, Rob," I said. "I guess it makes sense though."

"I'm always right; I don't know why you keep forgetting that," Rob said. *Some things never change...*

"Sure, Rob, I'm not gonna argue with you about it," I said. Nate and Aaron just looked on, but didn't say anything.

"Good, there's no argument," Rob reiterated. *Insufferable.* Jessica pulled up to Nate's driveway in her grey Buick. Hannah got out of the car and ran up to me and gave me a big hug. She pulled back away from me and held my hand.

"Hey, Billy, can I talk to you?" *You are talking to me.*

"Sure, what's up?" Hannah led me away from everyone down the street to the point that no one could overhear us.

"Do you think it's a good idea for Rob to be in a car with Jessica for an hour?"

"I don't know...I guess so. He has to be over it, right?"

"Why not have Rob ride with Aaron and you can come with us?"

"Aaron's my best friend..."

"And I'm your girlfriend, and I think it would be best if..." Jessica walked up to us and interjected.

"So..."

"He wants to ride with Aaron."

"Jessica, just take one for the team. Rob's not gonna bother you."

"Oh, fine, but you're gonna owe me. Aaron too..."

"You got it. I'll be sure Aaron makes it up to you," I said.

"Are you sure about this?" Hannah stared at Jessica. "Because you told me that..."

"It's fine. I just hope he doesn't try to talk to me," Jessica responded.

"Ok, if you're sure," Hannah said.

"He knows you're with Aaron; he's not gonna talk to you. He'll probably just look out the window the whole time," I said.

"Yeah, ok, I'm good; sorry I made a big deal out of this," Jessica said.

"No worries, let's roll out," I said. We walked back over to Aaron, Nate, and Rob.

"Are we ready to go?" Aaron said.

"Yeah, what's the hold up?" Rob said.

"It's nothing...Just Hannah worried about her parents," I said.

"Yeah, I don't know what would happen if I got caught."

"That's not gonna happen, right Jessica?" I said.

"Ummm, yeah, my parents aren't gonna say anything, they're not like Hannah's parents."

"All right, let's go. Aaron, to the band van!" I hugged Hannah and then walked over to the passenger side of the van and got inside. Aaron got inside and started the van. Rob came over to the window.

"Follow us. I know where it is so I'll give Jessica directions," Rob said. *I guess he'll be talking to her after all, well shit.*

"Ok," Aaron replied. Rob got into the Buick and sat behind Jessica. *I hope he doesn't say something stupid.* Aaron followed Jessica out to the 198 and then to the 99 North. We were on our way to Fresno and our first real show.

It took 45 minutes to get to Shakey's. It was close to downtown Fresno in a pretty sketchy neighborhood. Aaron followed Jessica onto an alley to get to the back entrance of Shakey's. Homeless people lined the alley and tents were set up everywhere. *We're gonna park back here? This doesn't seem like a good idea.* "Hey, man," I said to Aaron. "This is super sketch."

"Yeah, seriously, I think that guy over there is taking a shit against the fence." Aaron pointed toward a thick area of tents, stopped the van, and parked next to Jessica's Buick.

"That's just nasty," I said while shaking my head. I got out of the van and walked over to Hannah. "How'd it go?" I whispered.

"Good, he didn't say anything to Jessica," Hannah whispered back. Aaron opened the back of the van and we all grabbed a piece of equipment and took it into the restaurant. We were greeted at the back door by a large man who identified himself as the owner.

"I'm Tyrone," the man said, "but you can call me Ty." Rob stepped up and said,

"I'm Rob and this is my band, Anarchy."

"Yeah, your dad and I go way back...Anyway, let's get your equipment inside, you're going on at 2." Tyrone led us into the back of the restaurant and we brought all of the equipment in piece by piece. After we got everything inside, we set it all up in one of the corners. There weren't any people inside yet, but we could see a line forming outside.

"Hey, man, there are a lot of people outside," I said to Nate while helping him set up his drums. Nate looked out toward the street.

"Shit, that is a lot of people. It's not even a night show." Rob brought in a couple of cymbals and set them down.

"Hey, Rob, did you tell people about this show?" I said.

"Yeah, I told a few people," Rob said. I pointed outside toward the street and the crowd that was becoming more robust by the second.

"That's more than a few people," I said.

"That's a good thing, right?"

"I guess so, but these people have never heard us before. What if they don't like us?"

"Well, they're paying to see us...Don't mess up!" Rob said. *Really, that's all you've got, don't mess up? Some things never change...Or some people...Is that how it goes?*

"Right, I'll keep that in mind." Tyrone came back around a few minutes later.

"Do you guys need anything? We're gonna have you start setting up pretty soon."

"Nah, we're good," Rob said.

"Hey, Ty, it's Ty, right?" I said.

"Yeah, man, what's up?"

"Why are there so many people outside...I mean, it's cool and all, but we're just a local band...How do these people even know who we are?" Ty laughed.

"We promoted you as a Nirvana cover band. People love Nirvana." *God dammit...Rob!* Ty walked away and I turned to Rob and shook my head.

"What!?" Rob said indignantly.

"Rob, we're not a Nirvana cover band. We write our own songs now," I said.

"Do you think that all these people came to listen to your weak ass songs...Tread safe!? Yeah right," Rob said. "The people want Nirvana and that's what we're going to give them." *Fucking asshole...*

"So that's how you booked this show...Using Nirvana to do it?"

"Whatever it takes," Rob said. "Stop whining and start moving shit."

"I'm sure Kurt Cobain would have loved this..."

"We're never going to know because he fucking blew his head off." *Damn...*

"I have a feeling he wouldn't have condoned this..."

"Don't be such a bitch. We're gonna play this set list." Rob handed me a piece of paper with a list of 15 Nirvana songs. "we're gonna get paid, and that's it." *So, it's all about the money...*

"Fine, whatever, Rob," I said and walked away. I grabbed my guitar and plugged it into my amp. I turned the volume down and started tuning it up. I looked at the list that Rob gave me. *Mostly*

E standard all the way through; a couple of half-steps and a drop D.
Well, that's not too bad. Ty came backstage again and said,

"All right, guys, we're ready for you to move everything on stage." I moved my guitar and amp to the stage and then went back to help Nate move some of his drums.

"Have you seen Hannah?" I asked.

"Yeah, she got a seat with Jessica," Nate said and pointed out across the restaurant. "I think they we're going to get some food or something."

"Shit, I wasn't even paying attention. I was too busy arguing with Rob," I said. Aaron came over to help with the drums too. "Hey, man, did you know that we we're playing an all-Nirvana set?"

"Nope, but it is Rob, so, yeah," Aaron said.

"Shit, what's that word where you're doing something obvious and totally expected?" Nate asked.

"Cliché?" I said.

"Yeah, this is totally cliché," Nate said. I laughed.

"I guess it is...and I should have expected it."

"As long as he's singing, I guess he controls what we play," Aaron said. *Hmmmm. Aaron's right...* "And let's be real, he does sound exactly like Cobain."

"Yeah, he does...Can't argue with that...I have an idea," I said. I looked around to see where Rob was. I could see that he was on stage setting up the PA system. "Let's play Tread Safe..." I glanced down at the set list again. "...right after 'About a Girl.' I'll just start playing it and Rob will have to go along with it. What's he going to do?"

"Not sing it," Aaron said.

"Yeah, he'll be pissed. He's stubborn as hell. He'll probably just stand there," Nate added.

"Fine, then I'll sing it," I said. Nate and Aaron laughed.

"Dude, you can't sing for shit," Nate said.

"And Rob knows that too, so he'll be forced to sing it to save face."

"Save what?" Nate said.

"Save face...You know...to avoid embarrassment."

"That's a stupid saying."

"Yeah, it doesn't even make sense," Aaron said.

"I learned it in English class so, yeah, it does."

"I don't remember that," Aaron said.

"I'm not making it up; I don't think I could make it up."

"That's true, who would make that up?" Nate reasoned.

"All right, damn, let's get back on topic here, shit...So do you guys have my back? Tread Safe after 'About a Girl?'"

"Yeah, sure, why not?"

"Yeah, I can't wait to see the look on Rob's face," Aaron said.

"Perfect. All right, let's finish setting up," I said. We grabbed the floor toms and the cymbals and placed them on the stage. I looked into the seating area and saw Hannah and Jessica sitting at a table eating some pizza. Ty asked us to do one song for a sound check. Rob chose 'Teen Spirit,' and we played through it. We sounded pretty good and Ty must have agreed because he gave us the 'thumbs up' and then walked to the front of the restaurant. He opened the doors and started letting people in. There must have been at least a hundred people. They all streamed in and most of them crowded in around the makeshift stage and sat in the booths closest to us. Every other person was wearing a Nirvana shirt. *Maybe Rob was right. But, who cares if he's right? I don't want to just be a cover band.*

"Will...WILL!" I heard someone screaming at me while strumming away on my guitar. I looked out at the crowd. *Oh shit, what is Vicki doing here? And, oh shit, Angela, too?* I waved at them and then looked over at Hannah and saw that she wasn't paying attention. She was laughing at something Jessica must have said. *Good, maybe they won't even see each other. Maybe it's all cool...shit, I don't even know.* Everyone got settled in to the restaurant. Some people ordered pizza and some people were just hanging out. Interestingly, most of the people were seemingly there just to see us play. *This is crazy.* We had played in front of more people before at school, but because that was a captive audience, it didn't really count, at least not to me. But these people wanted to see us play. They paid to see us play. After a few minutes of us doing our final tuning, Rob stepped up to the Mic and said,

"Thanks for coming out, we're Anarchy." *We're Nirvana...* Rob pointed at me and I started playing 'Teen Spirit.' The crowd of people roared to life. People were screaming 'yeah,' and 'fuck yeah,' and I heard my name too. *That was probably Vicki again.* I could hear everyone. They were all so close. We continued playing through the set list and finally, after a few songs in, we were playing 'About a Girl.' Rob started playing the solo and I looked out into the audience and caught Hannah's eyes. She smiled at me and I could feel that she really loved me. It was a pure, innocent smile. It was as if she was proud to be my girlfriend, something that I continued to have trouble believing. *She is so beautiful. It's almost time for Tread Safe...I hope Rob's not too pissed...nah, I don't care.* My attention was diverted to the front of the restaurant where I saw Hannah's dad bruising his way through the crowd. Jessica's dad followed. *Son of a bitch! Shit!* I tried my best to keep my concentration, but my playing got sloppy as we were closing out 'About a Girl.' Hannah's dad approached Hannah and I could see him yelling and pointing his finger at her angrily. I could tell that one of the things that he said emphatically was 'Now!' Hannah and Jessica got up from the booth and they both waved at us. Hannah's dad turned and pointed his finger directly at me. His gaze pierced right through me as I played the final E chord of the song. I stepped up to the mic and said, "I love you, Hannah." Hannah smiled and mouthed the words 'I love you.' Hannah's dad snarled at me and then turned around. They all left out the front door of the restaurant. The crowd watched them leave and then turned around back to the band. *Shit.* I looked over at Nate and he raised his eyebrows at me as if to confirm my mini-insurrection against Rob, but without Hannah there, I really wasn't feeling it. I shook my head and waved my hand in front of my throat in the classic 'kill' motion. Rob walked over to me and said,

"Hey, man, are you all right? I saw what happened with Hannah..."

"I'm fine," I interjected. "Let's finish this show."

"All right, cool." Rob walked back over to his mic and then started playing 'Son of a Gun.' Nate came in and we were back at it. The crowd came back to life and started singing along. They sung the chorus over and over again, almost overpowering Rob. I wasn't feeling it at all though. I didn't sing the backing vocals like I usually did. *They got this.* I couldn't really focus on playing when I knew that Hannah was in serious trouble. I never saw her dad look that pissed off. I needed to know what was going on, but it wasn't like I could just stop playing. I tried my best to forget about Hannah and did manage to play through, mostly because of muscle memory, but my priorities were elsewhere. After the final chord of 'Aneurysm' Rob simply said, "thanks," and put his guitar down. The crowd cheered once again and then individual people came up to us and thanked us for a great show. I pretended to be interested in what they had to say. I appreciated the compliments but I was more concerned about getting home and back to Hannah. As the crowd started thinning out, we began packing up our equipment. Vicki walked up to me and tapped me on the shoulder while I was putting away my foot pedals.

"Hey, Will, that was a really great show...I mean, you were great."

"Thanks, Vicki," I said with only a slight glance up at her.

"I'm sorry about Hannah, that was kind of embarrassing..."

"Look, Vicki, don't talk about Hannah."

"It's just, that must have sucked...you know, to see your girlfriend have to leave in the middle..."

"Just stop! You don't know how I feel, and I already told you, don't even say her name."

"Wow, fine, I thought I was being nice." ...*The fuck?*

"...I appreciate your concern," *No I don't,* "but, I'll be...we'll be fine."

"Ok, well, if you need to talk, you have my number." *Unfortunately.*

"Yep, I'll see you around then," I said. *Please go away.*

"Ok, umm, I was wondering...do you guys have any other shows coming up?"

"Vicki!" I said, raising my voice.

"Ok, ok, I can take a hint." ...*Can you?* Angela walked up to us with a slice of pizza in her hand.

"Hey, Will, great show!"

"Thanks, Angela. So, how's Chris?"

"Good. He's doing something with his church today or he would have been here." *Is that right...?* Angela looked over at Vicki and took a bite of the pizza. "Are you ready to go?"

"Yeah, I guess so," Vicki said.

"Ok, see you guys later."

"Bye," Angela said.

"Bye, Will," Vicki said and smiled as they both walked back across the restaurant. *Thank God.* I finished packing up my equipment and then helped Nate with his drums. We packed everything in the van including Rob and Nate who were now without a ride home. They had to sit on the floor. No seats. No seatbelts. They held on to some of the drums to stabilize themselves. *This is hilarious.* I normally would have been laughing out loud and making a fool out of myself about their predicament, but not that time. I was as stoic as ever even though it was objectively funny. I heard them sliding around with the equipment in the back of the van as we merged onto the 99 south...and nothing. I couldn't get the vision of Hannah's burly-ass dad out of my head. *What an asshole. Why can't he just let her be?*

"Hey, Rob, when are we getting paid," Aaron said.

"Tyrone wrote us a check, so I'll have to cash it. I'll get you guys your money on Monday."

"Ok, cool," Aaron said.

"Cool," Nate said. I wasn't thinking about the money at all but added,

"That'll work." The ride back to Visalia only took 40 minutes. It went by quick as I listened to the guys make small talk about the show. We pulled up to Nate's house and I was the first to jump out of the van. "Hey, man, can I use your phone?"

"Yeah, you wanna help me up off the floor of this van first?"

"Yeah, sorry, that's my bad." I grabbed Nate's hand and then Rob's and helped them both out of the van. Nate walked to his front door and unlocked it. I didn't want to seem too anxious but I practically ran over to the phone. I dialed Hannah's number and Hannah's dad picked up.

"Hello?"

"Is Hannah there?" I said. I heard a click. *That son of a bitch hung up on me!* I dialed her number again and the same thing happened. *This is not going to work. I have to go over there. Shit.*

"Hey, man, what happened?" Nate said.

"Her dad hung up on me."

"Shit, man, what are you going to do? He looked pissed at the show."

"...I'm gonna go over there and tell him how it is." Nate's eyes widened and his jaw slacked.

"Dude, are you on a suicide mission? You might want to wait for him to calm down."

"I have to make sure Hannah's all right." Aaron and Rob came into the kitchen and Nate glanced towards them.

"Dudes, Will's gonna do some stupid shit," Nate said. Aaron looked at me sternly.

"Let me guess, you're gonna go over to Hannah's house..." He said.

"You're gonna get dead. Her dad's gonna kill you," Rob added.

"Whatever. I have to end this nonsense now. Tiptoeing around her dad; this shit has to end."

"Look, man, we all saw him at the show. Maybe you should just break up with her," Rob said.

"What did you just say!?"

"Is she really worth all of this?" Rob said. *Yes, yes, and what the fuck?*

"You don't get it, Rob. You, especially, wouldn't understand," I said.

"Whatever." I turned to Aaron.

"Hey, man, I need to go."

"All right, let's go, but we should probably drop Rob off first since he's closer." *Shit, I need to get over there yesterday.*

"All right, later, Nate," I said.

"Good luck, man," Nate replied. Aaron, Rob, and I got in the van and we drove to Rob's house. We dropped him off and helped him unload his equipment.

"Call me later if you're still alive," Rob said.

"Sure," I said. *Asshole.* Aaron drove us back to his house and said,

"Maybe Rob's right, man...at least let me go with you." *Has everyone lost their mind? I know what I have to do.*

"Thanks, but I have to stand up to him alone."

"I just thought he'd be less likely to kill you if you..."

"...He's not going to do anything to me. I'm 17...Actually, I think I'm going to remind him of that fact."

"You think that's going to work? He doesn't look like the kind of guy that would mind going to jail..." *Shit...*

"I have to risk it." Aaron didn't say anything else for the rest of the drive and I looked out the window and watched the entire world flash by. When we got to Aaron's house, I jumped out of the van and ran over to the Malibu. I fumbled around with my keys and eventually opened the door and quickly fired it up. I revved the engine up in an attempt to warm it up faster, but I still had to wait for the idle to settle. Aaron came over to the passenger side and I rolled down the window.

"Hey, don't do anything stupid."

"I'll be fine, man, I'll call you later."

"All right, later," Aaron said and walked back towards the van. I put my car into gear and sped away. My mind blanked out during that drive. I was angry, maybe as angry as I'd ever been. It only took about 10 minutes to get to Hannah's house. I drove around the cul-de-sac so that my car was at the optimum position for a quick getaway. I parked across the street from her house and got out of my car. I didn't hesitate. I walked across the street and noticed that the Isuzu Trooper and the old truck were both parked in the driveway. I walked across their lawn and knocked on their door repeatedly until Hannah's dad opened it. He stared at me with piercing precision. His body blocked the entire doorway and he stood in it as if he were some sort of gatekeeper.

"I want to see Hannah," I said. I watched Hannah walk up behind her dad and look at me. She looked as upset as the last time I stood in front of her dad. She must have been crying for some time before I got there. Her mascara had run down her cheeks and smeared into a dirty smudge. I felt helpless, but that helplessness quickly turned to anger. My eyes moved from Hannah to her dad. "You can't keep her locked up like this," I said.

"I can do whatever I want. She's my daughter and she's my responsibility." I looked back over at Hannah as tears once again welled up in her eyes and slowly streamed down her face.

"Yeah, you're a real hero, look at what you're doing to her." I noticed that Hannah's dad was making a fist with his right hand. I could see him turning red and his arm began shaking.

"STAY AWAY FROM MY DAUGHTERRRRR!" He screamed at me. I was startled, but quickly regained my composure.

"What are you going to do old man? I'm 17. What are you going to do, hit me?" I could hear Hannah getting more upset and her tears became more prominent. Her dad stood in the doorway shaking his fist at his side as if he had Parkinson's disease. His face turned to a deep red color. "Go ahead, hit me; I'd love to see you locked up." Hannah's dad didn't say anything. He let out a growl more reminiscent of a bear than a human and quickly slammed the door. *Shit. What am I going to do now?*

Chapter Sixteen

Revelation

T HE GIRL...IT WAS ALWAYS about a girl. This girl was
different though...I felt Hannah slipping away from me. I
felt totally helpless. I sat at the edge of my bed and stared out the
window. It was the Sunday before the first day of my senior year
and even though I was looking forward to seeing Hannah again,
I didn't know what to expect. I didn't know if it was going to be
the same between us. I hadn't seen her since the night after her dad
slammed the door in my face. That summer went by excruciatingly
slow. When I called her, I got the message, 'this number has been
disconnected, please check the number you dialed and try again.'
In spite of that message, I tried every day. I also spent a lot of time
simply waiting for her to call. It didn't happen. *What in the hell
happened that night?*

I held Hannah's hand as we slowly crossed Court Street and
headed to Whitendale Park. We walked around the entire school to
avoid jumping the fence and then sat on adjacent swings. Hannah
looked over at me and grabbed my hand. "Oh, Billy, my dad...well,
I'm glad he hasn't gotten wise to me sneaking out."

"Yeah, I know...What happened, Hannah? Why was he even there?"

"My grandma's in the hospital...she's really sick."

"That sucks, babe, I'm sorry."

"It's ok...So I don't know what to do...I feel like I'm in prison. FUCK! I just want to scream. Why do they have to be so rejected?" *Rejected...Retarded?*

"I don't know...things have to get better though. You'll be 18 soon enough and then they'll have nothing..."

"I love you; I will always love you," Hannah interjected. "That seems so far away..."

"A year and a half."

"Do you think we'll be together forever?"

"We love each other...that's all that matters," I said assuredly.

"What if love isn't enough?"

"Then we fight for it."

"I just want to die. My life is shit. I can't handle..."

"Hannah, it's going to be fine. Where's the girl I fell in love with? That doesn't sound like her." I moved my hand up to Hannah's face and gently wrapped my fingers around the base of her neck. A slight smile appeared on her face.

"You always say the right thing, Billy, I should go back; I have a bad feeling."

"Ok, don't worry, babe, we're going to figure this out," I said and walked Hannah back to her house. I hugged and kissed her goodbye. Before letting her go I said, "I'll call you tomorrow...everything's going to be fine."

"Thanks, Billy...I feel a little better now," Hannah said and then slowly crept around the side of her house and into the shadows.

• • • ● ●• ● ● • •

The first day of my senior year didn't feel special. It didn't feel like anything. The only thing I cared about was finding Hannah. I parked my car and immediately headed over to the front of the band room where everyone hung out. Aaron and Nate were there but I didn't see Hannah. "Hey, guys," I said, "Have you seen Hannah?"

"Nah, but we just got here, so..." Aaron said.

"Shit, I've got to find Hannah. I think something happened."

"Like what?" Nate said.

"I don't...I'm not sure. Something doesn't feel right."

"All right, man, go find her," Nate said.

"Ok, I'll catch you later," I said and quickly made my way through the quad. I walked around campus looking around nervously until I finally spotted Casey. "Casey...CASEY!" I yelled and got her attention. "Have you seen Hannah?"

"Yeah, she was talking to Rob over by the gym." *Rob...Huh?*

"Ok, thanks, Casey, see ya."

"Bye." I walked as fast as I could without looking like a complete maniac. It was about 7:45 in the morning so it would look a little out of place for someone to be running through campus. *There she is, thank God.*

"Babe, there you are. What are you guys doing over here?"

"I don't know...we were just talking," Hannah said.

"But we always meet in front of the band room..."

"Yeah, we were just headed over there..." Rob interjected. *Ok.*

"Anyway, what happened this summer, Hannah, did your parents change your number?"

"Yeah, they did, and they kept the phone in their room. I'm sorry I couldn't call you. They kept me on lockdown as usual."

"No worries, it's not your fault. I'm just glad you're here. I thought for sure they would make you change schools."

"They were going to, but they always threaten that."

"Well, I'm gonna go to class; later," Rob said.

"Bye, Rob," Hannah said.

"Yeah, later," I added. Rob walked away and into the crowd of students diligently trying to find their classes. "Babe, you wanna get out of here?"

"You mean you want to ditch on the first day of school?"

"Yeah, who cares? I haven't seen you in forever. I think we need some alone time."

"That's sweet, but we can't miss the first day...maybe some other time..." *What the hell is going on here?*

"Ok, school it is then...How about Friday?"

"I don't know..."

"Come on, babe, I really need to see you."

"Ok, Friday," Hannah said. "We should get to class...don't you think?"

"Ummm, yeah, sure, I'll walk you. What do you have first period?"

"Math, but I'm fine, I'll walk myself." *What is going on? Who are you?*

"Since when did you not want me to walk you to class?"

"Since I'm not a kid anymore...I don't need an escort."

"Well, shit...so you were a kid last year?"

"NO! I mean...you know what I mean." *The hell I do.*

"What is wrong with you today?"

"Nothing, I'm going to class." Hannah turned around and walked away from me.

"See you at lunch," I said. Hannah didn't turn around or respond to me. *I'll take that as a yes? What the hell? Did we just have our first fight? What the hell is happening?* I walked over to the band room to find Nate and Aaron still hanging out. "I'm glad you guys are still here. I found Hannah and Rob...Hannah's acting really weird...like she's mad at me; she's never acted like that before."

"I don't know, man, maybe she's on her period or something," Nate said.

"...I'm not sure," I said. *I should know this stuff.*

"What was she doing with Rob?" I was wondering where he was," Aaron said.

"They were just talking, I guess."

"Why weren't they talking over here?"

"Yeah, they don't like us anymore or what?" Nate added.

"Shit, I don't know. Something isn't right though. Anyway, I'm going to talk to her at lunch and see what her problem is." The bell rang and we all went to our first period class. The morning classes all seemed to blend together. The teachers all did their usual first day syllabus lecture and all I could think about was Hannah. I had a feeling of dread. I wanted to talk to her to figure out what was going on and at the same time I was afraid that she was going to break up with me. I couldn't understand what had happened that would cause her to change so much. I didn't want to lose her. I couldn't lose her. I had to make things right. When the bell rang for lunch, I rushed out to the front of the band room and Hannah was there waiting for me. She did not look happy. There was a look on her face of what I can only describe as indifference. I walked up to her and gave her a hug, but she only haphazardly returned my affection. "Babe, what's wrong?"

"Nothing, I'm just having a bad day," Hannah said. *Yeah, no shit.*

"Did you have another fight with your dad or something?"

"...that night, the last night we met up this summer, my parents caught me sneaking back in my room...they were there waiting for me."

"Oh...shit."

"Yeah, so, I lost all of my phone privileges and you won't believe this...they took my bedroom door! I have zero privacy..."

"I'm sorry, Hannah, I know it's hard, but we'll get through this. I love you."

"I love you too, but I don't know if it's worth it anymore." A cold-chill spread throughout my body and I felt my heart sink deep into my bowels. I knew exactly where this was going. "And I was thinking...you're going to go off to college next year, and I'm going to be here all alone and..."

"No, you're not," I quickly interrupted. "You have friends here and I'm probably just going to go to Fresno State...so I can commute. I'm not going anywhere."

"I don't know...do you really think we'll be together forever?"

"Yes...you said it yourself...we were meant for each other. You said it...we were meant to be together. I believe that..."

"I don't know what I believe anymore." *That's all bad. What am I supposed to say? I don't want to lose her.*

"I love you," I said and slowly held Hannah's hand. "Let's get out of here. Let's go back to my house. I'll prove it to you." Hannah looked around and behind herself and then back at me. She gave me a strange, quizzical look and then reached for my hand.

"Yeah, let's go," she said. *Oh, thank God.* Holding hands, Hannah and I headed to the student parking lot and got in the Malibu.

When we got to my house, I didn't waste a lot of time. *I can't lose her...I just can't lose her.* I parked the Malibu sideways and then practically pushed Hannah upstairs and through my front door. I kicked the door shut and the force reverberated through the front windows. Without saying a word, I grabbed Hannah close to me and unbuttoned her jeans. I pulled them off with her panties in one swift motion. Hannah started laughing. "What's so funny?" I said.

"You forgot my shoes." I smiled.

"It seems I did..." I pulled the laces and then slipped her shoes off. "You can keep your socks," I said decisively.

"Oh, thanks," Hannah said. "I was really worried about losing those..." *Smartass.* I led Hannah over to the couch and lay down next to her. The sex was good but it seemed to be over before it even started. *Something just doesn't feel right.* I sat up on the couch and looked over at Hannah's half-naked body. Hannah looked back at me with the same quizzical look that she gave me at school.

"That's funny...I remember when we started with the top and worked our way down," I said. Hannah looked down at her perfectly manicured body. "Now we just go straight for the bottom."

"You mean you go straight for the bottom."

"Yeah, straight to the point, I guess."

"I have to tell you something."

"What's that?"

"I'm tired of sneaking around...I'm tired of my parents' shit. I'm just tired; mentally, emotionally...I'm just tired of it."

"I know...it's going to get better though...like when you get your license. I feel like we've had this conversation before."

"We have, and that's what I'm saying." Hannah sat up and then pulled her panties and jeans back on. "Nothing seems to change; it's not getting any better."

"I'm sorry...what can I do?"

"Nothing...there's nothing that you can do. You should take me back to school."

"Really? No second round?"

"No, I need to go back. I think I can get away with one period, but not two." *You never cared before. What's going on with her?*

"All right, I'll take you back to school." We got back in the Malibu and drove to school like nothing had even happened.

The next day at school, I saw Hannah sitting on a bench outside of the band room where we normally met up every day. I could see that she was upset and that she had been crying. *For fucks sake, what now?* "Hey, babe, what's wrong?"

"I'm in deep shit...My dad..." Hannah started crying uncontrollably.

"It's ok, I'm right here," I said and sat down next to her. I put my arm around her and said, "What happened?" *Is there ever a day when something doesn't happen? Wait, no, the answer is no. Stupid question.*

"Yesterday, my dad came to pick me up after lunch...My grandma died..."

"Oh shit, I'm so sorry Hannah." *Oh shit...*

"I wasn't here. They know everything now...my parents...my dad said he's gonna get a restraining order against you."

"Wait, for what? I didn't do anything."

"He said when you turn 18...he's gonna call the police...something about statutory rape." *The fuck!?*

"How does he even know that we're having sex?"

"He's not stupid, Billy."

"Well, shit. How does he know I'm turning 18?"

"That's my fault...I told them a long time ago." *Hannah, what the fuck?*

"Why would you do that?"

"I wasn't thinking about it then." Hannah's crying became even more intense. "I was so happy about the Libra and Aquarius thing...I just let it slip. I'm so sorry, Billy."

"This is not good..." *Wow, the understatement of my life.*

"I know...I don't know what to do. I'm scared."

"You're scared? Your dad wants to ruin my life with a bullshit rape charge."

"Statutory rape, and yeah, I know it's stupid."

"What's the difference?"

"I guess it means I'm too young to consent to sex." *For the love of all that is holy...*

"You're not even that much younger than me...and they can't prove anything."

"I don't think they have to...my dad..."

"Fuck your dad!"

"Billy, I know, but I'm worried about you."

"I've never been scared of your dad."

"This is serious, Billy!" *Yeah, I know, shit...I can't believe this is happening.*

"After all we've been through...What does he want from me?" Hannah paused for a few seconds and then said, "He doesn't want us to be together anymore."

"Well, no shit, what's new?"

"No, if we don't break up, he's going to call the police. I love you, Billy; I don't want to see anything bad happen to you." *Fuck.*

"So that's it then?"

"I don't know what to say. I don't want it to be over between us but we can't really be together if you're in jail." *Yeah, I don't think I would fare very well in jail.*

"This is such bullshit."

"I guess love isn't enough...The whole world seems to be against us."

"Yeah, it's never been easy."

"I'll always love you, Billy, forever...maybe; hopefully, we can be happy together one day...

"Like when you're 18?"

"Yeah...I'm sorry things had to suck out, but what else can we do?"

"I don't know, I guess you're right..." The bell rang and I watched as everyone around me moved in slow motion. It felt surreal, like none of it was actually happening. I felt like I was in a dream.

"Well, I've got to get to class...I guess I'll see you later," Hannah said and gave me a hug. I didn't want to believe it but I felt like that was the last time I was going to ever feel her that close to me again. An overwhelming sense of sadness came over me but I didn't want her to see me cry. *Don't be a pussy, Pussy!*

"Yeah," I responded and walked away from her. I didn't feel like going to class so I started walking back to the parking lot. *This can't be it. It can't be over. I can't lose her. Wait, maybe there's still a chance.* I stopped and turned around. Hannah was walking away and I watched as her hips flowed seamlessly from side to side. I yelled out, "I LOVE YOU, HANNAH!" Hannah turned around and smiled. She mouthed 'I love you too' and quickly turned around and continued walking to her class. *Shit!* I walked to the parking lot and got in my car. *This is not happening.*

When I got home, I sat on the edge of my bed and cried like I had never cried before. It was an uncontrollable kind of crying. It was the kind of crying where I could hardly get enough air into my lungs to breathe. *I will never find anyone as good as her...It's not possible. She's perfect.* As my crying subsided, I heard the front door open and quickly tried to get myself together. Larry walked in and said, "Hey, bro, why aren't you at school?"

"Why aren't you at work?"

"...Have you been crying? Yeah, you've been crying..." *Shit, is it that obvious?*

"No...just bad allergies," I reasoned. Larry laughed.

"Yeah, right, sure, so what happened?" Larry sat down next to me with a smirk on his face as if to say he was calling me on my bullshit.

"...My girlfriend broke up with me...or I broke up with her...or she convinced me to break up with her...I don't even know, but I guess we're not together anymore."

"That sucks, so why did she...or you break up with her?"

"You know how her dad hates me?"

"Yeah, I remember you saying something..."

"Well, she told me that when I turn 18 her dad was going to have me locked up for statutory rape."

"Damn, that does suck, bro."

"So, I guess we had to break up."

"Yeah, it's not worth it. No worries though, there are other girls. It's no reason to cry."

"You don't get it. I'll never get another girl like her. She's perfect."

"Damn, bro, I didn't know you had oneitis."

"What the hell is oneitis?"

"It's where you think there's only one girl for you in the world...get it? One 'itis;' like it's a disease." Larry laughed again.

"I'm glad you think this is funny."

"Trust me, you'll get over her." *No, I won't.* "And the best way to do that is to move on to the next one."

"I don't want anyone else."

"You need to trust something else too...you may not want to hear this..." *I don't want to hear any of this.* "She's gonna move on to someone else. She probably already has."

"What!? You're crazy." I stood up and walked to the other side of the room. "We just broke up. That doesn't make any sense."

"Just because you just broke up doesn't mean she wasn't planning this for a long time...girls always have a backup plan." *Wait...Hannah...No, no way!*

"Wait, are you saying that she's been cheating on me?" *Besides Keith?*

"I don't know. I'm telling you though, they always have a plan. Take it to the bank."

"Just because you got screwed over doesn't mean I did. Hannah's not like that..."

"They're all like that, bro, all of them. They're all the same and none of them are any different." *Wow, redundant much?* "At the end of the day, they're all going to do what's best for them, and you need to do the same."

"You're wrong about her, Larry, if it weren't for her dad..."

"You'll see, bro, you'll see for yourself. There's nothing I can tell you...I know that...Experience is the best teacher."

"Sure...now you're a prophet?"

"All right, bro, I'm gonna leave you alone. I can tell you're not in the mood for advice." *Really, it took you this long to figure it out?*

"Thanks," I said. Larry got up and closed the door behind him. I lay down on my bed and stared at the ceiling. *Shit, what am I going to do?*

The next day at school, I met up with Nate and Aaron in front of the band room. "Hey, man, sorry to hear about your girlfriend," Nate said.

"Yeah, that sucks," Aaron added. *What the hell?*

"Wait, how do you guys know?"

"...Rob told us," Aaron said. *Rob?*

"How would Rob know...unless Hannah told him?"

"Yeah, I don't know. I thought that was weird too."

"Where is he right now?"

"I don't know," Aaron said. Nate shook his head and said,

"He's been acting strange lately." I looked around campus and across the courtyard. I couldn't see Rob anywhere. *I've got a bad feeling.*

"Are we practicing today? I really need to get my mind off of this whole situation," I said.

"I'm always down to practice, but Rob didn't say anything about it this morning," Nate said. *Something is definitely wrong.* "We'll see him at lunch...we can ask him then."

"Shit, you know what, let's go find him right now," I said.

"Ok, but we only have like 10 minutes," Aaron added. We walked toward the courtyard in the middle of the school and then down each and every hallway of classrooms.

"I don't see him anywhere...what about Hannah? Have you guys seen Hannah?" Nate and Aaron both shook their heads and responded in unison with a simple,

"Nope." The bell rang and I said,

"All right, meet in front of the band room at lunch and we'll wait for Rob." We all agreed and then headed off to our classes.

The morning went by very slowly. All of my classes were exactly the same for me. I would sit down, take out my notebook, and stare at all of the scribbles and graffiti that Hannah wrote in it. *I Love U. Hannah + Will. Stussy. SK-8. Billy, I love you, Be happy. Keep your distance, fuck your girlfriend, love always, Hannah.* I turned through a few pages and read some of the lyrics for songs that I was working on. Every so often I would look up at my teachers. I would see their mouths moving but I couldn't hear any words. I would constantly look back at one line over and over again. *Keep your distance, fuck your girlfriend...What the hell does that mean and why did I not notice it before?* In my 4th period class, I just stared at the clock the entire period. Flashes of Hannah's beautiful naked body flickered on and off in my mind. *Her smile; her perfect teeth. The way her hips stress the fabric in her jeans. All the times we snuck out. Every time we laughed. Every time she cried...Every time I cried.* The bell rang. *Shit.* I got up from my desk and walked out of class. I headed straight for the band room. When I got there Nate and Aaron were waiting for me, but there was no sign of Rob. *Shit.* "Where is that dude?"

"Maybe he went home," Nate said.

"Without telling anyone? That's not really like him," Aaron said.

"No, it's not...something's up. If Rob were going to ditch, he'd tell anyone that would listen," I said.

"Well, fuck 'm," Nate said. "I'm hungry."

"Yeah, let's get out of here. I'm thinking about a Double Whopper heavy everything. I'll drive," Aaron said.

"Sounds good to me, let's go," I said.

"I got shotgun," Nate said. I laughed.

"Thanks, Nate, I needed a good laugh," I said. We walked to the parking lot in the front of the school.

"I didn't say it to be funny," Nate said.

"Dude, you're the...no offense, the smallest person, so, yeah, you have to sit in the back. I can't fit in the back seat of Aaron's bug," I said.

"Well, that's just not fair," Nate said.

"Sure it is; I don't fit in the back, so..."

"But I called shotgun."

"Doesn't matter, it doesn't make sense. I would have to put my feet up and sit sideways..."

"Are you girls done arguing?"

"It's not an argument, it's a logical discussion."

"Oh, is it? I think Nate's feelings say otherwise," Aaron said and we laughed.

"Hey! Not cool," Nate said. "I'll remember this when I get my license."

"When you get your license," I said.

"I am so gonna put you in the back seat." Aaron and I laughed again.

"All right, man, I look forward to it," I said. We got to Aaron's car and I moved my seat forward and gave Nate a little push on his back as he fell into the back seat.

"Not funny," Nate said.

"It is a little funny, Nate, and you know it," I said.

"Yeah, I guess, if it weren't me then...yeah."

"Exactly!" Aaron fired up his Volkswagen and we headed out onto Conyer Street. As we crossed Tulare, Nate yelled out,

"OH SHIT! Dude, there's Rob...and Hannah!"

"What! Where?" I said. Nate pointed towards the church on the other side of the street.

"They're over at the church...and dude, they're holding hands." I flipped my head around and caught a glimpse of Hannah and Rob standing behind the church.

"WHAT THE LITERAL FUCK!" I screamed. "Aaron, turn around."

"Oh shit, this is gonna be bad," Aaron said and slowed down. He turned around at the next street and then pulled into the parking lot of the church. Hannah and Rob were facing the church still holding hands. They didn't seem to hear us pull up even though Aaron's Volkswagen sounded like a tractor. I sat in the passenger seat for what felt like forever. Every moment with Hannah passed through my mind and I felt my upper lip tremble. "What are you gonna do?"

"I don't know," I said as I looked over at Aaron and then at Nate. "You guys got my back?"

"Oh, for sure!" Nate said enthusiastically.

"Yeah, let's do this," Aaron added. I slowly opened the door and without closing it, I yelled,

"WHAT THE HELL IS GOING ON HERE!?" Hannah and Rob turned around and looked surprised. They were about 20 feet away. I made my approach with Aaron and Nate following closely behind. Hannah dropped Rob's hand and looked down at the ground. Rob looked at me and seemed uncomfortable. He started looking around and fidgeting with the chain on his wallet. "What the fuck, Rob?"

"Hey, we wanted to tell you..." I looked at Rob up and down and felt a deep disgust at what was in front of me. I could almost smell the filthy greasiness coming off of him.

"Tell me what, ROB!?"

"Look, it kind of just happened," Rob nervously said.

"WHAT JUST KIND OF HAPPENED, ROB!?" I screamed. I had never felt so angry at another person in my entire life. I felt the reason and logic escaping from me. I didn't have words anymore.

"We've been talking for a while and..." Before Rob could finish his sentence, I clenched my right fist as hard as I could and delivered all of my rage to the middle of Rob's portly face. He fell backwards and tripped over his own impeccably placed backpack.

"Rob!" Hannah said as she knelt down next to him. "Are you all right?" *Is he all right? What the hell is happening?* Rob's nose was bleeding onto his white Misfits shirt. *I'm so glad it's white.* He didn't get up. He didn't attempt to fight back. It was over before it started. "We're not even together anymore, what's your problem?"

"What's my problem?" I looked at Hannah and raised my left eyebrow hoping to translate the absurdity of the question. I looked over at Rob and saw a smirk on his face. *What is he smiling about? What the fuck?"* I still love you, Hannah, and Rob...is; was, my friend...Bro code, Rob, shit!" I waited a few seconds but Rob didn't defend himself.

"I love you too..." *Yeah right...* "but what did you want me to do, wait an entire year for...?" Hannah said.

"Yes, goddamn it, yes, was that too much to ask?" I interjected. I looked behind myself at Aaron and then Nate. They both shrugged their shoulders. I looked back at Hannah and just stared at her waiting for a response.

"Well, I couldn't do that...I didn't want to be alone," Hannah said.

"Didn't want to be alone...and of all people...Rob...You know what, Hannah? You are a slut." Hannah's eyes got really big as if she never expected those words to come out of my mouth. She looked at Rob like she expected him to do something about it.

"Hey, man, watch your mouth!" Rob said as he picked himself up off of the ground.

"Watch my mouth? That's really funny, Rob, considering you were the one calling her a slut when we first got together."

"Oh shit!" Aaron said.

"I should have brought some popcorn," Nate said to Aaron.

"That's a fucking lie! I never said that. Hannah, I never said that," Rob pleaded as he tried to grab Hannah's hand. She quickly pulled away.

"Yes, you did! You said they're all sluts...You even said that she was probably cheating on me with Chris!"

"What the fuck!" Hannah said and started walking back toward the school. Rob picked up his backpack and followed her as she started crying. Rob tried to console her.

"He's lying, I didn't say any of that...please, Hannah, I would never..." His words trailed off as they got further and further away from us. I turned back to Aaron and Nate.

"Well, shit, this year is going to be awesome," I said.

"I know you're being sarcastic, but this year is going to be awesome...It's our senior year...forget about them," Aaron said.

"Yeah, dude, it may not be my place to say this but it seems like they deserve each other," Nate said.

"Yeah, I guess...I just never thought in a million years..."

"For real, no one did," Nate added. "By the way, what's the bro code?"

"Seriously? It's the rule that you never date your friend's ex. No matter what," I said.

"Oh yeah, I knew that, but I didn't know that's what it was called," Nate said.

"Yup, bro code, something that Rob obviously doesn't care about," Aaron said.

"That's exactly right, he doesn't care...and neither does she, I guess," I said while I looked down at my right hand and then flexed it out in front of me.

"How's your hand feeling?" Aaron said. *It hurts like a motherfucker!*

"It feels good. It's never felt better," I said. "Let's go get those Whoppers, I know Nate's still hungry."

"I am. I'm never not hungry," Nate said and we all laughed. *Shit, what about the band?*

Chapter Seventeen
Full circle

NATE, AARON, AND I were standing at the edge of the stage at lunch when Vicki walked up to me with a strange smile on her face. "Hi Will, I just wanted to wish you a happy birthday," she said.

"Thanks; wait, you know it's my birthday today?"

"Yeah, I've always known," Vicki quickly responded. She slowly moved her hair away from her face and wrapped it over her right shoulder. *She looks...really pretty...actually, kind of hot.*

"Did you do something with your hair?"

"I've been growing it out."

"Nice, it looks good."

"Was that a compliment? That sounded like a compliment..." Vicki said and looked at Nate and Aaron for confirmation. "That was a compliment, right, guys?" Nate and Aaron didn't say anything and looked at each other as if they were confused by the question.

"Yes, Vicki, it was a compliment," I said. She smiled and then turned to walk away.

"Wait, Vicki, what are you doing this weekend?"

"Nothing, why?"

"I was just wondering if you wanted to go see a movie or something..."

"Yeah, didn't you just break up with your girlfriend?" Vicki said rhetorically. *I guess everyone knows.* "I don't want to be your rebound...Don't you think it's too soon to get back out there? *What is happening right now? She's been in love with me since the dawn of time and now she's going to turn me down?* "Look, I'm flattered, but I think you should take some time...maybe be alone for..."

"Nah, it's cool," I interjected. "I understand." *No, I really don't.*

"Call me later, ok?" Vicki said and walked away.

"Ok," I responded and turned my attention back to Nate and Aaron.

"Vicki, huh?" Aaron said.

"Well, shit, I need a girlfriend, and I thought Vicki was a slam dunk," I reasoned.

"Obviously not, but she makes a good point," Aaron said.

"It's easy for you to say, you're still with Jessica."

"You don't need a girlfriend," Nate said. "Look at me; I'm good without a girl..."

"Yeah, man, sorry it didn't work out with Casey."

"Like I said, it's all good, I don't need..."

"Well I'm not good," I interrupted.

"You will be," Nate said. "We need to talk about the band."

"Yeah, for real, what are we gonna do?" Aaron said. "Is that it? No more band?"

"I have an idea," Nate said. "You guys know Andy Blackwell? He's the drummer in Scorched Asphalt..."

"Nate, you're the drummer... we don't need a drummer, we need a singer." *If that isn't the most obvious thing I've ever said...*

"No, we need a vocalist...and that can be me, and I can get Andy to drum for us," Nate said.

"Since when could you sing?" I inquired.

"Yeah, you've been holding out on us?" Aaron added.

"I can't sing," Nate said. "I can growl and yell...like Jonathan Davis. You know, Korn...Deftones; stuff like that."

"So, you think we should become a nu-metal band?" I said.

"It's not a bad idea, really, I like Korn," Aaron said.

"Yeah, I mean, I like Korn too, but that would be like starting over. Do you guys really want to throw everything that we've worked on out the window?"

"Yeah, and so should you," Nate said.

"Why is that?"

"Nirvana is Rob and Rob is Nirvana and, I don't really need to say it do I?"

"No, point taken..." I looked at Aaron and shrugged my shoulders. "All right, let's do it."

"Cool, I'll talk to Andy. Maybe we can get a practice together this weekend," Nate said. "Learn 'Blind' and 'My Own Summer,' at home. We can start with those."

"Sounds good," Aaron said.

"Yeah, no problem," I said. *Starting over...*

The weekend came around before I could even start feeling sorry for myself again. Nate got Andy to join our new band without too much resistance. I guess he wanted out of his band so he didn't need much convincing. Getting Andy to join our band also had a very big perk in that his cousin owned an auto body shop downtown that was closed on Sundays. He let us use the shop as a practice space for our newly formed band. Our first practice went really well. We played 'Blind' and 'My Own Summer' multiple times until we played them perfectly. Nate sounded beastly. He was definitely honing in on his inner Jonathan Davis. Andy, ironically, wasn't as good of a drummer as Nate, but he was solid. After practice that first Sunday, I had a heavy heart. The music we were playing was dark. It was hard. It was angry. It was exactly what I was feeling even though I didn't want to feel that way. It didn't help that Jessica was at that practice. Every time that I looked over at her it reminded me of Hannah and how much I loved her. *We were so in love...we had such great times together...Why did it have to end?* I set my guitar down on the stand and I walked over to Jessica.

"All right, guys, 'Killing in the Name' next week...Learn it," Nate said. "And maybe 'Bulls on Parade' too."

"Hey, Jessica," I said, "Have you talked to Hannah?" Jessica looked down at the ground and then back up at me.

"No, not since..."

"Why Rob? I just don't get it."

"I don't know...She didn't tell me, Aaron did. I didn't even believe it at first. I thought he was joking."

"I miss her," I said and felt an overwhelming sense of sadness.

"I don't really know what to say..."

"If her grandma didn't die none of this would have ever happened." Jessica gave me a somewhat perplexed look.

"Hannah's grandma didn't die," Jessica said. "I think that's something I would have heard about. "Oh shit, is that what she told you?" My heart sank even further into the depths of my chest. *If she lied about that...what else did she lie about?* Aaron walked over and put his arm around Jessica.

"What's up?" Jessica looked down at the ground shaking her head.

"Hannah...She lied...About everything," I said under my breath. "If her grandma didn't die then the whole thing...with her parents, with her dad...it wasn't true. Or was it?" *It seemed real. I know her dad hates me...or does he? Wait, of course he does. Why would she lie? It doesn't make sense.*

"Shit, man, that sucks," Aaron said. "What are you going to do?"

"I guess I'm going to confront her about it tomorrow at school."

"Are you sure that's a good idea?" Jessica said.

"Nope, I'm not sure, but I have to. I will literally go crazy if I don't."

"Do me a favor though...Can you maybe not mention me?" Jessica said. *She's not stupid, but yeah, sure.*

"No worries, Jessica, I won't tell her you told me."

"Thanks," Jessica said. Nate and Andy walked over to us.

"What's going on over here?" Nate said.

"Hannah lied. You guys got my back tomorrow?"

"Hannah lied? About what?"

"Everything. I'm gonna find out why tomorrow at lunch."

"Drama, man," Andy added.

"It is, but I won't be able to move on until she tells me the truth."

"How do you know she's gonna start telling you the truth now?" Aaron asked.

"Yeah, that's a good point," Nate said. *That is a good point. I really don't know. I guess I don't know anything.*

I didn't talk to Hannah the next day at school. I was deeply hurt that she lied to me, but I couldn't face her. I wanted her to tell me the truth to my face and at the same time I couldn't stomach the idea of watching her struggle through it. I still cared about her. I still loved her. I didn't want to see her hurt even if it was justified. None of it made any sense and at some level I still wanted to know why she went through all of the trouble just to get me to break up with her. She could have just as easily broken up with me. And the most daunting question I had was about Rob. *Why Rob...Why Rob...Why Rob?* It haunted my thoughts day after day. I would see them from a distance holding hands at school and that's the only thing that ever came to me. *Why Rob?* After a few weeks though, I cared less and less. I would still see them together on campus but I didn't hear that incessant question in my head. I would even pass right by them in the hall sometimes and Rob always looked straight forward. Hannah and I would always make eye contact. I didn't see anger in her eyes. I thought that I saw her smile at me one day, but that may have been in my head. I never said anything to either one of them though. I didn't have anything to say. I said everything I wanted to say at the church that day. The holidays came and went like they didn't happen at all. At the end of January, after practice, Aaron, Nate, Andy, and I were standing on the corner downtown across from Starbucks waiting for Jessica.

"Man, it's as cold as a witch's tit," Nate said and we all laughed. Nate had a habit of under dressing.

"Well, yeah, you're just wearing a beater shirt," I said.

"Shit...Where's your girlfriend, man? This sucks, I wanna go inside," Nate said.

"She'll be here in a minute," Aaron said.

"You can wear my jacket," Andy said and laughed.

"That's gay," Nate said. "I'll be fine."

"Then stop complaining," Andy said. We all shook our heads in agreement. Jessica pulled up in a parking spot just about right in front of us.

"There she is; happy, Nate?" Aaron said.

"Yes," Nate said. I looked at Jessica as she got out of her car and for the first time in a long time, I just saw Jessica and didn't immediately associate her with Hannah. Jessica walked up to us and looked at Nate.

"Nate, you look so cold, do you want to borrow my jacket," Jessica said. We all started busting up laughing and I almost fell off of the curb.

"Fuuuuuuu," Nate muttered without finishing the word.

"It's ok Nate," I said. "You can finish your thought." We all continued laughing. Nate looked indignant but he just stood there shivering with his hands in his pockets.

"Maybe we can all pitch in and buy him a jacket," Jessica said.

"I...errrr...have a jacket," Nate responded.

"He does, he's making a choice," I said.

"Ok, this is cruel and unusual punishment, let's go into Starbucks," Jessica said.

"Yeah, get this man a coffee," Aaron said.

"Yes, buy me a coffee," Nate agreed.

"I got it," Jessica said. "He's like my little brother."

"Thanks, I think," Nate said. We all crossed the street and walked into Starbucks. As we were standing in line waiting to order, I noticed Vicki and Angela sitting at a table next to the windows.

"Hey, I'm gonna go talk to Vicki, I'll be right back," I said.

"Do you want me to get your drink?" Aaron asked while putting his arm around Jessica.

"Yeah...Venti Mint Frappuccino."

"All right." I handed him five bucks and walked over to Vicki and Angela.

"Hey, Vicki, Angela, what's up?"

"Hey, Will, you're in a good mood," Vicki said.

"That's my cue," Angela said. *Cue for what?* "I've got to meet up with Chris. I'll see you guys later." Angela got up from her chair and seemed to pull it out for me. "It's good to see you, Will."

"It's good to see you too, Angela, tell Chris I said hi."

"I will, you guys have fun." Angela smiled and then walked out.

"So...when I said to call me later, I meant sometime this century." Vicki raised her eyebrows and crossed her arms. I smiled. *She got me there.*

"Yeah, I know, I've just been busy with the band...and trying to get enough units to graduate."

"Really?" Vicki seemed unconvinced.

"Yeah, you know, I still don't know if I'm going to graduate. My counselor told me that I had to pass all of my classes this semester and I would 'barely squeak by,' in her words."

"Ms. Mortenson?"

"Yeah, how did you know?"

"We have the same counselor."

"We do? Shit...Something else I didn't know."

"Yeah, you just haven't been paying attention."

"I guess not."

"So, how's your ex-girlfriend?" *Really?*

"Who? I mean, to whom do you speak?"

"Ha-ha, you don't have to be coy. I understand if you don't want to talk about it."

"Well, to answer your question, I don't have any idea how she is."

"You haven't talked to her?"

"Nope. I haven't talked to her." *Totally true.* "In fact, I haven't even thought about her." *Kinda true.*

"Really? Well, that's good, I mean, I guess that's good…moving on and all."

"Yeah, it's good. I've been much happier lately…Vicki, what are your plans for Valentine's Day?"

"I don't have any plans."

"Perfect, well, that's not how I…that sounded bad."

"Yes."

"Yes?"

"Yes, I'll go out with you on Valentine's Day."

"Cool, it's a date."

"It's a date."

"Hey, you wanna get out of here? Maybe go for a drive?"

"Yeah, I need a ride home anyway." Vicki smiled. "Angela drove us here." Aaron and Jessica walked over to our table and Aaron handed me my drink.

"Thanks, man. Hey, I'm gonna take Vicki home so I'll catch up with you guys later."

"Oh, all right, call me later," Aaron said.

"For sure," I said and led Vicki out with my hand on the small of her back. I threw a peace sign to Nate and Andy, who were still waiting in line for their drinks, as we walked out of the store. I took a sip of my Frappuccino and looked down Main Street where I parked my car. Vicki brushed her hand against mine.

"Can I have a drink?"

"Yeah," I said and handed it to her. I watched Vicki slowly bring the oversized green straw to her lips and take a long, almost exaggerated sip. "You good?"

"Yeah, that's really good; very minty." Vicki handed it back to me and I took a short sip.

"Yes, very good," I said. "My car is on the other side of Court, let's go." We walked across the street as our hands met in stride. I intertwined my fingers with hers and looked into her expressive, big brown eyes. She smiled at me and I smiled back at her. I wanted to kiss her and taste the mint on her lips, but I looked forward to the road to make sure that my path was clear.

Chapter Eighteen

Vicki

I HAD BEEN DATING Vicki for about three months when everyone started talking about the prom. It seemed obvious to me that I was going to take Vicki, but for whatever reason, I guess it wasn't so obvious to her. After school one day, about two weeks before prom, Vicki turned to me and said,

"So, Will, were you planning on asking me to prom or what?"

"Wait, are you serious?"

"Yes, I'm serious." Vicki looked quite perturbed. "You have to ask me."

"I just thought that because you're my girlfriend..."

"It doesn't matter," Vicki quickly interjected. *Ok, Psycho much?*

"Ok, Vicki, will you go to prom with me?" I asked half-heartedly.

"Yes!" Vicki said. *What a waste of time.* Vicki hugged me tightly. "We're going to have so much fun. We should get a limo...no? We can talk about the details later. I am so happy. I have to tell Angela! Hey, maybe we can get a limo with them. That's a good idea, what do you think?" *This girl is crazy...wait, you already knew that. Awesome.*

"Yeah, I haven't seen Chris in a long time. It'll be good to catch up with him."

"Perfect! I'll talk to Angela later and figure everything out."

"You do that," I said. "Hey, babe, I've got to get to practice."

"Ok, I'll call you later...Maybe I'll stop by...Maybe not. I've got to talk to Angela. We have to start planning now. I'm so excited." Vicki grasped my hand tightly and we walked towards the parking lot. I walked her to her car: a new, red Chevy Cavalier, which her parents bought her for her 18th birthday. *Must be nice...*

"Alright babe, drive safe." Vicki sat inside of her car and then shut the door. She rolled down the window and I leaned in.

"Have a good practice," Vicki said and then kissed me. "I'll call you tonight."

"I should be home by 8," I said and then walked over to the Malibu. I fired it up and sat there for a minute while the engine warmed up. *Vicki is really excited about prom...Why aren't I? It's supposed to be a big deal. Why don't I care? Do I even want to go? Shit, I kinda have no choice now...I wonder if Hannah and...Rob...are going to be there. Of course they are. I could ask Jessica. Maybe I shouldn't. It might look like I care...Shit.* I pulled out onto Conyer Street and drove very slowly across the intersection and looked over at the church. I expected to see them, but no one was there. *Shit. I feel so...I don't even know.* I made my way downtown and to our practice space. Aaron was already there and Jessica was with him. *Don't even think about it.*

"Hey, man, Nate and Andy aren't here yet?"

"No, I guess Andy had to do something real quick," Aaron said.

"Oh, all right," I said.

"So, Will, you're going to prom with Vicki, right?" Jessica said. *Well, shit.*

"Yeah, and get this...she made me ask her," I said. Aaron laughed. "What?"

"Of course you have to ask her," Jessica said impatiently.

"Yeah...I just thought it was obvious."

"It doesn't matter if it's obvious," Jessica said. *I wonder if they all take a course on not making any sense...*

"Yeah, well, I asked her and she said yes, so it's all good," I pointedly said.

"Wait, when did Aaron ask you?" Aaron smiled as wide as ever but didn't answer.

"It was so romantic. He got down on one knee with a single rose in his hand. He handed me the rose and asked me if I would do him the honor of being his date to the prom," Jessica said. *Fucking Aaron.*

"Shit, well done, Aaron," I said, "But don't tell Vicky. I'll never live that shit down." *Making me look bad.*

"Yeah, no worries," Aaron said.

"Vicki wants to share a limo with Angela and Chris, which is cool I guess. I haven't seen him in forever."

"Chris? Isn't that your old drummer?" Aaron asked.

"Yeah...Anyway, you guys want in? We could all go together and keep the costs down. *I'm glad I have some money saved, shit's gonna be expensive.* I would have to run it by everyone else, but I'm sure it's cool," I said.

"We can't," Jessica said. *Can't?* I looked at Aaron and then back at Jessica.

"Why? That doesn't make any sense. You guys just want to go alone?"

"No, it's not that," Jessica said. *Ummm, yeah, ok.* I just stood there with a perplexed look on my face. It's the same look I had during the Chargers/49ers Super Bowl when our safeties got burned by Jerry Rice for three touchdowns in the first quarter of the game. I looked intently at Aaron as he uncomfortably stared at Jessica.

"Just tell him," Aaron said.

"Tell me what?" I quickly responded. Jessica paused for a few seconds and when it became obvious that she wasn't going to say anything, Aaron said,

"It's Hannah." *Hannah? What the hell?*

"What about Hannah!?" I said angrily.

"Fine...I don't want this to turn into a thing but we're going to go with Hannah and Rob," Jessica said.

"What the literal fuck, Jessica, you hate Rob!" .

"But Hannah is my best friend and she..."

"And Aaron is my best friend," I interjected. "Aaron, you're ok with this? Rob's a piece of shit."

"I'm not ok with it, but it's what Jessica wants, so..."

"Hey, if you're not ok with it, maybe we shouldn't go at all," Jessica said and stormed off down the street.

"Damn it, Jess, wait," Aaron said and then ran after her. I stood there and watched as Jessica yelled profanities at Aaron as he stood in front of her without saying a word. She finally pointed back my way. Jessica continued walking down the street and Aaron walked back towards me. "Hey, man, I know this sucks, but it's just one night."

"Just one night, huh?"

"Yeah, and if I'm not on board, Jessica won't even go with me," Aaron reasoned. "I don't have a choice."

"You always have a choice, but I get it."

"We're all going to be at the same place so does it really matter what cars we take?"

"No, that's not it, I know that doesn't matter," I said. "I was just hoping that Hannah and Rob wouldn't even be there." *Well, just Rob actually.* "It's just drama, man."

"Yeah, it is, but what are you gonna do? You don't have to talk to them."

"I guess you're right. I've managed to not say anything to either one of them for three months. I think I can manage one night, right?"

"Right. I'm not planning on making much conversation with them. I don't really have anything to say."

"But, what about dinner? You'll have to say something then, I'm sure."

"Yeah, you've got a point...well, I'll say as little as possible. One-word answers. Yes, no, that kind of thing." I managed a brief laugh.

"Thanks, man, I feel a little better about it."

"Yeah, we'll figure it out. It won't even be a thing," Aaron said. Nate and Andy walked up behind us.

"What won't be a thing?" Nate said while heading over to the PA system.

"It's prom stuff," I said.

"Oh, fuck the prom," Nate said. "I'm not going to the fucking prom."

"Me neither, forget that noise," Andy added as he started setting up the drums.

"That's because neither one of you fuckers has anyone to go with," I said. Aaron and I laughed. Nate and Andy looked at each other and seemed irritated.

"I could get a date if I wanted to...But I don't want to. The prom is fucking stupid," Nate said and looked back over at Andy. Andy didn't say anything.

"Well, maybe you'll change your mind next year," I said. Nate looked around at everyone and paused like he was thinking about it.

"...Nope," Nate finally said. We all laughed. "So, are we gonna practice or are we gonna keep talking about our feelings?"

"Yeah, Nate, let's play. We can deal with this stuff tomorrow," I said. Aaron nodded in agreement. Aaron grabbed his bass and I picked up my guitar. Andy started playing the intro to Korn's 'Blind,' and any thoughts about the possible transgressions at the prom quickly disappeared.

Later that night, Vicki called me and told me that Angela and Chris were down to share a limo for prom and that Chris wanted me to call him. I decided that it was time to make amends with Chris, especially since the entire reason I hadn't talked to him in so long wasn't even in my life anymore. I dialed Chris's number and waited through the monotonous ringing.

"Hello?"

"Is Chris there?"

"Yeah, this is Chris."

"Oh, hey man, I didn't recognize your voice."

"Will?"

"Yeah, Vicki said you wanted me to call you."

"Yeah, it's been a long time, so, I guess we're going to share a limo for prom?"

"Yeah, it was Vicki's idea."

"Dude, this is crazy. Remember that night that didn't happen with Angela and Vicki? And now we're taking them to prom..."

"It is kind of crazy the way things work out."

"It's really crazy...Hannah and Rob? What's that all about? How is that even possible?" I laughed.

"I have no idea. I spent a lot of time beating myself up about it and then I eventually stopped caring."

"So, you broke up with her?"

"It's a really long story, but it ends with her lying to me about her grandma dying...and her dad threatening me...shit like that. I think she wanted to break up with me, but wanted me to do it."

"Damn, that sucks, man."

"I mean, I guess she's not my problem anymore, but I think there's something seriously wrong with her."

"I wasn't going to say anything, and maybe I shouldn't..."

"I don't think there's anything you could say that would surprise me at this point."

"Ok...That time, when I asked her out...I did it because, and I still know it was a shitty thing to do to you, but I did it because she was flirting with me something fierce...and so I asked her out, and well, you know, she turned me down. It didn't make any sense to me. And I ruined our friendship over it..."

"Wow...like I said, I'm not surprised. It was still a shit thing that you asked her out...no matter what she did."

"I know and I'm sorry; she was just so stupid hot."

"Yeah, I'm good. I'm over it."

"So, yeah, Vicki..."

"It just kind of happened, man. Valentine's Day."

"It's funny though...you couldn't stand her and now you're with her."

"I know, I know, but she's not bad to look at now. She got thinner and grew her hair out. She started wearing make-up at some point...She's still annoying as hell, but I'm not sure that's ever going to change." Chris Laughed.

"No, you're probably right."

"Well, hey, I gotta call her before I go to bed so I'll have to let you go. It was good talking to you."

"You too, man, give me a call this weekend."

"For sure, talk to you later."

"Later, man."

A couple of weeks after Vicki and I officially had our first date, we were alone for the first time at her house. It felt strange being alone with her. I walked into the living room and looked at all of the pictures hanging on the wall. There were pictures of Vicki's parents and some of her grandparents, which seemed obvious enough to me. There were pictures of all kinds of different people. *These can't all be her family. Shit...* "So, Vicki, are all of these people your family?" I asked. Vicki walked into the living room from the bathroom.

"Yeah. These are my parents, which you already know, and these are my grandparents in Mexico...and these are my cousins, and this is my uncle Fernando, he's my favorite." My eyes glazed over as Vicki pointed at each picture on the wall while practically naming everyone. *So many names...so many people. I'm not going to remember all of these people. Shit, how do I tell her to stop talking?*

"Do your grandparents still live in Mexico?"

"Yeah, on my mom's side, but on my dad's side, grandma and grandpa Hernandez, well, they live in Arizona. We don't talk to them much, but that doesn't mean that we don't love them. One time..." *I had to ask...*Vicki talked about her estranged grandparents for a long time. Something about them fighting about something, but I tuned her out. When there was finally a second of silence, I changed the subject.

"So, what do you want to do?"

"Wait, you don't want to find out what happened with Uncle Ricardo?" *Oh shit, Uncle who?*

"No, babe, I do, it's just maybe you can tell me later when we have more time. When are your parents getting home?"

"Oh, ok, yeah...uh, I'm not exactly sure." Vicki looked at me and smiled like she knew exactly what I was thinking. She grabbed my hand and led me down the hallway to her bedroom. I was immediately taken aback by everything I saw in her room. Her bed was pink. Her actual bed wasn't pink, but her comforter and blankets and pillows were. *This is ridiculous.* It looked like everything had been white at some point, but a terrible accident had occurred with a red something in the washing machine. I wanted to believe that. *Who would choose that color?* I looked around her room at the walls and saw an NSYNC poster, a Backstreet Boys poster, and a 98 Degrees poster. *That's a shit-ton of boy bands!*

"Wow, Vicki, I had no idea you liked the boy bands." I smiled and laughed. Vicki did not look amused and smacked my arm in protest.

"Do you have a problem with that?"

"No, I mean, it's fine, I guess."

"You guess, huh? Well, if you do have a problem then I'm going to have to punish you." *Ummm, ok.*

"And how are you going to manage that?"

"Like this." Vicki pulled her jeans down to her knees and then sat on the edge of her bed. She pulled them completely off and then took off her shirt.

"You said punish right? I think you and I have two very different definitions of punish."

"You'll see." Vicki smiled and then quickly unhooked her bra and tossed it into my face. She then slid her panties on the floor and stepped on them. I was aroused and disgusted at the same time. She lay back onto her bed and then motioned for me to come over to her. *Who just takes their own clothes off before sex and then lies there naked? Weird and...kind of slutty.* I stared at her for what must have seemed to her at least a minute, but in all actuality was only a few seconds. She had a fairly decent body, but I had been spoiled by Hannah so I didn't react the way that Vicki expected. "What's wrong? You don't like what you see?" Vicki sat up on her elbows as her breasts slowly moved forward. My eyes drifted down to her overgrown bush. *Hannah takes much better care of herself. I'm not impressed... Get out of your head! Who even cares? This girl wants to fuck.* I didn't know what it was that was keeping me from jumping on top of her, but I hesitated.

"No, it's not that, it's just I've got a lot on my mind. You know, graduation, my band... stuff." *Yeah, no. I've got nothing on my mind. I shouldn't be here right now. I feel like I'm cheating on Hannah...What in the literal fuck!* I looked at Vicki's ceiling and saw a bunch of stick-on stars that probably glowed in the dark. *How did I not notice those before? Hannah cheated...wait, no she didn't. We were broken up. But she did lie...shit!* Vicki must have thought I was going crazy looking back and forth at different stars on the ceiling.

"Are you ok? You're kinda freaking me out." I looked down at Vicki and realized there was a naked girl lying on a bed which snapped me out of my daze.

"Yeah, sorry babe, I just need to get out of my head."

"Well, lie down next to me and let me help you." Vicki smiled and then grabbed my hand. I sat down on the edge of her bed and then pulled my shirt off over my head. I kicked my shoes off and then pulled my pants and boxers off in a single movement. *This just feels wrong. Oh well.*

"Do you have any protection? I don't have any condoms on me."

"No, don't worry, I'm on the pill." *How often does she do this? Gross. I can't recall her having a boyfriend, but I guess it's possible. She sure isn't shy about any of this.*

"Oh, all right, cool." I got on top of her and kissed her...The sex only lasted for a couple of minutes, but Vicki didn't seem to care. I slid down and rested my head between her breasts. She pet my head like a person would pet a dog, but I didn't mind.

"How was it?"

"Good?"

"Just good."

"I mean, it was our first time, so, yeah, good." *I busted a nut, so it was good enough.*

"That's true, it'll be better next time...maybe longer too." I sat up and Vicki smiled.

"Ha-ha, very funny."

"Oh, I meant," Vicki pointed at my crotch, "that is plenty long enough, the time, I meant the time."

"I know, I get it, thanks." I grabbed my clothes off of the floor and got dressed. Vicki continued to lie on her bed naked. She didn't seem to notice, or care that she was soiling her bed.

"Hey, Vicki..." I said as I watched the wet spot grow more prominent. *Is she gonna get dressed or what? So weird.*

"Yes."

"How many, you know, guys have you been with?"

"Two. Counting you." Vicki smiled. *Yeah, right, two, and I was born yesterday.*

"Really? You just seem like you've done this...like, you have a lot of experience."

"I'm not a slut."

"I didn't say you were."

"I had...this guy, he goes to Golden West...we hooked up a few times, but we were never actually a thing."

"Did you want it to be a thing?"

"I don't know. Maybe. I just, I guess I wanted to be someone's girlfriend." *That is so sad.* "And since you couldn't be bothered..."

"No, I get it."

"And what about you? What number am I on your bedpost?"

"What? I don't have a bedpost." I laughed.

"You know what I mean."

"You're number three."

"So, Hannah's number two!?" Vicki laughed. *Very funny; actually, that's not bad.*

"I see what you did there. Did I ever tell you how much I hate puns?"

"Nope. I love puns." *Stupid dad jokes.* "How many times do you think you've had sex?"

"Like the actual number? I have no idea...A lot."

"Was that a lot with girl number one, which has no name..."

"Rebecca."

"Ok, Rebecca, or Hannah?" *It's not even close. Hannah by a country mile.*

"Hannah."

"How many times with Hannah?" *A hundred...*

"I told you I don't know."

"More than 10..." *So annoying.*

"Yes, more than 10."

"More than 100?"

"I don't know, Vicki, can we drop it?"

"Sure, I'm just making conversation." *Yeah, right...*

"Hannah and I are over, and I'd rather just not talk about her at all." *I miss her.* Vicki smiled.

"All right, I'll let it go. Sorry I hit a nerve." *Yeah, I don't think you are.*

"It's fine. So, I don't want to tell you what to do, but don't you think you should get dressed?"

"Got a problem with my naked body?" *This shit again?*

"No, you have a beautiful body." *Kind of.*

"Awe, thanks, babe."

"Yeah...anyway, I've got to get to practice." I looked down at my left wrist and nonexistent watch. "Are you coming?"

"Yeah, Sure. Do you want me to come?"

"Yes, which is why I asked you." *Fucking doopitydoo duh...*

"Well, if you want me to come, then I'll come." *For the love of all that is holy.*

Chapter Nineteen

Prom

CHRIS AND ANGELA WAITED in the limo as I anxiously made my way to Vicki's door. I rang her doorbell and was greeted by her mom, a jovial, overweight woman who looked much older than my mom. The first time I met her mom and dad, I thought that they were Vicki's grandparents. Vicki never told me how old they were other than to say that they had her much later in life, which was a huge understatement. Her mom smiled and leaned into me while I fumbled the corsage from my right to left hand. She gave me a hug and said,

"Will, you look so handsome." Chris and I got matching black tuxedos from Tux-N-Tails, Visalia's go-to tuxedo rental place.

"Thanks," I said. "I think they did a good job." *Yeah, they did a good job of making us all look exactly the same.*

"Vicki should be ready soon; you want to wait in the living room?"

"Sure." I walked into the living room and sat down on their couch looking directly across from Vicki's dad, who was watching the news.

"Will," he said, "what time are you gonna have Vicki home?"

"Frank, leave him alone," Vicki's mom said.

"What? I'm just giving him a hard time...Isn't that what I'm supposed to do?" Vicki's dad said and then laughed.

"Well, it ends at 12, so I guess like 1."

"That's fine, Will," Vicki's mom said. Vicki's dad seemed to agree and focused back on the news. "So, you guys are going to The Vintage Press for dinner?"

"Yeah, I've never been there before, but I guess everyone goes there for prom."

"It's really expensive," Vicki's mom said.

"Everything about this night has been expensive," I said and laughed. "It's a good thing I've been saving my money." Vicki's mom laughed.

"Yeah, it really is. I'm glad that Vicki's with such a responsible young man." *A responsible what now? I wonder...what it would have been like if Hannah's parents liked me as much as Vicki's parents. It doesn't matter now but...* "I'm gonna go check on Vicki, she should be ready by now." Vicki's mom walked out of the room and then came back a few minutes later with Vicki following close behind her. I stood up and her dad followed.

"You look beautiful, Vicki," I said and put the corsage on her left wrist. She was wearing a long black dress with spaghetti straps that had a floral pattern going down the front. Her long, curly brown hair rested neatly on her shoulders.

"You too," Vicki said. "I mean, you know, handsome, that's the right word, right? Damn, I already messed up. What am I thinking? So embarrassing..." Vicki's parents laughed.

"It's fine, Vicki, relax," I said. "It's not a big deal." Vicki picked the boutonniere up off of the kitchen counter and tried to pin it to my tuxedo jacket.

"I can't seem to get it to go through..." Vicki said. Her hands were visibly shaking. *What is she so nervous about?*

"Here, honey, let me get that," Vicki's mom said and pinned the boutonniere on my jacket without issue.

"Wow, what's wrong with me?" Vicki said. *Do you want me to answer that?* "That seemed like it was really simple and yet I couldn't do it." *Sheesh, relax, much.*

"It's ok, Vicki," I said and held her hand. Vicki smiled.

"Ok, you two, let me get some pictures and..." Vicki's mom said.

"Mom, we're going to get pictures there," Vicki interjected.

"I know, honey, but humor me." I wrapped my arm around Vicki and we posed for some pictures.

"Fine, but hurry up, our friends are waiting," Vicki insisted. *Oh shit, how long has it been?* Vicki's mom grabbed an orange disposable camera off of the kitchen counter, which she apparently bought just for this occasion, and exhausted all of the pictures on us.

"All right, that's the last of them. You guys have a wonderful evening."

"We will mom, bye dad," Vicki said while pulling me to the front door.

"Bye, have a good time," Vicki's dad said. "One 'O clock." Vicki opened her front door and then closed it behind us. We stood on her porch and looked out to the limo. Vicki looked at me and down at her corsage.

"Sorry about being such a spaz," she said. "And sorry about my parents...so embarrassing." I put my hand on her cheek and then kissed her.

"Relax, babe, it's not even a thing, and like you said, our friends are waiting...they've been alone in there for a long time, there's no telling what they're doing," I said and we both laughed.

"Should we give them more time then?"

"Nah, we have a reservation."

"Angela told me that Chris is pretty quick anyway, I think we're good." *What the shit?* Vicki laughed and looked back at the limo.

"Babe, she tells you that stuff?"

"Of course, I'm her best friend." *Shit.*

"What do you tell her about me?"

"Only good things." Vicki smiled and held my hand. *Yeah right, but whatevers.* I raised my eyebrow and flashed a half-smile at her. I wrapped my hand around her waist and we walked across her lawn towards the limo. I opened the door and helped Vicki inside.

Chris and Angela, much to my surprise, were not all over each other. "Sorry it took so long guys...oh my god, Angela you look gorgeous!"

"No you look gorgeous!" Angela said. *Can we just cut the shit?* I looked at Chris and rolled my eyes.

"All right, man, we're ready," I said to the driver. He nodded and then set off towards the restaurant.

It seemed like everyone and his brother and sister were at The Vintage Press that night. Cars, Limos, black tuxedos, dresses...cleavage...were everywhere. I had heard that it would be busy, but I really didn't know what to expect. The limo driver let us out in the middle of Willis Street and told us that he was going to find a place to park. I wasn't sure how we were going to find him after dinner, but that didn't seem to cross anyone else's mind. Chris looked at me with a somewhat concerned look.

"Hey, man, I'm starving," he said. "This is gonna take forever." Angela walked around Chris and took hold of his hand. She was wearing a red dress with a plunging neckline and a gaping leg opening. It made Vicki's dress look conservative by comparison.

"I made the reservation last week," Angela said. "I don't think they would have let me do that if there wasn't any space." *Are you sure about that, Angela?*

"All right, let's fight our way in there and tell them we're here," I said. I put my arm around Vicki and we made our way to the front of the restaurant. We continued to reception where they told us there would be a one hour wait and that was with our reservation. We all walked back outside and crossed the street into the Smart and Final parking lot. Other people were waiting there too so we weren't alone in our predicament. There was a slight chill in the air so I put my arm around Vicki. She smiled at me and started rubbing her hands together. Chris and Angela were standing across from us and Angela was looking especially cold. I smiled and let out a slight laugh at the absurdity of the red fabric that Angela considered a dress.

"Will, it's not funny, I'm freezing my tits off here," Angela said.

"Seriously? A little hyperbolic much?" I said. Vicki looked at me and smiled.

"It looks like someone's been paying attention in English class," Vicki said.

"Of course; Straight A's," I said and laughed. Angela turned to Chris and looked as irritated as ever. I had seen that look on Angela's face before and nothing good ever came of it. Chris seemed to know this fact as well and quickly took his jacket off and wrapped it around Angela's shoulders.

"Thanks, babe," Angela said.

"Very smooth, Chris," I said. *And more importantly, very smart.* Vicki looked at me puzzled.

"Do I have to ask?"

"Ask what, babe?"

"Your jacket..."

"It's not even that cold so if you want my jacket, then yes, you're going to have to ask for it," I said. *Payback's a bitch! Haha.*

"Nevermind," Vicki said. Chris and Angela looked at each other.

"Bro, just give her your jacket," Chris said. I started to take off my jacket and Vicki immediately pulled herself away from me.

"I don't want it now," Vicki said. *So much drama.* I looked around the parking lot at all of the people seemingly waiting for the same thing we were. *This is not good. People get pissed when they're hungry.*

"Aaron told me that they were going to Red Lobster for dinner," I said.

"Are you thinking about your ex?" Vicki said. *What the literal fuck? I wasn't before, but now that you mention it...I wonder...*

"No, what? I was just thinking that if we had gone to a normal place we would be eating," I reasoned.

"So it's my fault now?" Angela said. *Son of a bitch.*

"No, it's nobody's fault, I'm just making an observation."

"Well, keep your observations to yourself, ok, Will, shit!" Angela said. *Wow...This is going really well.*

"Look, we're all hungry...and some of us are cold," I said.

"Will, just shut up already!" Angela shouted. Vicki looked at me with disdain and I quickly looked away from her and across the street towards the restaurant. *I wonder how Aaron, Jessica, Hannah, and Rob are all going to fit inside of the Camaro. It's got four seats, but damn. Why would Aaron's step dad let them take that car? Wait. I bet Rob is sitting shotgun right next to my best friend! I wonder what Hannah's wearing...or not wearing. Why Rob? What the hell?* I looked back at Vicki. *This is fucked. I am with the wrong girl. She's all right...she's a pain in the ass. I don't like her. If you don't like her then why are you with her? I think I'm losing my mind.* Vicki wrapped her arms around me and whispered in my ear,

"I'm sorry...You're right, I'm just hungry. Sorry for being such a bitch."

"It's ok, I get it," I whispered back. *No, I don't.* I leaned in and kissed her.

"Hey, what are you guys whispering about over there?" Angela said.

"I would tell you but you don't want me to talk," I responded.

"I wasn't actually being serious. You really thought I was serious?" Angela said. *Fucking girls.*

"I just told him that I'm hungry so I'm not myself," Vicki said.

"Yeah, fuck it, let's go back in and demand they seat us," Angela said. We all agreed and walked across the street and into the reception area. Angela made her case with the receptionist about our reservation and when she said that nothing could be done, Angela raised her voice which prompted a manager to come over. He was very apologetic and offered us a table on the patio outside, which we reluctantly accepted.

"Nice work, Angela," I said. *I guess that disagreeable personality comes in handy sometimes.*

"Thanks," Angela said. The manager guided us through the restaurant and outside to the patio. We all took our seats and began to flip through the menus. We ordered almost as quickly as we sat down and waited impatiently for our food to arrive. Chris and I each ordered a steak while Vicki and Angela each ordered a salad. The food came out rather quickly considering how many people were there. We didn't say much to each other during dinner other than the side comment about the wait staff or our similarly-situated peers. We were all more focused on eating than talking. We also were thinking about getting to the convention center on time. Prom technically started at 9, but we were supposed to be there early for pictures and introductions. There was a tradition where all of the couples were introduced by name as they entered the ballroom. I had heard that this was a big deal. It was a status symbol of sorts. Even if someone didn't see who a person was with, they most definitely heard who was with whom. It was also an imperative that a person had a date. If they were there solo, that would be announced. Nothing could be worse. As we finished our food, the waiter brought us the check. Chris and I both placed cash inside the bill folder and we all stood up.

"All right, let's get out of here," I said. We made our way through a side gate and walked across the street to the Smart and Final parking lot with the hopes of finding our limo.

"These cars all look the same," Angela said.

"Just look for the driver," I said. We walked through the parking lot and looked into each and every limo that we came across.

"There he is," Chris said. "Look, he's waving us over."

"Oh, cool, that wasn't so bad," I said. We piled into the limo and the mood immediately improved.

"It's so warm in here," Vicki said. *Almost too warm, but I'm glad she isn't bitching about the temperature anymore.* The convention center was only a few blocks away from the restaurant so it only took ten minutes to get there. The driver pulled over to the side of Acequia Street and let us out. There were already hundreds of people outside waiting to be let into the exhibit hall for pictures. I looked around the plaza at all of the beautiful and not so beautiful people. I recognized some of them but, for the most part, they were strangers.

"This is really cool," I said.

"What's that?" Chris said.

"Visalia allows all of the high schools to attend the same prom. It's kind of crazy, but it's really cool. I don't think they do this anywhere else."

"Yeah, I guess I never really thought about it."

"We wouldn't all be together right now otherwise."

"True, true."

"Hey, let's see if we can go inside," Vicki said and grabbed my hand.

"Ok, I guess we're going," I said. We walked to the entrance and they were letting people inside of the exhibit hall. We walked inside of the giant room which was being used as the staging area and for pictures. Ms. Reddell handed us a piece of paper where we were supposed to write our names down. She then gave us a number. We were number 268. We wrote our names down and returned the paper.

"Ms. Reddell, 268 out of how many?" I inquired.

"Oh...We're expecting over a thousand, so maybe 500, but some people buy tickets and don't show up, so I'm really not sure."

"Ok, thanks, Ms. Reddell," I said.

"You kids have a good time tonight," she said and walked away. *Kids huh? Oh well, I guess old people just say that.*

"Hey, I need to use the restroom...Angela..." Vicki said.

"Yeah, we'll be right back. Don't move!" Angela said.

"Yes, ma'am," Chris said.

"I'm serious, Chris," Angela retorted. Vicki and Angela worked their way back into the hall to find the restrooms and Chris looked back at me.

"Hey, man, do you think Rob and your ex are going to show up?"

"You can say her name, man, I'm over it, and yes, as far as I know they're coming with Aaron and Jessica. I looked around the exhibit hall and didn't see any of them. "I guess they're running late."

"You don't care that Hannah and Rob are going to be here together?"

"No, I'm good."

"Are you sure? *No.*

"Yes, I'm sure. Why are you so concerned anyway?"

"I'm not, really; it's just, I can't believe it, I mean, how...why Rob?"

"I beat myself up too long with that shit...I guess...Well, Hannah is ridiculously hot and all, but she's, what's the word I'm looking for? Eccentric...she's very eccentric."

"What the hell does that mean?"

"Different. I don't know, strange. She's not like other girls, that's for sure." Chris laughed.

"What's so funny, you don't agree?"

"I don't know...maybe, but that's not why I was laughing. There she is." Chris lifted his head slightly and looked over my shoulder. *Shit.* I slowly turned around and made eye contact with her. *Shit, she looks beautiful...like a Disney princess. Damn it! Don't come over here...*

"She's coming over here," Chris said.

"Yes, thank you, I can see that."

"Rob's not with her either."

"Wow, Chris, do I need to pull out the captain obvious stuff again?"

"I'm just saying, it's weird right?"

"I don't know...shut up, she's almost here." Hannah walked slowly, but deliberately toward us, moving her hips like the models do. She never once broke eye contact with me. *I can't believe the confidence of this girl...wait, more like the audacity of this girl.*

"Hey Billy; hi Chris," Hannah said. "Ummm, Chris, do you think you could give us a minute?"

"A minute for what?"

"To talk...could you leave us alone for a minute?"

"Sure, yeah, Angela would be pissed if..."

"Yeah, she would," I interjected. Chris turned around and walked away.

"So, what's up, Hannah?" I said. "I don't think we have anything to say to one another. And where's Rob, by the way?"

"So, I hear that you and Vicki are a thing..."

"Yeah."

"That's cool."

"Yeah, it is."

"I miss you."

"Where's Rob, Hannah?"

"He's around here somewhere. We had a fight. We're always fighting. It's not like how we were, Billy."

"You can call me Will." *What is her deal?*

"Billy, don't be like that, you're gonna make me cry." *I should care why?*

"Why did you lie to me about your grandma dying? It doesn't make any sense. If you didn't want to be with me, you could have just said so."

"Lie? My grandma did die. Why would you say that?"

"Jessica told me that your grandma's alive."

"Jessica? She doesn't know. I didn't even tell her."

"Well, I don't know what to believe. Honestly, it doesn't even matter. I have to ask though, why Rob?"

"He was really nice to me. I was confused and, I don't know, frustrated with my parents."

"I'm sorry; it just doesn't make any sense."

"I guess, I mean, I guess I just couldn't face being alone."

"What are you even talking about, Hannah, alone?"

"I knew that you would break up with me eventually when you went to college so..."

"Nope. I don't think so. We went through all kinds of shit to be together and all of the sudden you think I'm just going to leave you?"

"Yes, I always thought about you leaving me. I started talking to Rob about it, and he was so sweet to me...and he's the same age as me...and my parents..."

"Great, Hannah, that's just great. So why are you standing here talking to me right now?" *And why am I standing here listening?*

"I had to do something...I had to do something to get my parents to leave you alone. I had to convince them that we were really not together anymore...and Rob...and I already told you. I miss you." *I don't believe you. I want to believe you, but, shit, why do I even care?*

"So all of this was for me? I just don't buy it, Hannah."

"It's true. I never wanted any of this to happen."

"And what about Rob?" *Not like I care...*

"Rob isn't who I thought he was." *That makes two of us.*

"It doesn't matter anymore. I should go find Vicki." Out of the corner of my eye I saw Rob walk by me and put his hand around Hannah.

"What doesn't matter anymore?" Rob said. "Why are you talking to my girl?" *Dude, you're so cringe and gross.* Rob was wearing a blue leisure suit that looked like it was straight out of the seventies. His greasy blond hair was pulled back exposing his terrible complexion. *I so badly want to punch him in the face again...such a punchable face...It's not worth it, though.* I stared at Rob with intensity while Hannah turned to him.

"I was just saying hi, Rob, I haven't talked to him in months," Hannah said.

"Yeah," I said. "Not since I punched you in the face."

"Hey, bitch, if you want to go, we can take this outside," Rob said. *Seriously, Rob, at prom? Read the room, buddy.*

"…Nah, Rob, I'm good. You two have a nice evening," I said and walked away.

"Fucking right!" Rob said with authority. I didn't turn around. I saw Vicki, Angela, and Chris standing on the other side of the exhibit hall. Vicki did not look happy as I walked up.

"Talking to your ex?" Vicki said while crossing her arms.

"Yeah, she wanted to say hi."

"Really? That's it? Nothing else? Should I be worried?"

"No; look, can we just have a good time? You don't have anything to worry about," I said.

"I don't trust that bitch," Angela said, "and neither should you, Will."

"Why so serious over here?" Aaron said as he walked up to us hand in hand with Jessica.

"Oh, hey, man; it's Hannah, you know, problems," I said.

"Speaking of…can I talk to you alone real quick," Aaron said to me.

"No, he can't!" Vicki said. "If you have something to say, then you can say it in front of everyone!" *Shit…*

"Yeah, man, go ahead."

"Hannah, at dinner…"

"Don't even say anything, Aaron; it's not your business!" Jessica said and let go of Aaron's hand.

"No, I want to hear this," Vicki said. I nodded my head.

"Hannah just talked about you the whole time; about how perfect you guys were for each other. She brought up all of the astrology stuff. Rob got pissed and they got in an argument," Aaron said.

"I don't know what's going on with her," I said.

"The funny thing is she didn't care that Rob was getting mad. She just kept talking. I almost felt bad for him," Aaron continued.

"If she thinks she's gonna try to sleaze her way back into your life, she's got something else coming," Vicki said.

"Am I going to have to kick that bitch's ass again?" Angela added. *I don't recall it going down like that.*

"No one is going to have to kick anyone's ass! It doesn't matter what she said. It doesn't change anything," I said. I looked back across the room and saw Hannah looking right back at me. I saw Rob pulling on her arm as if he were trying to divert her attention away from me, but it didn't work. I could see a sadness in her eyes. She was asking for my help without saying a word. *Stop feeling sorry for her. Shit.*

After a few minutes of standing around, they let us into the main hall one couple at a time. Hannah and Rob were in line in front of us by a few couples, but I could clearly see the back of Hannah's perfectly sculpted body and wavy blond hair. She looked back at me and smiled. I could feel Vicki's cold, hard eyes penetrating right through me. She grabbed my hand and squeezed it tight. It was the kind of grip where I knew I was going to be in trouble later. I didn't look at her though. I looked straight ahead at Hannah until the announcer called their names. I snapped out of my daze and looked over at Vicki. "Are you ok?" She whispered.

"Yeah, I was just thinking..."

"About your ex?"

"Yeah." Vicki looked at me like she was about to hit me. "Would you rather I lie?"

"So, you still wanna be with her?" *Don't answer that.*

"No, I mean, I don't know...No, the answer is no."

"I don't believe you." The line moved forward and they continued to announce couples one at a time. I knew most of the people in my class, but I stopped listening after I heard Hannah's name being called.

"I don't know what to say." *I really don't.*

"It doesn't make any sense...The way she treated you." *You just don't know...You can't possibly understand.*

"I know. It's just going to take some time."

"For what? I thought you were over her. At least that's what you acted like."

"We have history that you can't wipe away in a couple of months. I mean, shit, Vicki, give me a break."

"We have history, too, William! We've known each other forever!"

"I can't explain it..." 'Victoria Ramos accompanied by William Smith.' The announcer said. I could see Vicki smile out of the corner of my eye as the camera-man took our picture. *How fake are you, Vicki?* We walked into the hall where the music had already started playing. Third Eye Blind's 'Semi-Charmed Life' came on. It was probably the most popular song on the radio at the time. I didn't really care for the bubble gum pop-rock type of music, but it was kind of catchy. Vicki made her way towards an empty table on the other side of the room and I followed after her. She sat down and then slammed her purse on the table in front of her. "Are you going to be pissed at me all night?" Vicki looked at me with inquisitive iciness.

"Maybe."

"This is our prom...and may be the last time we're all together and you want to make a big deal out of this?"

"You're right...you know what, Will? You're right...Next year we'll be at Fresno State and Hannah will still be in high school and then it won't even matter." *You know that Fresno is what, like 30 minutes away, right?*

"That's right, so stop worrying about her." Chris and Angela joined us at the table. Chris sat down next to me and Angela gave Vicki an uninspired half-hug before sitting down herself.

"Are you still talking about that bitch, Hannah?" Angela said scornfully. Vicki looked over at me before answering.

"No, I'm over it," Vicki said unconvincingly.

"Good, because, we're gonna have some fun." Angela grabbed Vicki's hand and stood up. "Let's dance." Vicki looked at me as if she were waiting for my approval. *I don't care, Vicki.*

"Yeah, go ahead," I said. "I want to catch up with Chris anyway. I'll find you later." Vicki waved at me as she was pulled onto the dance floor by Angela. "So, how's Golden West?"

"It's good, man, pretty chill actually."

"That's cool..." I looked out and watched Vicki dancing wildly. *She can't dance for shit.* "I think I'm gonna break up with Vicki."

"Tonight? Don't do it tonight. Shit, man, Angela's gonna be pissed."

"You're worried about Angela?"

"Yeah, she's crazy and that's all I'll hear about for the entire summer. Is this because of Hannah?"

"No...maybe, I don't know, but I know that Vicki isn't working out, and, shit, I already know what you're gonna say..."

"You're right, I'm gonna say 'duh,' you never liked that girl for as long as I can remember." *For as long as I can remember too...*

"Yeah, it's really too bad her personality didn't change with her looks," I said and Chris laughed.

"I'm surprised you even care."

"Dude, she's annoying as hell, like a soul-sucking kind of terrible. I don't know how to describe it any other way. Being with her feels like a chore."

"Like a chore?"

"Yeah, like washing the dishes or cleaning the bathroom...yeah, let's go with that one. Being with Vicki is like cleaning the bathroom."

"Shit, man."

"Yep, that's it...somebody's got to do it but I don't want that someone to be me." Chris laughed again.

"Well, listen, don't break up with her tonight."

"I won't. Shit...maybe I won't break up with her at all. I didn't tell you..."

"Tell me what?"

"Vicki plans on going to Fresno State with me."

"Yeah, you're fucked. You might as well just get married to her. Vegas?"

"Shit, that is not going to happen."

"I think it would be cool. I could be your best man. Angela would love it."

"Yeah, we need to not talk about this, like, ever again." Chris smiled and then looked away from me toward the dance floor. "Dude, I'm serious, that girl will ruin my life."

"Hey, what's going on over there?!" Chris pointed towards a crowd gathering to the side of the dance floor.

"Shit, a fight? At the prom?" *It better not be...*

"Let's go check it out." Chris and I got up from the table and made our way over to the outside of the crowd. Vicki found me and wrapped her arm around mine. I couldn't see who was fighting so I pushed my way forward with Vicki trying to pull me back.

"Who cares who's fighting!?" Vicki yelled. The music was playing loudly and I could barely hear what she said. I didn't respond, I just kept pushing forward until I could see what was going on. It was Rob and Hannah. *Go figure.* It looked like they were arguing, but I couldn't make out what they were saying. It looked like Rob was yelling at Hannah. He kept pushing his stubby finger into her chest. Hannah was looking down at the floor and just taking the abuse. Vicki pulled on my arm and yelled into my ear. "Let them deal with their own shit." I looked back into Vicki's eyes and made it very clear that was not going to happen. I turned my attention back to Hannah. Out of the other side of the crowd, one of the security guys grabbed Rob's arm and led him toward the door. *Oh, shit, they're gonna kick him out.* The crowd of people quickly dispersed and Hannah was left crying by herself. Vicki continued pulling on my arm. Jessica walked up to Hannah and hugged her. "Look, she's fine, let's go." *Go where, Vicki?*

"I want to make sure she's all right. I need to talk to her. I want to find out what Rob said."

"Why do you even care? Oh my God, whatever..." Vicki let go of my arm and pushed me in the back before walking away. Hannah looked up and saw me standing there waiting for her. I looked over and saw Aaron waiting on Jessica. He gave me the 'what's up' head bob and I did the same. Hannah let go of Jessica and ran up to me and gave me a hug. It was as if nothing had ever changed between us. *What is happening here?* Hannah pulled away and then just stared at me. *She is so beautiful. Look at those big, brown puppy-dog eyes. What! Snap out of it, damn it!* Hannah grabbed my hand and led me outside into the hall and then outside of the convention center. *Where? What? Why?* Hannah stopped and turned around to face me.

"It's so loud in there, I can't even hear myself think."

"Yeah, you and me both, but what's going on Hannah? What happened with Rob?"

"I don't really want to talk about it."

"Well, I do...I'm pretty sure that Vicki is gonna break up with me over this, so, yeah." I laughed and Hannah looked at me perplexed.

"What's so funny, Billy?"

"It's just ironic. I was going to break up with her anyway."

"Why were you going to break up with her?"

"It's really simple actually. I don't like her." Hannah laughed.

"What's her sign, Billy?" I laughed.

"She just had her birthday, so, Taurus? I guess it's not a good match, right Hannah?"

"Obviously not a good match..." Hannah smiled. "Just like Rob."

"What happened?" Hannah sighed.

"I may have tried to get Rob to break up with me."

"How did you do that?" *Rhetorical question...*

"I told him how good our relationship was and how we're perfect for each other. *Present tense, huh?*

"Then why aren't we together? Why did any of this happen?"
I squinted my eyes, slouched, and let my hands fall to my side in
exasperation.

"...He said if I ever broke up with him, he would kill himself. I
believed him."

"Rob's a lot of things, mostly bad, but he wouldn't kill himself. I
know him pretty well and the one thing that Rob loves more than
Nirvana is himself." *Wait...Cobain...* Hannah laughed and grabbed
my hands.

"Billy, I lied to you." *Yes, I know.*

"About what?"

"My grandma didn't die." *I knew it!*

"Oh, I fucking knew it!"

"Don't be mad, please, I wasn't thinking clearly back then."

"Back then? How long ago do you think this happened?"

"I know..."

"And then you lied about lying...and that was like 5 minutes ago!
What about that? I actually thought that Jessica was lying for a
minute, but couldn't figure out a reason for her doing that."

"I know...I'm sorry...I haven't been myself since..."

"Since when? I mean, It's a good question...right?"

"I don't know...sometime between my dad threatening you, and
Rob...But it's good...being with Rob was a good thing." *What in
the literal twilight zone fuck?!*

"Are you ok, Hannah? You're not making any sense."

"No, I am...If it weren't for Rob, I wouldn't have realized how
much I miss you...how perfect we are together. I already knew that,
but I think I needed the reminder..."

"Well, shit, I should stop by his house on the way home and
thank him."

"You see, I miss your sarcasm, Billy, you don't get all mad like
Rob. "*I don't? Well, I guess not...*

"What about the whole statutory rape thing? Did that even happen?" *I would be so pissed off if...* "Because you said since your dad threatened me, but that could mean anything."

"Oh, yeah, he made that threat all the time. I just didn't want to worry you. I was worried about it, but I didn't say anything...until I did." *I don't know...* "It just didn't happen as recently as I..."

"So it had nothing to do with that night or your grandma?" *What the fuck...*

"No, I was just under a lot of stress and I was, I don't know, I don't know what else to say." *This shit is giving me a fucking headache.*

"What now, Hannah?" I pulled my hands away from her. "What's the point of all this? Are we just going to get back together and act like none of this happened?" Hannah looked away from me and then at the ground. "I think it's more complicated than that."

"I know, Billy, I know...I'm sorry for everything."

"We should get back to the dance."

"Billy, you wanna walk me home?"

"Without telling anyone?"

"Do you want to talk to Vicki? You said it yourself...do you think she's going to be happy right now?" *Ok, so you've got a good point.*

"No, but what about Aaron and Jessica? And Chris...we came in a limo together. That was expensive."

"Oh, fancy!"

"I'm serious right now, leaving without saying anything would not be cool."

"I know, Billy. Oh so serious..." Hannah laughed. "Aaron and Jessica will be fine and do you really care what Chris thinks?"

"Yeah, we worked things out."

"That's good..." Hannah looked at me and got really close. "Come on, Billy, like old times...walk me home. Who cares what anyone thinks? I think they know anyway..." *I wonder what happened to Rob... Shit, I'm going to have to deal with Vicki at some point. This is a bad idea...Just walk back into the dance...turn around.* Hannah stared intensely into my eyes waiting for an answer. *Turn around...Her eyes, shit, look away...turn around.*

"All right, fuck it, let's go." Hannah pulled me close and whispered in my ear.

"I'm so sorry, Billy, I fucked up." *Yeah, and...*

"I get it," *no I don't,* "I really do." *I think I do.*

"I don't want you to be mad at me. I just want us to be happy together..." *That's funny, then why do you keep lying to me?*

"I'm not mad at you, well, not anymore at least." I laughed.

"What's so funny, babe?"

"I was furious with you a few months ago and now, well, now I just don't care."

"What do you mean you don't care?" *I really don't care. I don't even know.*

"I'm over being mad at you. You made a mistake and I've accepted that."

"I don't know...it doesn't seem like you have," Hannah said and stopped walking.

"What do you want me to say?"

"I don't know. I'm so sorry. I don't deserve your forgiveness, but please...everything..."

"Let's just forget about it."

"Ok, so what do you wanna do?"

"Whitendale Park?"

"Yeah, let's go." Hannah wrapped her arm around my waist and we continued walking down the street heading toward Whitendale Park. We walked hip to hip without saying another word. Flashes of headlights constantly passed by as we made our way down Court Street. When we got to Whitendale Park, Hannah turned to me and said, "what time is it?"

"I don't know." We walked over to the playground and I sat down on one of the swings. Hannah sat down on my lap sideways and I started swinging.

"Do you still love me?" *Shit, yes...but why?*

"Yes, I still love you. I don't think that will ever change."

"Me too." Hannah dug her feet into the ground and stopped the swing. She stood up, slipped off her shoes and then pulled her panties off. She put them inside the front pocket of my jacket. *Fuck.* I removed her panties from my jacket and then gently placed them back in her hand.

"We shouldn't do this tonight," I said. "We should take things slow." *I can't even believe that came out of my mouth.*

"Are you sure? I've missed you, Billy."

"I've missed you too, but we don't have to...let's just be here together."

"Ok, if that's what you want."

"It's all I've ever wanted." Hannah leaned in and kissed me and then put her panties back on. She sat down on my lap sideways once again and then rested her head against my chest. After some time had passed, and the majority of my body was asleep, I brushed Hannah's hair from her forehead. "Hey, I'm gonna walk you home, it's getting late."

"Ok, Billy, let's go." We started walking back to her house. Before we got to Laura Street, Hannah took off her shoes. "These shoes are loud, it's time to go barefoot." *Smart.* We stopped right behind her parent's Isuzu Trooper. Hannah kissed me with an authority that I hadn't felt for a very long time. I pulled away from her and said,

"I should probably go, it's getting late."

"Billy... I'm going to call you tomorrow...early, like 8."

"Ok. Damn, we've got a lot of damage control to do, Hannah, this is going to be a god damn mess."

"I know, Billy, but we'll deal with it together."

"Ok, yeah, call me in the morning."

"All right. Billy, I love you. Don't ever forget that."

"I won't...Good night, Hannah." I kissed her one last time and then let go of her waist. I turned around and walked back towards

Court Street and headed home. I looked up at the sky and gazed at the dimly-lit stars in front of Blaine Park before moving on. *It's almost beautiful.*

Chapter Twenty

Staring at the Sun

"DUDE, WHAT THE FUCK happened last night?" Chris said. "Dude, are you even awake right now? Wake your ass up!"

"I'm awake, fuck, damn, what time is it?"

"It's almost ten."

"Fuck." I pulled the phone away from my face and stared at it for a few seconds before replying. "Hey, man, sorry about last night."

"Dude, everyone is pissed off."

"Yeah, I figured as much. Shit, hold on." I put the phone down and wiped the sleep out of my eyes. I let out an enormous yawn. *Fuck.* "Shit's complicated."

"I guess, so what happened?"

"Hannah. I think that Hannah and I are going to..."

"Dude, what?" What about Vicki? She was super pissed after you disappeared."

"Yeah, I need to call her, shit, man, I need to break up with her."

"Seriously? You think that's a good idea?"

"Yeah, man, shit, I spent the night with Hannah, so..."

"This is some crazy shit. What happened with Rob?"

"I don't know."

"You don't know?"

"Yeah, I mean, I guess he got kicked out of prom and then went home. I don't know. I don't care. I think Hannah and I are going to get back together."

"She cheated on you. I know she's crazy hot but damn, dude, what makes you think she's not going to do it again?" *I really don't know.* "Vicki was crying something fierce."

"Yeah, Vicki... shit, she's a good girl." *Vicki would never cheat on me.*

"And you're going to fuck that up?" *Yeah.*

"I think I already did. I don't know, man, I can't explain it. Hannah has me under some kind of spell."

"Well, snap out of it!"

"Damn, I need to call Vicki. I'll call you later."

"All right, man, handle your business." I hung up the phone with Chris and got out of bed. *Fuck, I should take a shower before I deal with all of this shit.* I got up from my bed and headed toward the shower, but before I shut the bathroom door, I heard a loud knock. *Oh, shit...who's that?* I poked my head outside of the bathroom and saw Larry get up from the couch to answer the door. *Oh, shit.* Larry opened the door and to my horror, it was Vicki. She asked for me and Larry turned around and pointed right at me. *Thanks, bro.* Vicki walked right up to me with the most serious look on her face that I had ever seen. *Yeah, I'm in some deep shit.*

"We need to talk," Vicki said and grabbed my arm. She pushed me into my bedroom and closed the door behind us.

"I didn't plan for any of this...I didn't mean to hurt you."

"How stupid are you, Will!?"

"Am I supposed to answer that?" *I thought that I was pretty smart.*

"Yes, shit, Will, what is it about that girl!?"

"Ummm, yeah..." I sat down on my bed and Vicki stood over me.

"Yeah, what?"

"I don't know what to say...I love her."

"She cheated on you with your best friend." *Well, Rob's not really my best friend, but whatevers.* "And god knows who else."

"Ok, wait a minute, that's a little much."

"Is it? Is it really!?" Vicki pushed her hand into my forehead. "I thought you were smarter than this."

"I know...I thought I was too."

"That is so weak."

"I can't explain it."

"Does she have nicer tits than me? Does she suck your dick better than me? I don't get it." *Shit.*

"No, I mean, it's not that."

"Then what the fuck is it?" Vicki cried hysterically and sat down next to me.

"I don't know what to say."

"You don't know what to say? You always know what to say. You always have something to say. And now, nothing!?"

"I think that Hannah and I..." Vicki immediately interrupted me.

"Don't even say her name."

"We don't have what, she and I, yeah, what..."

"Fine! I get it.... I need some closure. " *I thought that this was closure.*

"Ok, I don't think we should be together."

"Because of that whore!?" Vicki continued crying.

"It's not because of..."

"Don't say the bitch's name!"

"Fine...You and I...We...just aren't compatible."

"What is that supposed to mean?"

"I don't know...It's just hard. We don't get along like..."

"Seriously?"

"Yes, seriously."

"We're going to Fresno State together."

"We're both going to Fresno State at the same time, there's a difference. What's with you, anyway? Going to the same school doesn't mean we should be together."

"And the whore? You're ok robbing the cradle?"

"Oh my god, seriously!? She's one freaking year behind us."

"Whatever."

"What do you mean, whatever?"

"It's whatever...We belong together." *Says you.*

"I don't think so. It's over, Vicki, deal with it."

"You're making a stupid mistake. That girl is gonna break your heart again and I won't be around to pick up the pieces."

"That's fine."

"Well, fuck you then. And, fuck her, too. I hope you both get what you deserve." *I...hope so too?*

"Bye, Vicki." *I hope I don't see you.*

"Fuck!" Vicki got up from my bed and wiped her face. She looked back at me with scornful, bloodshot eyes. It was kind of scary. "Go fuck yourself." Vicki opened my bedroom door and then left. *Well, damn; could have been worse. Shit...I don't want to be with Vicki but she's got a point...I love Hannah, but...Oh shit, I hope Vicki doesn't do something shitty like slash my tires. That would suck. Nah, she's crazy but not that crazy.* I got up from my bed and walked out to the living room. Larry was sitting on the couch seemingly doing nothing. I opened up the drape in the kitchen and checked the parking lot for any debauchery. *I don't see her.*

"Hey, bro, what the hell just happened?" My brother said.

"I broke up with her," I said and continued looking out over the parking lot.

"I get it. That girl had a mouth on her."

"What does that mean?" I shut the drape and sat next to Larry.

"She cussed like a sailor." *Yeah, she's normally not like that.*

"...You heard?"

"Everyone within a three-block radius heard."

"Shit. Hey, Larry, do you think, hypothetically, well..."

"Cough it up."

"Do you believe in that saying...once a cheater, always a cheater?"

"Why? Did your girl cheat on you?"

"Maybe."

"Yeah, she did. That sucks bro."

"I guess technically she didn't, but I don't even know."

"Wait, that girl that just left here all pissed off cheated on you?"

"No, the other one. The blond one."

"Oh, yeah, I remember you telling me about her. The 'oneitis' girl..."

"Ummm, yeah..."

"So let me get this straight...Your old girlfriend cheated on you so you got a new girlfriend and you just broke up with her right now."

"Yeah, and my old girlfriend wants to get back together with me, but I don't know, which is why I asked the question."

"Hmmm, well, I think that a cheater will always cheat if they can get away with it. You see what I'm saying?"

"Yeah..."

"Get rid of her, dude. Anyway, I've got to go to work. See you later." Larry got up from the couch, grabbed his keys off of the table and left me standing in the middle of the room with what must have been the dumbest look on my face that I had ever conjured. *Well, fuck me. I need to get out of here. Take a shower, fire up the Malibu, and just go. But where? Oh shit! Hannah was gonna call me...she should have called already. Damn it. I can't call her. Her stupid dad. I should stay and wait...But I don't want to. Shit.* I got in the shower and let the water run over my face. *Why does shit have to be so complicated?* I just stood in place and watched the water hit my feet. *What am I going to do?* I finally found the motivation to grab the bar of soap. I stayed in the shower until the water got cold and got out when I couldn't stand it anymore. As I was getting dressed, I heard the phone ringing faintly over the bathroom fan. *Hannah...nah, let her wait.* I slowly pulled my jeans on and then put on my White Zombie T-shirt. The phone kept ringing. *Ok, ok, shit.* I opened the bathroom door, walked over to the phone and answered it.

"Hannah?"

"No, it's Aaron."

"Oh, hey, what's up man? Sorry about last night, shit got crazy."

"Yeah...no worries. So, Jessica is on her way over to my house."

"Ok, thanks for sharing." I laughed. "I kid, I kid."

"Yeah, you wanna let me finish that thought?"

"Sorry, man."

"Rob's in the hospital."

"Why is Rob in the hospital?

"I guess he tried to kill himself." *No fucking way.*

"I don't believe it."

"Jessica and I are going over there when she gets here."

"Why would Jessica even...wait...Hannah's already there isn't she?"

"Yeah. She's the one that told Jessica." *Which is why she didn't call me. Wow.*

"Shit, ok, I need to call Chris and I'll head over there too."

"All right, man, I'll see you there."

"Later." A sense of sadness came over me. *Why do I even care? He fucked me over something fierce. But for some reason...I feel sorry for him. I feel sorry for me.* I took my finger off of the receiver and dialed Chris's number.

"Hey, man, what's up? What happened with Vicki?"

"We broke up, but that's not why I called...I guess Rob tried to kill himself and he's in the hospital."

"No fucking way!"

"That's exactly what I thought."

"What happened?"

"I don't know yet. I'm gonna come pick you up right now."

"All right, man, I'll be here, shit, I can't believe it."

"I know...I'll see you in a little bit." I hung up the phone, headed downstairs, and walked around the Malibu to check for any sabotage. *Everything seems ok. No flat tires.* I sat inside but didn't start it right away. I stared out of the windshield and slowly slid the key into the ignition. *Hannah...He did this because of her, or for her...And it worked.* I fired up the engine and peeled out across Caldwell Avenue on my way to Chris. I pulled up to Chris's house about fifteen minutes later. He was waiting outside and ran up and got inside of my car.

"Dude, I don't understand any of this," Chris said. I put the transmission into drive and sped away toward the hospital.

"That's what we're going to find out," I said.

"I've got a question. What are you going to do?"

"What do you mean?"

"I thought you'd be happy about this...you know, because of your issues with him."

"That's a pretty shitty thing to say."

"You know what I mean. Not happy, but not overly concerned either, I guess."

"I know he did me wrong, but he wasn't the only one involved..."

"You mean Hannah?"

"Yeah, I mean, none of this happens without her. You said it yourself...she tried to get with you that one time, or pretended to. Shit, man, Hannah is fucking poison."

"Damn, man, I never thought I'd hear those words come out of your mouth."

"I've been thinking about this a lot. And it's hard, it's really fucking hard because she's so damn beautiful and nice and she always says the right damn thing. But...it doesn't matter. It can't matter. It's not what she looks like or what she says...her actions are...she's the devil."

"And here all this time I thought you weren't religious," Chris said and I laughed.

"Yeah, well, neither did I."

"Wait...Is Hannah at the hospital?"

"Yup, she sure the hell is."

"Dude, what are you going to do? It sounds like you're gonna make a scene. One minute you're telling me that you're gonna get back together with her and now all this."

"This isn't about Hannah."

"It's always about Hannah."

"Yes, it has always been about Hannah, but that's going to change today."

"That's what I keep asking you...What are you going to do?"

"I'm not sure yet."

"Well, shit."

"Rob was one of our best friends. We were a band. That's why we're going to the hospital. All the bullshit doesn't matter."

"I guess not...so are you going to get back with Vicki, or what?" I laughed.

"No, I'm not going to get back with Vicki. Where did that come from?"

"I'm just thinking about how pissed Angela was last night. She's going to give me shit for hanging out with you."

"That's what I'm talking about! It's always about a girl. These girls are ruining friendships, shit, ruining everything, and do they care? Nope, they do not give a single shit."

"I don't know, I think they care."

"No, they say they care, but they don't actually care."

"I'm sure some girls care."

"Maybe, but not the ones we want to be with. Think about it...Fat, ugly girls wouldn't pull this shit because they would never get away with it."

"So, you wanna date fat chicks now?"

"Nope." I lowered my eyebrows and gave Chris a stern look. "No way in hell. It sucks. I think I learned about this in English class. They call it a paradox or a conundrum. Some shit like that."

"So, what are you going to do?"

"I don't know. Look, there's the entrance to the emergency room." I pulled into the parking lot of the hospital and turned off the engine. "No scene. No drama. We're just going to go in, make sure Rob's all right and then get the fuck out of Dodge."

"It sounds like you have it all worked out...you think it's gonna go down like that?"

"Sure, why not?"

"I would say, but if I said her name, I think your head would explode." I laughed halfheartedly.

"I already told you, it'll be fine."

"Ok, man, let's go." Chris and I walked through the automatic sliding doors to the hospital and a stench of ammonia and death filled my nostrils. *Gross.*

"You smell that, Chris?"

"Yeah, what is it?"

"It's the smell of 'we won't be here very long.'"

"It's good you can still joke about this."

"You're right, this isn't funny. This is super not funny." We walked into the reception area that was adjoined by a half-empty waiting room.

"Can I help you?" A receptionist said from behind the counter.

"Uhm, yeah, we're here to see Robert..."

"Hey, man, his parents are over there," Chris interrupted while pointing at the other side of the room. I walked over to Rob's mom and it was apparent that she had been crying. She looked old and defeated. His dad was sitting next to her with his head in his hands. Rob's mom looked up at me.

"Will...Chris...oh my god." She choked up and started crying. Rob's dad looked up and finished her thought.

"Rob would be happy that you're here." *Somehow, I seriously doubt that.*

"What happened?" I said.

"Rob got home last night much earlier than we were expecting him...He didn't say why. He wouldn't talk to us. He went to his room and shut the door," Rob's dad said.

"Will, do you have any idea what happened?" Rob's mom muttered.

"Yeah, I think I do. Hannah broke up with him or was going to break up with him...I'm not really sure. They got into a fight at prom," I said. "He got escorted outside. That's all I know."

"But Hannah's in the room with him right now. I was the one that called her," Rob's mom said. "And two of her friends." *Aaron and Jessica...*

"What happened? Why's Rob here?" I asked.

"We woke up this morning and found Rob in his room." Rob's mom started crying again as she began to talk. "He wasn't moving...I found my empty bottle of Vicodin next to him. He took all of them...Why would he?"

"Is he going to be ok?" Chris said.

"Yeah, is he?" I reiterated.

"They think he'll be fine. He's asleep right now...and then..." Rob's mom said.

"And then?" I inquired.

"He'll be on suicide watch for 72 hours." Robs mom said. "Why does he want to kill himself?" She covered her face and cried hysterically. *Shit.*

"I don't think he wants to kill himself..." *I really don't know...* "Do you think we can go see him?"

"Yeah, but like we said, he's asleep," Rob's dad said.

"It's fine, we'll only stay a minute," I said.

"He's in the room at the end of the hall on the left."

"Ok, thanks," I said. Chris and I walked down the hallway. Chris stepped into the room before me and as soon as I crossed the threshold of the door, I saw Rob lying down on the hospital bed. His eyes were shut and I could hear his heartbeat over the machine next to him. Hannah was sitting by his side and holding his hand as she stared at him intensely. *She doesn't even know that I'm here.* Aaron and Jessica were whispering to each other on the other side of the room. When Aaron saw me, he walked over and shook Chris's hand and then mine.

"What's up, man, this is crazy," Aaron said.

"Yeah, it's...something; some twilight zone shit," I said. Hannah looked back and seemed surprised to see me. She nervously pulled her hand away from Rob and let his hand rest on the bed. She got up from the chair and walked over to me.

"Hey, Billy, can we talk outside?"

"I'm not sure that we have much to talk about, Hannah, it seems like everything's pretty clear."

"Please?" Hannah tried to grab my hand but I pulled away from her.

"Fine, Hannah, this isn't the place to have this conversation anyway." Hannah walked out of the room and down the hall toward the lobby. I looked at Aaron and then Jessica. I stared at her for what seemed like a lifetime. *I wonder what would have happened if she had just hooked up with Rob.*

"Are you ok, Will?" Jessica said.

"I was just thinking..."

"About what?" Jessica responded.

"Nothing...it doesn't matter. You can't change the past." Jessica looked back at me like she understood what I was saying. She looked over at Rob and then back at me. "I'm gonna go talk to Hannah." I looked at Chris and then Aaron. "Let me know if Rob wakes up."

"For sure," Aaron said. I walked out of the room and through the lobby. Hannah was waiting for me outside. She was holding a lit cigarette in her right hand. I watched her slowly bring it to her lips and breathe in the smoke. *That's just nasty.* She exhaled the smoke and then tossed the cigarette on the ground and snuffed it out with her foot.

"When did you start smoking?" I inquired. *I don't even recognize you anymore.*

"I don't smoke." *Of course you don't.* "They're Rob's."

"That's a pretty nasty habit, you know...That shit will age you something fierce. Wrinkles; you'll lose your teeth; I think your hair will fall out...And, yeah, well, you'll stink pretty bad."

"I know, I get it, sheesh. Thanks, Dad." *You're really gonna mention your dad right now?* "I'm just really anxious...I needed something to help calm me down."

"If I remember correctly, smoking does the opposite."

"I don't know...listen, Billy, I don't want you to get the wrong idea. I still want to be with you." *Are you serious right now?* I raised my left eyebrow and stared at Hannah suspiciously. "I'm just worried about Rob. I don't want him to kill himself. Shit, this is all my fault."

"Yeah, it is." I smiled. "That much we agree on."

"It's not funny, Billy, I'm too young to deal with all of this."

"That's actually really funny, like ironic funny, because I feel the same way. I'm too old to deal with this shit."

"What do you mean?"

"I just need this to be over with."

"What are you talking about?"

"Hannah, I love you...I'll probably always love you. I'll probably be 40 years old and still be thinking about you...about what could have been. But I just can't do this with you anymore."

"Are you saying you don't want to get back together?"

"I don't want to get back together with you, Hannah, I don't trust you...*yeah, that's it.* "I don't...trust you."

"I guess I deserve that. I don't even trust me."

"Well, yeah, see, that's a problem." I smiled and Hannah laughed.

"I don't think I'm ever going to find someone as good as you."

"Yeah, I don't think so either," I said and then laughed. "You should go back and check on Rob."

"I don't want to be with Rob...I can't deal. He's angry and now he's suicidal. He told me he would kill himself...And now..." *Yeah, not my problem.* Chris, Aaron, and Jessica walked through the automatic doors and stood between Hannah and I.

"Hey, did Rob wake up?"

"Nah, he's still asleep," Chris replied. "I don't know, man, I don't want to be here all day. It's not like he's going anywhere."

"Yeah, I was gonna get out of here. I think I need to be alone for a while," I said. *Shit...I do need to be alone.* "I feel like going for a drive."

"Can I call you later?" Hannah said.

"Yeah, call me later," I said. Hannah started walking back into the hospital lobby and then stopped in the middle of the automatic doors and looked back at me. *She looks so sad...defeated...beautiful.*

"I, ummm, I'm sorry, Billy, I...I'll call you later." Hannah turned back around and disappeared into the hallway.

"All right, shit..." I looked at Chris. "I guess I'll drop you off at your house."

"Ok, what are you gonna do?"

"I don't know...Maybe drive up to Three Rivers."

"Are you guys gonna get back together?"

"No, I don't think so, Jessica."

"That sucks," Aaron added.

"Yeah...anyway, I'll come by your house later, man," I said to Aaron and walked away with Chris following closely behind.

"All right, later, man," Aaron said. I heard a faint conversation between him and Jessica about them leaving as well. Jessica wanted to stay and Aaron wanted to leave. As Chris and I got into the Malibu, I looked over at the entrance to the hospital and saw Aaron and Jessica go back inside. *Well that figures.* I pulled out of the parking lot and Chris turned to me.

"Do you want me to come with you to Three Rivers?"

"Nah, I'm good. I just need to clear my head. These past couple of days have felt like forever."

"Yeah, so what should I tell Vicki?"

"Tell her the truth...tell her I just want to be alone. She's a good girl, I don't want her to think I broke up with her because of Hannah..."

"Didn't you?"

"Well, kind of, but, shit, I don't want her to think that. I want her to know that I'm not going to get back together with Hannah. I really need her to know that."

"If Rob didn't try to kill himself, do you think that..."

"I don't know," I quickly interjected. "I'd like to think I wouldn't have...but, I mean, I love her...I can't trust her, but I still love her. I think it's better this way, though, no matter how we got here."

"Yeah..."

"Hey, Chris," I said, "tell them that I'm really sorry about everything...that if I could do it again," *like just turn around and walk away,* "I would have made better decisions."

"I'll tell them, but, you know..."

"Yeah, but I just want you to tell them, whether they believe it or not." I pulled up to the curb in front of Chris's house. "All right, man, I'll give you a call later."

"All right, cool, later." I got back on the road and then merged onto the 198 East toward the Sequoia National Forest. It was a beautiful, sunny day and about 80 degrees outside. My windows were rolled down and the wind rushed through my hair with wild intensity. I cruised well below the speed limit in the slow lane all the way to Slick Rock. The Slick Rock recreation center was a local swimming and picnic area off of Kaweah Lake right before Three Rivers. We called it 'going to Three Rivers' even though we rarely went into town. I parked the Malibu and then walked down to the river, which only passed as a stream at that point. I followed a series of rocks across the trickling water to a large rock that would eventually, later in the summer, be submerged by the river. I climbed to the top of the rock and sat at the edge with my feet hanging over the side. The sun streamed down onto the water and reflected back into my eyes. I had never been to Slick Rock alone before. I had never been anywhere alone before. It was only me. I listened to the birds fly over my head singing their songs of hope. I listened to the sound of the water bouncing over the rocks. *Why have I never done this before? I hope I made the right decision...Hannah...Vicki...girls. I'm gonna have a lot of shit to deal with at school tomorrow...I wonder if we'll finally win a Super Bowl with Ryan Leaf? That was random, but I am looking forward to the football season. Fresno State should be cool...going to those games. Maybe I should be with Hannah...What the fuck! Get out of my head! Vicki's gonna stalk the hell out of me in college...shit. Always about a girl...It's always about a girl...Why is it always about a girl?* I sat very still on the rock and placed my hands behind me. I leaned back and stared at the sun as if I were searching for some truth from the gods. *You got nothing, huh? I didn't think so. Neither do I.*

About Author

William Michael Stephens was born in San Diego, California. He graduated with a B.A. in English from California State University, Fresno. He is currently teaching high school English in Salinas, California. He has been a teacher for 15 years and has taught grades 6-12 in Tulare, Fresno, Santa Clara, and now, Monterey county. His hobbies include, aside from writing; cars, football, and guitar. William has written poetry and short stories for the majority of his life and About a Girl is his first novel.

severlinepress.com

Please visit us online for additional content and be sure to join our
email list for updates on current and future projects.
Please consider leaving a review on Amazon:
https://amzn.to/3CCy8Mq
Thanks for reading!

www.ingramcontent.com/pod-product-compliance
Lightning Source LLC
Chambersburg PA
CBHW061925170626
46813CB00006B/2304